D1190895

CENTURY OF LOCUSTS

Century of Locusts

MALIKA MOKEDDEM

Translated and with an introduction
by Laura Rice and Karim Hamdy

University of Nebraska Press : Lincoln

Originally published as *Le Siècle des sauterelles*
© Éditions Grasset & Fasquelle, 1994. English-
language translation © 2006 by the Board of
Regents of the University of Nebraska

Publication of this book was assisted by a grant
from the National Endowment for the Arts

Cet ouvrage publié dans	This work, published
le cadre du programme	as part of the program
d'aide à la publication	of aid for publication,
bénéficie du soutien du	received support from
Ministère des Affaires	the French Ministry
Etrangères et du Service	of Foreign Affairs and
Culturel de l'Ambassade	the Cultural Service
de France représenté	of the French Embassy
aux Etats-Unis.	in the United States.

Library of Congress Cataloging-in-Publication Data
Mokeddem, Malika.
[Siècle des sauterelles. English]
Century of locusts / Malika Mokeddem; trans-
lated and with an introduction by Laura Rice
and Karim Hamdy.
p. cm. — (European women writers series)
ISBN-13: 978-0-8032-3254-9 (cloth : alk. paper)
ISBN-10: 0-8032-3254-3 (cloth : alk. paper)
ISBN-13: 978-0-8032-8306-0 (pbk. : alk. paper)
ISBN-10: 0-8032-8306-7 (pbk. : alk. paper)
I. Rice, Laura. II. Hamdy, Karim. III. Title. IV. Series.
PQ3989.2.M55S5413 2006   843'.914 — dc22   2005025551

Set in Carter & Cone Galliard by Kim Essman.
Designed by A. Shahan.

TO JEAN-LOUIS

And I know that one can end in the
peace and silence of some *zaouia* in the South,
end in ecstasy, beyond both regret and desire,
looking out over splendid horizons.

ISABELLE EBERHARDT, *Kenadsa*

CONTENTS

ACKNOWLEDGMENTS

The translators gratefully thank Sadeg Hamdi,
president of Hamdi-Frères Corporation in
Gabès, Tunisia, for his generous support
during their work on this book.

INTRODUCTION

Century of Locusts is the translation of Malika Mokeddem's second novel. Mokeddem, who immigrated to France from Algeria in 1977, is a physician-nephrologist by training and, when she started to write, a novelist by avocation. She is a daughter of the desert, born into a family of recently sedentarized nomads who settled in Kenadsa in southwest Algeria, one of the gateways to the Sahara. She was raised in a house at the foot of the large sand dune called La Barga, for which Kenadsa is famous. Now a well-established full-time novelist in Montpellier, France, Mokeddem draws on her Algerian origin and culture for many of her literary themes, landscapes, and characters. She received the Prix Afrique-Méditerranée in 1992 for *Century of Locusts*, the third of her novels to be translated into English. After writing eight novels, Mokeddem turned to autobiography and wrote *La Transe des Insoumis*, which was awarded the Grand Prix du roman des lectrices de Côté Femmes. In this memoir she relates the series of events that shaped her life and her writing. It takes the reader full circle, as we find in it the family members, landscapes, and experiences that shaped her earliest novels, the semi-autobiographical *Les Hommes Qui Marchent*, and her compelling tale of the desert, *Century of Locusts*. Of all her work to date, *Century of Locusts* most clearly reflects the narrative energy and imaginative scope of Bedouin life, with clear echoes of her own life experience in the Algerian Sahara.

Mokeddem credits her paternal grandmother, who told her tales late in the night about the nomadic life, with passing on to her a love of tantalizing narratives and open spaces. While there is a grandmother in her first novel, it is in *Century of Locusts* that Mokeddem captures the narrative power of her grandmother's voice, dispersed across the characters and events. In her memoir, Mokeddem explains that as a young girl, an *insoumis* (unruly one) suffering from *insomnie* (insomnia), she was relegated to the kitchen at night to share her grandmother's bed. There she was comforted and entertained long into the night by tales told amid the shadows of the flames of the kitchen fire flickering across the walls:

> Exiled from nomadism at an advanced age, [my grand-mother] has only words now as an escape from the immobility of sedentary life and as a way to discover once again her own rhythms of departure and arrival. Her words begin to dance in the night, to the rhythm of footsteps that long ago crossed the wide-open esparto grass steppes. She narrates. I see. I see the blue-gray expanse of esparto grass. I see its tresses swaying in the breeze. I hear the rustling of this mane when the wind whips around and howls with no obstacle to rest against. I feel her breath in which the names of aromatic herbs are beaded into poetry. I imagine the days of harried walking. There is the silhouette of Djebel Amour, a hulking dinosaur on the far horizon of the steppe; the shimmering of horses; the halo of red dust in their wake. Grandmother has a fantastic repertoire about horses, the symbol of the high plateaus. Before I know it the winged hoof beats are carrying me off to sleep.[1]

This is the inherited narrative voice that brings *Century of Locusts* to life: the enigmatic ancestor roused from the grave whose phantom self dances in the firelight, the aromas of women that permeate the moist air of the *hammams*, the poetic cadences of the caravans crossing the high steppes, the laughter of mad highwaymen and the squinting eyes of dangerous predators, the haunting melodies of wandering artists.

Many of the traits we find in her fictional heroine Yasmine are drawn from Mokeddem's own childhood experiences. Yasmine and she are children of mixed racial backgrounds and learn about racism early; Yasmine's father is Arab, her mother black, thus Yasmine is taunted as a marginal being by other children. Mokeddem's tribe, the Doui Minaï, are of mixed race as well. Both girls are isolated by their literacy in the midst of a culture that is deeply oral. Their love of the written word is mixed with traumatic experiences that drive them into exile, into silent scribbling on the sand and away from speech for Yasmine, and into creative writing for Mokeddem. Mokeddem tells us that she longed to escape from the confines of a familial and social system that suffocated girls in the interest of privileging their male siblings. Living in two or three small rooms occupied by eight siblings, her parents, her grandmother, and her uncle and his wife and baby, Mokeddem, the oldest child, rebels against losing her own identity in the larger body of the clan: she immerses herself in books, learns French, becomes a doctor, migrates to France, and becomes a novelist. Mokeddem's revolt involves a withdrawal from her mother, who worried that her grandmother's tenderness would weaken the girl: "The love of mothers is measured by their ability to strengthen their girls against life's hard blows; to do so without changing anything; to do so without becoming sullen. I would realize that much later."[2] Yasmine, in *Century of Locusts*, rejects the protective efforts of her adoptive mother Khadija, who wanted to draw her safely into the world of women, their work, their suffering, and their marriages. Instead, Yasmine withdraws into speechlessness and writing, and finally runs away to avoid the group pressure to conform to traditional female roles.

Mokeddem tells us: "Books were my first inviolable space. Neither my father nor my mother could read. They could not therefore control what I took from that cocoon of paper. When I wasn't busy arguing about some other constraint on my freedom, I subversively put the silence of books between my parents and me."[3] To avoid her mother's attempts to protect her by traditional means (heavy housework, marriage, motherhood), Mokeddem withdrew at night into the "guest room," a room in traditional Arab houses set aside especially for visitors. She would lock herself into the guest room and read all night. When her mother tried to get in to wake her in the morning, a battle would ensue:

> My appropriation of this room is the call to battle, a conflict still intense today between my mother and me. Every morning, she leaves her chores periodically to come pound angrily on the door: "Hey! *American*! There's work waiting for you. Get up! . . . Reading all night, living at a distance from others — *American style* — allowed me to escape as well from all the chores that devoured the days . . . to escape from being transformed into my brothers' slave.[4]

Mokeddem's escape, "American style," into the exhilarating but instrumentalist, individualist world of Western literacy has many negative consequences: it cuts her off from her family network, separates her from her native country, causes her to withdraw from her medical practice, and finally drives a wedge between herself and her French husband as she devotes herself more and more to the solitude of writing. On the other hand, this same literacy did open the way to escaping conservative customs concerning gender roles, to obtaining a medical degree, to marrying a person of her choice, and to savoring the solace and rewards of becoming a successful writer. Throughout much of *Century of Locusts*, Yasmine's line of communication to the world is also limited to writing. Writing is her protective cocoon, writing draws her into fictional worlds that serve as a shield from the gossip and criticism of the women of the tribe, the disapproving stares of men, the unwelcome leer of a potential husband. But writing also displaces the healing potential of speech and dialogue with others. When she finally regains the power of speech she is a wandering poet existing in the realm of legendary events.

In *La Transe des Insoumis*, the gender and political constraints that structured the early novel *Century of Locusts* are now presented as complex trade-offs. Mokeddem leaves behind her the conservatism of the "ayatollahs" of her village only to find that France has both its immigrant "ayatollahs" in the North African ghettos and even worse bigots among the *pieds noirs* who set her car on fire and leave her death threats. She tells herself: "You didn't fight for so long, you didn't follow such a long path to suffer this now. You didn't flee the ayatollahs over there to put up with them here. You'll never be Arab except by your own self-fashioning."[5] After France participated in the coalition that conducted the first Gulf War, Mokeddem wrote that she finally realized how complete her exile was: "Stateless this time in my adoptive country, France. I wanted to vomit for having taken French nationality. This France, one of the coalition of state terrorism, gave me a furious desire to rub out everything the word stood for, France. . . . Civilizing mission or self-appointed rangers of human rights, it is the same carnival of vampires. . . . The gulf war is simply the repeat of the 'civilizing' crusades of the colonial powers acting together."[6] Defending her love of the language, Mokeddem ends up arguing that the only community that is real is the community of ideas. For Yasmine at the end of *Century of Locusts*, the only world that was real was the epic space of oral poetry.

A final trait Mokeddem shares with her character Yasmine is a love for Isabelle Eberhardt, the turn-of-the-century writer who learned Arabic, converted to Islam, traveled across North Africa dressed as a male, joined a Sufi brotherhood, married an Algerian, and died at age twenty-seven in a flash flood in the Sahara near the desert region where Mokeddem was born.[7] Tragic, androgynous, and cross-cultural, Eberhardt embodies the marginality Mokeddem and Yasmine embrace. Introduced to the writings of Eberhardt in a dictation read by her French teacher, Mokeddem remembers how as a young girl she was astonished by her words: "In all the other classes, the readings, the dictations only refer to France . . . [but Eberhardt's] words in another language describe not only my village but above all my dune. That bowled me over."[8] Likewise, Yasmine finds in Isabelle Eberhardt a role model to provide support for her when she is lonely because of her literacy and her independence. Whenever she passes through the desert town of Aïn Sefra where Eberhardt died, she pays homage at her tomb:

> Then Yasmine also tells herself the story of Isabelle Eber-
> hardt. A belle called Isa, whose fair skin is bronzed, haloed
> by intelligence. Dressed as a Bedouin male for freedom
> of movement, she walks outside the beaten path. And on
> nights when the moon is opalescent, Isabelle has the ebony
> tint of her mother and her father's brio to tell her life story.
> When that happens, all the dead of the desert, both man
> and beast, rise up, throwing off their coverings of earth
> and, dressed in light, come on foot to the dune of Aïn
> Sefra to hear her.[9]

The language of *Century of Locusts*, and even its format, which includes a glossary of Arabic terms, reflects the complex cultural and linguistic discourses of North Africa, its code-switching between spoken Arabic and French. Mokeddem's first published edition of *Century of Locusts* (1992) is the product of a young writer, marked by mixed registers, mixed metaphors, and proliferating characters and stories. The version of the novel translated here is Mokeddem's revised edition of 1996. In this later version a character has been eliminated, long monologues have disappeared, and repetitive language and images have been pruned. So this early novel is now really the fruit of a mature writer much more in control of the text. *Century of Locusts* now reads with all the concentrated power of the oral world that once reverberated in the voice of her Bedouin grandmother.

NOTES

1. Malika Mokeddem, *La Transe des Insoumis* (Paris: Éditions Grasset & Fasquelle, 2003), 22–23.
2. Mokeddem, *La Transe*, 35.
3. Mokeddem, *La Transe*, 62.
4. Mokeddem, *La Transe*, 141.
5. Mokeddem, *La Transe*, 83.
6. Mokeddem, *La Transe*, 98–99.
7. See Rice and Hamdy's translation of and critical essays on Eberhardt's selected writings: *Departures* (San Francisco: City Lights, 1994).
8. Mokeddem, *La Transe*, 123–24.
9. *Century of Locusts*, chapter 10.

I

A small herd of sheep, three camels, and a donkey—behind them Mahmoud is walking lightheartedly. A stick swings about in his hand and pecks the ground in front of his chiseled calves. He is happy. Early that morning at the market, he sold his two oldest ewes. He could no longer keep them, much less eat them. No! They had been the very first of his herd. Together, through the years, they had roamed the steppes far and wide. In this immense solitude you become attached to your animals.

Up on the camel's packsaddles, a sack of flour here, another of semolina there, and several kilos of wheat are piled high. One of them also carries sugar, tea, and, of course, dates. For Nejma and Yasmine, Mahmoud bought bright dresses. Their dark skin delights in these contrasts.

Now the stick lies horizontally across Mahmoud's shoulders. His wrists drape easily over either end. His hands, hanging, bounce to the rhythm of his step. The air is light. The azure blue turning to violet announces dusk. To make the going faster, Mahmoud sings a poem he's made up.

Soon he sees his *kheïma* in the glimmer of the setting sun. And just then, the yapping of his dog reaches him. Soon she will race to meet him, just ahead of his daughter Yasmine. The only thing that will remain hidden until he nears the campsite is the dark, slender silhouette of his wife, Nejma.

Sitting in front of her kheïma, Nejma looks out over the land: a sky of slate and as far as the eye can see, desert.

The only shrub, over several hours of walking distance, is there in front of the kheïma. Oh! A tree? More like a crucified lie, the lone attempt at verticality, struck down. Everywhere else, the same flatness. After wandering for a long while, Nejma's eyes come up against a small moving shadow out there in the distance. She shivers and smiles.

"I'm so silly! Who could be coming from that direction?!"

In Mahmoud's absence, whenever a moment of idleness frees her thoughts, the anxiety hidden beneath the surface emerges. Nejma recognizes its damage. More than once she has let herself be dragged toward irrational fears. Strange silhouettes, unusual sounds, all imagined, obviously. Can it be otherwise? How can she expect to avoid anxiety when she wraps herself in silence and indulges in all sorts of excesses? Mahmoud has gone to the market at Aïn Sefra for the day. Until his return tonight, her gaze is only pursued by daggers of sunlight. It is haunted only by the flowing of mirages on the horizon. As for the *regs*, they will sleep on in tawny languor, in their damnation of light.

"Perhaps it is just the wind?"

Galloping imagination, cavalcades of wind, a world imagined? Nejma looks around her. She says:

"*El-rih!*"

In that piped "h" already there is breath, the beginning of a soaring flight.

"Let it come, let the wind come," she sings sadly to herself.

Nejma smiles. In her rediscovered dreams, the north wind is already beneath her skirts. It caresses her thighs. It hardens her nipples, surprising them in their warmth. Is it the wind? The present evaporates. She continues her song:

"Wherever it comes from far in the desert, the lover of dunes, the soul of sands, the wind . . ."

The wind? It is the only one who always finds them again. From north or south, the wind is the only welcome guest.

"Maybe it is *el-rih!*"

But the small shadow, barely larger than a fly, persistently stays out there where the sky ends.

"It is not the wind. It's my own wretched fear!" That's what remains from her contact with others, from her experience with communal life. A terror that stalks her and pursues her even into the far reaches of the desert. And yet, and yet, she has no reason to worry! She knows that. Her best protection is just that rampart of emptiness, those limitless flat spaces. She knows that. Mahmoud reminds her of it often, and as he tries to convince her, his tawny eyes take on the look of a serene tomcat certain that his territory is inviolable.

Nejma closes her eyes. But her anxiety is not dissolved within their darkness. So she opens them again and tries to ignore the horizon. She keeps busy. Before her the *kanoun* turns red. She puts a *tajine* on it. When it's nice and hot and begins to smoke a little, she puts bread on to cook.

Her baby is sleeping under the tent. He will not wake up for a long time for his next nursing. Her eldest, Yasmine, is playing a bit farther away near the tree of wrath, so named because of the bristling sharp thorns. The little girl is eight and is the spitting image of her mother. She has her full lips, her liquid eyes, her fierce air. She differs from her only in the bronze tint of her skin. Yasmine has no toys, nothing in her hands. She simply plays with some pebbles taken from the heap her father made when he was clearing the campground.

Sitting on the ground, the lop-eared dog, Rabha, gazes longingly at the tajine. Salivating, she licks her chops. The smell of hot bread rises and fills the air. Soon it reaches Yasmine and fills her nostrils. The bread is already done. On a purple *mendil*, it makes a golden flower starred with sesame seeds.

Suddenly the dog Rabha pricks up her ears, leaps to her feet, and starts barking. Nejma's eyes return to the troubling horizon. No more doubt! Someone is coming in her direction from the west. It can't be Mahmoud; he will come from the south.

3

Yasmine's eyes scan the horizon, too. Nejma had already confirmed that her father would not be back until nightfall. What will she find hidden in his hood? But the horizon is completely empty in that direction. Her eyes sweep the open spaces without detecting anything, return to question Rabha, then go looking again into the distance. In a few moments Yasmine begins to see something very small that seems to float like a hawk at the edge of the sky, in the direction the dog's muzzle is pointing to.

It is not a caravan, no. It can't be more than two or three people, maybe mounted. For the time being, it is only a halo of dust wavering in the light. Anxiety comes back to Nejma's distracted gaze, to her trembling hands. She places the last portion of bread dough on the tajine and waits. Mother and daughter keep their eyes fixed on the little cloud that is slowly approaching.

"Perhaps it's a shepherd looking for a lost animal," the mother suggests.

Instinctively, Yasmine hides behind the heap of rocks. Nejma removes the tajine from the kanoun. Off the fire, the bread will continue to cook slowly.

"Or other nomads going to Aïn Sefra," she adds, still trying to convince herself.

She laughs at her fear. Laughter releases her, for awhile, from its grip. Nejma's eyes turn away from the people arriving and seek Yasmine. She senses her hiding behind the rock heap.

"Our solitary life has made us both wild. A trifle, the sudden appearance of travelers, is enough to frighten us," she thinks tenderly.

Then her eyes turn back to the people heading straight toward the kheïma. Now she can clearly make out two mounts, two camels that she recognizes by their amble. Who are they? What purpose, what chance leads them toward her? She gets up, goes into the kheïma, and quickly comes out again, her head and face veiled with a *fouta*. Then she squats again by the kanoun. She waits. Time stretches out. Time clings to the steps of the strangers. The silence, rent by the dog's barking, explodes and falls back to earth again, its weight intensified. And the high plain is there, vast and devastated, at the crossroads of nothingness and unreality.

There are two of them—men—coming toward them on this late autumn morning. Now they are not far away anymore. And suddenly everything is altered. Suddenly it's as if this isolated kheïma were now on a busy path between two *douars*, or as if some relatives, knowing when and where they would set up camp, were coming to pay them a visit. They don't have any relatives. They live and roam the land alone. However, let it not be said that in the abode of Mahmoud the poet, travelers are not treated with the consideration that is their due. But in his absence, Nejma is not at all used to dealing with such a situation, that's all.

"May Allah help me!"

She puts a kettle of water on the kanoun for tea.

One of them is bony. The other tall and robust. Their faces are hidden by dirty white turbans. Rabha circles them, showing her fangs.

"Woman, don't be afraid. Tie up your dog. We only need some water and a little time to rest!" says the emaciated man.

Despite the firm but reassuring tone of Nejma's commands, Rabha takes a long time to calm down. She finally gives in and lets herself be taken away, but not without persistent growling. The woman ties her tightly to one of the posts of the kheïma. Then, with a carafe in her hand, she heads toward the *guerba*, the goatskin bag hanging from a wooden tripod. Then she walks back toward the men. They are already dismounted, their camels kneeling. If she hadn't been so preoccupied with scrutinizing the strangers, Nejma would have seen the full *guerba* swelling insolently behind one of their saddles. The men grab the carafe, one after the other, rinse their mouths and noisily spit out the

5

first mouthfuls. Then they drink a little without showing any of the satisfaction that occurs when thirst is at last quenched.

"Slave, where are your masters?" asks the skinny man.

"I am not a slave. Mahmoud, my husband, is over there with his herd," Nejma answers carefully, with a vague gesture toward the large plain.

"Mahmoud? Mahmoud who? What is his family name?" asks the big one, exchanging a meaningful look with his companion.

She almost says, "Mahmoud Tijani." Then, catching herself, she declares, "Mahmoud the poet," her voice strengthened by a note of pride.

"The poet! Ha, ha. Ridiculous! One of those who prattles away all day like a puny little woman."

The false thirst, the feverish looks, the violent reply are all splinters in her anguish. For a moment the intruders scrutinize the plain without a word. A person's gaze unreels tediously across this bleak, uniform flatness. Not a shadow of life for a thousand leagues in all directions. Horrifying silence cinches fear's girth a little tighter. Nejma is suffocating. The skinny man bursts out laughing, causing her to tremble.

"Is he a slave, too? Did you escape together from your master? *Ya sidi*, we are going to remedy that infamy!" decrees the lanky one.

"We are not slaves, either of us. And my husband is white," retorts Nejma.

"Ah! So he bought you! But tell me, you must be very pretty then!" he argues.

He glances furtively at his companion, who is still silent, before adding:

"Uncover your face! I want to see you!"

"That's enough," his companion interjects. "I want to drink some tea first. Slave, make us some nice tea."

Nejma obeys. Her legs are jelly. Inside the tent the baby is still sleeping. His closed fists frame his head. His sucking mouth seems to nurse a delicious dream. A handsome dimple creases his chin. A searing grief shoots through Nejma's mind at the thought that these scoundrels might kidnap her children. She takes the baby in her arms. After a brief hesitation, she hides him behind a pile of cushions and covers that serve as their bedding. Thus, he cannot be seen from the entrance. Then she leaves the kheïma with the utensils for tea. As she approaches the kanoun, she throws a furtive glance at the pile of rocks. Yasmine remains perfectly invisible.

"Oh God, Oh God, don't let her show herself!" she begs with silent fervor.

She makes tea. The men say nothing. Nejma puts the teapot and glasses down in front of them, then retreats. The skinny one gets up and, with an ungainly stride, goes toward the fire. He grabs a loaf of hot bread, cuts it in two, and holds half out to his companion. They both eat and drink. They help themselves to more tea.

"Slave, come drink tea with us!" demands the other man after voraciously gobbling up his half of the bread and swallowing three cups of tea.

"I am not in the habit of drinking tea with strangers! Especially when Mahmoud is absent," Nejma answers curtly.

And for several moments indignation overpowers fear:

"Drink the poison of your own contempt! Your words prove you are no guests of God!"

"*Ya sidi*, she has a sharp tongue too, the hussy! But that whets appetite! I'd have preferred her to be white, obviously. White with a milky breast and a calf like a sugar loaf. She's just a negress. But for poor travelers like us . . . Have you ever screwed a black woman?" he suddenly asks, addressing his accomplice.

A guffaw is his only response.

"She must have the taste of game, the scent of waterfowl."

Saying that, he moves slowly towards Nejma. She retreats. He leaps, seizes her by the neck opening of her robe and pulls.

7

The cloth rips sharply. The noise sounds like a sharp cry of terror. Then a round breast appears, showing a large cranberry-colored nipple. It takes the man's breath away. His arms drop to his sides. Nejma quickly covers her breast and leaps back.

"I beg you! I beg you! Tell him to stop!" she pleads, turning toward the other man who is still seated, sipping his tea.

His hands and face jumping with tics, this man has the look of a lunatic. Nejma understands she can expect no pity from either one or the other.

"If you touch me, my husband will kill you," she threatens.

Desperately, she rushes towards Rabha. The dog, scenting the danger, strains against her tether, barking furiously. Nejma might have a chance of escaping them if she managed to free the dog. The man catches on to her intentions immediately. Pulling himself together, he leaps on her, pushes her down, and pins her to the ground. Nejma struggles, screams, hurls insults, begs, cries, and scratches. To no avail. Already with one hand, he has torn open her robe all the way down the front. His partner, who has so far kept his distance, his insane eyes almost hypnotized by the scene, gets up and comes to help him. He kneels at the woman's head. Holding her wrists with one hand, he grabs her fouta with the other. In short order she finds herself bound. His sidekick is already on top of her. In a final surge of defiance, Nejma raises her head, bites the left arm of the man, and won't let go. A howl of pain pierces the air. The man slaps her savagely, trying to release his arm. The trap of her teeth does not spring open. The woman's eyes are frightful. Horror and fury join forces violently. Blood spurts through her teeth, staining her lips. From the corners of her mouth, it flows toward her neck. With his right hand the man grasps her throat and squeezes. The entire weight of his body shifts and presses down on his hand. Nejma's head falls back. Her eyes roll up. Her mouth drops open at last. Once freed, the man's left hand comes to the aid of the one strangling the woman. He stays locked spasmodically onto his prey, hallucinating, drooling onto her headdress. A long time.

When the two men finally get up, Nejma stays on the ground, inert, eyes bulging, mouth spattered with blood. Without a glance her way, the men straighten their clothes and get ready to leave.

Nailed to her hiding place, Yasmine has witnessed the entire scene. Body twisted, face pleading, her mouth is wide open but no sound emerges. On the far side, the dog Rabha still strains against her rope in a frenzy. Her barks hammer time and space. They reverberate against the blue of the sky. They ricochet off the stones of the *reg*. They roll uselessly across the emptiness of the plateau.

The two men hurry toward their mounts. Midway there, the large one turns back and runs toward the kheïma. The only furniture he finds is a little wooden box, which he overturns with a big kick. The family's possessions scatter on the ground: nothing that would bring cash. Three small rugs spread out near the box are the only objects of any value that the kheïma has to offer. Even those are no longer brand new. The man takes them just the same. In his hurry, he doesn't see the baby sleeping next to them. He goes out immediately. The kneeling camels, looking off into the distance, are quietly ruminating, deaf to the men's frenzy. Exasperated by their sluggishness, the men get them up, beating them to start them moving. They hurry off.

From her hiding place Yasmine watches them flee. She stays there, curled up in a knot, without tears, without a call for help. But cries quake inside her. Stone teardrops spread to infinity, the weeping of the reg. The thorns of the tree claw with blind fury at the emptiness. The vast sky is ready to burst out sobbing. The brigands ride off into the distance. Behind them flows a wake of dust.

It is only much later, when the fugitives are only two flies between sky and earth, that Yasmine brings herself to move. With unsteady legs, her body completely numb, she walks toward her mother. She circles around without daring to touch her. Although the men have disappeared, an overwhelming violence still hangs in the air. It is something she can neither name nor place. It has frozen her mother's features in horror. It's crouching there, stock-still, sealed beneath the heavy shroud of silence. Yasmine doesn't understand. The men are far away. Where is the danger now? Death? She's never even heard of it. How is she to recognize its lineaments in the disfigured traits of her mother's face? She looks at her: a hideous grimace, trails of blood on her mouth, on her cheeks, the expression in her eyes . . . Yasmine feels her stomach heave. She narrows her scope of vision, trying to exclude the nightmare. Her eyes come to rest on her mother's breasts. Their blackness gleams in the sun, scintillates with glints of bronze. Yasmine throws herself forward, collapses on her mother's body, and buries her face between her breasts. Her small hand reaches out, searches gently. With a trembling caress she touches Nejma's face and, avoiding the blood, finds her eyes. She brings down the eyelids. She closes off their demented stare. Then, her face still nestled between the breasts, she no longer moves. A few silent tears roll down their harmonious ebony curves.

The wild yapping of the dog abates. From time to time she gives a long howl that spreads out over the plain before finishing in a sort of death rattle. Attuned to them, Yasmine's tears also abate.

All that remains is earth face to face with sky. Between the two, just the arc of the void held in tension by silence. The knots of anguish slowly come undone. Yasmine's muscles relax. Her body sags, overcome by great weariness. And then, from inside the kheïma, the cries of her little brother reach her. She shuts her eyes tight to take refuge in the blackness, hoping to sweep away all outside events with a blink of her lashes. Yasmine does not want to move. She wants to stay there, against her mother's immobility and, like her, she wants to forget the rest. But the baby's cries persist, seek her out even in the darkness beneath closed eyelids. They disturb her weary exhaustion. Reluctantly, Yasmine sits up. She glances quickly at her mother's face. The terror in her eyes is hidden behind her eyelids. But her expression is still horror-filled. Yasmine turns her head away and, with both hands, feebly shakes her mother. Getting no response, she gets up and walks reluctantly toward the kheïma. She looks around for the baby. Guided by his crying, she finds him in an unaccustomed corner. He cries, waving his fists. The small circle of his pouting lips sucks the emptiness from time to time, between his cries. With one hand, Yasmine pushes the small swaddled body to rock him. His cries and tears redouble their vigor. So she resigns herself to taking him in her lap and tries to calm him by swaying her infantile body along with the baby's. It doesn't work. She goes out and takes the baby to their mother. With a pleading look, she holds him out to her. Her mother remains oblivious, inaccessible, given over to a bloody rictus. Yasmine cries in distress. Her silent tears accompany the cries of her little brother. Then, through her tears she again catches sight of the superb roundness of bared breasts offering themselves. Yasmine goes back into the kheïma and quickly returns with a cushion. She places it against her mother's side. She always saw her mother do it this way when she stretched out at siesta time. She puts her brother down, his head on his mother's shoulder, his lips to the nipple. Right away the hungry mouth lays hold, fills itself greedily and nurses, finally, for real. The tears soon stop. For the first time a flash of pleasure shines in the teary eyes of the little girl. A feeble smile wavers on her full lips, stops her tears. For a moment she looks at the baby, sucking calmly on the breast, his eyes closed. Then, confused, she scrutinizes her mother again. Disconcerting spectacle. Yasmine tries in vain to undo the bonds on her wrists. At a loss, she turns away from her and rests the small of her back against her mother's other side. She looks out over the plateau. It is once again cloaked in its usual heavy silence. There it is, without the contours of joy or anger, without laughter, without grief. It is simply there, like death.

Dismounted, Mahmoud kneels by the body. His eyes alone reflect his distress, trying to understand. Understand? Tracks, farther on, violate the earth all the way to the empty horizon. Empty to the east. Empty to the west. Empty in the north as in the south. His head, empty. Empty. Vertiginous nothingness, nauseating, to the point of imminent death. His eyes meet Yasmine's mute gaze. The girl's eyes torment him—they are unblinking. They stare, yield no answers. They are filled with unspeakable questions. They are penetrating. Mahmoud sees her tears welling up. Slowly they water her sorrow. Another brutal event taking place in silence. Mahmoud's eyes, hallucinating, turn back to the body. The marks on her neck are like two large, motionless scorpions. The baby, his mouth still filled with his mother's nipple and his small hand resting on the curve of her black breast, is asleep. Mahmoud looks away. At last he manages to get up. Like a sleepwalker, he goes to untie her wrists and cover her face with the fouta. Then he bends over the baby and takes him in his arms. The little mouth makes the sound of a suction cup when pulled from his mother's breast. Three sucking motions in the void, and movements of the head and tiny fists before he is once again fast asleep. Mahmoud enters the kheïma and lays him down. He picks up a sheet and comes back out. With gestures that don't seem to belong to him, he covers the body.

All at once the camels begin to complain. They are still fully loaded. The sheep, lying on the ground, reply with a few hesitant bleats. These manifestations of daily life seem incongruous, almost grotesque. The camels keep on repeating their protestations. Haggard, Mahmoud walks over, unloads them and makes them kneel. Going back to the kheïma, he sits down and takes Yasmine in his arms. Slowly swaying his torso back and forth, he rocks her and rocks himself. Suddenly all the aridity of the plain and of the desert penetrates him. He slips down into a sort of trance. And this absence is the worst torture of all. Soon, maybe tomorrow, all the suppressed despair will reemerge. For the time being, there he is as if outside himself. Like someone who stopped, mute for the moment, at the edge of an abyss into which he knew he would let himself fall.

He rocks Yasmine and rocks himself.

But another sound pulls him out of his torpor. Rabha, the dog, gives from time to time a sinister howl. Mahmoud finally puts Yasmine down and unties the dog. She goes to sniff her mistress. Getting no response, she drops her head, laying her muzzle near Nejma's shoulder, and stares tiredly at Mahmoud. Yasmine is once more in her father's arms. Occasionally a dry sob still convulses her chest.

The night is serene on the plateau. It is one of those nights with a full moon that fills the atmosphere with a phosphorescent steel-blue haze. Its soft luminescence beads up on the clear thorns of the tree like so many drops of dew. And they remind Mahmoud of all the tears his eyes can't shed. He is grateful to the tree for crying that night for him. Scattered tears of the moon, an opaline dawn for a black nymph. From the depths of Mahmoud's memory other lost faces surge up, other sorrows. His thoughts, fleeing the intolerable, return slowly along the twisted pathways of his life.

2

At first it is his mother's face that imposes itself upon Mahmoud. His mother, adolescent widow, sylph of memory. Her youthful grace, her large eyes glowing with fathomless love in which there ran, without eddies, fear for Mahmoud. Her smile interfused with nostalgia. Mahmoud can still hear her advice. He can see her again, slender, bending toward him as they parted. She was the one, however, who insisted that he be educated, first at the school in Tlemcen, and then at El-Azhar.

"May your father's wishes be fulfilled, my son. Go, my blessing goes with you."

Mahmoud remembers their brief reunion at the end of his studies in Tlemcen. He had felt her impulse of sorrowful joy. But she hadn't wavered. He must leave again, this time for much longer. Much farther away from her affection. She inflicted upon herself, then, the worst of absences. Sending away her only child drew her out of her own adolescence. His absence had matured her. And it had killed her.

Upon his return from Egypt, Mahmoud's joy was shattered on her tomb.

"I never should have left her alone for so long! I should have come to get her once I was able to earn some money. She has already been dead three years, and I knew nothing about it."

His mother was very much alone. She had nonetheless many suitors from allied tribes as well as from her own. But she adamantly refused to be remarried and resisted the diverse pressures from her relatives. A widow in the bosom of the clan represented not only a danger, an element of instability, but also an insult to honor. And then, on top of that, that she dared to rebel was yet more intolerable. All that spared her from a forced marriage was respect for her deceased husband's prestige. In addition, she was lucky enough to have a son. Still, they never missed an occasion to punish her refusal to submit. She faced all sorts of vexations and criticisms.

During the brief vacations he spent with the tribe, while he was still at Tlemcen, Mahmoud became aware of the differences, each time more pronounced, that separated him from the tribe. Their attitude toward his mother was one major cause, of course. But in all truth, their practice of always sacrificing individual liberty to the interests of the group repelled him. His studies continued to distance him from the tribe. Once his mother was gone, he felt himself a complete stranger among the Tijani. He no longer felt the least patience, the least consideration for them. Their compassion in the face of his despair only irritated him. And to complete the work of those infernal days, they gave him what his mother had left him: a letter from his father. A father he had never known, a father dead before his birth. A letter written on the eve of a *jeich*. For at that time, from Labiod-Sid-Sheikh to the desert, men were rising up against the violation of their territory by Lyautey's soldiers. And each time, at the very beginning of this century of uncertainties, these lonely lands exacted their blood tribute. What if he should die, Lakhdar Tijani, without achieving a noteworthy feat? That was his only fear each time he left for *baroud*. His wife was pregnant. Another cause for worry. His only hope as well. So he decided to leave a letter for this child-to-be. A letter he left with his wife with the express wish that she not give it to him until he reached adulthood, after having seen that he had received a proper education. Lakhdar Tijani died that day under the fire of the *roumis*. That was in 1901. His wife had hidden the letter for all those years.

A moment of panic, fingers trembling on the seal of the paper.

Liberated from their long imprisonment, his father's words riddle Mahmoud with their silent burst of fire. Salvos from beyond the grave, voiceless words whose impact nonetheless would be etched in him forever.

"*Ejjrad*! The most harmful locusts in our history have always come from the sea, not from the desert . . . Your grandfather, Slimane Tijani, brave disciple of the emir, could not do otherwise than to respond to his call for jihad. He died in 1843, my son, my blood, with a sword in his hand, along with a number of the bravest men of the tribe, defending the *smalah* . . ." And further on, "In retaliation the roumis expropriated our lands. We became nomads because of injustice, my child, my blood. And now, see how they want to control even the lands where we wander. But this, alas, you must already know . . . Tomorrow, if I die beneath the roumis' guns, my last thoughts will be set afire by regret for dying before your birth, before hugging you in my arms. They will be troubled by remorse for leaving my mother, your grandmother, alone back there, my blood, on our usurped lands, given over to be trampled by the roumis. However, she has visited me in my dreams many times. And she always makes the same request: 'I want to rejoin my own people at Labiod-Sid-Sheikh.' But from jihad to jihad, I have never found sufficient peace and time to carry out this task. From jihad to jihad, I've shirked this responsibility like a coward. To be honest, the idea of returning to the land of my childhood was too high a price. It could only be carried out at the cost of a massacre: my own by the colonizers, or that of the roumis, parading around on my ancestors' lands, by my own hand. Thus it is to you, my offspring, because you will have more distance from these grievous events, that I dare to address a request: when you reach the age of reason and understanding, lend your hands and a few moments of your life to this task. If you bring my mother's bones to Labiod-Sid-Sheikh, my own bones, wherever they may be, will at last find peace," said these words from beyond the grave, thirty years later. Death's unreasonable demands, yet again.

His mother's face, his father's words are afloat on this moonlit night. Violence and death are present once more. Once more they lash Mahmoud's thoughts. He had believed his life well protected by a thousand leagues of desert, by years of solitude wandering across the steppe.

"The most harmful locusts in our history have always come from the sea." From whence came today's locusts? They left only devastation in their wake, only a child paralyzed with horror. Here he was now, on this land that had been his refuge, shipwrecked.

He rocks Yasmine and rocks himself.

If only he could cry! If only tears would deign at last to rescue him. And the words of the poet? The ones that jostle each other, sing out with an ineffectual pomposity. They, too, leave him empty. They're only words. Dry, naked words like the steppe itself. A few words without luster, trying to express what they cannot tamp out. Just to master it. He would say them very low, without revolt and without crying. If he could.

He rocks Yasmine and rocks himself.

Out of this paralyzing grief, other memories rise up. As if memory were venting:

That bitter winter spent with the Ouled Sidi Sheikh. They gave us a small plot of land not far from a well. Typhus, cholera, and other fevers had decimated both men and beasts. We had nothing left to barter for food. No more wool, no more clarified butter. We had to try everything, even the impossible. That land? Scorched earth cracked by frost imprinting its fissures on the land's emaciated body. All the survivors of the tribe attacked the ground, however, with their rudimentary tools, spurred by the energy of last hope. At cock's crow, already they were clearing

17

land, smashing rocks, wresting from it a strip of soil. At nightfall they were still at it. But every morning, it seemed that the earth was taunting us, for such labor seemed ridiculous in the face of all that remained undone. As if, profiting from the cover of night, the earth had sweated out, excreted tons of rock from the entrails of hell. I remember those early mornings pierced by cold. A cold that shot its icy dart into the heart of sleep, even into the unconscious. Days were centuries. Evenings wasted away in cosmic, cyclical despair. Then, that spring. First shoots appeared tufted and scattered among the rocks. Then locusts and still more locusts. Then, nothing left—nothing—only a bitter and paralyzing derision that ate up the last straw of will.

However, that brief moment of being sedentary brought me a luminous revelation. Until then I only knew the French as the squadrons or camel corps that occasionally crossed our path, the former along the border of the *tell*, the latter along the frontiers of the desert. Usually they ignored us and continued on their way. But we were so afraid of them! *Ejjrad*! *Ejjrad*! the adults would say, for whom this vision of the triumphal conqueror reopened old wounds. The result being that when I saw them riding away, I associated them with a true swarm of devouring locusts who had spared us this time. Raised with this fear of the roumi, I held them responsible for the terrible need for vengeance that tormented me. I thought that if our lives were spent shuttling endlessly between the edge of the tell and the edge of the desert, it was because the locusts tracked us from the north and the south. The roumis were for me a dangerous cloud on the horizon of my liberty.

On the first day we arrived in Labiod-Sid-Sheikh, I was at some distance from the camp when I saw a man coming toward me in long pants, his blond hair uncovered. "A roumi!" Fear propelled me back to the camp. All my relatives were standing together uneasily and waiting. Hands in his pockets, the man approached us with an untroubled step. When he reached us, he said "salaam" and sat on the ground and looked up at us smiling.

"I am a teacher; my name is Meunier," he said affably.

My group looked at him with undisguised hostility. My mother, who had been fixing tea, had left her dishes and stood with her arms around me. She was the first to be conquered by the stranger's good nature. All of a sudden, she turned and went toward our kheïma, returning quickly to offer tea to the man. Furious, one of the Tijani hurried to take the tray from her and put her in her place. But Sheikh Ma'mar intervened. He pushed him back and, taking the tray from her hands, went to sit down near the roumi.

"Welcome. You are my guest."

The others stayed at a safe distance. In spite of the reticence toward him, the man made it a habit to visit us toward the end of the day. Not finding in him the least bit of aggressiveness, with each of his visits I came a bit closer to hear the conversation he was having with Sheikh Ma'mar. One day, after he had left, the sheikh said to me:

"This roumi is a good man, a great man!"

That idea imposed itself on me bit by bit. But up until then I had denied it guiltily. I was thankful to hear the wise sheikh's words, for they allowed me to acknowledge the evidence. Reassured about my opinion, the next day I went to the small school and waited the whole afternoon for the Frenchman to come out. When he saw me, a smile spread over his face. He motioned me forward.

"Come, I'll show you the school. You really should come here. I know that you are learning Arabic. But you should also have access to French!"

That day he did not come to the camp. Rather I stayed late with him. I told him about my family's history, about my fear of the roumis, the locusts.

"Wars, invasions, the warlike nature of man will nourish for a long time to come such fears in children. I'd like to hope that one day that will change. Only knowledge, learning, will be able, perhaps, to cure man of this fault. Only educated men can become the artisans of that new future."

For the first time I had a friend, an adopted father. My mother and Sheikh Ma'mar, united against the rest of the group, had decided to have me educated. Alas! The arid land kept us from living among the sedentary. To survive, we had to find food for the animals through nomadism, a path we trod only because we'd been dispossessed. That explained my distress at leaving. But even if the land had stymied our efforts without giving us any harvest, thanks to Meunier I took with me an enormous harvest of faith in humanity. Meeting him opened for me a spell of fair weather along the northern horizon that until now had always been menacing. His lofty mind and dignity taught me that even just one person could sometimes make up for thousands of others trapped in contempt. No longer being constrained by a colossal hate helped a little to ease my fears about the future. And when the tribe returned to Labiod-Sid-Sheikh to visit the *marabout*, I always headed off to visit Sheikh Meunier.

Once when we had just arrived in Labiod-Sid-Sheikh, I ran off as usual toward Meunier's house. I pounded impatiently on his door. How surprised I was when it was opened by another man. By all appearances, this one did not speak Arabic as Meunier had. When he finally understood my question, he said to me:

"Gone! Gone! *M'cha* Constantine.

In despair I turned my back on him and fled. It was the twenty-seventh night of the month of Ramadan. I must have been just twelve years old and was fasting for the entire month for the first time. I would have loved it so much if Meunier knew that feat. I kept my pain to myself far from the camp that was preparing to celebrate that special night.

That night, after having broken the fast with some dates and a bowl of *h'rira*, the men left camp to go to the mosque of the sheikh. They would pray there until dawn. The women would be busy feeding the small children, who during the month of Ramadan were only fed frugal snacks during the day. Later they would prepare the *sfifa*. Large *guessa'as* were sent to the mosque. When their chores were done, the women would gather in one of the kheïmas. With a tray of tea before them, and the last-born still at their breasts, they would sing together. Songs and *bendirs* singing the praises of Allah and his prophet.

Squatting outside, I listened to their song. Their impassioned voices, vibrating in unison in a sublime sob, thrilled me and kindled my own grief. All the children watched the sky. At the least noise, they'd jump. The twinkling of the stars fed their impatience as they waited. They waited, oscillating between pronounced anxiety and entreaty. Because on that night when angels revealed the sum of human acts, God might elect a chosen one and rend the heavens in two before their astonished eyes. Awe and ecstasy! But beware of these outpourings of emotion. Beware of the traitorous swoon and other cowardly escapes. Don't waste time on either awe or zealous devotion; they are useless when heaven itself carries you to its heights. Salvation lies in keeping a cool head and in nurturing heartfelt wishes. Wealth, glory, honor, redemption . . . All that was once coveted will seem like mere ornamentation in life and in death.

Crouching in front of the kheïma, eyes riveted to the sky, I waited. Though the biting cold pierced me with a thousand needles, I did not move. If the heavens chose me, I would only ask for the return of Meunier. But the heavens remained obstinately calm. The myriad of stars glittered serenely in the dark. I barely noticed the occasional shooting star. It would shoot away like an ironic burst of icy laughter. And the women's voices made me ache with longing.

"Almighty God, let a violent wind carry these devastating clouds of locusts far from us."

Their pleas caused a sob to well up in my throat. Caught in the throes of depression after being abandoned by my only friend, I felt pessimism unfurl in me. That evening I was aware of my sins, of my falling short of the code of honor. How dared I still await a liberating rent in the heavens? All that was unbearable assailed me. In my world, where one only existed by his bravery, his virility, his willingness to sacrifice, I would be scum if I did not avenge my family, if I did not take seven wives, if I did not . . . How much all these ideas terrified me! How would I find a way out?

My mother was looking for me, calling me. Finding me immobile in the cold, she came anxiously toward me. I threw myself impetuously against her breast and cried in distress:

"*Oummi*, I swear I will avenge my grandfather and my father."

In fact, I was trying in this way to ward off fear of divine retribution, more than trying to convince myself of the merits of this tragic assertion.

"Don't say stupidities," scolded my mother. "Has Meunier's absence affected you so much? Listen to me, your being a *taleb* here can bring you nothing more. You must continue your studies in Tlemcen and then Cairo, according to your father's wishes. If there is any debt toward him which you must acquit with honor, it is that one, my son. And the best sign of friendship you could show Meunier would be to learn his language. He said that all teachers were nourished by the same ideas as he was. He said that each language learned was a new opening onto the road of freedom and dignity. I would like to see you take that road, my son. I don't want to lose you. I don't want the future that destiny has in store for you if you stay here. Go discover *el-mashreq* and the easier life of the cities. I want you to be noble, as your grandfathers were.

Sheikh Ma'mar, the least intransigent of the Tijani, had died recently. As for the others, more rebellious, delivering a boy over to the influence of the French signified allegiance with the enemy. Mahmoud's education continued in Arabic only. Tlemcen for a few years, then Cairo. Urban life raised its walls, wove its perfumes, erected its rampart of noise around Mahmoud. His sensibility, until now stripped down by the immensities and all the unbounded spaces of deserts, crushed by the weight of dogma, possessed by hallucinatory, nomad myths, found sanctuary in these clamorous cities sealed round with greenery.

"Here, feeling grows like a sensuous water lily along the ripples of a thousand paths, beneath the shimmer of delicate sensations and enchanting sounds," Mahmoud noted in amazement.

El-Azhar, even more than the school at Tlemcen, blessedly filled his days. His contacts with some of the founders of the Nahdha movement overwhelmed him with hope and enthusiasm. Reading varied texts other than those to which he had been limited until now by his taleb helped to free him from the iron collar of liturgical dictums. He hurried to taste the *narghila* and wine. It didn't take him long to magnify the "fault" by losing faith and virginity in a Cairo bordello blessed with all the sins.

Finally, with the discovery of poetry, there grew in Mahmoud that sensibility that had first taken shape upon meeting Meunier. Little by little, his focus shifted. And with this delivery from obsessions and dreadful projects of vengeance, time no longer weighed upon him.

Had he, then, forgotten his mother? No. All this time, his mother meant, for him, the certainty of return. He could cope with her absence. That certainty alone had allowed him to carry on peacefully.

Upon finding his mother gone upon his return, and then reading his father's words, all the ills of the past rose up. Time reared up again. Life fell apart, got tangled up in knots of remorse and regret.

Pushed by words from beyond the grave, Mahmoud got ready to leave to carry out his father's wishes. Primarily, getting ready meant buying a new horse at the peak of fitness. As for the rest, he still had the same *baluchon*.

Mahmoud set out and galloped for days upon days, blind to the landscape, the same images always before his eyes. In his head, always the same firebrands of words. Chastised as ever by his conscience, haunted by the manes of his ancestors, he galloped through the realm of death. His grandfather, his father, all those formidable warriors. Horrendous journey.

However, Mahmoud resisted, tried to keep at a certain distance.

"I, myself, am different. I will not allow myself to be caught in the trap of vengeance. For far too long, and with an almost morbid accommodation, I've endured the tug-of-war between the duty of vengeance and my own deep aspirations to live in peace. What vengeance and whom to avenge? The dozens of my tribesmen cut down by the roumis? And how can we take back our lands from the colonial settlers at this point? My good-wife conscience no longer corners me with her biases."

Born with the century and now in his twenties, the idea of violence repelled him completely. As gratifying as they were, the various insurrections had ruined his tribe, decimated its men, with no other outcome than successive generations of orphans given over to reprisals and misfortune.

"A war, a real war — yes! If an uprising throughout the entire country, methodically structured and organized, came about to break through the wretched lethargy that has beaten down the *'arbis*, I would work for it with all my heart. But not with arms. I am a poet."

However, the current context was hardly propitious. Pitiless repression had crushed the rebellions. The country was "pacified" through humiliation and misery. By the denial of the most elementary rights. But he knew himself to be incapable of starting a widespread insurrection. As for the punitive expeditions of small *jeich* or individual actions, no way! It was out of an innate aversion to violence rather than cowardice.

"Clean hands and jihad? Pen in hand. Head full of dreams, heart full of joy and jihad? Poet? Poetry, what a miserable dodge when courage is lacking!" he taunted himself.

What torture! Despite the ramparts of reason, despite the banner of poetry, a guilty conscience clouded his horizons. How ridiculous this ride toward his grandmother's bones. His mother's absence suddenly became real, and the pain it brought blotted out the reality of the landscape. He galloped through a thick fog in the midst of blazing days. He galloped without being able to cross through the land of remorse. When he stopped, brought low by fatigue, he nibbled several hunks of bread and a couple of pieces of *khlii*. But everything was tasteless to him. So, rolled up in his burnous, he was engulfed by melancholy. All around him on the plateau, silence loomed. A silence so heavy with mystery that it only increased his anxiety.

After several days, he arrived in the region where his family's land was. Often, he stopped to ask the older Algerian farmers he encountered if they knew the former lands of the Tijani. They would nod their heads sadly and show him the direction. The last one asked replied:

"Yes, today the estate belongs to the Sirvant family. Beautiful lands. Keep going straight ahead on this road. You'll see twin hills, curved and rounded, covered with vineyards. They will swell up before you like breasts filled with milk about to nurse the sky. The elder Sirvant, the father, died several years ago now, crushed by work. His children boast they make the best wine in the region."

From a distance Mahmoud saw the gentle contours of the hills striped with soft green. At their foot, the leaves of large olive trees shimmered. Yet farther down, the springtime sun played over the burnished wheat. Here and there, the vermilion necklace of a eucalyptus burst forth in scarlet splendor. In that full light, they seemed to be crackling with smokeless flames. Mahmoud stopped his horse to contemplate them.

"Did they look like that when my people left? Beauty can inspire a deadly ecstasy. In troubled and uncertain times, sight may have an almost demonic, eleventh-hour lucidity.

He imagined his tribe leaving this place fifty years ago, and he felt their distress in rediscovering these lands. He had to force himself to put away these thoughts and continue on his way. A little farther on, he came to the estate's entrance. The simple Arab house described to him no longer existed. Instead, there was an imposing edifice several stories high. White as snow, it had large windows shielded by sky-blue shutters.

"Beneath the first olive tree to the right of the house," said his father's directive.

The tomb of his grandmother.

Mahmoud shivered. Snapping back to reality, he became conscious of his bizarre behavior. Throughout his long return to the verdant tell, absorbed in gloomy meditations, he had not thought for a moment about how to behave once he reached his destination. How should he set about retrieving his grandmother's bones buried in usurped ground? Would he have to introduce himself, the descendant of the rightful owners of these lands, to the thieves the laws of might-makes-right protected?

"I've come for my grandmother's bones."

What an outrage! The very idea of negotiating with these settlers revolted him. What could he do? He wasn't going to hang around the premises waiting for nightfall so that, like a thief, he could insinuate himself in the dark into the property to dig up the ground a couple of meters from the house. No, no! For a few seconds, he felt a terrible desire to retrace his steps, to flee. These enchanted lands were foreign to him. The only memory they aroused in him was the agony, now mythic, of his people. Yes, leave again, keep on moving, wear out all torments, exhaust the dead, bury them once and for all, and escape once more from their clutches. Yes, go back to the austere calm of the plateau. But a force at once obscure and more powerful compelled him to continue on. He reined in his horse and walked him into an alley bordered by a double row of palm trees with whitewashed trunks. It led straight to the house, dazzlingly white and sky blue. Two men were working nearby. As soon as they saw him, carbines in their bandoliers, brows furrowed, they swooped in upon him.

The Sirvant boys, clad in military jackets and boots, their carbines at an arm's reach inside the house, or banging against their flanks whenever they plowed the fields, had the reputation of being good shots. Game was abundant. Yet, shooting wood pigeons or pheasant was not for just anyone. It was a talent reserved for the chosen few. Hunting always gave the men an opportunity for bragging at anisette time. And the aroma of waterfowl enlivened the daily fare for the guests around the Sirvants' table. Beneath blue shadows woven by the grapevines, meals became celebrations. Legs spread, planted in the earth, as motionless as tree trunks, then bang! the Sirvants' bullets reached their flying targets just as they took off over the fields or the olive trees. In addition, firearms discouraged the Arabs roaming "like jackals" around the property. Just a few days earlier, from a second-floor window, the elder boy had seen one of them around the entrance at nightfall. A dark silhouette whose gaze—threatening, he imagined—was focusing on the house and on the opulent orchard. Seeing him emerge with his gun, the man turned and left with the easy step of a Bedouin who has a long way to travel. Sirvant ran in the hopes of catching him. But when he reached the end of the long alley, the other had already disappeared, snapped up by night suddenly fallen like a heavy curtain over the grandiose theater of the valley.

"What do you want? You're on private property here," the elder one burst out.

"I am a son of the Tijani whom your family dispossessed."

Already on their guard, the men pulled out their guns. But at the moment, Mahmoud felt no fear. He continued calmly:

"Before his death, my father wrote down his last wishes. He asked me to come, when I became a man, to gather my grandmother's bones that remained here."

The men looked at each other in astonishment. The enormity of the thing left them flabbergasted for a time. Then their suspicious eyes scrutinized this man who, with brazen assurance, tried to feed them such a lie. The elder pulled himself together first, exclaiming:

"Arabs never let themselves be buried outside cemeteries."

"Is that so. Then what do the nomads of the high plateaus and the desert do? Perhaps they have ambulatory graveyards? My grandmother asked to be buried on her own land!"

"But as luck would have it, there is no grave here."

"Yes, there is. She's got to be over there, beneath the first olive tree, to the right of the house."

"There is nothing there, I tell you," the man thundered.

"Was the house built on the site of the previous one? Were any olive trees sacrificed during its construction?"

"Well, Grandfather said that where the house stands there was only a *dechra* he wouldn't have used as a henhouse. He razed it. Cutting down trees was hardly his style, especially an olive tree. On the contrary, just look at what he planted. Don't imagine it looked like this before. He . . ."

"If the house is in the same place as the other and no olive tree was cut down, then the bones must still be there, under the first olive tree, on the right!" interrupted Mahmoud.

Three women came out of the house and joined the men. All of them stared, nonplused, at the old olive tree, as if just discovering it. It stood, massive and solitary, at a distance from the field. Its superb mane was shimmering mother-of-pearl. Across the entire, carefully cultivated field, the whitewashed bases of the trunks contrasted prettily with the red-brown clods. Not a trace of a weed, not a hint of a barrow, anywhere. Skeptical, they turned back to Mahmoud. He didn't let himself get flustered. He calmly reasserted:

"She must be over there."

"What's this story you're feeding us? What is this tale after so many years? What is it you're really after?" exploded one of the Sirvant men still clenching his teeth.

Anger made his moustache quiver. The carbine was trembling in his hand. Just then a woman's voice was heard behind him.

"Jean, please, give him a shovel and a pick and let him dig," she said in Arabic in a soft but firm tone.

It was a tiny old woman, all wrinkles. And in the midst of all those wrinkles were ancient eyes, like clear water. The others looked at her, disconcerted. She repeated:

"Give him a shovel and a pick. Let him dig."

"But Mother, even if it is true there's still a grave over there, you don't have the right to go digging up the dead. There are laws, you know," protested one of the men.

"Our laws we imposed on them along with all the rest. We took all they had. We will not also take their dead!" she shot back sharply, this time in French.

"Let him do it," added the youngest woman. "Now that I know there is a grave there, in front of the house, I'll be afraid when night falls. Surely I won't be the only one. And besides, it's the grave of one of the . . ."

She left her sentence unfinished, wringing her hands nervously, faced with the cold stare of reproof the old woman shot at her. An elderly Algerian, probably one of the workers, standing at a distance from the group, went away toward the grange. He returned carrying two picks and two shovels.

"I'll help him dig," he said for the benefit of the others.

Mahmoud took the tools from his hands and said in a dull voice, categorically:

"I want to dig alone!"

29

Mahmoud walked over to the olive tree and caressed its trunk with a distracted hand while looking at the ground in the shadow of its parasol. He took off his burnous and hung it on a branch. Then, pushing back the sleeves of his 'abaya, he spread his feet and gave a first blow with the pick. Behind him, the silent, motionless group kept their eyes riveted on him. A woman's voice blurted out:

"Thank God the children are not here!"

Mahmoud dug energetically, more than a meter deep. The earth had been worked. It opened easily under the fang of the pick. But the shovelfuls only uncovered the brown, woody roots of the olive tree. Exhausted, his face covered with sweat, Mahmoud put down his pick and shovel and sat down nearby to catch his breath. His disillusioned gaze roamed over the area. He caused a stir among the Sirvants who were gathered on their terrace. After a few whispers, the entire group turned their backs and disappeared into the house. Several moments later, the old woman came back out. Her body barely curved by age, she walked toward Mahmoud with a sure step. She had a carafe of water, which she held out to him. Mahmoud's gaze, acknowledging neither her presence nor her gesture, brushed over the outline of the hills, caressing the dark, sturdy trunks of the olive trees, the rippling iridescent silk of their foliage. They paused for a long time over the foliage of the orange trees with their snowy profusion of blossoms. Mahmoud inhaled it all in one voluptuous breath. Then, his gaze returned to the imposing house. In its place, he imagined an old Arab house with its central courtyard ringed by rooms. In front of it, a well and a low stone wall where women were sitting. He thought he even heard laughter, the sound of water, a pulley squeaking faintly. All around, kheïmas of greater or lesser importance were pitched. Havens where men could take refuge and receive their relatives, friends, neighbors, and travelers. Special havens far from the house, from needy hives of women, riddled with the cries of babies. Mahmoud imagined the fantasias performed during the great *ou'adas*. Warriors in hand-to-hand combat, at one with their horses, sharing in the glossy shimmer and the winged, purebred motion. Soaring ululations of women followed in their wake, all across the valley. Clouds of sparkling trills launched forth, dizzying the skies . . . Nothing was left of all that. In its place, this immense house that could easily shelter an entire tribe. Its size, its excessive whiteness, its too-cheerful shutters, and even its style offended his eyes, assaulted his history.

The old woman had put the carafe in front of him. Leaning back against the trunk of the olive tree, she watched him.

"Where does your family live now?" she asked in a soft voice.

Her question brought Mahmoud back from his reverie. The wrathful lightning bolt of his glare was unspeakable. Without touching the water, he took up the pick again and returned to digging, a cubit farther on. But the woman was not to be put off yet:

"You know, if you need something, we might be able to help you. I've often thought about that."

Mahmoud snapped upright. He threw the pick, burying its churlish fang in the pile of dirt. Eyes blazing, Mahmoud burst out in an acid voice:

"You would like to give us back our land, perhaps, dear madam so full of generosity? Or perhaps you would accept us now as servants? Well, well, what's one more Fatma, one more Ali or one more Mohamed! Excellent for one's reputation, isn't it? The best antidote against the haunting fear of returning, one day, to things as they were, is to try to domesticate the true landowners! Because nothing in the world could make you want to revive that past. Spit out on our shores by an angry sea one black day, lousy beggars in worn-out shoes, that's what you were, all of you!"

"Violent words, full of rancor. You are saying whatever comes into your head and you know it. In any case, the military expropriated your ancestors. We ourselves had nothing to do with it. And we had nothing to do with the fact that your ancestors preferred to use the language of gunpowder."

"You had nothing to do with it when you agreed to take the land of others?"

"These lands have been ours for a long time now. They belong to us because we took them, wrested them, strip by strip, from the underbrush and the dwarf palm. More than half this land was scrub."

"Yes, yes, I recognize the lullaby that rocks and reassures the colonizers! Nevertheless, even in a state of almost total abandonment, occupying land is theft. One of these days, you'll have to give it back."

"Never! My father-in-law and his brother devoted their lives to this hard labor . . . Don't let yourself be blinded by the past. We can help you. Gall . . ."

"I am gall and you are all honey. Venomous honey, of course. I have nothing to say to you, and even less to ask of you. I only want to satisfy the last wishes of a dead man and transport the bones left all alone here. Now get out of here. Let me finish my task in peace, otherwise I'll have the pleasure of burying you alive in place of my grandmother!"

He returned to digging furiously with the pick. He detested her, that tiresome little old woman, and seeing her, in spite of everything, carrying on with an affable, reasonable air exacerbated his anger. He hated himself for not being able to get rid of the idea that if he had met her somewhere else and hadn't known who she was, he would surely have found her likeable. Maybe even, in different circumstances, they would have become friends. That idea exasperated him completely. Wasn't it a sign of weak character? A perverse and twisted temperament, imagining itself blessed with a discerning mind? Because after all, look at the affront he had just suffered. Scandalous propositions, the worst of insults proffered with a serenity grounded in certitudes. Certitudes based on the rejection and enslavement of the other. He cursed himself. He cursed all that old woman stood for in his eyes. He even damned her for being so impertinently old and spry, so impertinently lively for all her snowy hair. His own people had all been decimated in the flower of youth, either in various uprisings, or by fevers and illnesses during the migrations of his diminished tribe. But his people had never compromised. That was the real difference between them and himself.

Better a thousand straightforward hostilities, better a thousand wounds, than this contempt disguised as condescension. A bad conscience trying to whitewash itself at bargain prices, Mahmoud thought to himself while digging in a fury.

Discouraged, the old woman had turned on her heel and gone to sit on a bench in front of the house.

Get this over with quickly and get out of here! Mahmoud told himself.

All of a sudden, in a clump of earth . . . there, on the shovel, a bone! Mahmoud stopped, momentarily hypnotized. It was a long bone, chalky white and very clean. With a thousand precautions, Mahmoud put down his shovel and headed quickly toward his horse. The horse, thinking they were about to leave, pawed the ground and tugged at the reins. From a small satchel hanging from the saddle, Mahmoud pulled out a cloth bag, dazzling white and carefully folded. He had purposely made it into a shroud. Retracing his steps, he opened it up and placed it beside the grave, which he climbed back into. Kneeling down inside, he felt around with his bare hands in the yielding soil. Little by little the entire skeleton appeared, there, embedded in the earth like a dead root from the olive tree. Mahmoud sat down.

What did I come for? My grandmother? He gave a short, derisive laugh. What remained of her? An anchor incrusted in the soil that soon would crumble all together. Her soul? What is a soul? A small breath of air diluted for so long in the atmosphere

33

that finally is inhaled innocently, by other lungs, and then taken away again by the wind.

He shrugged his shoulders and once again was lost in thought.

Did the torment of another, himself long dead, justify this uprooting from the cradle of such a beautiful place? And why? To remove her from the soft shadow of this magnificent tree to an Arab cemetery, burnt by day, frozen by night, naked beneath the acrid frost of dust, a hell beneath whatever heavens. She had wanted to be buried here. That was her wish. Her apparition in my father's dreams never translated anything other than his own agony. And I, a third party, what am I doing?

Beneath the parasol of the olive tree, several reddish splashes of sunlight moved slightly like giant fireflies busily harvesting the nectar of the thick shadow. In the wavy hair of the tree, a heedless nightingale was performing its concert. Mahmoud raised his head.

Maybe her soul is there, like a kitten of light capering when the leaves whisper and shimmer, cavorting in the diaphanous ring of wind, gorged by the splendid anthem from that gay and fluent nightingale.

He heaved a sigh of resignation. The dead never troubled themselves with answering his questions. He had not come so far, he had not disinterred this skeleton to leave it here. No, he could not do that.

"Maybe she would have liked being protected from this violation, from the intrusion of my gaze, by a *hijab* of Qur'anic verses. But I just cannot do that. Not that I don't know the Qur'an; my childhood teacher drilled me so much it even shapes what I forget. But I would be a hypocrite if I engaged in such a parody. And for you, Grandmother, it would just be one more profanation. In Labiod-Sid-Sheikh, a *jema'a* of the taleb will recite them for you," he promised.

In the face of this pure death, devoid of stench, unconse-

34

crated, Mahmoud recovered his perspective. He suddenly felt serene and clean, his conscience purged of all opprobrium.

"A blessing from my grandmother in consideration of my efforts to find her," he liked to think.

"Blessing?" mocked a perfidious little interior voice at once.

"Yes, blessing, even if it contradicts my usual habits of thought. So what?" he joked ironically.

Now Mahmoud was no longer in a hurry. Sitting in the grave, he contemplated the remains of his grandmother. He filled his eyes and his thoughts with this pure death, light in spite of the weight of the earth on her smile, on her eye sockets, all the clawed-at openings. He looked at her, the deceased, her commonplace anatomy, her simple destiny. She was at one and the same time his grandmother, his father, and all those brave warriors unburdened at last of their worries, cast into mineral outlines. She was there, the derisive, earth-filled eye, the toothless smile, cheeks smoothed of the flesh's rictus, strong in her immaculate silence.

What kind of woman had his grandmother been? How he would have loved to make her talk, have her recount her life in this green and rolling land, have her tell him her joys and sorrows, have her describe death. With a slow gesture, Mahmoud caressed the bones of her hand. They must have been long and beautiful with fine wrists. At present, without their envelope of flesh, they looked like antique carding combs. And this bowl, a hull where life had blossomed. Now, even death had deserted it.

Frozen beneath the eucalyptus, the old woman had been fascinated by his protracted immobility. She had stretched her neck, straightened her back, but the interior of the grave remained inaccessible to her gaze. After a short time, when she could bear it no longer, she got up and walked, with a soft step toward the olive tree. Sitting in the bottom of the grave, his eye reflecting a sweet melancholy, Mahmoud caressed the skeleton. This spectacle made the old woman shiver and caused her hair to stand on end. The other Sirvants, both men and women, were above, on the upper floor. Hidden behind the window drapery, they were following the scene. Mahmoud sensed her presence.

Her again. Cursed old woman.

Mahmoud's eyes flamed. Rage cut into his reverie.

Some peace! To be alone! Alone to converse at last with his grandmother.

He got up.

Go! Go!

The shroud was there, nearby. Nearby, too, was his grandmother. Fragile, chalky bone fixed in the earth. Mahmoud tugged on it. The hand fell apart into disjointed phalanges and splinters.

"Fragments of a shattered memory. Pulverized, beyond the memory of a gesture. Debris. One, two, three, all loose, anonymous in the sack. Amputated skeleton. No tears, no weeping, absorbed in the plenitude of the earth's embrace," Mahmoud exclaimed, overcome by a sort of joy.

He continued to disinter the skeleton. The joints gave way, snapping.

Destroyed, our final identity in the communal skeleton. One, two, three, all loose, anonymous in the sack.

Some of the bones grated. Others had that hollow sound that announced their imminent future as dust. There was nothing left in the ground but the head and one foot.

How odd are that head and foot lying there with no body. Head that once was capable of thought, you see how you are taken care of now! Head, what of your dreams once upon a time of flying away? Here you are crumbling, knit into the soil, robbed forever of all desire, a couple grains of sand your only sense. And you, foot, forever shackled to one certainty, the measure of your days, the length of your journey, you are now in your turn trampled. And while the head is invaded by earth, you dig your toes in like so many small roots in order to plant yourself there. A head full of dreams and pretensions, or a foot used to advantage or to take a bow—just look at them now united in the same mockery, equally decrepit.

Mahmoud laid hold of the foot, which also broke apart.

"How many bones! How many in a foot! One, two, three, four, five . . . The head now. A fragile roundness, white as chalk, eyes of avid shadow, a smile so beatific and empty. Into the sack with it as well."

Mahmoud bent over to put it down. He thought better of it, and straightened back up.

"No, no, my beauty, you will travel in the open air, to the great displeasure of the living. I'll take you on a journey through life. May our travels be the bridge into yours. May your death cross back into my days with the sweetness of friendship."

With anxious eyes, mother Sirvant backed away. Then, turning around, she went toward the house with a lively step. However, given the curiosity and fear competing inside her, she stayed hidden behind the front door barely ajar. Her retreat delighted Mahmoud. He let go a mocking laugh, turning toward the facade of the house. The movement of the curtains put him once more at ease.

"You see, Grandmother, how the living, however boastful they are, however fearless they pretend to be, panic before a corpse. Why are we so afraid of the dead?"

The bones rattled on his back. Held in his hand, at shoulder height, the skull fixed its derisive sockets upon those in hiding. His head bare, his moustache and clothes covered with dust, with a surly eye and an arrogant smile, Mahmoud had something demonic about him. He seemed to taunt the living, make fun of death and all its rites. Was he an unreal being, a phantom? Maybe he was Dame Death herself, come in the guise of a Bedouin, a shade demented, to mock the living.

Mahmoud had already turned his back on the olive tree and was getting ready to leave when, from the depths of the hole, something unusual drew his gaze. Vertigo. Dizziness. He saw himself stretched out in the grave. A corpse wrapped in a dirty winding sheet, a sickly countenance with shameless eyes, as if petrified in morbid hilarity between life and death. The shock made Mahmoud close his eyes.

"Oh, Grandmother, here I am once more prey to hallucinations. Just when I thought you had delivered me from them. Just when I feel such calm! Just when . . ."

He opened his eyes to discover that it was only his *chèche* still in the grave. A chèche, spotted with mud, as wrinkled as a castoff snakeskin. Mahmoud burst out laughing.

"It's hunger, Grandmother. So many days of riding and scarcely anything to eat. So much solitude. Neglecting the needs of the body so much, the mind becomes corrupted. Feeding thoughts with nothing but bitter food, constraining them to austerity, the imagination rebels and throws itself into folly, hoping to taste there an impossible fantasy, to burst all the iron collars. Maybe it's fear, Grandmother. I have no more courage than those at whom I laugh. But they won't possess me yet, not anguish, not folly, not death, at least for now."

He put down the sack of bones, skull on top, and fumbled in the pocket of his pants, pulling out a folded paper.

"See, Grandmother—Father's letter, into the hole," he exclaimed emphatically.

He picked up the shovel again and set himself to refilling the grave feverishly, crying:

"Father's letter, buried! Let it rejoin him then. The remorse that overwhelmed me, buried! My own memory, buried. The rules of the tribe, buried! Their cretinism, buried! Buried! You are witness, Grandmother! I leave all this here and start afresh! You will tell them, won't you? And when I've taken you to them at Labiod-Sid-Sheikh, I'll be finished answering to the conventions of the clan, finished bowing to the wishes of the dead, finished."

Despite the energy he'd expended, he still felt the need to revolt. The grave filled in, he threw aside the shovel, put the skull in the hood of his burnous, which he draped over his back, and headed quickly toward his horse. The horse greeted him with a long whinny that, in these circumstances, reverberated eerily. Mahmoud put his foot in the stirrup and mounted. Glancing at the rustling window curtains, he let out a derisive hoot of triumphant disdain, gave the horse its head, and raced off through the alley of palm trees.

"Run, Nassim! Away, friend, hurdle over men's ignominies and continue on. Go, my courser, fly over the floods of the mountains, cross the deserts of time, scale the wandering winds and continue on. Red stallion, gallop through space where our traces are lost, ford the sky and continue on. Faster, my companion, outrun all the chaos, the worries, and carry me galloping away from the rictus of life toward the quiet, mocking smile of death."

He disappeared across the fields.

3

The jackals are howling. Rabha, the old dog, sits up, muzzle pointing into the night, and answers them. Her barking pulls Mahmoud away from his escape into memory. His gaze bumps against the white-draped form on the ground. The present opens its maw. Mahmoud falls into its depths. He closes his eyes. Lightning bolts zigzag in the darkness. The movement of blood pulses at his temples, roars in his ears. Then slowly the turbulence fades, dies out.

Silence falls again, completely. The jackals must be far away. No shadow troubles the brightness of the moon.

"I must bury her," Mahmoud tries to convince himself.

Suddenly, a strange sensation draws his attention to the right. He has the impression of a presence there, nearby. But, all the way to the edge of night, crouched there at the moonlight's limit, nothing. The same thing happens on the left. Mahmoud scrutinizes the area. Nothing. And yet this rustling sounds familiar, an icy hand stirring up a familiar feeling in his guts.

Mahmoud thinks again about the olive tree, about his encounter with the Sirvant family. He shrugs his shoulders and says in a vexed tone:

"I was so stupid! I swallowed it whole with the self-importance of a sheikh attracted to an impossible mission. I always made fun of my people, but my behavior certainly was just like theirs. That ride with Grandmother . . ."

Once more, he slips away, letting himself be carried off into a welcome past.

He rocks Yasmine and his memories.

Mahmoud rode at a gallop at first, then a trot, avoiding farms and large villages during his long descent toward the south. But whatever his pace, he talked continuously. To whom did he speak? Why this sudden flood of words? He was all alone with Nassim, his red horse, and the crumbling bones of the dead. Was it because he had held his silence for so long? Was it out of fear of this silence? The staccato pace of his journey, the flat spaces of time, would finally calm his overexcitement.

Mahmoud jumped from the saddle and walked. It was a more radical remedy against what tormented him, a reflex welling up from the old habits of his childhood.

Nightfall found him dead tired but calm, absorbed by his journey and by careful contemplation of the landscape. Now and then the bones rattled against each other in the sack, left to the mercy of the bumps in the road, attracting his attention. Mahmoud gave them a compassionate smile. Perched on the saddle above the sack, the skull seemed to be enjoying this excursion through life. The cloud of his chèche encircling his long silhouette, Mahmoud walked beside the horse.

The shadows of night fell slowly, erasing the outlines of things bit by bit. The hungry horse balked at going on. Mahmoud stopped to look around for a place to camp for the night. He collected a little wood and some brush for a fire and put water on to boil. For the first time in a long time, he felt he could eat with appetite and sip several glasses of tea. He even had a sudden desire for some *kif*, quite an improvement in his spirits. His horse was already grazing on the meager grass. Mahmoud gave him a little grain. Then, with the sack of bones and the skull of his grandmother nearby, he made tea, ate a bit of stale bread and some pieces of *khlii*. Across from him, the eye sockets of the skull, now darkened by night, had the slight air of charming attentiveness.

"You'd think it a figurine in an immaculate drape with a still unfinished head," he thought.

Pulling a pouch containing tobacco and *kif* from the pocket of his *saroual*, he smoked, slowly, savoring his tea. The night, dark, was leaning with all its weight against the firelight. The sky was streaming with stars. The silence was heavy with an innate voluptuousness. The distant yapping of jackals, out on the chase, suddenly interrupted him. They resounded, long quavers in the night, after which the darkness sank once more into a deep sleep. His head resting on one of his sacks, Mahmoud slept.

What a strange red dream came upon him. Up early in the morning, his grandmother tidied herself before the rest of the family was awake. She was a slender, brown woman, dressed in the bright red hues of madder. Holding his breath, hidden behind a fig tree, Mahmoud contemplated the feminine gestures he loved. Her eyes still filled with sleep, she scraped dried henna off the bottoms of her feet and the palms of her hands. She then dipped them in water to wash them. The slightly earthy odor of wet henna filled Mahmoud's nostrils. Water brought to life the fire of her fingers, the saffron of her nails. The woman combed her long hair, stroked it with both hands dipped in olive oil. The aromas of cloves and orange blossom were plaited into her long braids. Outlined with *kohl*, her eyes had the velvet luster of two deep pools of night on that fresh morning. She rubbed her gums with *messouak*. Her teeth were gleaming in her mouth, a pomegranate flower. She admired, deliberately, the curve of the hills, the green of the valleys, the twisting bed of the *wadi* filled with glossy laurels. She listened to the rustling of the trees, breathed in with delight the scents of the orchards. Then she lit a fire and made tea, which she drank in great sips. While she savored it, behind her, the flames of the fire were rising. They grew higher, roared, growled. Soon they formed an incandescent wall. Showing no surprise, the woman rose and stood for a moment contemplating them. Then, with a sweet smile on her reddened lips, she began to sway her hips, to rock her body, which soon was just a small flame dancing in the front of the enormous brazier. All at once, the huge colonial house of the Sirvant clan, as blinding as a *sebkha* in the sunlight, emerged from this incandescent crown. Great tongues of fire licked it avidly, lapped it with loud smacks. Ululations burst out from all sides, filling the sky, rising and swelling, like the flight of starlings. *Bendirs* sounded, keeping time with the dance of the flames and with the ever more spirited dance of the woman.

Mahmoud awoke when the sun was already high in the sky. Clouds of insects, swirling in networks, came to rest here and there with a metallic brilliance. The sack of bones, the chalky skull, the dead fire . . . it took Mahmoud a moment to come back to the present, so engrossed had he been in his dream. After a simple breakfast, he was getting ready to take to the road again when he saw a sooty cloud welling up in a break between the hills. At first he thought it the smoke from some remote camp of nomads. But the cloud was turning, twisting around itself in the quiet air. A flock of migrating birds? The summer was already heating up and, with increasing arrogance, was disputing the last moments of spring. The cloud was growing, spinning, advancing rapidly, in great spasmodic leaps. In this somber, swirling cloud were small glitters, here and there, of bright silver, fugitive, like sparks.

"Locusts!" He stood speechless for a moment.

"Locusts!" he repeated. "One of my greatest childhood fears. Terror and fascination combined. The sky would turn black with them. They transformed the earth into a hideous, pustulating crust. They crashed into everything. They covered everything. They got in everywhere. The locusts were like a sandstorm, that other inundation of the desert. That other inferno of the desert. No protection defended you against them. They were in the kheïmas, under the covers. They fell in cooking pots the moment you lifted the lids. They fell into the fire. The smoke tainted every meal with their fiery substance. They made your hair stand on end. They devoured all, down to the last minute trace of green. They chewed holes in your attention. They crawled over one another by the thousands. They were as fat as my finger, as large as my fear. They could lose their wings, become amputees, and still they didn't stop swallowing everything! Nothing could contain their voracity. A dementia of the mandibles. Number, aspect, insatiability — everything about them filled me with fear. I had the terrible feeling that they were going to ingest everything. That after the leaves and the grasses, they would gobble up the tree trunks. Then humankind! Then the entire earth! Then, they would devour each other."

Mahmoud contemplated the tornado's advance. It was approaching quickly. He could already hear a great rustling. A noise like the sound of wind in the tamarisks or the reeds. Soon the cloud would be there. Soon it would be bursting over his head. Soon it would vomit its devastating vermin all over the place. Toilers from hell, clouds of small chlorophyll vampires.

This kind of invasion put a crimp in Mahmoud's plans. Stubbornly continuing his journey in these conditions would be a risky undertaking. Mahmoud knew the curse of the locusts would last some time. Unless a contrary wind forced them to fly back to where they came from. So he decided to delay his journey and go instead to Sebdou, the closest village. He would wait it out there. But how could he go off on a visit to any town whatsoever with the bones of his grandmother in a sack? They'd think him an idiot! They'd accuse him of sorcery, at the very least. In any case, the risks were great. On the other hand, the idea of letting these disgusting insects soil his grandmother's remains distressed him. What to do? How to avoid that? Only a grave could preserve them. A grave? Yes, a grave! Under a bush, in a sandy place, Mahmoud dug a hole a cubit deep. In it he put the bones and the skull. Then to mark this temporary tomb, he planted a stick and attached a strip of cloth to it. No sooner had he finished than the demonic insects were there.

The sky darkened. The air quickly became saturated. In great salvos, they pelted the ground. The trees whirred. Time became murky and so did Mahmoud's thoughts. His ears were filled with their hallucinatory flittering. His skin crawled with repulsion. The locusts were clinging to his chèche, to his *'abaya*. They even hurled themselves against the only uncovered parts of his body, his eyes and hands. With icy horror, he tore off the worst of them. They resisted. They were so firmly hooked onto his clothing that often their back legs would detach from their bodies and remain stuck in the weave of the cloth. Sometimes his maddened hands threw their disjointed wings to the ground. Without their wing sheathes, they hung from him, hideous charms, armor-plated worm abdomens topped by blind heads. Heads with large, pro-truding, opaque globes that were not eyes, guided by antennae, impressive sonars.

Terrorized, his horse reared and neighed madly. His long tail lashed his flanks, whipping the locusts. With the help of a tamarisk branch, Mahmoud rubbed and brushed his coat. Huge masses of insects fell off. He crushed them under an enraged foot. Among his affairs he had a large piece of cloth that he would use for different purposes as needed, a cloth in which he would wrap up various things. He covered the horse with it. Then, mount-ing, he took off quickly in order to calm him and to keep from being trampled. Body protected by the providential caparison, eyes and ears sheltered by the branch of tamarisk that Mahmoud shook constantly, Nassim calmed down, settling into a regular trot. Mahmoud headed back along the road he had followed the day before. But nothing around him looked the same. He was now traveling amid a swarm of insects. The acacias and laurels in the wadis were covered. Soon, completely stripped, they would present the spectacle of final cataclysm: woody skeletons and a chaos of stones covered over with locusts.

"Ugh, ugh! *Ejrrad*! *Ejrrad*!"

From all the cultivated fields garlands of smoke arose amid the clamor and cries. All the farmers were burning green grass and banging on anything that would resound in the vain hope of making the clouds of insects flee. The pestilential odor of locusts grilled by the flames infested the air.

Upon reaching Sebdou, Mahmoud took refuge in the town's only inn. Gloomy day. To protect the room from a massive invasion of locusts, a heavy curtain was hung, darkening it. The air was close. At the least movement, the men exuded suffocating odors that vied intermittently with the aromas coming from the kitchen. Nevertheless, mint, basil, and coriander resisted bravely, to the great delight of the noses and lungs that lay in wait for their wafting freshness. With fighting words and lower lips almost always bulging with great tobacco quids, the players of dominoes and *ronda* seemed sealed off from the rest. Mahmoud immersed himself for a moment watching them. The ability of men to lose themselves in a game, for hours at a time, fascinated him because he knew himself incapable of it. From time to time, one of them would turn his head slightly and, from between clenched teeth, launch a large, yellowish jet of saliva record distances. The floor was spotted with them. The continual hubbub wove a protective net around Mahmoud. His daydreams huddled there happily. And, soon tiring of the quips and somewhat repetitive jockeying of the players, his thoughts drifted toward what his life had been like these past days.

He had returned from Egypt with a project. He wanted to start a *medersa*. Education being the seedbed of liberty, he felt he could be of some use to his country in that field. With this goal, he had tarried in the tell on his journey back to his tribe. Alas! His prospecting in Mostaganem as well as Tlemcen had been depressing on a number of counts. The few schools there had been closed, one after the other. The teaching of Arabic had been reduced to just the Qur'an. Spirituality itself withdrew into the *zaouias*, abodes of fatalism and archaism, run by religious leaders who were completely under colonial influence. Watching the lives and actions of a certain number of these individuals confirmed a thought that Mahmoud had sensed deep down already when he was in Egypt:

"Invaders, no matter how strong they are, cannot establish themselves and continue to hold on in a foreign country unless there is local complicity. And a few handfuls of men, greedy and corrupt, are enough to subjugate the better part of their fellow citizens, better than the most powerful army. Illiteracy and misery, those were our first two colonizers. The Turks and then the French, after so many others, needed only to gather in and exploit the weaknesses that fit their greed. We have been colonized because we were colonizable."

Attempts at clandestine *medersas* had, for the most part, been dismantled. People were in prison because of that. Well-meaning contacts had counseled Mahmoud to abandon his projects. His name, all by itself, seemed to them to symbolize defeat and danger. The town was already unsafe in his view. Mahmoud had only liked city life in Egypt because it gave him a temporary refuge and because he was a stranger there. He had never been at ease except in the role of outside observer, in anonymity, in transitional situations. In Algiers, Oran, Tlemcen, and Mostaganem, he was immersed in his extended tribe. He should have felt at home. But he could find there no place, no space for action. He caught no glimpse of any possible future. Disenchanted as he was by these realizations, the pleasures of the city left him cold. And the daily spectacle of the *'arbis*, humble and crushed by a few despicable zealots of colonization, was unbearable to him. Never had his feeling of isolation been so great as in the feverish and boastful crowds of these cities. And so he had fled.

His reunion with the high, lonely steppes was a consolation. Their austerity and silence matched his bitterness so well. But he had needed distance and withdrawal in order to realize how important their hold on him was. He had needed to visit busy cities such as Cairo or Alexandria to realize that. There, in spite of the distance, in spite of the soothing melody of the most merciful twin of the desert, the sea, in spite of the years that magnified space, the steppes unfurled within him like gusts of wind in a sandstorm, acrid and burning. He was restored each day by their love. And even in the heart of the tumultuous crowds of the Middle East, their silence, at times, swooped down on his thoughts like a warning against any betrayal, like a prayer of fire that set his memory ablaze. Thus, his absence had been completely marked by the absence of the high steppes. He found them again in the image of melancholy that they had forged in him: bleak and infinite, imbued with light. And he experienced, then, the fantastic revelation of having reached a threshold. He left behind countries, torments, but entered into nothing. He was merely a lookout, a surveyor. The vast expanses that offered themselves to him were only a luminous respiration, a site of passage, a theater of encounters, separations and departures. Brave souls, hot-tempered and full of *baroud*, were capable there of the greatest weakness, loving. There the horse, the star of the parade, walked alongside the camel with its heavy, persistent steps conjuring up in the imagination the drunken enchantment of their journeys. There the Bedouin exchanged his goods and those of the north for the African commodities of the "Blue Men"—the Regueibat, or Touareg. There was the threshold of the desert for the former, and of the tell for the latter. It was not only extremes of temperature that reflected this duality. The days burned there with the flame of the desert. The winter nights there outdid the north for frost. In all truth, it was a place of waiting, a staging ground. Quests did not come to an end there. Journeys could only be broken by brief halts. A zone as sublime and unbearable as lucidity. For that reason, in the area from Kheïder to Aïn Sefra, songs never spoke of honor unless it was deadly, of friendship or love unless it was impossible or one was thunderstruck by the certainty of its being forsaken. The steppes were an opening, the "nowhere" where truth is. And Mahmoud could only see himself as existing in between, between the sedentary and the nomadic, between orality, the camaraderie of stories, and the solitary bewitchment of writing, between flight and revolt, always at the junction of complementarities, always at the point of contact between contraries. The in-between suited him.

Mahmoud understood the demonic effect these empty spaces had on his imagination. But for the moment, he was prepared to hold them in check, to throttle their excesses. His daily work with words lessened these fears. There was no void that he could not drape with their contours. No absence or lack he couldn't fill up with their rich sensations. Armed with this knowledge, he had a vantage point on humanity. From there he could embrace it in its diversity, at times play on the most subtle of its vibrations. When the days wavered, when his thoughts vacillated, words came to him, sustaining him. Thanks to words, Mahmoud could maintain his calm at the heart of turbulence, in the very abyss of collapse.

After his mother's death, Mahmoud had only one desire. He wanted to be the father of a girl whom he would watch grow up, whose childhood he would watch over, whose thought he would nurture. His daughter would have a real childhood. Childhood, that sublime fragment of time before getting mired in adulthood. His daughter would laugh. Her eyes would not know shame. Her nights would not be filled with nightmares. His daughter would be schooled, free and blossoming. She would avenge his mother. Before being born, she already gave him the immense hope of love and the words to express it.

Evening fell without Mahmoud realizing it. Alone amidst the din, he wrote. The players, intrigued, cast furtive glances in his direction. His demeanor was serious. The innkeeper, who came to offer to put him up at his home, drew him away from his writing. Mahmoud discovered it was evening. Preferring the anonymity of the nearby *hammam*, he gracefully declined the man's invitation. Lacking a true caravanserai, that's where every traveler crossing the *ksar* found shelter to sleep. After having drunk a bowl of *h'rira*, Mahmoud left his horse in the care of the innkeeper and headed toward the baths.

Night, having folded the locusts' wings, ruled the skies alone. The insects clung to the earth and trees. Those still moving seemed to be in agony. In the narrow streets, the least breath of air stirred up a whirlwind of wings and legs suspended in dust. The feet of passers-by ground up the locusts with a horrible crackling. Even in the dark it made Mahmoud nauseous, because he couldn't help imagining the burst bellies with their disgusting juice, a cross between snot and pus, beneath his soles. From time to time, a curse from an angry voice rocketed into the night. The sounds of a fall immediately followed. Slipperiness was on the lookout for the imprudent and the hasty. The victim picked himself up, his hands and clothes splotched and sticky. The odor of grilled locusts continued to stink up the air.

Three other men were in the hammam. Stretched out on the floor, using sacks full of their clothing or other items as pillows, they slept deeply as evidenced by the choir of their snores.

"Men who came to the *souk* and were caught by the invasion of locusts," thought Mahmoud.

First, he inspected the place carefully. He didn't trust hammams. They were often home to those small beasts fond of clammy scum, the inescapable parasites of misery. At the mere thought of them, he began to scratch himself and cast suspicious looks around him.

"No way! Locusts are more than enough upset for today. Lice, crabs, fleas . . . No way!" he bristled to himself.

The room looked clean. Reassured, he lay down. He stayed awake for a long time. To divorce himself from the concert of snores his neighbors were inflicting on him was no easy matter. They applied themselves, a round for three voices: first, a duet of bass and baritone thundering with the farting and belching of innards in love with heavy carousing. Next, a tenor that, with

a leap, whined on a higher note to attain a singular register between a rattle and a hiccup. And finally, the echo of the hammam
blaring back the ensemble in vibrato. How was he going to stand
this racket? The fluttering of his nostrils flaring in the suffocating heat rescued Mahmoud. There was rich matter for the sharp
noses of even less apt stalkers. So, as his sense of smell rummaged
through the dampness, it slowly blocked the insult to his hearing.
It was as if, led by his nose plunging into the mass of effluvia,
Mahmoud distanced himself from the snoring, separating himself from it by the thickness of odors. He thus applied himself
to identifying the curious mixture. Some were easy to identify,
others were unrecognizable. He recognized the agreeable smells
of the stone overheated during the day, of *ghassoul*, that clay that
left the hair of women so supple and shimmering. He searched
in vain for the smell of damp bodies, probably now disguised
among the heady odors of musk and amber. There were also,
now and then, gusts of staleness, of dirty clothes. The persistent
vapor of detergent. All was awash in the rank humidity that
made the atmosphere oppressive, almost unbreathable. But that
night, it was preferable to the locusts. The locusts! Several had
managed to penetrate into the baths, in spite of the vigilance
of the proprietor. Mahmoud could hear their wings rubbing in
the dark during the brief pauses between snores. He thought
about the previous night, sighed with regret for its silence, the
starry vault of the sky, the aroma of the brush, even the uncanny
presence of his ancestor.

"Grandmother is there in a makeshift tomb because of these
cursed locusts," he thought.

For the first time, his dream of the previous night returned
to him. He tried without success to remember the features of
this woman. The failure of memory to recapture the fullness
of sensations, the totality of dream images, had always upset
him. Sleep had never been for him anything but a constraint
he was forced to submit to. These moments of mysterious ab-

sence from himself were illuminated, at times with the halo of a dream or the violence of a nightmare. That he was denied even those landmarks always frustrated him. However, still floating like a cloud in his memory was a long silhouette in brown and madder, a small flame at the forefront of an immense brazier. Then suddenly, the Sirvants' house burst forth from the center of the hearth. And bursting forth from the heart of his dream, the same wave of sweet vengeance filled Mahmoud. Then his thoughts turned toward the current conflagration, the locusts. He imagined the Sirvant domain given over to their jaws. What he imagined so delighted him that he burst out in a sonorous laugh whose echoes ricocheted off the walls of the baths, waking one of the three men. He lifted his head, leaned his elbow on his sack and scrutinized his companion.

"It is raining locusts, and you find it funny? You have no shame," he admonished him with ill humor.

At first embarrassed at having forgotten himself that way, Mahmoud apologized to the stranger.

"To have the shamelessness to laugh in the midst of an invasion of locusts?" That phrase astonished him. "*Ya sidi*, why?"

Mahmoud was in no mood for morality to mix itself into this intimate moment. On the edge of sleep that was stealing him away from himself, he was only attuned only to the feeblest of sounds rising up from within.

"What a grumbler! Did I complain about the orgy of snores myself? Degenerate morals! Morals are to the spirit what farting and belching are for the intestines, what snoring is to sleep. The flatulence and musty smells of tainted digestion is what they are, he said to himself. Laughter! . . . I am not going to hold forth on sorrow and laughter at this hour of the night! No way!"

An idea had germinated in his mind during his insomnia. Mahmoud at first thought it ridiculous. But it persisted, obliging him to reconsider it. After some hesitation, he had to admit that it was very tempting, as witnessed by the fact that he had, once again, become oblivious to the moist, suffocating, heated atmosphere. And there could be no doubt about it when it awakened him in the morning. He had to force himself to wait for the arrival of the *tayyab*. But the moment he heard him open the door to the hammam and begin moving around, he got up. His three neighbors slept on, swallowed up in the obscure darkness. Mahmoud could scarcely distinguish their motionless forms. The *tayyab* was in the process of relighting the fire that would heat the water and the steam room until the end of the day. Here and there, torches shed a feeble light beneath which shone the wet gray stone of the hammam. The temperature in the steam room was beginning to rise. Mahmoud took advantage of it to wash before the atmosphere became too suffocating for his taste. Then he paid and went to eat at the inn. The previous evening, when leaving his horse in the care of the proprietor, he had told him that he would wait until the invasion of insects abated before leaving. When the proprietor saw him up before dawn, he simply thought him one of the many pious people who sacrificed the best part of sleep to do the optional prayer of the *fajr*. So, when Mahmoud asked to pay the bill and get his horse, the man's eyes opened so wide that Mahmoud felt obliged to justify himself by telling him his dream and the project he had created based on it.

Worse than the flowing waters of antediluvian rains, worse than the greatest floods that in mere moments submerged entire countries, worse even than the strongest bursts of hail that, with their grapeshot, beat down the vegetation, nothing so devastated nature as locusts.

Rocked by the easy trot of his horse, Mahmoud rode back north. The locusts, still frozen on the ground, looked like lava flows. It was the celebrated hour of their copulation. The males, small and yellow, became one with the females, large and brown. And no matter what happened, nothing could unhinge their obstinate lovemaking. They could remain that way, without moving, for several hours, at times for two days running. And neither the surrounding noise, nor the menace of trampling or imminent massacre, could unsolder these unions. However, the female was first of all a mother. A conscientious mother. Threatened by whatever peril, in the pathetic effort of a final agony, she tried always to plant her eggs in the earth. Sometimes she had just the time to expel them from her abdomen before dying. The hooves of the horse crushed under their stride the coupled males and females.

More even than their great numbers, their deaf and ferocious urge to ingest, copulate, and reproduce, so terrifying, so fascinating and unexpected, frightened Mahmoud. It seemed to him to be part of a dark instinct, an exterminating determinism.

Later on when the sun warmed up, they would fly off whirring. And the sky would soon be full of their winged flittering.

Suddenly, the sound of galloping behind him brought Mahmoud to a halt. Instinctively, he hid himself behind a bush. Bandits plagued the roads, and a solitary traveler was easy prey. It was then that he saw three riders emerging from a loop in the road hidden by a grove of trees. Two of them were pursuing the third. This last rode ahead of them, mounted on an impetuous chestnut. When he sensed that his pursuers were about to catch him, he did an abrupt about face. With dazzling rapidity, he unseated the first and then the second. He circled them, roaring with laughter. His laughter snapped like a whip. Then he made his horse rear, and with a prodigious bound, took off. A superb horseman. A dashing steed, quivering nostrils intoxicated with the cavalcade, the bravado. With a more than perfect harmony, the evident complicity between the rider and his mount turned danger into a game and, all afire, battle into a parade. They commanded admiration. Mahmoud was so amazed by them that he had to make an effort to restrain his applause. The two men, still on the ground, snorted with surprise. Remounting their horses, they shot off once again on his trail. From his hiding place, Mahmoud saw one of them bend over toward his right stirrup strap and pull out, probably from a holster made of the saddle strap, a cutlass whose blade flashed in the light. Without a moment's thought, Mahmoud picked up a nearby stick and waited. When the men reached his level, he jumped out from behind the bush and gave a violent blow to the arm with the weapon. The cutlass fell to the ground. The man cried out in pain. His companion, after a few moments of fright, spurred his horse toward Mahmoud. It was then that a shot rang out, cutting off his trajectory. The fugitive had made a half turn and was closing upon them, a carbine in his hands. At once the men turned tail and fled. The one Mahmoud had injured was still whimpering.

"Peace be with you, friend. Whoever you are, you are above all my friend. You helped me to get rid of those two pigheaded fellows—I thank you for it," said the man in a voice winded from his ride, nodding his head.

That gravelly voice . . . For several seconds, he searched his memory to identify it, but without success.

"May the peace that seems to have abandoned you, temporarily I hope, be with you again to your destination. As for ridding you of your pursuers, you had no need of me for that. Focused on your assailants who had the advantage of numbers, I hadn't seen your arm, a far more dissuasive one. You had a good laugh at their expense."

The man was large and solidly built. His white chèche covered almost his entire face. All that emerged were his piercing eyes. The two men looked at each other for a moment. Then, with a sudden gesture, the other took off his turban uncovering a face etched with clear-cut features. The face, completely unknown to Mahmoud, subdued the struggle of his memory to find an identity, a context to associate with the timbre of his voice.

"Which way are you headed? Maybe we could keep company

for part of the road. It surely would be less miserable than riding alone on these roads covered with all kinds of locusts!" the stranger suggested.

"I'm heading toward Aïn Témouchant," Mahmoud responded.

"Very good, I'll stop long before then, but I'm headed in that direction, too."

"I am Mahmoud, son of Lakhdar and grandson of Slimane Tijani. Were those two men bandits who attack travelers?"

"If we stick strictly to the usual meaning of words, the bandit would be me. But isn't it true that everything is relative. And exceptional minds differ from the minds of the vulgar. They call me El-Majnoun, "the demented"! Ah! Ha! The demented, yes, because there is no act, no thought that the common morality of men censures, that religion bans, that I consider taboo. I lie without shame. I abhor all forms of decency. It limits men to what's bloodless and narrow. Why decency? In the name of what justice? Cowardly conduct, that's all. I look down on the poor man who stays that way, because after all, his poverty is a reflection of his undeveloped mind, his immaturity. As for me, graft, looting, swindling, robbery of all sorts are my favorite pastimes. I drink wine. I smoke opium and I rape. Fighting gives me great pleasure. My life is a dangerous and entertaining game. My life involves none of the hypocrisies of men who behave like marionettes. Me, I gamble with my life. As for them, they are played upon by fear of God and the myth of a beyond, by decency, which is, in fact, just pure travesty. They are shackled. Me, I'm completely free!" concluded the scoffer.

This tirade, as insane as it was unexpected from a stranger, left Mahmoud aghast. The other burst into strange laughter again.

"Murder?" Mahmoud inquired ironically.

"It could happen with me," replied El-Majnoun in a soft voice that had lost none of its good humor.

Exasperated by such vanity and furious at having helped out

someone so depraved, Mahmoud took off down the road at full gallop. He rode like wildfire. His disdain would have discouraged even the most presumptuous of pests. It had no effect on El-Majnoun. Behind his back, Mahmoud heard his satanic laugh and the galloping horse he was spurring on. Mahmoud decided then to slow his horse to a trot. A frantic ride would surely only flatter the conceited fellow. He'd be quite capable of thinking him terrified on his account. And besides, at that speed the locusts became formidable projectiles for the eyes. The man soon arrived at his side.

"My friend, you can't get rid of me that easily. Our meeting today was not just a matter of chance. Finding myself yesterday at Sebdou, I spent the night in the hammam. When I arrived, two poor wretches in rags were lying stretched out there, commenting on the disaster caused by the locusts. Judging ahead of time that I wouldn't make any profit from their empty purses, and even less from their more impoverished minds, I fell asleep soon enough out of boredom. Late in the night, when I was deep asleep, I was awakened by peals of laughter, one after the other, which the empty rooms of the bath repeated, like empty-headed shrews. It ended up waking me up completely. That good humor intrigued me. I sensed, rather than saw, a fourth man, who'd arrived while I slept. I asked him a question he didn't deign to reply to. It could only have been him laughing. The two others slept the imperturbable sleep of the poor. Who was it then so cheerful in spite of that day darkened by locusts? Some clever merchant enjoying the ruin of the farmers from which he would make a profit? Or an adventurer like myself who would have flown, at a moment's notice, on the contingencies of the instant, down the open roads? Whoever he was, he interested me. The next day I got up early. But the man had already taken off. Some important project had made him keep night watch for the dawn. I hurried to the innkeeper who told me that he had taken the road going north. I had a pressing problem to settle in the village. That done, and pursued by two vicious malcontents, I took the same road thinking to catch up with him.

Although more and more stunned, Mahmoud nevertheless controlled himself. He continued his ride. Once the first moments of irritation passed, he gave in to curiosity in his turn. Soon he started to laugh beneath his chèche, thinking about how outrageous the fellow's discourse was. The fantastic situation certainly did not lack spice.

"Whether lying and boasting are the only vices of this braggart is debatable. Perhaps I am in the presence of a true madman? That would explain the last name that he takes pride in as if it were a glorious title. Though somewhat excessive, his statements couldn't be more structured nor his conduct more coherent. Only his tormented and unsteady gaze seemed at times to betray a certain lack of reason."

Mahmoud didn't know what to think.

They rode on for a long time without a word. Dealing with the locusts, they did not in fact have time to talk at ease. But they didn't fail to spy on each other in secret. Each of them stopped from time to time to drink a few mouthfuls of water straight from the *guerba* hanging from the saddle. After whirring around them, the locusts, stirred up by their passage, landed immediately. Caught by the jagged edges of their long legs, the locusts clung to their clothing, to the manes of the horses, with the voracious serenity of a predator finally triumphing over a long-stalked prey. They shook themselves at once to escape the dreaded contact. To calm the terrorized horses, they brushed them vigorously with small branches they were holding. Then they set out again.

The sun was long past its zenith, but its oblique rays still penetrated their clothes and felt like burning embers on their tired bodies. El-Majnoun said:

"I know a spring with wonderfully fresh water. We'll be there in a short time. It will be on our right, coiled beneath a bunch of laurels.

Exposed to the incessant assaults of the locusts, Mahmoud's concentration was a band tightening around his temples, strained by the twitching of muscles fatigued by the long ride. A bit of fresh water would soothe the bruises, the irritated eyelids, the traumatized throat and mouth. So he spurred his horse, following El-Majnoun when he took the right fork. What a huge disappointment for the two men when they discovered that the small water hole at the head of the spring was full of locust carcasses. Floating on water that had become fetid and brown, they spread their pestilence all about them.

"I should have known better!" Mahmoud thought, angry with himself.

They had to fall back once more on the water in the guerbas, but the skins, having dried out long ago, did not keep the little water they held cold any more.

"I'll be getting to my kheïma soon," El-Majnoun announced. We can quench out thirst there and finally eat something to settle our upset stomachs, revolted by these horrors. Will you do me the honor of being my guest for the night?

"I have an urgent appointment . . ." Mahmoud countered.

The desire to see the Sirvant domain in ruins thanks to the vengeful jaws of the locusts pressed him to hurry. And the desire, no less vivid for being unacknowledged, to see the impact in the eyes of a certain old woman, made him refuse to be turned aside by any obstacle and prevailed over all other plans. But Mahmoud recognized also that the curiosity wakened in him about this fantastic traveling companion would be unappeased if he dropped out of sight. Try as he might to lecture himself about the proverbial "wheat" and to warn himself about the evils of "tares," his intense curiosity worked diabolically, countering his reason.

"He is probably less a danger than he is a braggart. And besides, how could a man who is in such complete communication with horses be truly base?" he ventured, trying to reassure himself.

Whatever the case, the fascination that El-Majnoun held for him won out over his hesitation. Aware of his hesitation, El-Majnoun awaited his response without lowering his gaze. After a moment's silence, Mahmoud added.

"But my task will be soon done. So, if I won't bother you by arriving a bit later in the evening, I'll let myself be seduced by your invitation."

"Not at all. We'll wait for you. My home is your home, whenever you get there. I can lend you a horse for the rest of the journey. That way yours can enjoy a well-merited rest. And should you have need of my help, I'd be happy to accompany you after I've changed my mount."

"I'll gladly accept lunch, a glass of tea for dessert, and even the horse. However, I want to continue on alone. As for the rest, I won't run into any problems other than these insects. So please don't disturb yourself! But I am obliged to you for so much care."

"As you wish, recalcitrant loner. At the least, keeping your horse means I'm guaranteed to see you again."

Soon they were in sight of two superb kheïmas in front of which three women were working. One of them, a bucket of water in her hand, sprinkled water on the ground in front of the tent. The second, holding a tuft of esparto grass, swept the wet space, brushing away the carcasses of dead locusts. A third, squatting, blew on a kanoun from which the smell of grilled locusts arose, their blind flight having landed them on the coals. When the men appeared, the three women abandoned their tasks and ducked into one of the tents. Appearing suddenly from behind the tents, a man came toward them on quick, stealthy feet. His eyes shot glances, at times feverish, at times icy. He had a receding chin, and a large, black moustache hid his lips. Given his lanky silhouette, he truly had the air of a mangy *sloughi*.

"*Salaam 'aleïkoum*," he said bowing before El-Majnoun, all the while fixing Mahmoud with a stony look.

"Hassan, take good care of our two horses," El-Majnoun ordered, and without looking at him, he handed him the reins.

Then, turning toward Mahmoud, he added:

"Don't pay any attention to him. He's so jealous of everyone I am friends with one would think him capable of assassinating them. But he's never committed murder other than by his looks. Beyond that, he'd never injure a woman in any way!" he concluded in a tone of biting contempt.

Mahmoud, who was watching the man, saw a demonic lightning flash streak across his eyes. It gave the lie instantly to El-Majnoun's assertions.

"That guy is the worst sort of vermin!" Mahmoud said to himself.

A chill ran down his back. Ruse or the blustering of a braggart? Was El-Majnoun trying to reassure him by talking that way? How could you ignore or underestimate the implacable cruelty of this man so obvious at the first glance? Whatever the case, and however formidable the verbose El-Majnoun pretended to be, he was a pale figure next to his silent servant. Given this fact, Mahmoud's misgivings returned.

They entered the second kheïma. It was even larger than it seemed from the outside. His eyes, still adjusted to the intense outside light and inflamed by the dust of the road, were blinded for a moment. It was a mollifying blindness, however. The shadow and the impression of many hot colors mixed together had a soothing effect. Soon Mahmoud began to focus on the outlines of things. A *zarbia* of red and black wool was spread on top of an esparto grass mat covering the beaten earth. On it were scattered cushions of wool and silk of various colors in patterned disorder. To the right, next to the entrance, two wooden trunks decorated with colored inlays and with miniatures stood next to each other. Not far away, hung on a tripod, a burnous, a *kheïdous* and a *hadoun* fell into line, their supple, majestic silhouettes side by side, white, rust, and black. Their great hoods, adorned with threads of silk, hung softly against the capes. To the left of the entrance was a whole row of swords with silver scabbards inlaid with enamel and coral. Reigning over the center, a large red tray of copper, superbly engraved, rested on wooden legs. Wherever the eye wandered, there was luxury. Since his return from Cairo, Mahmoud hadn't seen such a rich interior. With the eye of a connoisseur, he examined the objects. It wasn't so much the display as the delicacy of taste that he appreciated. For a moment, he was tempted to tell himself, as earlier in the case of the horses, that a man capable of such refinement couldn't be . . . The thought triggered an ironic smile.

"A treasure no doubt constituted from years of pillaging!"

El-Majnoun, delighted to see this cheerful face, invited him to sit and did the same. Hassan of the deadly stare came in bringing a towel, ewer, and copper bowl. He put them down so he could quickly lower the flap of the kheïma behind him to keep out the locusts. Several were already flying around inside, bumping here and there against the roof of the tent. Eyes obstinately lowered, the man poured out water for each of them. They washed their faces, arms, and hands, and dried off with the same towel. Next, they drank tea and ate flat bread still warm, served by Hassan, who soon withdrew.

The heat radiated softly. Outside, one could hear the brushing of innumerable wings and the murmur of women returning again to work. In quasi-religious silence, the men drank their tea. The peace of being sheltered from the insects and the hot, sugary drink, wafting the fresh aroma of mint, slowly relaxed the tensions of their weary bodies sprawled on the carpet.

"Perhaps I should forget obsessive dreams and the locusts and close my eyes to sleep for a bit," Mahmoud said to himself.

Drowsiness had anesthetized his limbs and spread little by little throughout his body. If he weren't careful, he would be engulfed in deep sleep. He shook himself and got up.

"Already!" El-Majnoun couldn't help exclaiming.

With a light bound, El-Majnoun also arose and walked toward one of the trunks. Pulling keys from the deep pockets of his *saroual*, he opened it.

"Come see!" he said, his eyes suddenly lighting up before the spectacle of its contents.

Normally, family linens were kept in this kind of chest. This one, so prettily adorned, might have belonged to a young bride. Mahmoud walked toward him. But wafts of amber and musk did not greet him. From the depths of the trunk arose the scarcely perceptible odor of greased metal and powder. A number of well-oiled guns and ammunition were arranged inside. El-Majnoun took one, loaded it coolly, and held it out to Mahmoud. The latter, with a surprised look, shook his head no and asked:

"How did you acquire such an arsenal? There's enough there to arm an entire squadron!"

"Some of them, like this one, were purchased secretly and at high price. There is an entire network, well-organized, that gets its goods from Tangier! Others . . ."

He left his sentence hanging and made a vague gesture with his hand. But the smile that crossed his lips was most suggestive. Then, he held the gun out once more to Mahmoud.

"I'd have no use for it! I carry nothing on me that could attract bandits. And I don't hunt either. So . . ."

Irritated by his refusal, El-Majnoun shrugged his shoulders and put the gun back inside the chest. With a sharp gesture, he slammed down the lid.

A low building made of *toub* was sheltered beneath some large pine trees, which hid it almost completely. It served as the stable. Besides their two horses, it contained four other superb stallions as well.

"They are all equal. Take your choice."

While stroking Nassim, who swished his tail without raising his muzzle from the manger, Mahmoud looked at the other horses. They were truly magnificent. He chose a black one whose least movement made his coat shimmer with silver.

"That one is El-Essoued."

Mahmoud thanked him and took off. Hassan's stare, leveled at his back, gave him a frightful chill that stayed with him for a long time.

4

Tears rend the silence.

"It's the baby. He doesn't usually wake up like that during the night. He must be hungry. Tomorrow at dawn I'll bring the goats. I'll give him milk!" Mahmoud promises, speaking to his wife's body.

But the promise of future nursings has no effect on the present. The baby cries louder. Mahmoud feels helpless. Usually, he would share the household tasks with his wife. He would make bread, tea, cook the *rob* . . . take care of Yasmine. But when it concerned the baby, he would become clumsy. And if, bringing her authority to bear, Nejma put the baby in his arms, he'd stand there petrified with fear. A baby is so fragile. After a moment's indecision—his limbs, stiff from staying in the same position, all needles and pins—Mahmoud gets up with difficulty. Carrying Yasmine in his arms, he goes toward the tent and lays the girl down. Then he tries to comfort the nursling, rocking him in his arms. The baby is burning hot. On touching him, Nejma would have quickly lit the oil lamp. His flushed face and the redness of his mouth would have alarmed her. Mahmoud doesn't see all this. Then he remembers something: Nejma occasionally gave the baby sugar water. That's what he would do, too. The diapers are wet. Mahmoud searches around the tent, finds clean diapers and changes him. Suddenly, the baby doesn't move anymore. Mahmoud puts him back to bed and goes out. Outside, the moon is still there. A pearly glow snaring the hours. The sheet covering Nejma is an incredible white. It implants itself, a splinter in Mahmoud's aghast eye.

"I should bury her," he says to himself without much conviction.

He sits down by her feet and caresses them through the cloth. In spite of the heat, a shiver runs down his back. He feels eyes aiming at his back like a weapon.

"He is there, it's Hassan!"

Past and present converge inside him.

Mahmoud reached the Sirvant domain at the end of the day. The property had been transfigured. Dusk gave the final touch of disaster to the estate. The oblique rays of the sun highlighted the layers of locusts sculpting them with coppery tints. But in this instance, the sight enchanted Mahmoud. It was as if during his long ride toward this final goal, he had restrained his gaze. His eyes had only skimmed over the devastation of other estates, without focusing on detail, as he rode through the countryside. They were only a prelude to the scene awaiting him upon arrival. He saved himself for it. Only now did his gaze settle, linger over the details, savor the metamorphosis. The vineyards were stripped bare. The orange trees? The orange trees whose snow of flowers had blinded his eyes, whose aromas had filled his nose, were all charred! The other fruit trees? Peeled and bristling, swelling with locusts. The wheat was crawling with them. Only the olive trees with their thick, rigid leaves still resisted the destructive jaws. For the first time in his life, Mahmoud applauded the ravaging jaws. And the glory of the setting sun, that made the magma of vermin gleam, was the crowning touch.

Walking his horse, Mahmoud slowly rode along the perimeter of the property. Here as everywhere, there were fires. Here as everywhere was the same acrid stench of grilled insects that for two days had filled his nostrils. For two days, smoke and noise. Ridiculous methods! Nonetheless, men, women, and children continued to light fires, to shout their heads off, to bang on metal pots and pans. Doubtless the increasing pandemonium was less a matter of bolstering a hope that got weaker and weaker, than of putting to flight the terrible feeling of impotence, of checking the descent into complete despair.

The sun had bled dry its fury. The locusts grew quiet and settled on the ground. The stupefied silence and immobility were a sort of cosmic asphyxia that paralyzed, for a brief moment, both nature and man. When the last flamboyant gleams of dusk died out completely, the sky suddenly turned to periwinkle, a color so pure and deep it restored space and allowed lungs to breathe. Heads turned toward it voluptuously as if emanating from it was a divine promise of tomorrows without locusts.

Night fell softly now. Mahmoud looped the reins of El-Essoued around the branch of a tree. Sitting not far from the entrance to the estate, he observed it. He had come back for this. As long as there was a gleam of light, no matter how feeble, he would fill his eyes with it. When the darkness took over completely, he would leave, never to return. By Allah, the spectacle of this disaster erased the bitterness that previous images had left in him. It was as if the forces of nature had become judges. His gaze locked on the estate, Mahmoud poked a careless finger into the ground. His finger penetrated a gelatinous mass. Mahmoud quickly pulled it out and saw that at about a centimeter deep, the earth was infested with the eggs of locusts. Clustered in spikes, they were like grains of rice, grayish and gleaming.

In forty days, they'll hatch into clouds of locusts, Mahmoud thought, horrified.

He returned to looking at the property. Suddenly, in the alley, he saw a silhouette he thought he recognized. He jumped up, his heart pounding. It was the old woman he'd been waiting for. Two days of locusts had overwhelmed her, broken her. Misfortune suddenly added the weight of truth to her years. She advanced slowly, with an uncertain step. Haggard, she stopped at times and looked around her. Then she continued her inspection tour. Unaware of his presence, she walked unknowingly in his direction. Without realizing it, she was walking to a second fateful confrontation.

Behind her, the house lit up abruptly. After arriving, preoccupied as he had been with enjoying the metamorphosis of the fields and orchards, Mahmoud had paid but very little attention to the house whose magnitude and splendor had so irritated him two days before. Admittedly, the naked vines and trees had marred its panache and scratched its whiteness. Only now that the night had swallowed up its surroundings and an artificial light separated it from the rest, foregrounding it, did he see it again. But it no longer made him angry.

"One would say it was a ship that, having escaped a tempest in which all its escort perished, was sailing along on waves momentarily calmed by the night. And in its luminescent wake floats the ghost of an old woman," Mahmoud said to himself.

Completely preoccupied, she did not see Mahmoud until she was upon him. She started, then drew herself up abruptly, full of defiance, her eyes blazing.

"You see, I had to see you again. I couldn't miss such an occasion! Why do you bristle like that? Are you afraid of me, O lady of great pretensions?" Mahmoud said ironically.

"I'm afraid of no one!"

"Nevertheless I saw you tremble." She relaxed and shot back:

"Why are you here? Forget a bone maybe?"

"I came to behold your ruined efforts and your pain. To each his own locusts!" Mahmoud replied in a honeyed tone.

She broke into a bitter laugh.

"I am certainly ruined for this year. But the locusts will leave. The land will always be there. Listen to me, ibn Tijani.

Mahmoud no longer listened to her. Something unusual behind her caught his eye and demanded his attention.

"By all the *jnoun*!" he blurted out, astonished.

Was he prey to a hallucination he'd at first taken for a dream? He closed his eyes at the shock. But when he opened them again, the unimaginable was still there. Then, as if to rid him of any doubt, characteristic sounds reached him. Old lady Sirvant couldn't fail to see the sudden and radical change in his expression. All trace of sarcasm had disappeared and in its place was great bewilderment. Intrigued, she turned in one motion to see what so fascinated this man, frozen there in the darkness.

The house was on fire!

A long cry exploded from her body. With a sudden burst of energy as if propelled by her cry, she ran toward the house. Mahmoud stood paralyzed by astonishment.

The men were still in the fields where several fires were finally burning out. These had to be watched until they were completely extinguished. Spring had been stingy about water. An intense drought was raging. So, without some care, what had escaped from the locusts would be ravaged by the fire. There still wasn't the slightest breath of air. Better to be on the lookout nonetheless.

"Wind! Wind! Let the wind rise! Let it come! Let it blow!" challenged the settlers.

While waiting for the last red embers to go out, the men gathered huge piles of grass in different places once more. At nightfall, these would be transformed into giant nests of insects. Later, after supper and some rest, the men would return to set them afire. And, by the light of these enormous torches, they would scrape the land with rakes and shovels in order to burn the multitude of eggs infesting it along with the gluey locusts. But then the cries of the women reached them. Turning toward the house, they saw above the trees an immense screen of smoke.

From all the windows on the ground floor, wide open to the night, great crackling flames burst out. They grew taller and jumped by fits and starts. They roared, spreading here and there. They braced one another, slackened, and then with a sudden leap, they caught on higher up. Demonic trance. A lunatic smacking. In an enormous convulsion, they spit out eddies of black smoke, sputtered salvos of sparks. Soon all the windows were nothing more than maws of fire. Soon, the crimson stampede galloped across the facade of the ruined house. Next to the house, the grange too was nothing more than a blazing firepit. And as the finishing touch to this tragic ballet, the matter being cremated seemed to emit death rattles. The parquet floor and the woodwork cracked like broken bones. From time to time a garbled whistle burst out. It spiraled, growing ever louder, and ended with a frightful blare. The plasterwork burst like bombshells. Running and crying out, gesticulating grotesquely and impotently, men, women and children swirled around as if moving in some archaic dance.

Was it dismay at witnessing the scene of a dream fulfilled? Was it fear at discovering, all of a sudden, the gifts of clairvoyance? Mahmoud felt no pleasure. He was even depressed by it. The shouting, agitation, and flames were at their height when the acrimonious words of the old woman, out of her mind, startled Mahmoud.

"It's him! It's him! He's over there, by the entrance. Kill him!" she cried, hysterically.

"Who?" a man's voice inquired in a shout.

"Him, the son of Tijani! He's come back!"

"Bastard! Bastard!"

Brandishing arms, the men were already running in his direction. The shock of those words and the immediacy of danger electrified Mahmoud. In one bound, he reached his horse, threw himself in the saddle and took off. Shots rang out. El-Essoued reared up with a mournful whinny. Then he collapsed, taking Mahmoud with him in his fall. The latter untangled himself quickly. The animal stayed on the ground, inert. His head in an uproar, Mahmoud rushed down the hill. After a brief moment of headlong flight, he sensed a horse galloping on his right. He dodged quickly to the left. But, hammering through the night at a furious gallop, a horseman closed in upon him. Mahmoud felt he was lost. How could he escape this determined assailant? How could he hide in these immense fields? What good was it to run anymore? He stopped and turned around. Better to meet death head on. Better to see it coming. With astonishing speed, the horseman was upon him. Mahmoud jumped back falling in the stubble.

"Quick, Mahmoud! Mount, mount!"

That voice! That silhouette! El-Majnoun!

"Quick, mount! They are coming!" the other urged, one hand held out toward him.

Head spinning, Mahmoud got up. El-Majnoun helped him mount behind him. In control, he put a gun in Mahmoud's hands. Then spurring his horse, he shot off into the night.

"But where did he come from?" Mahmoud asked himself, thunderstruck.

"You followed me?" he asked stupidly, once he had gotten his breath and wits back.

"Ah! It wasn't very hard. One could even say that I did a bit more than just follow you. I carried out your intentions," he said, with a gesture toward the fire.

The awful significance of his words stunned Mahmoud.

"But why did you do that? Why?"

Several bullets crackled, far behind them. Deaf to his questions, El-Majnoun spurred his horse.

"Giddyup! Giddyup! We have to get out of here to the cover of the woods right now."

The hiccuping of the bullets stopped. A moment passed, broken by the pounding of horses' hooves.

"I don't hear them anymore. They must have doubled back. They are going to divide themselves between fighting the fire and tracking. As for the fire, I can promise you they'll be able to do nothing. Tracking is a question of nerves and ruses. Tracking is my specialty, not, most certainly, theirs. Those who are going to take off on your tail have gone to look for horses. With two of us on the same horse, they'll catch us easily. I inspected the environs earlier. There is a wood, over there on the right with a thick cover. We'll hide ourselves there to wait.

"Why did you do that!"

El-Majnoun didn't bother answering. Soon he tugged on the reins and stopped his horse. Dismounting, both of them had to make their way through the rugged underbrush. They chose to hide themselves behind a copse from which they could see the fields lit up by the fire. The silence was broken only by the rubbing of the locusts' wing sheaths.

El-Majnoun jumped up, covering Mahmoud's mouth with his hand:

"Shh! Don't yell! You're going to give us away. They aren't far. I did it because you didn't have the courage yourself!"

"And what gave you the right, not even knowing I existed this morning, to attribute this intention to me, even repressed? Even impotent?"

"The visions that haunted you, you described to the inn-keeper, remember? The visions that made you laugh, one dismal night at the hammam. The visions that woke you before dawn. Because of you, I had to rough up the innkeeper a bit. Luckily, nobody was at his den yet. He ended up telling me the reason for your sudden departure. I concluded that your dream had given you ideas. These ideas I found exciting, I'll confess. And your refusal of my offer to accompany you only strengthened this feeling. So I decided to join the celebration.

"You are truly mad!"

"If pushing one's ideas and desires to their limit is mad, then I am. But how do you explain your behavior? And please, don't tell me that you came back from so far away simply to look at the locust damage!"

"Leave my behavior out of it! We're going back to the Sirvant place now! You're going to confess your crime!"

Saying this, Mahmoud pointed his gun at the man. El-Majnoun laughed with amusement and sat down. He dug his hand into the pocket of his saroual.

"Yours isn't loaded. I'm not that mad. I wanted to test you before giving you these."

He pulled out some cartridges and showed them to Mahmoud. With a muffled laugh, he added:

"On the other hand, mine is. Maybe you prefer this!" A cutlass gleamed in his other hand. "Pal, I find you a bit ungrateful. I flew to your aid. I've provided the strong arm you lacked. I gave you the spectacle you panted after in dreams. Beyond that, I saved your life and lost one of my best horses thanks to you and look how you repay me!"

Furious at himself, furious at this madman, Mahmoud threw his gun violently to the ground. Still full of irony, El-Majnoun continued:

"Go back to the settlers! Their bullets will transform your body into a sieve before you can say one word in your defense! I followed you happily. You were so intent on your goal you heard nothing around you. Not once after you left my kheïma did you look back. I applauded your haste. I shared the fever that shut out even the locusts. Your determination cured my weariness and excited my admiration. An admiration that was, alas, disappointed upon arrival. Once there, you didn't carry out the deed. I saw you prowl around with hesitation and end up sitting down. The only thing that made you jump up was greeting an old woman who comes from your enemies with *salamalecs*! A failure of will? The scruples of a degenerate Bedouin? What hampered you? But I myself was there! And I didn't forget my debt to you. Especially since I had only to pick up the embers, kindly provided by the fire, and place them in a few strategic places. Which I was able to do in peace, the house being empty. The women and children were still outside hooting like barn owls. Such smooth sailing bordered on provocation. Why would I have resisted? Why deprive myself of such a pleasure?

"Never have I met anyone so vile, you . . ."

Mahmoud couldn't finish his sentence. El-Majnoun clapped a hand over his mouth. Putting a finger to his lips, he listened. Nature seemed to be sleeping. Far off in the distance, the enormous torch of the fire was still raging. The ferret gaze of El-Majnoun fixed next on his horse's head. At the same moment, the horse pricked up his ears, confirming the suspicions of his master. El-Majnoun caressed him and whispered some mysterious words of connivance. Then he crouched down, alert. The sound of a trot became perceptible. Then the moving silhouettes of two riders detached themselves from the night, searching through the wheat burnt by the fire. They approached cautiously, sounding the shadows of the woods on either side. From time to time, attuned to the rhythm of their riding, the glow of the fire shone on their metal weapons. Mahmoud and El-Majnoun stayed completely invisible. The horse, no doubt accustomed to this sort of ambush, turned to stone.

"They're going to go by without seeing us," thought Mahmoud, reassured.

The riders were very close now. Turning his head toward El-Majnoun, Mahmoud suddenly realized that he was getting ready to fire on them. Just a few more meters and they would be easy targets! Horror made Mahmoud leap up. He threw himself at the barrel to divert it. El-Majnoun fought back. For several seconds a mute struggle was waged between the two men. Then all at once they froze, alert: the riders had stopped. All ears, they peered into the darkness in their direction. Then, quite close to them, a night bird broke the silence and took flight with a great beating of wings. Reassured, the settlers continued their ride and disappeared into the night.

"That's it now! I've had enough! When those men are far enough away, we are leaving. I'm not going to let you commit another crime, harming me even more," Mahmoud whispered, shaking El-Majnoun.

The two were still grasping the same loaded gun. Mahmoud ended up letting go and crouching down. He was determined not to let himself lose control again. Full of resentment toward each other, they shut up and waited. They were ready to leave their hiding place when, once again, they heard the sound of distant galloping. After searching about for some time and listening in vain among the shadows, the riders were returning. The most pressing task, obviously, was to muster all forces to counter the infernal fire. The culprit would gain nothing from the delay. Knowing his identity, they would find him in no time. Hidden behind their bush, El-Majnoun and Mahmoud listened to the progress of the galloping hooves passing behind the curtain night hung along the border of the luminescent fields. The sound subsided, disappearing completely. It was only then, upon leaving their hiding place, that Mahmoud took off with long strides into the night. El-Majnoun gathered up the two guns and, jumping in the saddle, rejoined him.

"Mount," he bid him.

Mahmoud ignored him and continued on his way.

"You need to mount if you want to escape," the other argued in a coaxing voice.

"I myself had nothing to do with this fire. So why flee? You know I had nothing to do with it.

"Then why did you run away so quickly? And why do you keep on running? Isn't it because you know they wouldn't even take the time to listen to your explanations? And do you think that I'm going to clear you by denouncing myself? I remind you, my madness is not without method. Anyway, everyone is busy accusing you! You were seen on the grounds, I wasn't. They know who you are. They've never seen me. You have a clear motive. I don't have any! They'll find you sooner or later. How will you prove your innocence? Next to a formal accusation by settlers, an Arab's word isn't worth much, and the laws are tailored for them, as you well know. In their view, any Tijani, no matter how weak and rubbed out, remains an outlaw.

He was silent for a moment. Mahmoud was too caught up in his thoughts to answer.

"I have several reasons to carry a grudge against the Sirvants. But him? I strongly doubt that this guy, who hasn't an ounce of altruism, would do what he did simply to avenge me or please me. Is this the work of a madman? Or does he have some other motive I don't know yet? What venal logic, what pugnacious project makes him tick, causing him to dog my footsteps?"

El-Majnoun was suddenly shaken by a spasmodic laugh.

"It was magnificent! Admit it. No matter how you look at it, that fire was grand!" he said arrogantly, turning slightly toward Mahmoud.

"Have you set other properties on fire before?"

"Maybe, but nothing can compete with the pleasure of the present. I am a man of the moment. Today, all the conditions came together for a great success!"

"It's a pity to see you waste so much energy and potential on all sorts of foul deeds! If you can't stand the settlers, if their actions push you to revolt, fight them! Launch a true revolt, rather than these small-minded actions that do nothing more than dirty the reputation of all 'arbis!

"The reputation of the 'arbis! No, please, not you! Leave harangues for those who lack creativity, for the usual *khourda*. You and I are from a different mold. I cannot set myself up as judge or apostle of the rights of anyone else! If I take up arms against the colonial settlers, it will be for my own profit. But I'll need brave souls with me for that, not khourda.

"Bandit, yes. Avenger, never. If you used your gift at oratory wisely, you'd have followers in your crew."

El-Majnoun let loose one of his sonorous, guttural laughs before answering:

"Give me libertines, joyful pillagers and pagans, and even useless poets! To seduce those, I'd rack my brains. Just as I did with you. But, alas! To stir up men who are already dead because their minds have atrophied for lack of oxygen to the brain, you need only talk to them about Allah. Look here, the company of those mystics of twaddle, those fanatics of feeblemindedness and failure, would drive me, a veritable fount of good humor, to suicide, so dirty and encrusted is their discourse. What khourda! Friend, they are grumblers, boasters, and dunces. Allah is in their putrid sputtering a thousand times, ten thousand times a day. They only know how to bark out: Allah! Allah! Allah! So they think of themselves as extolling moderation and humility. Truly, in their excess they make Allah into the rattle of their presumption, into a hiccup of that interminable anguish that is their life. Friend, they are so narrow that from the first taste great Allah remained ill-digested. His name got stuck in their throats. Allah! Allah! Allah! It's as if they were trying to touch, palpate, extract, or spit out a shooting pain. Allah, Allah, they have become stutterers under the weight of their useless prayers and prostrations. Allah, Allah, because enormous frustration is fermenting in them.

As for the rest, Allah or no Allah, do you think that if the 'arbis came to power one day they would be just toward their fellow citizens? I doubt it! If I wanted to start a mass uprising, it would rather be to women that I'd turn.

"What a Proteus!" Mahmoud burst out, laughing in spite of himself.

"Never mind. On the other hand, if I have gone to lengths to dog your tracks and, if to please you, I have shown so much zeal, and to conquer your hesitations, made good use of glibness, it is because I recognized you as one of my crew, as you said. Your family name was a guarantee from the start, obviously. And I don't think I was mistaken, although your behavior just now threw me off. Your explanations will surely dispel this misapprehension. Listen, I have in mind a difficult but promising project for which your assistance is indispensable."

"Oh, yeah? What project?" Mahmoud inquired derisively.

"I won't reveal it to you until I am sure that you are with me. But feel free here and now to tell me your financial requirements. They'll be accepted."

"I take care to avoid associating with individuals of your kind. You cannot buy me! I am not for sale!"

"It is only a matter of *touisa*. An emergency *touisa*, so to speak. My project has an element of risk in it, making it more attractive. Right now you're in danger of losing your freedom. Help me, and your defense and protection become my business. Otherwise, the roumis will have no problem taking you, believe me. Seems to me you don't have much choice. And anyway, *ya sidi*, everything in life has its price, even dreams," he concluded with a triumphant laugh.

"That's why you set that house on fire! You were hoping, in that way, to corner me into accepting your deals. You thought you'd incinerated in the flames of that house all possible escapes from your odious blackmail. Look, I won't knuckle under to your threats. I dare you to put them into action! Go on, try to make me shoulder responsibility for your infamous deeds!"

Mahmoud seethed. He clenched his fists with such rage his nails gashed his palms. His feet pounded the ground. Locusts were crackling under their fury. He slid on their gluey mass and barely escaped falling. Once again El-Majnoun let loose a sardonic laugh.

"I'm going to grab that madman by the foot, unseat and pummel him. I'll thrash him until he gags on his arrogance!"

Body energized and thoughts boiling, Mahmoud leaped

toward El-Majnoun. For a second time, he barely missed losing his balance and only saved himself by clutching the bushes lining the road. In doing so, he knocked his forehead against a branch. The sharp pain made him see stars. The pain, and more than that the sense of shame he'd suffer making himself into such a spectacle in front of El-Majnoun, brought him back to his senses. He moved away from the bushes and put his hands to his forehead.

"I am pitiful. It wasn't only the locusts that made me almost fall. I am reeling with weariness. That pirate would be all too happy to rejoice at my humiliation. And then, I am so stupid. He is armed and generally better endowed than I for battle."

He indulged in a small, cruel laugh at himself. He never would have thought himself capable of such a blinding need to be violent. "The beast"—that's what he called violence—had surged up, leaped from his depths as if it had always been there, awaiting its moment. This new awareness started him thinking.

"So then, 'the beast' never dies in us. Rather, except in dangerous moments, it hides its lion's fangs. And so we think we have completely conquered it. But it triumphs once more in the very word 'conquered.' Can we conquer without violence? Derision! And whatever noble resistance we might make to that violence lying hidden within us, how can we protect ourselves against it in others? Is conquering one's own aggression, only to disarm, thus exposing oneself to being snuffed out by the violence of others?"

His inability to master the situation plunged him into bitterness and ill humor. He walked on for a long time. The "beast" had apparently gone back to its lair. The night was pitch black. Only the wing-scraping of the locusts and the rustling beneath his feet and the horse's hooves accompanied them on their bizarre epic. Reining in his horse, El-Majnoun kept it alongside Mahmoud. And in spite of his impatience, El-Majnoun left him in peace, hoping that the strenuousness of the walk would quickly wear out Mahmoud's rage. After a bit of silence, he tried reiterating his invitation:

"Mount, Mahmoud. Please mount."

Mahmoud didn't answer. He meditated upon what fortune had thrust upon him. A letter from the beyond, a dream, the locusts, a perverse being, and his life turned upside down.

"You should mount. As soon as they are done with the fire, they'll organize a posse to look for you," predicted El-Majnoun.

Mahmoud continued to ignore him.

"What should I do now? First, get a couple of hours of sleep; otherwise I'm going to collapse from fatigue. I have to get Nassim, my bay. To do that, I'll have to go to this madman's home. So, better to go without any more balking. Put his suspicions to rest. That's the only way I'll succeed in getting rid of him. I've been negligent, letting this madman get to me this much. The extravagance, impetuosity, and even the glibness of this guy appall me, that's for sure. I thought myself in the presence of some exuberant joker, a live wire. But his bellicose nature doesn't limit itself, alas, to words. Under the mask of the brave knight, beneath the facade of the hothead, insolent and arrogant, lurks a greedy and demonic soul. First, I've got to get away as soon as possible. After that, I'll try to figure out my other problems."

So, when El-Majnoun, who had adopted a conciliatory tone, reiterated his offer to get in the saddle, he hoisted himself up behind him without a word. El-Majnoun spurred the animal. Anesthetized by bodily fatigue and nodding to the trot of the horse, Mahmoud let his thoughts drift. What he'd just undergone, including this journey guided by a man who was now his enemy, seemed to him surreal.

"It's just a nightmare. A delirium caused by the combined effects of a long journey, the discovery of my mother's death, the reunion with a tribe among whom I always felt myself an exile, the satanic effect of the steppes on my imagination. Soon, tomorrow, I will wake up in the kheïma of some peaceful tribe of the high plateaus. The men will be sitting at a distance on the bare ground. The women will be working with wool. The children will have gone out, following the herds. There will be no locusts. The steppes will unfurl their drab, mangy hides as far as the eye can see. The rays of the sun will continue to delouse the esparto grass, relieving its misery. I won't reveal my dream. I won't let fate appropriate it. I won't tell my dream. I'll tame it. I'll feed it drop by drop to silent words. I'll separate it from myself by writing it down. Horrible nightmares are only for children. I never had a childhood except for nightmares. I never was a child because I had such a young mother. My mother is dead. Am I touched by incurable dreams? Am I among those whom the despotism of dreams over reality condemns finally to the status of elderly child? I need a wife and a daughter. I have always been rescued by women."

The remainder of the trip was carried out in silence and without problem. They approached the kheïmas. Although dawn was not far off, the oil lamps and kanouns were still glowing. Emerging from the night, a feverish shadow came toward them. Hassan took the reins of the horses and melted into the shadows toward the stable. The two men entered the same kheïma as earlier in the afternoon. Soon, Hassan brought them once more the ewer and copper bowl. They washed their hands. Mahmoud's gestures were now those of an automaton. His anger had given way to an immense anguish. Out of the corner of his eye, he watched Hassan pouring out the water. The flame of the oil lamp burned in his grim eyes, which shot him angry looks. His hate-filled glare was paradoxically at odds with his submissive behavior. This dissonance reinforced his unsettling mien. His syncopated and silent gait gave the singular impression that he was floating above the ground.

Hassan left and soon returned, carrying a *guessa'a* of steaming couscous. At a different time, the gleaming alabaster of the grains, dotted with raisins, would have delighted Mahmoud's eyes; cumin, caraway, and the aromas of the vegetables would have made even a full stomach hungry. But tonight Mahmoud was indifferent to their aromas. He had to force himself to make a show of attacking the meal. While he was nibbling, El-Majnoun was eating with gusto. On his plate were a carafe of water and another of wine. A thick wine with the velvet glow of pomegranate. El-Majnoun drank it in great gulps.

"Let him sink into a deep drunkenness!" Mahmoud prayed, inciting him with frequent servings from the carafe, while he only drank a few drops.

After the meal, Mahmoud refused tea. At the first onslaught of sleepiness, he stretched himself out and was engulfed. After an unknown stretch of time, he awoke with a start. He didn't know how long. His host was snoring loudly, not far from him. Mahmoud was about to get up when he saw the flaps of the kheïma open. He was able to distinguish Hassan's silent silhouette. Mahmoud closed his eyes, pretending to sleep. For several seconds Hassan scrutinized the two motionless men. Then, reassured by the snoring of El-Majnoun, he went toward the chest where they had put down their sacks upon arrival. From the slight rustling that reached him, Mahmoud guessed he was going through their contents. He preferred to let him go ahead. Better that he believed him sound asleep. After all, there was nothing of importance in his own bags. What could be the point of this search? Robbery or simple spying? When he was done, Hassan knelt down in front of Mahmoud. The latter had to make a supreme effort to stay calm, feigning sleep, under the keen and ghostly eye watching him in the dark. He heaved a sigh of relief when the man left the kheïma in the same furtive way he had entered. Waiting for him to go back to sleep too, Mahmoud bided his time before trying to flee. The hoot of an owl broke the silence. In spite of himself, Mahmoud shivered and hunched his shoulders involuntarily.

"First the itch of violence, now superstitious fears running through me. This is completely absurd! How can the cry of a night bird be a bad omen? A characteristic of obscurantism is to fill in the gaps of backward thinking with arbitrary, incongruous stigmas. It's funny how in extreme situations, distant memories surge up in us. I am among those who back off or flee in the face of danger."

He got up. Shouldering his bags, he left noiselessly. Outside, he paused for a moment. All was quiet. As much out of repugnance as to avoid making any noise, Mahmoud carefully avoided stepping where there were large accumulations of locusts. Stealthily, he entered the stable, detached Nassim, his bay horse, and, reassured at not having provoked any whinnying among the other horses, he went out with him. He did not mount him until he was relatively far from the kheïmas. Luckily, El-Majnoun had no guard dog. Just as he loosened his horse's reins, a rock whistled past his ear barely missing him.

"Hassan! There's the guard dog," he thought, hurrying his horse.

As he tacked back and forth across the path to dodge them, other projectiles fell at his sides.

Greeted by a few distant crows of the cock, dawn was born from the evanescent scrolls of the night. It took its time. The sky slowly turned navy blue. The navy became iridescent, and dissolved. Then, the sun was born in rosy phosphorescence. A rosebud of vermilion, with vermilion tendrils, adorning the skies. Before blooming, it showered the earth with a mist of warm, golden light. But soon enough, it would open the inferno of its coral red corolla. Soon its wrath would come. It would blind the eye, scorch the skin with its firebrands until the dying of the day. Its first rays sounded the hour of lovemaking for the locusts. Limbs still stiff, they began moving about on the ground in search of partners. Hesitant steps guided by sure instinct, they climbed over each other, trying. Then amidst a monstrous crush, males and females found each other, gripped each other, melded together. A bizarre coupling, immobile, indifferent to the crowds of loners who bumped against them and climbed over them. At once, moving and astonishing.

Was he, Mahmoud, beyond reach now? He thought so, when suddenly he heard the sound of hooves.

From nearby farms the Sirvants' neighbors, alerted by the glow of the fire, had come to the rescue. The first on the scene were the Paulhans. Blood relationship linked them to the Sirvants. Alas, all efforts were deployed in vain. Fire burst out on all sides, immediately reaching a climax.

"Luckily, there's not a breath of air! Luckily, there's no wind!" the men were repeating endlessly, in a daze. Had there been, the disaster would have been even greater!

In spite of the suffocating heat of the night exacerbating the flames, this thought froze the soul. How could you not be gripped by fear at the idea that all those magnificent orchards could have been consumed in several hours? Fear had been balanced by patience keeping them going and watching over them. Patience that verged on religious devotion. A house? "By God, that could be rebuilt!" A few months of work, and it would rise up there in the light with more panache than ever. The work ethic was a defining feature of the Sirvant household. The opulence of these lands, which, were it not for the locusts, would have as usual scattered its fragrances into the night, was testimony. The locusts always headed for the other side of the desert, after having devastated a season's harvest. But next season, the resown fields would produce their riches anew. Locusts left the trees stripped but alive. Alive? The winds of winter, the sap of spring, and there they would be without any aftereffect. Alive? Life was preserved.

Soon, the moment they realized they could do nothing about the house and the grange, the men dedicated all their energy to containing the fire. Thanks to small water tanks mounted on carts brought from the neighborhood, they could sprinkle the ground liberally as well as the trees around the fire's two central locations. From the farm next door, they brought tall ladders and saws. A cluster of giant eucalyptus trees brushed the facade of the house. The fire licked at them hungrily. The men did not allow them to be consumed. Climbing the ladders and the trees themselves, they pruned off the branches. True enough, the trees grew a bit red. It was nothing serious, however. A good pruning and they would take off again next year.

When the police and the firemen finally arrived from the neighboring village, the fire was beginning to die down. There was nothing else to do. So they talked. They told stories of other fires, other plagues of locusts, other fevers, other Arab misdeeds. They had been busy for hours. But now that the impotence and uselessness of their efforts had stopped them, they were overcome by exhaustion. Some of the Sirvants sank into deep lethargy. Their eyes, riveted on the sad tableau of the familial home, told their nightmare. After a long pause and a twinge of conscience, the oldest among them, Jean, looked around for his youngest brother. A while earlier, at the beginning of the blaze, he was there in the crowd.

Everyone got up, looked around, called out. He was a taciturn and fierce person, Pierre. He had the habit of hiding himself in various places in the orchard to dream, read in peace, and escape the constant criticisms of his older brothers. Was he maybe once again at the home of Farès, the guard? He went there often, too often. What pleasure, what interest could he have in visiting with Yamna and Farès for hours on end, instead of courting the girls from the neighboring farms? They had bewitched him. For a long time, Pierre had been talking in an odd way. He, the silent one, had begun to hold forth: Arab rights, dignity . . . Hadn't the settlers contributed to that dignity in bringing them progress, in giving them work? His speeches had begun to unsettle his mother, who favored him over the others. His brothers had at one point contemplated firing Farès. But they knew their mother would oppose that.

Pierre was not with Farès. In fact, Farès was with them. So they searched the orchards and the bushes. Maybe he had withdrawn to some solitary place to nurse his pain. No response to their shouts, and their empty-handed search, brought their anxiety to a head. The men turned apprehensively toward the last cracklings of the flames, now quite small.

"I'll go see if he went to see Yamna and the children," Farès announced.

He came right back.

"No, they haven't seen him."

"He didn't go into the house, did he?"

"No! Impossible. The fire there was impassable from the start."

Everyone searched the darkness, called out his name in the silence. One group went toward the fields. Another went, once again, toward the orchards. Two policemen and two firemen went off toward the grange, which was still smoking a bit. There, from haystack to haystack, the sparks had ignited a cavalcade of flames whose growls were almost bestial. In no time at all, the grange had become nothing more than a gigantic torch planted in the side of the hill. Here and there, several small fires were still burning. The grange? All that remained were blackened walls streaked by fire. The frame, the roof, and all its contents were a heap of hot rubble, just cinders and blackened iron. Suddenly one of the policemen called the rest of his group. They knelt down. Appalling spectacle. Consternation. The nauseated silence of men. There, at the threshold of the small door behind the grange, lay a charred silhouette.

"It's Pierre—see there, that's his father's signet ring he always wore."

"He must have been trying to save God only knows what!" suggested a voice trying to make sense of it.

A beam, falling from the frame, had crushed his skull. The flames did the rest. A young farmer who had joined them began to vomit. The other Sirvants, searching across the way, saw that the group was growing larger and larger behind the grange. They came running. The men prevented them from approaching, from seeing. They lashed out, let loose heart-rending howls, tried to free themselves with their fists. Everyone kept a firm grip on them. The corpse wasn't even approachable in the magma of embers and blackened iron. It wasn't right to inflict this nightmarish spectacle on close relatives or to risk another life. Alerted, the women came running, too. It was only to spare them from such an atrocity that the Sirvant men allowed themselves to be led away. The farmers guided them back toward the entrance of the property. Some of them went to get one of the firemen's water tanks that was still full. They had to hose down the pile of debris and embers to be able to get the body out without danger. Someone went to get the priest. One of the neighbors was a carpenter. In addition to other things, he made all the coffins in the region. With all the illnesses, the endemic fevers all around, with all the accidents, he always had some extras on hand: pinewood or oak, right for everyone's purse. The firemen were finally able to extract the body. An oak casket was quickly brought. As soon as the priest arrived, they began putting him in the coffin.

In front of the house, sitting at the foot of an olive tree, Serge Sirvant was crying. Tumultuous sobs shook his huge body. It was shocking, a bit terrifying. It was as if pain's fury grew in proportion to the weight of the prey caught in its trap. Those around him suddenly felt more vulnerable, more dispossessed and humble, because his sobs rang out like a terrible warning. The older one, Jean, stocky, stiff-jawed, and dry-eyed, seemed focused on silent fulminations. Far away, under the trees, Yamna's sobs were interspersed with her praise of Pierre. Yamna's grief accentuated that of the roumias.

The priest arrived. Then everyone expedited things, and the coffin was closed. The men lifted it to their shoulders and carried it to the entrance. They had no difficulty doing that. The fire had absorbed the weight of the body. There was almost nothing left to carry but the oak casket itself. They put it down in the main alley. Everyone got up, mute, their heads heavy and buzzing.

The Sirvants' mother, following a brief bout of madness, was nothing more now than a tiny thing, she too being consumed by the fire. Empty-eyed, an unintelligible soliloquy on her lips, she no longer budged. Her children tried in vain to rouse her, to entreat her, but she didn't respond. And if at times her eyes glanced over them, they didn't focus on them.

The squeaking of wheels was heard. Soon afterward, crossing onto the property, two carriages started down the alley one after the other. The women were returning. At first they had come with the men. But because the firefighting was limited to several firebreaks only requiring a few people, they had gone back to get together a meal. The Sirvants hadn't eaten anything since noon. They came back with wine, brandy, sausage, *soubressade*, pâté, some *tapenade* and some *mouna*. They already knew about Pierre. The carpenter's wife was with them. During the journey across the bumpy roads, they had had time to shed some tears, to speak of the tragic event while searching the surrounding shadows with unquiet eyes. Two men of the group had carbines across their knees. At their arrival, all the men moved around, dispersed, and began to talk to each other again.

The women crossed themselves and stood for a time before the coffin. After a moment of prayer, they moved on quickly to escape the immobility and silence where fear was lurking, spreading its tentacles. Then, pouring out consolation and condolences and promising to give support without fail, they settled down to distributing the victuals. The alcohol did the men good, rekindled their spirits. The women drank, too. Its fire pulled their bodies from the grip of horror, helped trick fate. The Sirvants scarcely touched the food in spite of the urging and solicitude of the crowd. But the others, even if they had already eaten, suddenly felt a terrible hunger. It was true that a number of hours had passed since their last meal. But more than that, in the face of such a misfortune, in the presence of death, hunger arose as a survival instinct. And biting with all one's teeth into a loaf of bread suddenly became a powerful symbol of life.

"He couldn't have gotten very far! I shot his horse at the first try!" said the eldest Sirvant son, Jean, between clenched teeth, as if talking to himself.

"He must be hidden somewhere out in the dark. They do that, those jackals. They're jackals, all of them," added one of the farmers.

"Wherever he is, I'll find him!" Jean swore with force.

"Give us his description! What does the guy look like?" asked one of the men.

"Dark *saroual* and a red *chechia*. Light *saroual* and a white *chechia* or chèche. Always swarthy with a moustache," quipped a voice.

"This one is tall. His height is well above average. He's wearing a black chèche, like men from the South. A tan face with a shocking yellow gaze! I'd recognize him among a thousand," Jean declared.

The men regrouped, debated, got all excited. Little by little the tension and anger mounted. They'd divide into groups and scour the region. Concerned to avoid excesses, the sergeant in charge tried to put one of his agents at the head of each group. But first of all, they needed to tend to the coffin, to the old woman sitting mumbling, unhinged from reality, to the children who were sleeping outside, lying side by side on a blanket. It was decided that the women and children would go to the Paulhans'.

Their house was large. By squeezing a little, they would all fit. The women would put mother Sirvant and the children to bed. And, for what remained of the night, they would watch over the body. The men would go with the police to search for the culprit. They would find him! By God, they would find him!

5

When he heard hoof beats, Mahmoud pulled on the reins and turned around. Three riders raced toward him at full tilt.

"Already!" he thought, stunned.

After a moment's shock, he took off again, spurred on by fear of being caught. Despite pressing on without stopping, he couldn't get away from them. His pursuers seemed determined not to let him get away. Mahmoud looked around feverishly. No help from the landscape, not even the least wood to shield him from this new pursuit. As far as the eye could see, the flat land wove its grapevines like an immense latticework. How could he escape, where could he hide? For three days he had done nothing but flee, pursued by locusts, by a madman, and now the roumis were at it, too. Three days with hardly any sleep, wearing himself out on roads infested with locusts and brigands. Mahmoud couldn't take it anymore. He was dead tired, exhausted. Mahmoud jumped down and waited.

When they got near him, Mahmoud raised his hands to signal surrender. Two civilians and one policeman approached him cautiously.

The tall, thin man in a black chèche was surely the guy they were looking for. A dangerous man. In just a few days, his legend had spread among the settlers, fed by rumors quickly ignited by all the myths, by all sorts of anger. Each time he was alone. Did he have accomplices? Now they were only a few strides away from him. That untamed gaze with its piercing bronze tint . . .

It was him, not a doubt of it! One of the farmers leaped forward and pressed the barrel of his gun to his head.

"Are you Tijani?" asked the policeman.

Mahmoud responded with a nod of his head.

"Hold out your hands!" he ordered, visibly delighted by this capture that was so much easier than he had dared to hope.

"I didn't burn the farm! It wasn't me," Mahmoud protested.

"Oh, yeah? Hold out your hands just the same."

Mahmoud stretched his hands out toward him. The man put on the handcuffs.

"If you try to get away, we'll shoot without warning."

"It wasn't me!"

"Oh, no! It wasn't you? Mother Sirvant saw you! Get on that horse or I'll plug you with one of these slugs right now," thundered one of the farmers.

Mahmoud did so.

"Quick, let's go find the others," another farmer suggested.

"No! The chief's orders are clear. First I have to put this guy behind bars at the station. If one of the Sirvants had seen him first, it would have been all over for him!"

"We'll skin this devil of a bugger alive!"

"The law will decide his fate," the officer cut in.

"The law! If we have the bad luck to run into a 'bleeding heart' judge we'll never be done with it! You don't understand anything about the realities of this country. You're not from around here. What do you know about Arabs?!"

"I surely know less than you about this country, but I know my job and I know French law. And I have my orders. He's going to the jail. Let me do my job. I don't try to tell you how to make wine!"

"Laws are made to protect us, not to be used against us! Each time one of these buggers does a dirty deed, we need to liquidate him. To serve as an example. We have to keep them in their place by fear, otherwise they'll continue to burn down our houses and kill us!"

Mahmoud hadn't hoped to find among his pursuers a man who would try, for whatever reason, to protect him against the anger of the settlers. He turned around to look at the face of the other man who was threatening him.

"You, get moving! Did you hear what's in store for you?" the man in uniform said, giving him a shove.

The sun was high in the sky. Though the trivial, miserable vibrations of the locusts diminished its luminosity, they did nothing to attenuate its burning heat. No sooner had they gotten to the village jail than Mahmoud's handcuffs were removed and he was put in a small cell. In spite of the threats about his destiny flying around him, Mahmoud tasted, almost with relief, this peaceful interlude. Now and then he heard the noise of footsteps muffled by thick walls in the next cell. He concluded that he wasn't the only prisoner. But, other than this presence revealing itself only intermittently, silence reigned. It didn't take long for tranquility to grow heavy. Aided by the shadows, he drifted helplessly toward sleep, too weary to resist.

"I must stay awake in order to be prepared for any eventuality," he tried to persuade himself with one last twinge of consciousness before being engulfed.

The officer who had captured him soon left to take the news to his chief and to put a halt to the other searches. It took a long time, however, to find the entire group of those who had, since dawn, been out beating the countryside. They all gathered again at the Paulhans'. The men's eyes were weary, hollow dark rings. Two-day old beards shadowed their faces. They drank coffee and chewed on biscuits in silence. It was going to be a long, tedious day. Pierre's burial would take place that very day. The suffocating heat increased the pain and disrupted the mourning. In spite of several hours of sleep, the old woman awoke filled with the same vague absence. And so, someone had to go get a doctor.

Brought up to date on the actions and intentions of the arresting officer, the farmers growled with discontent. What disagreeable stroke of fate saddled them with "bleeding hearts" for officers of the law?

"Snivelers claiming they want to apply the same laws here as in France! What next?!"

On the other hand, the chief of police was relieved by the news of this clean capture. Taking him aside, he congratulated the officer who'd contained the settlers with him, avoiding the worst. When the men in uniform got up, the Sirvants and several other farmers got up also. And despite protests and repeated assertions that they wouldn't be allowed to approach the prisoner, they dogged their heels. By the time they got to the jail, the sky was afire. Myriad flashing locust wings were bursting there like sparks. Disputes fermenting during the walk blew up violently at the front door. The tumult grew louder, exploding into an extraordinary din: shouts, threats, slamming of doors. Then, suddenly, calm again. The help of several officers who'd stayed put was just enough to manage to evacuate the noisy, demonstrative crowd from the police station without conceding to any of their demands.

Awakened by the sudden clamor, Mahmoud imagined the scene: the Sirvants looming there, loudly demanding his skin and crying out for legitimate vengeance. Now he heard only the indignant responses of the officer who had arrested him, and another lower, heavier voice trying to calm everyone down while seeming, albeit weakly, to agree with the attitude of the settlers. The doors to the offices opened suddenly. A number of men in uniform surged in and looked Mahmoud over curiously.

"So that's our Arab!"

Squatting down propped against a corner of the cell, Mahmoud looked at these worn-out, gloomy, unshaven faces. How ironic! Thrown into the fray by a demonic compatriot. Saved from imminent death by men in uniform, symbol in his eyes, if not of death, at least of injustice.

"But saved from death to what end? To be put immediately behind bars where I can wait for someone to come up with a fitting demise for me?" he thought bitterly.

"Let's go have lunch and rest a while before interrogating him," the commander suggested. "He can cool his heels just where he is."

He didn't need to say it twice to the exhausted men. Alone again, Mahmoud didn't worry over things for long. Irresistibly, his eyelids closed. Soon, he was sleeping once more.

The hour of the siesta had emptied the village streets and delivered them over completely to the locusts. At the police station, the tired men rested each in their separate rooms. Down below in the offices, a policeman tried to fight off the wave of lethargy sweeping over each and every one of them. In the suffocating heat, even if one abstained from drinking wine at noon, profound apathy drained the body of energy, sucked out its will. Even the loosest tongues ceased to wag. A fog rolled in, damping the spark in every eye. Dogs lay down in the shrunken, bleached shadows of trees. They didn't budge after that, not even when touched by the rough legs of locusts, not even under the assault of numerous fat flies that, vampirelike, sucked the rheumy discharge from their eyes. Only the vibrations of the locusts and the shrilling of cicadas were stoked by the furnace of the day. Drunk with heat, the cicadas broke loose, punctuating the infernal trance of the locusts. Strange celebration in the dead heat of the day. Slumped over his little table, the officer slept.

A jingle. Someone was once again opening the door between the cells and the offices. Starting from his sleep, Mahmoud turned his haggard eyes toward the entrance. Then he jumped up. El-Majnoun! Yes, El-Majnoun! It was really him. Mahmoud was not prey to some hallucination. Nothing stopped this man, then, not even guarded doors. Wherever he was, he could swoop in on him like a nightmare invading sleep. The lower part of his face still veiled by his chèche, El-Majnoun shot him a triumphant glance. His gun barrel pressed against the officer's back, he was pushing him, shove by shove, ahead of him. Already, with the bunch of keys in his hand, the man was opening the cell door. As soon as he finished, El-Majnoun hit him twice on the head with his gun butt. The officer dropped to the ground, inert. All this happened very quickly, in silence. El-Majnoun took off his chèche and, tearing it lengthwise, used half to gag the unconscious man. With the other, he bound him hand and foot. That done, he gave the signal to leave. Mahmoud didn't waste time with questions. He followed him.

"Nassim! I don't know where they put him," Mahmoud said anxiously.

"We've no time to lose! Mine isn't far, hurry!" El-Majnoun cut in.

Quickly, he closed the door behind him. Then, putting the keys in his pocket with a mocking air, he pushed Mahmoud toward the exit. "Get going," he said hurriedly.

"Go that way—we are going to the home of a family on the outskirts of town. Don't be afraid, they won't breathe a word."

In the small streets, the locusts reigned once again. Still groggy and numb from his long siesta, dazed by the luminosity, and stupefied by the situation, Mahmoud followed silently. When they were far enough away from the post, El-Majnoun burst into roguish laughter.

Arriving at an Arab *douar*, he guided Mahmoud to the last house along the edge of the fields. He knocked lightly on the door, which opened at once. An older man, dressed only in a large *'abaya*, stepped back to let them enter. El-Majnoun's horse was in the courtyard beneath a *zriba*. Thanking the man, he tended to his horse. His host came to offer him a small sack with supplies and a chèche to protect him from the sun.

"I would have preferred you to have given me a horse!"

"*Allah ijib, si* El-Majnoun."

"*Allah ijib*! In all the time you've been praying, Allah didn't even bring you a horse! Keep on praying and you'll never mount anything other than your mare of a wife!"

That said, and without another thought for the man, he went toward the end of the courtyard where a second door opened directly onto the fields behind the village. They would leave from there. El-Majnoun was already in the saddle. After a brief goodbye to the man, Mahmoud got up behind him. Treading over clods baked by the sun and spotted with locusts, they took off at an easy trot. El-Majnoun heaved a sigh of relief, letting loose a string of his usual bursts of laughter. Then he began to hold forth:

"Insisting on fleeing from me and obstinately refusing to accept my help and friendship very nearly succeeded in causing your ruin. That scoundrel Hassan, nonetheless, had strict orders. I suspect the double-dealer of having knowingly allowed you to get away. He wanted to get rid of you too much. I have keen hearing, like an animal, luckily. I can hear hoofbeats for a radius of a thousand leagues! But by the time I got up, your hoofbeats were already pounding far in the distance. I took off on your track. Alas, I reached you at the same time they did. At that point, any intervention on my part would have been dangerous and would only have served to reinforce the surveillance around you. So I preferred to wait, following your progress from a distance. I was delighted when I figured out your destination. Discreet and useful alliances I can count on in that village reinforced that feeling. I let the police go parading on into town, and while invisible to the rest, I knocked at that same door we just left from. Then I had only to send my host's children to keep watch in front of the jail with instructions to keep me instantly informed about all comings and goings. Everyone knows that the street doors to the police station are kept open all the time. Sometimes a policeman does sentry duty at the door. Other times, the sentry is satisfied with sleeping inside while others busy themselves with daily concerns. Life is very dull here.

Mahmoud didn't see the point in responding. How absurdly hollow the bragging of this possessed devil was! At present, he felt in top form, with a clear mind. The brief stay in the cell had at least had the benefit of forcing him to rest. And the profound sleep of abdication and letting go of his will had renewed hope. Here he was once more following the pathway of fate, but his desire to escape it was stronger than ever. His stomach growling made him aware of his hunger.

"Do you have anything to eat?" he asked.

A forgiving smile lit up El-Majnoun's face. He handed him the little sack their host from the village had given them. In it Mahmoud found bread stuffed with black-olive paste, an onion, a tomato, and some hard-boiled eggs. He began eating. Mind filled with contradictory possibilities, he applied himself to chewing slowly, as if grinding all the difficulties of his situation between his teeth.

"I know another family not far from here. They'll lend us a horse. It's funny how I always have problems with time and horses when you're around. It's in our best interest to get out of here quickly. Some streaked walls are all that remains of the farm we set on fire. One of the men in the family was burned alive. The old woman seems to have lost her mind.

He laughed. Mahmoud, who'd been unaware of this tragic course of events, shivered with horror.

"How do you know all this?" he asked anxiously, overcome suddenly by doubt.

"Isn't he trying to paint a blacker picture? The idea of binding me to him through growing fear would probably please this madman."

"I didn't even have to ask questions. The police and the farmers spread the news. Even the man who kept my horse knew it.

Friend, the challenge we are facing is enormous, equal to our status. We have sown panic in our wake." He laughed again. "Since meeting you, I've regained my sense of humor!"

He burst into gales of laughter once more. Mahmoud tried to remain calm in order to think.

"What sibylline project does he have in mind, thinking he has found in me an irreplaceable partner? I can no longer bear the logorrhea of this consummate *majnoun*. *Khayi*, does he really believe I'm in the same sticky situation as he is?"

The memory of the old Sirvant woman imposed itself on him. The course taken by their last meeting had, from the start, confused him.

"I had nothing to do with it! I only wanted to enjoy the spectacle of her defeat," he argued to himself. "Damn! She and her people took the light of hope away from mine, plunging them into the darkness of disinheritance. They robbed them even of life itself. At the twilight of her days, because chance landed me in front of the door to her troubled conscience, she tried to whitewash it by throwing me a crumb. That takes the cake! The parasites offer the original owner, whose portion they've taken, charity in the form of a miserable pittance drawn from his very own riches! Let the devil take all of them! They won't catch me, not a chance, not El-Majnoun, not the settlers, not the police. Peace for me lies far away from these lands. I'm going to go collect the bones of my grandmother and take them to Labiod-Sid-Sheikh. Then, I'll head off to the land of endless evasions, my desert steppes."

For the moment, even though he was under the thumb of El-Majnoun, he'd nevertheless escaped from prison. But how was he to escape from the yoke of this madman? His eye fell on the gun knocking against the man's side. In spite of himself, he stared at it with sudden fascination. Then, with a smile, he drew back. It wasn't a matter of letting the "beast" bite him again. What to do with guile being held in check like this? He would find a way, if he remained alert, to outsmart the vigilant surveillance of this man. In any case, for the moment, El-Majnoun represented a lesser danger than the settlers and the police. He would find a way. He would find a way.

Soon they arrived in sight of the home of El-Majnoun's acquaintances. It was a small farm. They dismounted. A dog barked. Soon an old woman and some children appeared. They came to meet them. After the customary salutations, El-Majnoun made his request.

"The men are at the *souk*. It's market day. No, they took the three horses. There aren't any others on the farm. We don't have the mule any more . . . sold. The men won't be back until the end of the day."

El-Majnoun turned toward Mahmoud with a look of great disappointment.

"Hold the reins, I'm going to look in the stable!" he called out before going around the corner of the house.

Scarcely had he disappeared behind the house than Mahmoud's foot was in the stirrup. Heartbeats filling his head, he spurred the horse and took off. Damnation, if El-Majnoun's falling victim to his own distrust weren't the height of comedy. His suspicion about what the woman was saying had taken precedence over his watchfulness concerning Mahmoud. This opportunity wasn't to be missed! No other horses? What a blessing! No police in sight, no El-Majnoun glued to him. What luck! Freedom regained sooner than expected! For the moment, he needed to secure it, to safeguard it. In the distance to the east was the outline of the mountains of Tlemcen: his goal in order to hide himself. Far behind him there was a cry, the sound of shots. Too late!

"Ha, ha! El-Majnoun surely isn't laughing now! The settlers, still thinking I am under lock and key, will busy themselves with the locusts, their mourning, and the funeral. The police are resting in good conscience, having finished a job well done. Upon waking up, they'll look all around for a good while trying to find their colleague before thinking to open or break down the cell door. When they discover him gagged and locked up in my place, I'll already be out of reach. As for El-Majnoun, he'll have to await the return of the men from market. The sack of provisions containing the bread stuffed with olive paste and a small water skin are attached to the saddle. I can ride for the rest of the day."

Mahmoud felt a twinge of regret for Nassim, his bay horse back at the police station. Mane flying in the wind, the fire of his coat burning up the day, his energy . . . he'd miss him terribly. But it wasn't the time for nostalgia! He hurried to suppress his grief and focus on the journey. El-Majnoun had handed him a switch along with the reins, and he used it to brush off the horse's speckled coat, ridding it of the most obstinate insects. In any case, the horse was no more bothered by the locusts than by the equally numerous and irksome flies. Living with them had dulled the terror.

"I've got to get back to the only healthy territory, my only refuge, writing. I must carry it beyond the reach of chance, beyond the misadventure of random encounters. I must collect my scattered thoughts there so to avoid plunging into the wild helter-skelter of anxiety. Only then can my dreams be serene. I want to return to the humility of the steppes, to the sobriety of their bare flatness, to their language of silence. I no longer want to ride along like an unbridled dreamer. I want to walk. Walk as if writing. Writing the steps into words, the words into steps, on the high thresholds, the plateaus, the pedestals of the desert. And in the quietness of writing, in its wide-open spaces, I will seek nothing, embrace everything, at one and the same time. I want to rid my life of its burdens. I want my life to be a threshold, open and crisscrossed by contrasts. I want my life woven through with writings, blending in memory all its wonders, and the spoken word. I want it to be a mosaic scintillating with differences. Then, in the wide measure of poetry, it will display its finery, deploy its seductions, and offer itself at each moment like a conquest begun anew. But I will not let life fool me, either. Words and their mockery, the difficulty of walking on the high plateaus and in the desert, will control my life and will also protect me from excess. Moreover, in those 'nowheres,' glowing with eternity, death is the measure of time, a grain of sand its unity. From grain to grain, a warning that extends to infinity, discouraging any attempt at vanity. Death is only the last frontier before the crossing of another threshold. Death is only the briefest of nightmares I have yet to live through. But while the mere approach of sleep often seizes me, scratching me with its icy tremors, I want to be able to mock it, mock death. I want to be able to rid myself of this fear, to confront it at some time and peel away its veils of horror. Death is a tragic, mysterious, solitary dame crushed by her own fatal nature, yet at times I long to lose myself in excesses of rapture over her. And, unfaithful, I want to drift into sleep in her arms on the bed of my most beautiful muse, Poetry."

Mahmoud continued on in that way, his thoughts rejoicing, his body at ease. Each time he came upon a hill along the way, he climbed to its crest. From the summit, he surveyed the horizons marked out by locusts. For the moment, no one was on his trail. Reassured, he chose his direction as he went along. His goal: the blue line of mountains in which he hoped to lose himself. It was from the height of one of these vantage points that he saw huge black clouds appear from behind the mountains of Tlemcen, climbing over the crests and then spreading themselves down upon them.

"Storms?"

The possibility filled Mahmoud with uneasiness, because here, storms vomit waterfalls in seconds. Then, the spontaneous generation of rivers and torrents begin roaring, tumbling over the slopes and devouring the roads. Mahmoud glanced frequently at the mountain as well. Turbaned by the dark mass of clouds, the mountain loomed larger, closer. An abnormal silence suddenly swallowed up the multitudinous wing-scrapings of the locusts. Birds and insects flew close to the ground. The atmosphere, suddenly thickened, pressed down on his chest. All of nature gave the strange sensation of being braced in uneasy expectation.

Soon clouds covered the crests, overflowing them and running down the sides of the mountain. They approached very fast, soon blocking out the plain. It was as if a fantastic herd of dinosaurs, drowning in clouds of dust, were coming. Detaching themselves from this monstrous front, which was growing darker and darker, elongated feathery white escapees arrived at full speed. The golden light turned ashy gray. The lid of clouds lowered a bit and clamped down on the lower slopes of the hill.

Suddenly, rushing down the mountain and bellowing with convulsive and apocalyptic fury, the north wind began to blow. It clawed at the *maquis*, scratched the earth. With demented wailing, it gathered up clouds of locusts in compact whirlwinds and, breath raging, hurled them into the distance. Cursed insects, fanatical devourers! Torn asunder, they flew about in gusts with the sound of dry autumn leaves. On high, the clouds were still expanding. Soon the sky was nothing more than an amorphous swelling.

Crouched over the withers of his horse at first, Mahmoud tried continuing on toward his assigned goal. Soon, holding on to his chèche, barely able to keep his eyes open, he had to give up and let himself be carried along by the current of the storm. Lightning rent the murky sky. Thunder began to pound. Amid this apocalyptic chaos, as if in the process of crumbling to pieces, the earth was shaken to its very core. Then the storm broke. You would have said the thirsty earth was swallowing the drenched sky in great gulps, so enormous were the drops, so hard were they falling, beating down. A warm, moist breath rose from the earth. Very soon, torrents of rain were falling. Within moments, tumultuous flash floods were careening down, following the slopes of the mountains. All nature seemed to waver on the verge of being carted away by a muddy flood.

Soaked and blinded by the whipping rain, Mahmoud moved ahead slowly. He was forced to admit that he could no longer continue his journey. He looked a long time for someplace to take shelter when, through the torrential streaming, he saw the ochre mass of a group of houses. Battling the rage of the downpour, he hurried in that direction. It was a small *mechta* roughcast in mud. Mahmoud went from one house to another, calling out. The first two seemed empty. When he got to the third, a woman came out. Her face covered with a fouta, she walked out a few steps to look around. She was black, from what little Mahmoud could see of her. Suddenly, she turned and went back into the house, shutting the door precipitously behind her. Disconcerted, Mahmoud went toward the last house. But just like the first two, it appeared to be deserted. He backtracked to the one where the woman had come out. Dismounting, he knocked at the door.

"Please, could you give me shelter for the duration of the storm? I will leave as soon as the rain has stopped."

Receiving no response, and harried by the rain that was stinging him in its fury, he shouted to be heard above the raging wind:

"Don't be afraid if you are alone. I am a peaceful man. . . . I swear . . ."

With a creak the door opened once more. The woman reappeared in the opening. Face veiled, eyes modestly downcast, she said:

"Put your horse on the side. A mule and some sheep are there. Secure the door firmly with the outside bar."

Mahmoud did so, then returned. Another scraping of hinges and the woman moved aside to let him enter. He went directly into the room. The humid semi-darkness blinded his eyes. He remained with his back to the door, harried by the storm and wind, not daring to budge with so much water trickling off his clothes. The woman had taken refuge against the far wall. She was watching him fearfully.

"Salaam 'aleïki," said Mahmoud.

She replied with a timid nod.

"Are you alone? Don't be afraid, I won't harm you. As soon as the worst of the storm is over, I will leave," he repeated reassuringly.

She didn't budge, didn't make a peep. Gradually becoming accustomed to the semi-darkness, Mahmoud could see that the room was a sort of kitchen. On the wall to his left were hanging some goatskin bags. In a corner there were a few basic cooking utensils, canvas sacks, and a small pile of dried roots. The back of the room was hidden by the fine, close web of a weaving loom secured by two beams, one fixed to the roof, the other set on the floor. On the right-hand wall, a door led to the next room. A puppy came across the threshold and wound around the ankles of the woman, wriggling. After a long moment of embarrassed silence, the woman moved away noiselessly, followed by the dog. She picked up a large earthenware kanoun and filled it with charcoal taken from one of the sacks. Then she put a few roots in the center and lit them. Twisted and dry, they caught fire quickly, emitting crackling sounds, sweet to ears drunk with the fury of the storm. The woman turned her back to Mahmoud, uncovered her face and blew on the coals to ignite them. When they began to glow, she covered her face again and, turning toward him, said in an almost imperceptible murmur:

"You can dry yourself if you wish."

Actually, it was so warm that his wet clothes were really a blessing for his skin. But, even if impractical, the kindness touched Mahmoud. Moreover, he wanted so much to appear docile in order to ease his hostess's anxiety that he accepted her offer right away. He even was careful to approach slowly so that he wouldn't scare her with a sudden movement. With her crouched down like a great bird on a branch, he feared that at the least alert, she would disappear on nimble wings into gale.

He sat down near the fire. She raised her eyes to look at him. Her elongated eyes tapered toward her temples. The captivating flutter of the thick arc of her eyelashes seemed to set them aglow. And, along with her timidity and her fear, this wandering gaze engendered a feeling of vertigo in Mahmoud. A burst of sparks illuminated the sleek violet ebony hue of her forehead. Mahmoud, completely won over, forgot his wet clothes, El-Majnoun, the police, and his unfinished flight.

"What good fortune to be here, under the protection of this woman. What good fortune to be alone with her. Where is this sudden feeling of having at last reached my destination coming from? It seems as if the search for the bones of my grandmother were only a pretext. As if the journey through a land of locusts, topped off by a madman, were only a trial I had to undergo in order to merit the fullness of this moment. A black nymph was waiting for me in this sanctuary whose final defensive rampart was a raging tempest. If writing is my country, could a woman be that part of myself missing in life? Would a place in her heart make me settle down? But I am wandering. Above all, she mustn't see that I am disturbed. That might make her uneasy."

Outside the rain and the wind mixed their fury. The battered door, martyred, vibrated in every plank. Thundering squalls blew in through the cracks. A wave of water outdid the wind. It crashed down, spitting great red splashes inside. Then the wind picked up, swelled again in fury. In a brutal charge, bucking, it hurled itself into an assault on the house once again. The roof became nothing more than a sieve. It was raining almost as much inside as out, but with a soft, muted sound. The roof seemed to be there only to stop the fits of the wind and absorb the rattling of the rain rather than to stop the course of the water. The rain loaded the roof with mud, making it heavy. It transformed the roof into huge ochre tears that ran down the walls, making ravines in the mud plaster as they went. The walls became more and more coated. Then, pulled down by excessive weight, they detached themselves and fell with a soft "plop" that was almost inaudible given the chaos outside. The floor of beaten earth swelled with water. It came in under the door as well. The woman unfolded her limbs and rose. Mahmoud was fascinated by her silhouette. Her figure was full beneath the magic shadows of her skin. A complexion that would drive mad the senses of even the most ascetic man. His own, already doomed to perdition, cried out their hunger in silence beneath the iron rule of a sharp-edged but exquisite pain. The woman went to look at the adjoining room. Stopping on the threshold she said in a quiet voice:

"It is raining there, too. It is raining everywhere."

She went to the entry door and pulled back the bolt. She went out pulling it shut behind her. Lost cause. One brutal blow and the blaring trumpets of the squall blew into the interior. The woman came back to the room.

"We'll have to go in with the animals. It is the only dry place. The roof over their two rooms has always kept them dry. It will hold up this time, too."

The animals' shelter consisted of two rooms in a row. The one on the far side served as a stable. The one entered first served as a sheepfold. Mahmoud herded the sheep in with the horses. Going back to the kitchen, he picked up the huge sack of charcoal and put it in front of the door between the two rooms, where it served to keep all the animals in the far room. The earth was covered with a carpet of manure. The woman brought an old mat of esparto grass, which she spread over it. They also gathered up perishable foodstuffs. These efforts uncovered the face of the woman: high cheekbones, a fine nose with quivering nostrils like petals, the humid rim of a lip. . . . Busy fighting the bad weather, she wasn't concerned with the fact that her face was unveiled, to Mahmoud's great delight. Coming and going in the rain wet her light *melehfa*, which stuck to her skin, molding to her form. On the satiny jet black of her skin, the drops of water became iridescent ochre and blue. Thus, fertile and rustling, a naiad riding the storm, she awakened Mahmoud's sensuality from its long period of lethargy. And the spectacle of her beauty lit the heavens of Mahmoud's dreams, blinded for so long. How he would have loved to ask her the questions spinning in his head.

"Who is she? Why all alone in the mechta left to the mercy of the storm? Does she really exist? Is she a figment of my imagination yearning for a woman's presence? She holds the key to one of those dreams, opposing the drought of the land and the imprisonment of the senses. A divine creation. Is she not a hallucination, a stroke of black lightning inlaid in the jewel box of my mind by the thunderbolts of the storm?"

Mahmoud was so afraid he would wake from this dream, so afraid of seeing her disappear, that he silenced these questions. Outside, the patter of the storm grew drier and, like a multitude of sharp teeth, cut through the fits of the wind: hailstones!

Huddled in silence, they listened to the salvos of the hail and the dripping of the water underneath the bombardment of the hail. Sitting each in a corner of the room on the old mat, they hardly dared look at one another now. She held the puppy against her breast and caressed it with a distracted hand. The kanoun gave off a faint red glow. The odors of manure, old urine, sweat, and hides, heated up by the warmth, saturated the air. But under the circumstances, these musty odors had nothing disgusting about them. The suffocating heat wove around them a buffer that separated them from the raging of the elements. And this atmosphere charged with animal smells seemed to contribute, in a singular fashion, to the growing turmoil in Mahmoud. Over to the side, the animals were also quiet. From time to time the muzzle of a sheep would materialize above the sacks blocking the connecting door. It would fix an empty, round, reddish-brown eye on them before disappearing.

"I could make tea. Would you like some?" she asked timidly.

Mahmoud nodded. In the room, there was a *qolla* containing water. She put some on to heat in an old kettle. While she was doing these things, Mahmoud, captivated, was admiring her. Suddenly, she began to laugh. Mahmoud smiled at her happiness.

"They are going to say now that he caused the hail to fall," she commented in a soft voice.

"He?"

"Yes, he. The man who dug up a body, burned down a farm, and terrorized the settlers. A roumi perished in the blaze. That's too bad! They say that he championed the 'arbis . . . They are even saying that it was his curse that sent the locusts to ravage the land! So, this hailstorm, completing the disaster, must perforce be of his doing. When I heard you calling out, I imagined that maybe it was him. I don't know if I was disappointed or comforted when I saw the speckled coat of your horse through the storm."

"Was it out of spite that you almost denied me hospitality?" he couldn't keep himself from asking.

"He has a bay horse, they say!" she went on, ignoring his question. The others are all afraid of him, even the Arabs. As for me, his legend has so filled and obsessed my mind these last few days that it spurred on my hopes, willing him to come my way. I looked for him on the horizon. I looked for him from the threshold of my weariness and my solitude. I looked for him in the darkness beneath my eyelids when I could finally close them to dream. I even saw him with my eyes wide open, like truth. When the raging of the wind filled my head, he came to rescue my thoughts . . . One night, I had a strange dream."

"What did you dream?"

A smile broke her concentration. Her teeth were a crescent

shining in the night of her face. She lowered her eyes. The tea was ready. Gazing at the kanoun, the irises of her eyes sparkling, she avoided his question once more and continued:

"Around the well with the other women from the mechta, we invented a song for him: 'The man on the bay horse who returned from the past . . .'"

Stunned, the beating of his heart filling his ears and drowning out the chaos of the storm, Mahmoud reached out to get the glass of tea. Then he returned to his place and drank it slowly. He felt a sudden need to smoke. For two days at least, he hadn't taken even a puff. A little *kif* would do him good calming his shattered nerves. He felt feverishly in the pocket of his *saroual* looking for his tobacco pouch. Confiscated by the police! He'd forgotten. He'd have to be content with a glass of tea. The thought that he was in the dreams of this young woman, the way she spoke of it, brought the already considerable commotion inside him to a peak.

"What do they call you?" he asked in a voice that quavered with emotion.

"They call me Bent el-kelba, the daughter of the dog! No, no, don't be surprised. That is my first and last name! That was apparently a more than adequate name for a slave. Why give her a name more dignified or simply more accurate? What need was there for a true heritage in a life devoted to abjection and humiliation? Slaves all emerged from the damnation of shadows. And as if it weren't enough that the color of their skin was black, it had to also color their days, feelings, and thoughts. They have no history, no roots, no hope. They are nothing but that black."

Her voice had lost its suppleness. Bitterness, indignation, and aloofness gave it an unexpected inflection that was violent and biting. It made Mahmoud shiver. Dazzled by her beauty, he had never thought for a moment that this magnificent color could shackle her, too. Alas! The word 'abd, meaning slave, was still used to designate blacks. And even if one now had more scruples than to sell them like animals, they remained, solely because of their black skin, as if branded with a shameful mark that made them fodder for the cretinism and arrogance of whites.

"Even in my own tribe, however fallen, dispossessed, and wandering, there were still *'abid* when I was young. What shame! Now each one has his slave. The roumi has his dirty Arab, the 'arbi has his *'abd*. And for everyone, Jew, or *ihoudi*, is an insult. What a mess! Intolerance and racism are, finally, the measure of the stupidity of a people. Neither the wealth of the one, fruit of plunder and contempt, nor the misery of the other, sunk in ignorance and fatalism, is fertile soil to nurture caring for others. Why don't you flee!? You were here all alone before I arrived," said Mahmoud.

Her head enthroned on her long neck, with haughtiness and defiance in her look, she drew up her body and exploded:

"Flee to go where? To fall into the hands of a stranger, perhaps even more evil? Or to find myself in a bordello, site of the worst slavery!"

She hadn't raised her voice. But her tone was cutting. She added:

"I have thought the situation over fully. I have been in chains since my birth thanks to the tyrannical vanity of men. In escaping, I would change 'masters,' but I wouldn't change conditions. The people who went off to a wedding this morning, serenely confident, know that. They left me alone in the shackles of my skin. Only death will free me. Dreaming is my only freedom, my only sanctuary, my only wealth."

"But why 'daughter of the dog'?"

"The people I live with, my 'masters,' were nomads before settling here. One day when they were traveling, they found a black baby, guarded by a she-dog, by a spring. The nursling was me, and the dog, the mother of this female pup here. They say that they had to coax the dog, offer her food, pet her, before being allowed to approach me, so fiercely did she defend me with her fangs. Not far away they found the remnants of a recent camp. Thus I became the daughter of the dog. No one thought about giving me a name. A slave nursed me. It's a mundane story after all. It gave rise to a thousand suppositions, a thousand more interpretations. As for me, I like to think that my mother preferred to leave me to die rather than seeing me added to the growing wave of slaves, rather than delivering me into an existence like her own. An aborted attempt, but what does it matter. I guess it must take a lot of courage and a lot of despair to get to that point. I've been of the same mind since my childhood, and I have adored her in her burning absence. I still agree with her today. And love for her has grown inside me, as a thirst, always unslaked, for the touch of her hands on my body, and as a bottomless, gaping abyss opened up in my hearing, in my soul, by the absence of her voice, and by the sad certainty that I'll never know her face. The immense suffering embodied in that act shaped my childhood and caused me very early in life to reflect upon our condition. No one suspected the precociousness of my thoughts on these questions. A slave works herself to death without sullenness. She doesn't think, she bends. And I rarely talk about myself. If I did so today, it is because you are somehow 'extraordinary.' A horseman come out of the storm who will disappear in a few hours without leaving a trace, like my dreams. You must be unreal, because you are the first man who has not acted like a 'master' with me. The first with whom I have had any desire to talk. Maybe I will make up a song for you, the man of the storm, the man who listened to women, even to an ʿabda, once you have gone."

The hail had stopped. A heavy night drowned the rain, but the violence of the storm continued. Beneath the odor of the animals, only for the briefest moment, the smell of mint tea reached their nostrils before being inundated by heavy emanations. Oblivious to all the horrors of the previous days, Mahmoud silently savored the rebirth of his senses. The woman got up and lit an oil lamp. A wavering light illuminated, feebly, the beauty of her blackness from which the evening seemed to flow as if she were herself the source of night. A source from which Mahmoud's eyes drank deeply as if quenching an insatiable thirst.

"For dinner I can only offer a few grains of couscous and ewe's milk. Aside from the semolina and the milk, everything else is locked up in the houses of Sidi's three wives."

Mahmoud shook his head no. He had no desire to eat. How could he eat with this knot in his throat? Standing, at a loss at this refusal and suddenly ashamed at having talked so much and so openly, she turned and sat down in a corner of the room. For a long time they remained silent and still. Only their elongated shadows gave themselves over, on the wall behind them, to a strangely syncopated ballet, to the rhythm of the small flame in the oil lamp that the wind, filtering through the door, sent into trances.

Mahmoud drank his tea. He was at his fifth or sixth glass. It was very good tea whose sweetness bathed his palate. When he lifted his glass to his lips, the perfume of mint penetrated his nose. The glass also lent a welcome disguise to the stupid shaking of his hand. And the obvious contentedness of this sipping offered, in addition, a pretext for his silence. However, they had stayed silent too long. Soon embarrassment weighed upon them. Mahmoud noisily drank the final sip of tea, cleared his throat.

"Do you think that man, the rider on the bay horse, is really only a legend?" he finally asked.

"Oh! Certainly not. It's as sure as the fact that you can't return from the dead. I don't know where he comes from or what his purpose is. Whoever he is, he is a man who is very brave or completely mad. As for the rest, it simply speaks to the need for myths and legends in keeping men alive."

"Because we are only kept alive by our myths and legends?"

"Yes. Life itself is only a myth made of smaller or larger legends, depending on the person. The only truth is death."

"Putting that aside, what would you ask of this man if ever his journey took him by your mechta?"

"I can only endow that man with that which my own group is sadly lacking: a spirit of equity. I see myself leaving with him. In one fell swoop, he annihilates all the pain of my existence. A dream is the most vital of lies."

Shaken, Mahmoud thought over the prodigious spiral of their fantastically interwoven dreams. His dream of fire, the one that El-Majnoun had plundered as his own, spawned all the setbacks of his journey. Then there was this young woman's dream of escape, imprisoned as she was, first by the blackness of her skin, second by her being a woman.

"Look, in the first place, I . . . cannot bring myself to call you by such an ignoble name. For me, you will be Nejma. Is that okay? You are the star that guided me on my flight on a terrible, terrible . . . no, no, not terrible. On a magnificent night filled with a raging tempest. I must tell you now the truth: I am the horseman you were awaiting, even if my bay horse stayed behind as sole prisoner of the roumi police. And, at the risk of disappointing you, in the name of gallantry, I continue to resort to trickery in the attempt to escape my pursuers."

The woman's eyes opened wide with fear.

"Don't be afraid. I am nonetheless a peaceful man. I didn't commit even a quarter of the crimes they attribute to me. I'll explain it to you by telling you not a legend but the true version of what happened."

He told her about his family's being expropriated, about his father's death before his birth, about his mother, about his stay in Cairo, about his return . . . and then about El-Majnoun and about the long flight that had brought him to her.

She listened to him. Only the entrancing music of the gusting of wind, the fury of rushing waters, accompanied Mahmoud's murmured tale.

"Because of the bad weather, they must have had to call off their search. I have never seen such a storm. This flood will certainly get rid of the locusts, but unfortunately, it will destroy as well what little they left. What a disaster! I was waiting for something fantastic to happen, and with your appearance and this cataclysm, my wishes have been more than granted."

She fell silent for a moment and listened to the noises outside. Mahmoud poured out more tea.

"El-Majnoun is a very dangerous man. His name is well known throughout the country. He is often suspected of any number of criminal acts without ever being caught in the act. Sometimes people attribute magical powers to him, sometimes the most evil ones. He is elusive and well armed, with numerous accomplices and munitions in every nook and cranny, including with the roumis. That is to say, he is feared by all."

"He will not get me. He will not catch me! As soon as the weather clears, I'll go find my grandmother's bones. When I've buried her in a sepulcher at Labiod-Sid-Sheikh, I'll travel to a place where no one will ever find me. You see, the man of your dreams is no hero surrounded by an aura of mystery and glory. The very idea of violence terrifies me to the point of paralysis. I am nothing more than a fugitive in the grip of ill fortune, a utopian dreamer reeling among life's dangers. First the terrible fire, then a man's death. El-Majnoun seems to have done these things in order to make me bend to his will. If I don't give in to him, he's capable of denouncing me. He knows how to get his vengeance. Everyone is blaming me for these acts. All my life I will have to be on the lookout to protect myself from the claws of one group or the other. They are not going to give up the search so easily. That's the man you dreamed of running away with. But if all that hasn't frightened you, if going away with a horseman with no aura, and not even a bay horse, still interests you, I would be the happiest of men."

"Are you serious? You'd really take me away with you?"

"Yes," he responded in a voice choked with emotion.

"You'd be good to me? You wouldn't treat me like a slave?"

"You'd only have to put up with an immense amount of love, if you wished," he replied in a husky whisper.

The woman's lips trembled. Her eyes grew misty. Large tears glistened on the ebony of her cheeks. To hide her emotion, she got up and went to make more tea. It was very late. Suddenly, beneath the brutal assaults of the wind, the door opened wide, letting in the cascades flooding the night. Great gushes of water rushed into the interior, running upon the carpet of manure. They both rushed to close the door. They wedged it shut as best they could, with whatever was at hand. In their haste their bodies brushed against one another. They froze instantly. She raised her large fearful eyes to him.

"What a night!" she said weakly.

"Don't be afraid. It is a beautiful night. The most marvelous of all nights, he murmured in a husky voice, pulling her softly to him.

She pressed her trembling body against his. He embraced her passionately, caressed her. Soon, burning with desire, they lay down together beneath the exquisite surging of other skies.

6

The next day was a dismal one covered with mud. The squalls had finally conquered the resisting roof. Large drops were dripping at the corner of the room. They fell heavily and were absorbed into the manure. To keep dry, Mahmoud and Nejma put a bucket under the spout. In contrast to the weather, they were radiant. The chaos of the storm overflowed into desire. The subtle light wove a cocoon of pleasure. A little heated milk and stale bread suddenly took on incredible savor. They opened the door for a moment. The sky and earth were one heaving swamp. The vomit of dirty waters had drowned everything. Beaten down by the heavy rains and the hail, a multitude of dead locusts were decomposing in the puddles. Ripped away from the wings and legs, disemboweled, lacerated stomachs created horrible cesspools.

The rain was less violent now. The houses of the mechta, built on the crest of a small hill, were saved from the ravages of the torrents that seemed to gush out from the earth. Edged with a boiling red foam, the torrents tumbled down the slopes, swirling.

Mahmoud and Nejma latched the door. Quickly, returning to the shadow and the warm odor of the animals, they closed themselves away once more in intimacy. The little dog stirred, let out a few yaps, then went back to sleep next to them on the mat. For the entire day, they made love and drank tea. They told each other about themselves.

"Nejma, I want you to know that I am a solitary man. I want you to know that I have nothing to offer you but a life of solitude.

I have no wish to live among my tribe. In any case, they would never accept you. Nejma, from my earliest youth, writing has been my land, my exile."

She said:

"At the time of my birth, I entered the exile of my skin. I was born into a black solitude, abandoned even by my mother. With you, a bit of love and tenderness will rescue me from despair."

He said:

"Nejma, so that we may be two in our solitude, I must teach you, initiate you into writing. Otherwise, the wave of passion will have thrown us onto the shore of habits, and we will run aground far from each other. Far away and alone. Nejma, solitude becomes unbearable when filled by another's indifference."

"You say that written words are steps. I want to follow you, if you keep me from getting lost."

The gloomy day that many found oppressive and long was for them only ecstasy. The demonic fits of the wind, its long, humid, convulsive arms knotting themselves around their refuge, wept and brooded over their love that hatched from the muck on the night of the great storm.

At the end of the day, the wind suddenly shifted to the west. The compact mass of clouds separated and burst apart. The thousands of white, gray, and ochre tufts burst forth and scattered rapidly. Radiant openings to the heavens appeared. Great sunflowers of light edged with gold grew out of them. They lit up all the muddy waters on the land, which twinkled like constellations. On this mysterious day when nature reversed itself, the sun was born from the blaze of dusk. Great clouds hurled themselves upon it, spurring it, gutting it. Red spurted out everywhere, ran all over. It flooded the blue, dyed the ochre, and swallowed up the gray. Then the clouds, ferocious mastodons, each dragging a quarter of the sacrificed sun, made off. They left behind them a bloody mess in which all new clouds were immersed.

Mahmoud and Nejma took note of the changing weather.

Alerted by the sudden appearance of the sun, they emerged. For a moment they were silent, fascinated by the brilliance and violence of the colors of the setting sun.

"In this country, everything is always excessive," Mahmoud exclaimed. "Drought rages and year after year after year is burned to cinder. Storms are inevitably wild. In just a few hours they pour out the rains of several seasons. They drown the thirsty earth. Scarcity and excess are the realities of our cruel lands. Harsh winters, infernal summers, invasions of locusts, endemic fevers, everything turns to catastrophe here. Even the dispositions of men are ruled by this principle of extremes. Men? Either they bake in the sun their whole lives long, backs glued to the wall, eyes blank with stupor, or they are bitten by the demon of wandering whose only remedy is death. . . . But look, Nejma, the sky is clearing up. It is time to go. Tonight there is a full moon. Ricocheting from pool to *guelta*, the moon will celebrate the night with flashes of daylight. They won't catch me, Nejma! The full moon and my star-woman protect me. My pursuers are going to wait until tomorrow to track me. Tomorrow we will be far away. Tomorrow the *wadis* will still be overflowing. The roads will be miry and slick. Let's go! Let's take advantage of the respite offered us. You will guide me, my *nejma*. You will chase away my obsessions. I will deliver you from your cares. You will wear your skin like a divine flower, like a dazzled eye carries light. We will take our dreams far, far away from men. I don't want to go to prison, Nejma. I need the steppes. I need to return to the desert. I don't want to die, Nejma. I have still to love you, to teach you, still so much more to understand and to write. I am innocent, Nejma. To whom else could I say this? They are deaf, Nejma. Deaf and blind to all that does not come out of their molds. If we ride all night, by dawn we will reach my grandmother's bones and we'll bury her. Is this a dream or a delirium, Nejma? Look at the sky, a passion, a crimson pleasure."

Nejma gave grain to the animals and watered them. She hurried. Her gestures were nimble, her eye splashed by the symphony of light. Then, a waterlogged bundle under her arm, she said:

"I have my entire fortune here. Two old dresses and a *saroual.*"

"Leave those, Nejma! Jettison everything that could bring you unhappy memories. You'll buy more becoming clothes."

"I am taking the puppy Rabha! I can't leave her behind. She is, one could say, my sister!" she commented ironically.

"If you wish. And the mule as well. It's not worth a fraction of the endless labor you endured during your childhood and adolescence. I will ride it. You take the horse. We'll go faster that way. Let's hurry!"

They brought out their mounts. A little water in a guerba, some milk in a *chakoua*, what they needed to make tea, and some dates in a sack, and they were soon ready. As they left the place, the clouds were in retreat. The sun was shining in crimson glory. The animals trotted carefully through the mud. In addition to the bodies of dead locusts, the ground was littered with broken tree branches, uprooted plants, and a thousand other snares.

The wind had picked up again. Its raging scoured the evening. Mahmoud and Nejma had it at their backs. It railed at their heads. Bent over the withers of their animals, they advanced carefully. They forded a number of torrents. Their mounts floundered in them, sinking up to midshank. Then the moon rose in a sky swept clean of clouds. Far above the tumult of the earth, she reigned in radiant and serene sovereignty over obedient tribes of faint stars. Myriads of stars, like ordinary subjects, who celebrated their queen from a respectful distance. The sky arched up, uncovering the tops of the mountains. On the pools that flooded the earth, in the beds of the wadis now voluble, on the rippled surfaces of the waters, the incandescence of the sunset died out, only to be replaced by the sparkling of reflections, like silver filings. Then all the cocks began to crow in celebration of the wet opalescence of the drenched day. And the hyenas and jackals dug themselves in quickly, afraid, thinking the night had ended before it had begun. A night blown by squalls beyond the realm of the moon.

Overcome by hunger, Mahmoud and Nejma had to stop in the middle of the night. They ate some dates quickly and drank a little milk. Mahmoud held Nejma in his arms:

"The storm will die down. See, already the sky is calm once more. Be brave, smile, my star. Soon our flight will transform itself into a stroll. Tomorrow, the sun will shine on our journey."

Nejma, in fact, was not at all afraid. The immense, blustery wind that filled the earth breathed its energy into her, expanded in her chest. She was like this wind coming out of nowhere, neither black nor white, without the limitation of color. She had left trusting to chance, but looking into the distance, she saw a horizon silvered with happiness.

Unable to afford the luxury of resting for a few moments where it was dry, they took up their journey once more, driven by gusts plashing in the gueltas and the wadis.

Day broke on a mollified nature. On this blue morning, washed clean of locusts, heady perfumes filled the air. And the mounting heat stirred up puffs of intoxicating wind that spread out on the diaphanous air. This peace, this silence suddenly filling their heads, their ears, after the clamor of the hours past, suddenly opened up inside them like the edge of an abyss. Vertigo. Then Mahmoud and Nejma dismounted and walked for a while, clinging to one another, staggering. Drunk from the great libations of the wind, they walked on, pulling their mounts by the reins until the last echoes of the tempest left them, until their very limbs were stiff.

When they left the tell, morning was already well advanced. Before them the maquis, shiny white tufts with roots sunk in mud, spread out like whitecaps as far as the eye could see. And the cicadas, those other shipwrecked castaways, trilled away again as if they had never stopped.

"We will soon reach the place where I hid the bones of my ancestor! I camped near here," Mahmoud said.

He looked in vain for the stick marking the small hole. Carried away by the wind. And the flash floods had erased all trace of his passage. They got down from their horses and separated to explore in the tangle of brush. Although one tangle of bushes looked just like all the others, Mahmoud was nonetheless certain about the spot. At the end of their strength, they sat down on a pile of broken branches.

"Help me, Grandmother, please, help me to find you again. I have to get going. They must already be after me. You can't abandon me now."

Discouraged, Mahmoud fell silent. Suddenly, he saw a turtledove there, near a bush. She cast a round and flaming eye on him. Then she lifted her beak high, puffed out her throat, settled herself with a ruffle of feathers, and cooed.

"She is magnificent!" exclaimed Mahmoud to himself.

The bird sang out again like a fanfare. Amused and astonished, the couple burst out in laughter. The turtledove ignored them, pecking here and there in the mud with short hops. Then she filled her throat again and sang out another sweet melody.

"It's as if she were a public storyteller parading before an adoring crowd . . .

Mahmoud stopped suddenly in midsentence, then added:

"That knotty trunk, split open at the top, there behind the bird, I recognize it! Nejma, that's where my grandmother is!"

"Where?"

"There, where the turtledove is!"

He ran forward. The bird took wing, circled above them, and disappeared into the blue.

His grandmother! The sack containing her bones was in such pitiable condition that Mahmoud was sick at heart. It was a mere scrap of dripping cloth. The bones didn't clink any more. Soaked with water, they made a muffled, feeble sound. Mahmoud took the sack in his arms and carried it gently as if it were a sick child. Then they continued their way south under a sparkling sun.

By evening they reached the northern side of the high plateaus with their infinite straight lines and weave of esparto grass and aromatic plants. On a bed of wet sand, Mahmoud and Nejma made love eagerly; they made love tenderly; they made love in harmony. Then, exhausted, they slept snuggled against one another.

The next day, as they made their way toward the south, the ground became more and more barren. At the end of the afternoon, they walked on naked ground. A flat desert land where the eye conjured up landmarks in order not to go mad. From birth to death, the high plateaus draw out the nomad's steps, from empty space to empty space. Sad plateaus with no other wealth than an astounding light that hurts the eye to the point of blindness.

But there, Mahmoud was finally out of danger. Neither El-Majnoun nor the others, neither the roumis, nor even ubiquitous chance, would come to look for him here. He had reached the ends of the earth, the most absolute of escapes. He was on the threshold of the desert, the threshold of the tell, the threshold of love. He was in that "nowhere" where he hoped to find a place for himself. The ills that cripple the spirit in other places, the speech that under other skies possesses the power of the gods, here cannot withstand the corrosion and derision of the empty spaces and silence expanding within them. And the triumphant fury of this mineral immobility harries the steps of men and fills their heads with only one wish: to persuade death, in its inexorable realm, of man's stubborn will to survive. Thus, day after day, year after year, bare feet cracked and exposed, skin tanned by the sun, sand, and sweat, souls all bruised, the nomads inscribe their ephemeral traces upon the forsaken land. A unique cursive script. A fugitive testimony to the dignity and courage of men, confronting hostile nature, erased by the first gust of wind. And when death comes to gather them up, walking or squatting amid these solitudes blinded with light, they have fought her so long with their emaciated bodies, fascinated her with their lives on the march, that she feels no victory. She will come simply, this muse, sometimes glimpsed, often desired. And, with a gentle kiss of deliverance, she will close their eyes burned by dreams that, like the mirages on their journeys, endured amid the purgatory of their lives.

The day dawned softly.

The arc of memory had thrust aside the present. Because of the impossibility of bearing this grief, thought had immersed itself in memory and circled round the pain. But dawn broke, pitilessly. And the noxious odors that assailed Mahmoud's nostrils allowed him no escape.

"The day is breaking, Nejma, tearing me away from our shared life. How can a star be put in a hole? Nejma, I'd no sooner found you in memory than I lost you in real life. My mouth had scarcely again tasted desire than pleasure was already nothing more than a corpse stretched out before my impotence. Nejma, black will be my tomorrows without your light in my eyes, dismal will be my nights without the sun of your laughter. Nejma, blind will be the pathways of my life, my hands barren wastes without the touch of the oasis of your body. Nejma, Yasmine will wake soon. And the baby, Nejma!"

He raised his eyes and looked at the tree:

"Tree of wrath, how am I to survive the day that is dawning? Tree, in your prison of charred thorns, tell me by what mourning rite, by what magician's spell, are you suited to this poverty, these barren lands? By what fortune does aridity tolerate you? By what magic are you spared by this flaming sky? A fraudulent sap maintains the life of your tortured branches. Tree, my friend, at your foot, twice life was born. You saw the birth of my Yasmine and her brother. You cried over their mother's death last night. Tree of life and of death, between life and death in the passion of your crucified thorns. Nejma, in labor, tied a knotted rope to your strongest branch. To deliver her children, she passed the blade of a knife through the flame. She spread beneath her a square of cloth. Then, her two hands gripping the rope, she pushed and pushed outside herself that other life longing for the world. Tree, without crying out or weeping, she delivered at your foot the flower of her blood, while crippled by fear I hugged the ground far away. The cries of newborns entered your thorns and returned sweet hope to my heart. But today, friend tree, my soul like your trunk is burned, and my heart like your branches is filled with pricking darts."

The smell of the corpse, which had attracted jackals throughout the night, becomes an intolerable stench with the first rays of the sun. Clouds of enormous flies circle over the body and collect on the white shroud. Mahmoud shivers in horror. The sheep bleat now and again and peer with empty eyes over a makeshift enclosure. The plateau is nothing more than dead remains offered as fodder to the light. Each grain of sand, each pebble, reflects to infinity the idea of death. Armed with a small pick and a shovel, Mahmoud walks toward the tree. He digs at its foot, feverishly. The ditch opens quickly, too quickly. Soon, there it is, hole gaping open like his resignation.

As the last shovelful of earth falls on the body of his wife, Mahmoud collapses on the mound, sobbing at last. The heat is staggering. After a short time, Mahmoud feels its stings through his clothes. Then he remembers the baby.

"He has not cried. I must feed him. Usually he wakens his mother early in the morning."

Completely dazed, Mahmoud runs toward the kheïma. The nursling looks ashen, and traces of greenish drool have dried at the corners of his mouth. An acrid odor rises from his little motionless body. He is not breathing.

"Milk from the dead! A day of sun!" Mahmoud suddenly realizes.

Terrorized, he rushes to Yasmine. Her face still etched with grief, she is breathing quietly.

"Save Yasmine! At all costs, spare her from any additional grief or fear."

Mahmoud's will, strained to the breaking point by a desire to protect his daughter, propels him. He goes back out shaking. He picks up his tools and once more opens the earth.

A small grave right by the first one.

Mahmoud stands up. The horizons seem to tilt. Like a sleep-walker, Mahmoud goes back toward the kheïma. He drops down by Yasmine, holds on to her small hands and founders. In his nightmares, vultures threaten him with their talons from which hang shreds of dried flesh crawling with vermin. Other birds of prey circle in the sky. Mahmoud moves through a jungle of beaks and claws upon which pustules of putrefaction are blooming.

The day is shining with all its fury down upon the motionless plateau when, with a small nudge, Yasmine pulls Mahmoud out of his lethargy. He opens his eyes onto hers, large, filled with pressing questions.

"Nejma's daughter! Protecting her is a reason to survive. Protect?"

He sits up, holds his arms out to her, hugs her, clasps her to his breast. But she pushes away, struggles, escapes from his embrace. Then, with her small hand, she pulls him, her small body curving back with the effort. He gets up and lets her lead him. She takes him outside. Her eyes sweep over the plateau and return to Mahmoud, like pincers. The truth is enormous, impossible. The lies he could pour into the ears of the child choke in his throat.

"*Kebdi*, don't look for your mother. She is gone."

"Where? Where?" her restless eyes ask, scanning the barren land.

Yasmine takes off running straight ahead. Mahmoud runs to catch her and walks by her side.

"No, she has not gone looking for aromatic herbs. See, she has your little brother with her. She couldn't leave him behind. He needs milk to grow."

"Where? Where?" her exasperated eyes ask.

"Kebdi, she has gone looking for her own mother. To find her, she must go to the country of the blacks. It is a marvelous place, but very far away, very far! Kebdi, from those countries you inherit the blackness of your eyes and the dreams that haunt them. Your mother must go to the farthest point on the Bedouin's circuit. Then she will trade her white robe for a blue one in order to join a Touareg or Regueibat caravan. On the far side of the desert, she will find her people. The darkness of your eyes will be moistened by her kisses, lit up by her memory. Kebdi, we will rejoin her, but more slowly. We have to give her time to find her mother, the mother she never knew. And above all, during our long journey toward her, we must cleanse our hearts with dreams and plant and nurture the most beautiful of them. All sadness, all anger will lead us away from her. The serenity of dreaming is really the only route possible, the only path to lead us to Nejma."

He is talking for her sake. He is talking for his own sake. He talks in an effort to reach the inaccessible. Yasmine stops and looks at him with eyes full of grief, indecision. Mahmoud keeps talking, talking for a long time. The steady flow of words tries to erase the child's terror. Words are his tears. Words are his arms. Words rock Yasmine, rock himself.

"Come, you must eat. You've had nothing in your stomach since yesterday morning. Then we'll fold up the kheïma, we'll drive the donkey and the camels and sheep before us. And we'll trace your mother's footsteps. But remember: no distress, no grief, if you want to find her. In fact, let's start right now—smile for me!"

Yasmine's eyes fight back tears and she tries to smile. Together, they return to the kheïma.

"I will make tea and prepare some *ma'akra* for the journey. You like that, don't you?"

Mahmoud gets busy. Yasmine watches him with an innocent air. While he is lighting the kanoun she goes over to the small tree. At its foot, she sees the mounds. Intrigued, she circles around them. A vague anxiety, an elusive suspicion, invade her and torment her. She hastens to chase them from her spirit where her father's advice still resounds. The dog, Rabha, is there between the two graves. Yasmine joins her and leans back against the larger mound. With sad eyes she scrutinizes the plains. The desire to see her mother again soon wins out over terror. Hope makes her search her memory in quest of a dream for a calmer future. What she likes best in their travels are the stops at some oasis. She forces herself to focus her thoughts on those enchanting oasis stopovers. In the stifling heat, she imagines walking in a wadi. The wet sand feels so sweet beneath the arches of her feet. Cool and teasing, the water caresses her legs and thighs. Its happy babble is a joy to hear. The palm trees rise up. Dignified, they display to the sky the rich trophy of their luscious dates, stolen victoriously from a greedy aridity. Their arched fronds fan out with the endless songs of nightingales. A weak smile crosses Yasmine's face and, softly, the flow of the wadi carries her off toward her mother.

Mahmoud prepares the *ma'akra*, the simple but nourishing food nomads provision themselves with for long journeys. Semolina is cooked on a tajine that after a moment is transformed into a multitude of small grains of gold you must cook just long enough for them to become a uniform reddish brown.

Then the semolina is mixed with a gooey paste made of dates

and ewe butter. Peppered and rolled into small balls, the mixture stays good indefinitely. That done, Mahmoud takes down and folds the kheïma and gathers the cooking utensils into a bundle. On the back of one of the camels, he puts an 'atouch, a small palanquin covered with thick cloth, for Yasmine. That way, the small girl will be protected from the harsh rays of the sun. Quickly, he loads the animals. At the moment, he is in a hurry to leave. It is already almost noon, and Nejma's assassins are a night ahead of him. As they drink their tea, he tries to question Yasmine, to get some description of the men. Mute, she fixes him with her large eyes that, suddenly, do not blink. Mahmoud quits talking.

Mahmoud knows there were two of them. At daybreak he'd inspected the grounds and discovered the traces of their feet and those of their horses. They'd come from the west and disappeared toward the north, probably toward the town of Mecheria. That is the direction they're going to take.

Before stowing the guerbas with the rest of the baggage, Mahmoud fills a large carafe from one of them and symbolically waters the small tree. Nejma always did that before leaving. The sheep are out of their enclosure; the donkey and the camels, charged and ready to leave. Making the one carrying the palanquin kneel down, Mahmoud seats Yasmine there, giving final instructions. Yasmine's eyes are sad but calm. Her muteness, which has lasted since the previous evening, begins to disturb him.

It is time to leave, abandoning the dead to their fate while the living carry with them their suffering and remorse. The herd moves off slowly and Mahmoud follows. He turns back toward the tree. It is a place to celebrate life. He looks then at the two graves. Will he, Mahmoud, ever have the courage to return one day to this place? At the foot of the tree, he suddenly sees Rabha. She should be behind the herd worrying the laggards among the sheep with her muzzle. Lying in the same place since dawn, she is completely indifferent to their departure. Mahmoud's heart tightens. He goes back to her, tries to coax her to follow the herd. She fixes him with a gloomy eye, immobile, as if deaf to his words, resolute. The stubbornness of the animal exasperates Mahmoud. But he quickly realizes that his irritation stems less from her behavior itself than from the feeling of guilt that suddenly fills him. The loyalty of the dog toward her mistress seems to denounce the way he himself hurries to abandon the corpses. The instinctual devotion of the dog seems to him profound and unwavering, not like the fickle, egotistical sentiments of humans who whine or conquer, always expansively, but who adapt themselves easily to all circumstances.

These thoughts leave Mahmoud full of bitterness. How distant and longed for was his deft touch in handling the remains of his grandmother. Death was robbed of its cruelty, even rid of its horrible odor, and made remote. Right now, death is there, enormous, in his head and in his nose. It fills him completely like a nauseating temptation.

"What men pompously call reason is nothing more than massive boasting. Cheating! Cowardice!" Mahmoud says to himself.

"You are copping out, Mahmoud," an acerbic voice within him goads.

He concentrates to hear this voice. He recognizes it. He knows it to be sincere, without indulgence. Usually it speaks to him to cut his illusions down to size. Is it the voice of reason? It doesn't matter.

Mahmoud rouses himself.

"Stay, dog, if you wish. After all, you are old now. You must be tired of walking the deserts. Here, you will find a worthy death. Your mother protected Nejma at her birth. You are watching over her and her baby in death. If you want to accompany them, go with them. Rest in peace, all of you. I can do nothing more here. I have a child to raise. I must find the guilty. I'll make shade for you. I'll leave you some water. May your death be nothing more than sleep. You will awake in my memory."

He'd left the shroud covering Nejma overnight beside the grave. He takes it and spreads it over the branches of the tree to give some shade to Rabha. Soon, the smell of corpses permeates the place. Mahmoud runs to get Rabha's bowl. He fills it with water and puts it in the shade. Yasmine, in her palanquin, sees nothing. Mahmoud collects the scattered herd. He walks in the wake of the men. The camels, noses sniffing the horizon, set the pace.

7

Mahmoud and Yasmine follow the paths of absence. Though early in the day, it is late in terms of pain when a sandstorm catches up with them. The dreaded wind strikes the *ergs*. Twists round the *regs* in ruddy convulsions. Snuffs out the sky with an opaque rattle. Clawing the paths, erasing the footprints of the assassins, it scratches furiously. Eyes closed, Mahmoud and Yasmine keep walking through these fits as if borne by clamors of suffering amid the collapse of a disintegrating world. But, whether surrounded by silence or shot through by the shrillness of the wind, Mahmoud is constantly gnawed by a question:

"What am I to do given that I can't take my case to court?"

"In any event, what can I expect from colonial laws, laws sullied by the worst inequities? They declared me guilty a long time ago, and they wouldn't consider my denials. Going to court would just lead to my imprisonment and to the abandoning of Yasmine, condemning her to complete isolation. Should I take the law into my own hands? An eye for an eye? Not that! It wouldn't bring back my Nejma. And that is how I am. Vengeance will always be for me just a rotten word, a word to condemn to oblivion.

This dilemma is so implacable that Mahmoud feels bursts of unbearable anguish flaring up in him. He walks to the point of exhaustion. The hammering of his feet matches the burden of his torment. In the evening, when he finally gets Yasmine to sleep, he writes. By the light of the oil lamp, with the *calame* and the *midad*, written words pierce his suffering. *Calame* and *midad*—to blacken the cadaverous white of the paper is to gain a day of life; it is to win back a breath of air from anxiety. *Calame* and *midad*—the words are fertile, filling in absence; they bring Nejma back just a little. Writing is the nomadism of the spirit taking him through the desert of his need, along the dead-end paths of his melancholy.

At the end of two days of nonstop walking, Mahmoud and Yasmine finally reach Mecheria, a small *ksar* perched naked in the midst of maddeningly straight expanses, solitudes braised by the ferocity of the skies and eaten away by the winds. Amid this orgy of wavering lines, even the imposing mass of Jebel 'Antar hardly catches the eye. Just a piece of flotsam in relief, it's been washed up and inserted into the stretch of the land. Just an illusion of verticality, an unreal blue, an ethereal chimera. No sooner does the eye touch it than it falls to perdition along a landslide of infinities. And in the solitary confinement of this country, hardly does a silhouette bead up from the nothingness before all the inhabitants are there already awaiting it, with the whetted curiosity and the sharp eye of those condemned to immobility. To them, each traveler is a messenger from real life circulating beyond the deprivation of the sedentary. Thus, there is no chance that they wouldn't have seen the assassins, had they passed through there. But no sooner had they dismounted than Mahmoud and Yasmine learned that they are the "first strangers to come to the village in a very long time."

"The wind erased the traces of the assassins. Maybe at a given moment they had to turn off toward the southwest, toward Labiod-Sid-Sheikh or toward El-Bayad," Mahmoud decides.

The arbitrariness of this thought does not matter. At least it has the benefit of giving an immediate goal to Mahmoud, of responding to the urging of his conscience. Is luck for or against Mahmoud? He and Yasmine reach Labiod-Sid-Sheikh the day after the great *ou'adas*. How are they to find the trail of the two travelers when so many people are passing through the *douar*?

He feels, at first, a moment of despondency and indecision into which a glimmer of deliverance timidly inserts itself. But scarcely has it flickered in Mahmoud before the lightning bolts of guilt strike at it. The ambivalence of his expectations plunges Mahmoud into a deep malaise. Mahmoud shudders. With a flick of his hand, as if he could chase away the threat of the future with this gesture, he pushes his chèche high on his forehead. And, leaping up, he confronts these specters with a banner of words:

"I will find them!"

The numerous vestiges of the ou'adas littering the douar offer a good escape from the disorder of his thoughts. In Mahmoud's youth, ou'adas provided some of the rare moments of relaxation his morose people allowed themselves. The rupture they caused in the gray monotone of the everyday routine rescued him from his habitual nightmares. But Mahmoud had not participated in them since that time. A number of times he would suggest to Nejma to go to them, not because of the cult of whatever *marabout* it might be, no—rather to take part in the celebration, to find once more the savors of long ago. But Nejma had such fits of panic, such a phobia of crowds. When he insisted, she would object:

"Do you want to go to prison? Ou'adas don't bring together only followers. They also attract all the greedy and all the informers in the region! And besides, in each old black woman, I'll start again to search for my mother, while in the solitude and emptiness of the plateau, in their quietness, I can finally bury her. Do you want . . ."

Mahmoud no longer wanted . . .

The *qobba* of Sid-Sheikh, from time immemorial an object of great veneration, had become the site of renewed celebrations after a French colonel profaned it in 1881. On the eve of these festivals, the Amour from Aïn Sefra, the Hamyan from Mecheria, the Trafi from El-Bayad, and even sometimes tribes from far-off countries camped around the village. Mahmoud remembers that effervescent night when the pilgrims would prepare for the procession of their arrival at the settled villages. He rouses himself and tells the story to his daughter:

"They would bridle the horses. The men would get out their best saddles. They would wear their chèches loose as on auspicious occasions. When the hoofbeats were thundering, their burnouses would open like sumptuous wings over their mounts. With their enormous loads covered with flamboyant cloths, the camels bearing carved *'atouch* would seem to surge up out of the memory of the sands. Donkeys, herds, overexcited children, men and women, all would make their majestic entry into the village. Then the fantasias would begin and the *baroud* would boom out. A multitude of dances, poetic chants. The flight of ululations bridged differences, and in the oblivion of these skies, would reconcile warring tribes. Hollow *bendirs* and the fluid nasal whine of the *ghaïtas* competed in the town and in the camps all around. I used to walk around, smelling the acrid scent of gunpowder, the smoke of grilled *mechouis*, the emanations of spicy dishes, the exhalations of incense. These aromas . . . a celebration of all the senses. The prayers for the dead would buoy up the steps of the living. Offerings to the poor reinvigorated unfulfilled dreams. People would barter foodstuffs. They would buy and sell animals, cooked ewe butter, articles made of esparto grass, cotton cloth, wool woven into many forms. They would swap their high spirits for a hope of peace. They would feast on the rare abundance, the memory of which would quell their appetites when nothing of it remained inside their heads, under the weight of silence, in the wicker traps of solitude, but the memory of the hallucinating roll of the *bendirs* and the magical rippling of a great choir of ululations.

Although Mahmoud throws himself into his narration with zeal, Yasmine doesn't react. He's worried. Since her mother's death, she hasn't said a word. She has gotten thinner and looks drawn. Her silence increases her father's distress. The fever that ceaselessly makes him take to the road is henceforth completely pointless. Not a clue is left to act on, no trace of the assassins. A stopover for several days would certainly do them good. So, best to take advantage of the caravanserai and of the friendliness of these towns. The quarters are deserted. In there they'll find peace and quiet, but with the assurance of being able to escape quickly from anxiety just by opening and stepping through the door. Now Mahmoud dreads long, solitary sojourns. In the great courtyard, its earth beaten smooth by so many feet, the number of closed rooms and other forms of waste exude an air of contagious desolation.

"It is in our eyes, my daughter's and mine, that the affliction is lodged. Our gazes are what contaminate everything they touch. My daughter has also lost her childhood. Now she has the same tragic face that I had at her age. If only she could speak at least. Why doesn't she speak? It would relieve her!"

Mahmoud no longer knows what to do. If it weren't for Yasmine, he would have been engulfed by his grief. He shakes himself, gets up, and leads his daughter toward the street. But the respite delivers his spirit over to the torture of thoughts. Thoughts that are sometimes exalted, sometimes contradictory. Thus Mahmoud dreams, at times, of trying to find El-Majnoun.

"That madman certainly would be delighted to see me again. He would help me to find the assassins. Maybe he even knows them. A fellow who has scoured an entire region must surely have accomplices in neighboring regions. What would he ask of me in return? He spoke of a mysterious project, however, after which he was thinking of leaving the country. Could I find him? Nothing is less certain given that so many years have gone by."

The evocation of El-Majnoun plunged him into an undefinable state. Over the last eight years, he'd often recalled his name to memory. For a long time, the specter of seeing him suddenly reappear would cause him sleepless nights. Then the silence of his nomadic life, the flow of days in the fullness of love, had slowly erased these fears. So that now, in his memory of this "madman," nothing remained but the laughter and boasting, the cavalcade through a country of locusts.

But Yasmine was there, somber and tormented. Look for El-Majnoun again? That would expose her to still other dangers.

"What a ridiculous idea! To go turn myself over to the settlers or to that madman while leaving my daughter alone in the world? Pure folly!"

"What a great excuse, gratuitously invented. A soothing balm for the painful rough edges of your cowardice!" taunts a small mocking voice within him. Mahmoud rears back.

"I will find them!"

For fear that his suffering might become despotic and govern him entirely, Mahmoud exorcizes that part of it that is egotistical and introverted. His preoccupation with his daughter soon takes precedence over his own grief. The most urgent matter is to cure Yasmine of her pain. The invocation to dream, the lullaby of stories, the curing properties of medicinal plants in various infusions, the purgative of the desert bitter apple . . . He even tried bleeding, at the hand of a pious and learned sheikh. No use. So, in order to move about more quickly, Mahmoud sells his flock. And guided by informed advice, he resolves, even though he usually stays a thousand leagues away from any occult practice, to take Yasmine to a renowned magician.

"Your daughter is inhabited by a *jinn* who is a deaf mute," the master sorcerer pontificates. "These are the most pernicious of all the *jnoun*, because the power of men has no effect on them. Nevertheless, with time and through observation, I will find its weakness. I will manage to make contact with it. Only at that moment will I be able to impose my will and make it leave. I'll try to do it at the least possible cost. But in order to do that, you must stay here near me for the time it takes," says the man, whose gravity allows no sign of incompetence to show through.

"Jackal, vampire of suffering and distress. I have absolutely no desire to become part of the cohort that follows and adulates this opportunist everywhere he goes. I am already ashamed of having confided my child to him. How was I ever capable of such weakness!"

But his reproaches do not free him from the sense of impotence eating away at him. In Mecheria, they praise the competence of a roumi doctor whose office is in Saida. He's a last resort, this *nasrani*. After a long journey to the north, Mahmoud and Yasmine reach Saida finally, at the edge of the verdant tell. The French quarter is extensive. Uniforms are all over the place. Mahmoud and Yasmine find lodgings in the black quarter.

The *tabib roumi* examines Yasmine. He looks carefully at her throat where words have run dry. In a private conversation, he asks about the circumstances surrounding the symptom's appearing.

"The day of her mother's death," Mahmoud explains, hiding the brutal conditions of the event, however.

Having finished his examination, the man admits his impotence in a deeply grieved tone. He can do "nothing to cure the intangible illness of the girl. Her body is completely healthy. Something is knotted inside. Maybe over time . . ."

"Time? Men of all kinds place their failures and their ignorance in time's hands. A wise and patient witness, it will manage one day to untangle even the most tangled of skeins. And, even if that doesn't always happen, at least it keeps alive a flame of hope that helps you go on. The flame may die out slowly, of old age, almost painlessly, over time. Over time, even the greatest of disillusions is swallowed more easily," Mahmoud tells himself bitterly.

He rages in a fit of anger:

"I'll find them!"

As if that promise embodied within it an act of vengeance. As if its repetition alone were already an act promised to the future.

Sometimes Yasmine seems stifled, at other times tortured by

horror. When her breath quickens, when her small body trembles, when her heart thumps like a frightened bird in the cage of her ribs, when her eyes become fixed, Mahmoud takes her gently in his arms. With a gentle swaying of his torso, he rocks her and rocks himself. He sings to her about the land of desire, her mother's country.

"From this world come the blackness of your eyes and the cinnamon of your skin. Kebdi. I see her, happy, in my dreams. We will go to that country so far away in terms of pain but so close through the secret of love."

Does their movement from place to place, now more rapid and unremitting, contribute to creating the illusion of a long voyage toward her mother? At times you'd say that Yasmine believed in it. Her mother? What does she have left of her? Mahmoud has given away all her belongings. Yasmine kept only a small bottle of perfume, which she always carries under her dress, against her chest. She feels it there, over her heart, where it's in touch with the pulsing of her blood. Sometimes she opens it and inhales. The strong aroma penetrates her body with force. Little by little, she is permeated by the memory of her mother and immersed in her melancholy like a perfumed kiss. But often, Yasmine seems so closed off. A rictus appears on her lips. Smiles of forgetfulness are soon clawed away at by infallible memory. Is it suffering, grimacing, exposing itself, in spite of silence's veto?

Father and daughter walk across the plateau until they reach bodily and spiritual exhaustion. They halt at death's door, and when they get to their feet again, they simply continue walking. At sunrise the torments reawaken, and they move on quickly through landscapes without traces, quickly through the shroud of their light. Yasmine is far ahead, she doesn't hear Mahmoud's song.

"Deaf to the grind of daily life, my heart beats a retreat and huddles in the shadow of its memories. Let the hours pass or let time stands still, it remains indifferent . . ."

Or again, a plaintive melody about time:

"So long, so long, this time plagued by melancholy questions. So slow, so slow, these days that accompany the journey, heavy, a century of steps in one day . . ."

Now, nothing hurries them. They have nothing to do but to wander in order to forget and lose themselves in the solitude of these lands. So they buy more sheep and tramp behind them, eyes as empty as those of the animals who are ruminating on nothingness. To move on again, to be once more among those whose faces reflect nothing of the hopeless duel that pushes them toward a single end.

While Nejma was alive, Mahmoud had already begun to teach Yasmine. He spoke to her of the future role of women, of Nahdha, of the early voices of feminists in Egypt and Tunisia and their claims. Yasmine listened without understanding much, without distinguishing between fact and fiction. As for writing, she only had the beginnings: numbers and the alphabet. But having stopped speaking, the child clings to written symbols. Her father pronounces them for her. The echoes of their sonority ricochet against the wall of her silence. They vibrate in her ear like a promise. She presses on, so that by this means she will be able to give life to all the feelings she has hidden inside her. She will be able to ask the questions that trample around inside her without finding a way out. She feels them there, these words of silence, these scattered fragments, words dissolving at the tips of her fingers. Patiently, she settles down to crystallize them in order to grasp them, to carve herself an opening in the spherical tower of her silence. At first it is in the sand, during their stopovers, that she tries to construct them. Tirelessly, Mahmoud pronounces them for her, corrects her, encourages her. Squatting down or lying flat on her stomach, her eyes riveted to the ground, which her forefinger does not leave without coming right back to poke at it, Yasmine makes progress day by day. With each word written completely, with each approval from her father, a lightning flash of triumph streaks through the sadness of her eyes. Then she stops and looks at her father with a boundless love. She knows he has initiated her into an art, a rare one. Few men have access to it, so the uninitiated besiege them with questions, devour them with looks at once both curious and suspicious. The written word does not match their unremarkable existence, an existence that does not leave much to be proud of. The written word has the pretension, the durable sufficiency of all the structures of sedentary life. It is a frozen moment, a silent but telling betrayal. As soon as a man becomes versed in writing, he is, in their view, a dangerous man. He is in league at one and the same time with God and the devil, with whom he is the only one able to communicate in this sly, roundabout way, this word that disguises itself and hides itself away. And besides, aren't talebs often sorcerers as well?

It is above all during their encounters with other nomads that Yasmine suffers from her handicap. The solitude shared by her father and herself, "without a tribe and even without a mother," is such an anomaly in the clannish structure of nomadic life! That's why the children assail her every time with a multitude of questions. Yasmine's silence excites their curiosity even more. Its persistence seems a violation to them and arouses insults and curses.

"*Hartania*! *Hartania*!" clamor the vengeful voices.

Hartania means mixed race. Hartania is a curse, the banner of the impure, the emblem of a betrayal: treachery toward black blood, insult to the pride of the whites whom it splatters with its spots. So, Yasmine runs to the protective refuge of her father's embrace. And from then on, she avoids the cruelty of the children who are already imbued with the prejudices of the adults and armed with their most sectarian ideas. She will stay near Mahmoud in the group of men at a distance from the camp. To reduce her anxiety, Mahmoud has become accustomed to cutting short those meetings that are unavoidable. Besides, he is always plagued by questions that engulf him once more in the most somber depths of himself. He too prefers their isolation, where his daughter has him all to herself.

During the day, while guarding the sheep, Mahmoud keeps busy teaching her, introducing her to poetry. At night, he tells her stories and tales. He often says to her:

"You know, telling stories is an immediate escape. It is refusing to be nothing more than a channel for its flow. Telling stories is to capture time completely. It is to spread it out into a fan of words. You fan yourself with it and mock it. Then you fold it back up and enclose it in the knot of your narration. It's finished off, this captured time. You take a deep breath. You smile at the page or at the audience. You pick another one and you begin again to pluck off its leaves. Thus, you reverse the roles. By marking out time with your thoughts, you make it your object.

One day, Mahmoud told Yasmine the fascinating story of an unsettled sea and a terrible windstorm that had paralyzed the migrating birds:

"When I was in Tangier, I loved to go walking by the sea. You haven't seen the sea yet. I'll take you there. We'll go together to Tangier. The sea . . . Imagine, imagine, my sylph, a desert of calm water with the brilliance of our salt marshes, always talking. Imagine marine dunes beneath a caressing wind. Beneath the north wind they become crystalline crests, in which the skies are swallowed up with divine fury. And just as the wind of the desert lifts the sands, so too the wind of the sea turns, churns, and spits out its violence as dirty foam. One day in Tangier, I witnessed a tempest. The worst of the century, according to those who lived by the sea and who feverishly addressed their prayers 'to the greatest of all sovereigns, Allah.' The wind was coming from the west. Gibraltar had capsized, foundered in the tempest. The sea was attacking the earth churlishly. The sky was dirty, all smeared with mud. Imagine, imagine, Kebdi, thousands—what am I saying?—hundreds of thousands of migrating birds sur-

prised there as they prepared to fly across to the other conti-
nent. Imagine birds of fire, birds of ash and shadow, birds of
gold, silver, sapphire, emerald . . . All blazing with the desire
for flight and immobilized by the tyrannical breath of the wind.
Gathered in clouds along the coast, they were chirping in feverish expectation. They opened their wings, took off against the
wind, and were thrown against the shore like so many scraps of
cloth. Imagine, spark of my life . . ."

Yasmine shivers at her father's words. She awaits their blossoming in his mouth. Her father's words slip out and fall one
by one into the successive layers of her being: first, they pierce
the flawless surface of her silence, where they make concentric
circles like stones thrown into calm water. Then, they plunge
toward the depths of her being where they stir up strange eddies
for a long time. She imagines this multitude of anxious and impatient winged creatures, petrified by the fury of the elements.
In his description, her father has just given her a vivid image of
their sensations. Her own private hurricane is silence. Arising
from the void at the same time as two pirates, it has pillaged her
solitude, taken away her mother, shipwrecked her sensibilities,
paralyzed the words in her innermost being. Her own words
are those birds, feverish and powerless, with rainbow plumage,
their song wavering between *raï* and Andalusian, like a huge
tear about to drop. She listens to these interior words. She hears
their prisoners' roundelay behind the clapper of muteness. She
feels beneath her skin the trembling of their broken wings and in
her deepest being their drops of blood. Thus, it is the sonority
above all, the pronunciation of the words, that sets her entire
body vibrating with a frustrated voluptuousness. This is more
precious to her than the content of the story itself. At the sound
of words, the way in which their echoes find her own particular
resonances, Yasmine does not merely adorn them with adequate
hues, she finds in them as well an aroma, a savor, a weight and
a speed. They are alive. They caress, brush against, or collide

with her intoxication in different ways. However, there is one story where the facts seem to have the same importance as the rhythm of the narration. It is that one about the roumia Isabelle Eberhardt. Isabelle is a word like a bird with long, light wings of azure blue. "Isa" only shortens *'aziza* in order to lodge in the most tender part of her coiled heart. Isa warbles, a beautiful unfolding of two *l*'s and, like a swallow, her song takes flight. Eberhardt is rough and violent, like the rale of a sandstorm, like the fury of flash floods in wadis. Nonetheless, with the evocation of this name, a sweet dream of filiation holds Yasmine's thought in its embraces. A dream in which a woman walks and writes. A roumia dressed as a Bedouin man with the aura of all sorts of eccentricities. So, disguised as a male and motivated by a singular desire for identification, Yasmine walks in her footsteps, in the same landscapes, and in the world of writing. In fact, Mahmoud, who tells her often of the roumia Isabelle Eberhardt, knows this well. And when he speaks of her, Yasmine's eyes grow large with interest and her breathing stops as if her whole being were reaching out for this woman. It is as if at the invocation of this story, she were trying to perfect, through physical contact, her affectionate admiration for this woman.

Yasmine loves these moments when, by the light of the oil lamp, Mahmoud sets himself to guessing and to formulating replies to questions that she would have put before him. She loves his way of passing time. From writing to stories, from moving on to stopping over, years, one after the other, go by.

Many times, upon approaching villages or mechtas, Yasmine's gaze bumped up against the strange contours of small mounds. Sometimes she stops, intrigued by these small humps of earth about a foot in height, often grouped together in great numbers. Their elongated form with rocks one or two spans high at each end remind her of something. She doesn't really know what. Something that always awakes shivers of apprehension in her memory and that she hastens to forget. There, at the entry to Labiod-Sid-Sheikh, which they have just reached, is another great concentration. And suddenly, there that curious memory is again. Yasmine can no longer ignore it. She remembers brusquely having seen two just like them, far away, under a small tree. With this revelation her malaise increases once more, still undefinable but plagued with suspicions. It is . . . it was the day her mother "went away." Upon waking in the morning, she saw two mounds at the foot of the thorn tree. It was as if they had sprouted during the night. One of them was tiny. Before, there had been that pile of stones collected by her father during the course of many stopovers in this place. But those were definitely not there at all. She is sure of that now.

She looks at the strange field where nothing grows but earth. As if full and fertile on its own, it is growing beneath the grim eye of the sun. You would have thought it a camp of nomads who, after some terrible curse as in some of her father's stories, had suddenly undergone a mineral metamorphosis while they were deep asleep. Was it a punishment of the plateau weary of their tireless trampling that pounds its barrenness into dust? A damnation of the light, jealous of their darting looks that ceaselessly project their feverishness along the horizon, igniting hallucinations? Now they are there, lying side by side. Lying there, unfinished, a rough stone as a head, another for the feet, a heavy *gandoura* of earth, now tamed. After having traveled far and wide in their search for the impossible, they accept and finally become one with the plateau in its unbroken immobility, in its unique reality, in its very essence: earth and rock. Yasmine takes a long look at the strange red soil where nothing moves. Then she raises her head and fixes Mahmoud with a questioning look.

"That is a cemetery," he responds.

In the eyes of the little girl, the question still remains. She doesn't recognize this word that undulates like this landscape without finding an echo inside her.

"It is the place where the bodies of all those who have gone to that land beyond dreams rest. When they have been trying for a long time to stay on the paths of dreams, they decide one day to slough off, to rid themselves of the burden of flesh and bones that weighs us down and keeps us earthbound. Only then can they go off beyond everything, toward that faraway land. Come on, we'll visit the graves of my mother and grandmother. They are over there."

So that's what it is. That is the origin of the anxiety so rightly felt. The graves of her ancestors? How does her father recognize them? They are all just alike, without any inscription, simple wrinkles of earth littered with a smattering of rocks. Yasmine does not bend down to write the question that is burning at the tip of her index finger. The discovery of the unexpected purpose of this land disconcerts and frightens her. "An eater of bodies?" Her finger can only taste words of life, wants only to gather words like jewels, setting them as an adornment into the fan of time. And besides, her memory has nothing left of these two women who remain unimaginable to her spirit. They are only a couple of diaphanous words, inaccessible to desire, unintelligible to writing. Existences just like her words, shrouded.

Suddenly, a group of people, behind which some small boys are running, materializes from the edge of the douar. No fence surrounds the cemetery, so Yasmine can easily follow their progress. There are no women with them. Four men walk at the front, each carrying on their shoulders planks of wood made into a litter. They are all chanting the *shahada* in a manner so terrifying that the oneness and greatness of Allah thunder in vengeful accents. Their steps are quick, their faces impenetrable. On its litter, covered only with a white sheet and bounced by the jostling of the crowd, a corpse jounces. The procession chooses a path that bleeds its dust between the tombs. In spite of the entreaties of her father, Yasmine follows them. At the back of the burial procession, a man turns back:

"Get away, get away, you, girl," he says in a vexed tone.

Yasmine, her eyes fixed on the movements of the shroud, ignores him and continues on. Irritated, the man turns toward her again. But Mahmoud is there beside his daughter and takes her hand. The man shrugs his shoulders and once again takes up the *shahada* in which all his swallowed anger rumbles. The grave is ready and hasn't cost one bead of sweat, so sandy is the soil. Setting the litter next to it, the men, straight and solemn, pray a last time. Then the body is put in the earth.

"Her tomb is spacious! She was a good woman," someone notes.

It was a woman.

A few shovelfuls of earth directly on the body, a large stone at each end of the ridge, and it is all over. A small boy comes forward, puts his hands over his mouth, and leans over the grave. He puts a wood rosary on the headstone. In his face, clawed by grief, his eyes full of tears look too large. But the group is already far away and doesn't wait for this overflow of sorrow. After some hesitation, the child runs to rejoin it. The only ones left amid the silence of the dead are Mahmoud and Yasmine. There is in this haste to get rid of the dead something that chills Yasmine's sensibilities.

"Spacious? . . . So that's how it is."

The little girl's memory returns to the solitary tombs, far away, at the foot of the tree. She opens her little bottle of perfume and inhales eagerly. It prickles in her nostrils, a heady whiff that does not manage, however, to chase away her dull sorrow. How can you leave when you are locked under the earth? Her mother? Her mother moves about in her mind with such flexibility that, depending on her movements, her beautiful ebony skin is illuminated like a soft watered silk, sometimes cinnamon, sometimes a shade of blue. How can she imagine her otherwise? How can she imagine this body concealed forever in the bosom of the earth?

"That's where you were born. That's where your brother will be born!" Nejma used to say.

Her mother in childbirth, herself and the dog trembling, the first cries of the baby: she sees again this place at the foot of the tree. She sees again the earth full with the grimace of death, and the dog Rabha lying down nearby. If only she had had the keen sense of smell of that faithful animal. When they left, she thought Rabha was behind the herd as usual. And then there was the wind. She couldn't call her. That evening when they stopped to camp, she didn't find her. She shivers once more thinking of the horror of those days following their departure—the terrible sensation of something monstrous, of an evil power unleashed on them by those two thugs. Each morning the sensation was there, impalpable, undefinable, but heavy on her small chest. Harrowing awakenings when a terrible panic would seize her from the first moment of consciousness, before she even opened her eyes. The dread of discovering still other disappearances waylaid her at the break of day. This feeling of insecurity and moral destitution was aggravated even more by the loss of the herd of sheep. Without their needy and reassuring tramp, without their eyes so empty that they drained anguish bit by bit and calmed torments, without the soft udders of the ewes to milk, without all the little lambs so happily comical with their hesitating steps and their silky wool, Yasmine felt even more isolated, still more vulnerable. Thus, the purchase of a new small herd brought the first joy she had felt in a long time. A parade of banal, every-day chores slowly reinvigorated life. Then there was writing! Writing that braided her letters into words. Drop by drop, the letters nourished her. In the shipwreck of time, they allowed her to survive, no matter what. Now she gives words to time. She gives time to words. And writing makes itself indispensable in the face of silence and the anguish of absence. Writing feeds in her a voluptuous hunger such that each word gained, far from bringing satiation, only makes it sharper. Her first words had been cast down, in isolation, on the sand like cries of deliverance, like the truncated grunts of some primitive people. Like a first stammering in which the rest of the phrases, unwritten, collide and press down with a strange weight on the few words that escaped from the inextricable and mute tangle. Expression given to mute sand, suddenly ennobled, they had spilled out all over one another, at first incomplete, undisciplined, but sounding out her father's responses insistently. Like the twinkling of stars, like the bursting of sparks, words flourished above the black landslide of her silence. Little by little, these stammers grew and ripened. They covered the sand, progressively, with more coherent, more elaborate phrases. Now both father and daughter have left their solitary confinement.

Yasmine makes a small, rough sound. Mahmoud turns. Is it a cry? Is it a laugh? A cry that tries to forget by sliding, unexpectedly, into the exploding sonorities of laughter. A laugh that chimes, a small bell soon cracked by the implacable dagger of memory.

"Come on, let's go," Mahmoud cuts in.

In walking across the plateaus and through stories to push back the narrow contours of the days, has Mahmoud lost all sense of time? Or is it time that has gotten lost in the expanse of his pain and of his stories? Lost in the knots of his narrations? Now the need to count the years sometimes occurs to him: "Three, four, or five years?" He no longer knows. He's been a long while journeying with his little girl amid the crush of men and beasts, from market to market. Sterile attempts, vain searching of unknown faces. Yasmine's eyes seem to recognize no one. So, without losing hope, they continue on their way. They move toward the tell in the summer, toward the limits of the desert in the winter, to the east or the west in midseason.

With the milk of ewes, Mahmoud makes butter, a customary ritual. The sale of butter and raw wool, as well as some lambs, gives them enough money to provide for their meager needs.

The succession of months and years, this time that innocently meshes with the thread of steps and stories, works its art, bringing forgetfulness, a first sign of death. Still, how sweet this forgetfulness is. Because of it, questions that dig away secretly at the foundations of peace arise less frequently. It allows the re-seeding of interior deserts. It pours a sip of water upon the thirst for solitude, and even if it often has the bitter hint of derision, it helps nevertheless in crossing life's arid regions.

Their way of life makes them into singular beings in this crude, nomadic world of the high plateaus. Their constant presence at the markets in the region is intriguing. This father, always a widower, nurturing his daughter like a mother; this daughter, a hartania, but a superb hartania, staring at men with such gravity, never saying a word to anyone, and only communicating with her father in writing; they arouse curiosity and feed rumors amid the dust of the souks.

In Mahmoud's thoughts, Nejma exists as a tamed despair. However, for some time now without anything new having happened, nightmares return to plague Mahmoud's nights. Sitting with her dog under the thorn tree, Nejma is nursing her baby. It is always blistering hot in these dreams. Nejma's face is all wet and wears a mask of suffering.

The unbearable howling of the dog Rabha ends by waking Mahmoud up. He knows this sense of guilt that plagues him so results from his inability to avenge his wife's death. But try as he might, he can think of no way to protect himself from it. One day, as he is walking along, a clever idea comes to him.

He is silent for a moment.

"Completely ridiculous," he ends up declaring.

With a sharp, unsympathetic laugh, he mows down a thought

that's crossed his mind. But it grows again, stubbornly. Little by little it loses its absurdity and seduces him more and more. Soon it begins to buoy up his steps, to make them dance with joy, to gleam and frolic in his gaze suddenly turned mischievous. It keeps him busy and keeps him going throughout the long day. It is with jubilation that he hatches the plot, figures out the details, distills the end product. Yasmine, sitting in her palanquin on one of the head camels, cannot see him at the back of the herd, behind a halo of dust, mischievously smiling, laughing at his idea.

Before the day ends, they come to Aïn Sefra, the aptly named "yellow spring." The panorama of the superb countryside fills Mahmoud with ease. As you leave the grim flatness of the high plateaus, Aïn Sefra is truly the first royal banner of the desert, glorified by its colossal tawny and bronzed dunes, coiled at the base of the violet mane of Jebel Mekter. At the foot of the dune, the palm grove and the bluish haze of the gardens appear. Seen from a little closer, the ksar built of mud reddens in the light. You have to reach there to be able to see, at the top of the dune, an old abandoned fort. Like the wreck of a ship insecurely adrift on the swells of the dunes, it opens its empty sockets onto flat horizons. The noises of the ksar rise gently toward them. Across from it is the upper village, the roumi quarter.

Other nomads are there, come in pilgrimage or simply awaiting the next day's souk. Their kheïmas are adjacent to the qobba of Sidi Boujemaa. Mahmoud and his daughter put theirs up a ways away. And, while Mahmoud takes the sheep to Meftah for the night, Yasmine walks in the palm grove. Nothing is more unexpected in these dry lands than this green harbor. There are even weeping willows that softly dip their tresses in the humid *seguias*. Stirred up by the stone and sand still gorged with heat, the bitter, peppery aroma of fig-tree milk spreads its vapors around the tree, fanned by leaves shaped like the open palms of hands. Yasmine enters the profound shadow of their parasols, inhales deeply, and fills herself with this extraordinary atmosphere. The pomegranate trees are starred with purple and golden fruit. Farther on, above their pretty white trunks, the poplars' jade and pearl leaves are trembling. There are also oleanders. Mahmoud's return catches Yasmine red-handed in her delight.

"It is so beautiful, come, we'll walk in the ksar. But you know, you've grown. The men are looking at you now. You used to dress as a girl when we stopped in the city or when we met other nomads. From now on, you'd better do the opposite and dress always as a boy. I'll rest easier," Mahmoud suggests, smiling. "Have you noticed that in your *jellaba* men don't notice you?"

Yasmine agrees. "Like the roumia Isabelle," she thinks with a smile of complicity.

Dusk illuminates the crests of the palm trees and fills the orchards at their feet with black shadows. The summit of the dune is an immense firebrand while flowing amber shadows carve outlines in the sand, darkening the tufts of esparto grass sticking up here and there. Mahmoud and Yasmine abandon the wadi and take the main street of the ksar. Shopkeepers and *qahouajis* have generously watered the ground and swept in front of their shops. The air is a mixture of the scent of wet earth and basil wafted from several pots sitting behind the bars of narrow windows. Cinched tight in their uniforms, their enormous shoes grinding the dust, soldiers wander in the narrow, twisty streets of the ksar. Small groups of men cluster in front of the *qahwa*. Seated on small benches or on old mats, some chat quietly, others play *ronda* and enjoy flying into false rages against their partners. They are all experts in the art of spitting large yellow globs of tobacco juice great distances, where they land on the beaten earth like fat cockroaches. Among them are three or four roumis. Sitting cross-legged on a mat, their gazes calm, their gestures stamped with the slowness of desert folk, a glass of tea in their hands in which a sprig of mint floats, they seem happy and at ease among the Arabs. The sharing of tea is always a symbol of peace and friendship.

After a lazy walk around the ksar, Mahmoud and Yasmine return toward their kheïma.

"Tonight, I am going to make a couscous with whey!" Mahmoud announces, influenced by the indolence of the ksar dwellers and excited by the luminous fullness of his idea.

Couscous? Mahmoud has gotten into the habit when they meet other nomads of bartering several armfuls of wool or measures of cooked butter for dry, rolled couscous. So they always have it on hand. Couscous with whey is Yasmine's favorite meal. He likes it too. It is easy and quick to make. A small fire, three stones around it to hold the pot, and soon the two of them are sitting around the *guessa'a*. The couscous is hot, and the fresh, lightly acidulated whey fizzes on your tongue, the rounded mouthful slides down, smooth and savory to the palate. A meal as nourishing as it is refreshing, tonight it is a true festival for them because they enjoy eating it so much. The meal finished, Mahmoud pulls his pouch of tobacco and kif from his saroual. With an affable look, he meticulously rolls a cigarette and asks his daughter:

"Would you like to go visit the small tree tomorrow after the market?"

Yasmine nods her head eagerly.

"Nejma needs to see us again. I think she wants us also to build a shelter for the tombs. The flimsy shade of the thorn tree spares them neither from the burning summer nor from the freezing winter. A qobba worthy of a venerated marabout which would be visible from a distance, pink, crenelated, against the sky. What do you think?"

Yasmine agrees once more.

"The herd will stay with Meftah as long as necessary. The good man has already agreed to rent us some camels and guerbas. So we can carry a lot of water with us. Next to the tree, we'll make some *toub*. We'll need a board to make a mold. When we've used up the water, we'll return for more. We'll need to make a lot of trips back and forth, but the tree is barely a half day's journey from the closest well. Above all, we have all the time we need. Here's what we'll do. When the qobba is done, it will be seen from afar and will attract nomads. They will think it is a marabout. We'll keep our secret. It is neither a great wrong nor a sin. People need a stopping place, given their lives of perpetual movement. A place of prayer and celebration. It doesn't really matter to them who's beneath a few shovelfuls of sand. What they are looking for is already in their heads. They only need the pretext of the place to halt their steps and begin that other journey within themselves. In any case, Nejma was a saint. They will come from all over. They will chant praise to God. They will say prayers. They will celebrate ou'adas. I already see old women beautifully tattooed, with dignified wrinkles and ample headdresses, singing plaints. Nejma will love that!"

It is still there, the small, tortured tree, clawing the unmoving air with its hooked talons. At its foot, two mounds spread out, crumbling.

"It is because of the sandstorm, and maybe the feet of jackals and hyenas as well."

Mahmoud looks for the body of the dog. He finds it a little farther on: a skeleton reduced to only anonymous bones. The vestiges of a death, now long past and mundane, which, if it no longer inflicts a horrifying sorrow, nonetheless breathes into him an insidious feeling of being mocked.

"The jackals . . ." Mahmoud says, again invaded by the sensation.

He reshapes the rounded domes of the two graves. At their foot, he digs a grave in which he buries the remains of the dog.

"Nejma will like that."

He unloads the animals, puts the guerbas on the ground, and

puts up the kheïma. Mahmoud gets busy and hassles Yasmine in order to chase away a prowling, threatening melancholy.

"Nejma, here we are again. I am sure that your qobba will please you."

It is moving to find themselves there again. Driven by incessant twinges of conscience, they had looked for the two men, caught between hope and fear, along the straight paths of their will, along the twisted roads of their fears. Fleeing others, fleeing themselves, fleeing far from this place and its memories, for a long time. They start their project. The raw mud bricks are laying on the ground. When they are turned over, they expel a small, warm breath like a sigh of pleasure quickly absorbed by the hot, dry air. They dry out and soon become hard. Mahmoud and Yasmine go to get water and return immediately to work. The walls rise up quickly, soon surrounding the little tree. This task that occupies the body and the spirit, this work that emerges and takes shape, slowly exorcizes any hint of sadness. It becomes the purified sanctuary of other, more merciful memories. Their evenings flow by quietly in the softness of voluptuous October nights full of distant stars.

8

Having finished the walls of their building, Mahmoud and Yasmine make a final trip to Aïn Sefra to buy three palm trunks and some palm branches for the roof. Immersed in their project, they have completely forgotten it is the season, usually eagerly awaited, when dates are harvested. So, the seasonal joy and excitement that have overtaken the people in the palm grove running along the wadi are an agreeable surprise when they arrive. Other nomads from the region have come to bag up dates for the year. On all sides the aromas of cooking rise. The spectacle is such a feast for the eyes, such an exquisite promise for the palate, that Mahmoud and Yasmine decide to take the day off. They spend the day there strolling and savoring the succulence of dates.

While Mahmoud talks with some men in the shade of the date palms, Yasmine, seduced by the atmosphere, wanders along the wadi's bank.

"This is the wadi that killed the roumia Isabelle."

This thought strikes so brutally at the heart of this moment of well-being that Yasmine stops suddenly, incapacitated.

"She loved this place, as my mother loved the tree of wrath. She, too, died a violent death here."

At the evocation of her mother, she thinks once more about her tomb, about the qobba being built there. A smile brightens her pinched lips.

"I'll visit the tomb of the roumia again," she promises herself in order to maintain her fragile serenity.

This decision triumphs over her apprehension. Yasmine regains emotional clarity. She continues her walk slowly, smelling the sugary sweetness of dates. Colored a lustrous cinnamon, they swell with just the right softness. Some still are the beautiful honey gold of July fruit. In the mouth, they melt into large drops of honey. Their sight drives the last vestiges of sorrow away from Yasmine. The men who climb agilely up the straight trunks fascinate her. Dark-skinned and wiry, they ascend quickly, eyes riveted on these jewels in the firmament. Heavy bunches hang from bronze stems, as if proffered specially, in the crystal bowl of the heavens. These climbers possess the prodigious skill of reaching the crests of these high trees. And from the clouds where the jade crowns are swaying softly, they bring the savory harvests from the sky. Those who remain earthbound admire them and comment on their prowess. Laughter, jokes, and name-calling break out and accompany their climb. Children, eyes eager and mouths watering, make a racket and dance with impatience. As soon as they are on high, the climbers shake the bunches and a rain of ripe dates is caught on palm fronds spread at the foot of the trees. Immediately, those lying in wait rush forward. Chirping like nestlings at the sight of a beakful, they begin to fight over them.

Yasmine looks around the place with interest. At first her gaze is always drawn toward the dunes piled at the base of Jebel Mekter. When the sun blazes, the light cascades down them in blinding white flashes. Under the effect of their incandescence, the air trembles on the heights. The sands themselves burn up, creating mirages of vapor. While she walks, Yasmine caresses the flask of perfume bouncing against her chest, through the fabric of her dress. The ambient sounds only reach her muffled by the density of the dream into which she slips little by little. Suddenly a voice clears a path through her dense reverie. It is a woman's voice. A voice singing. It is mellow, warmly hued. Yasmine cannot see the woman. Slowly she traces the flow of the melody to find her.

157

"She is in that kheïma over there," Yasmine thinks.

Although finding her is easy for Yasmine, it takes a long time before she is able to see the woman, so shadowy is the kheïma's interior in contrast with the outside. Sitting across from the opening, the woman grinds grain, intoning her plaintive song. A gentle swaying of her bust accompanies her slow circular motions as she turns the grindstone in front of her. The crunching of the dried grain under the weight of the grindstone, and the rubbing of the upper and lower stones, produce a continuous and monotonous sound over which the modulated voice of the woman unwinds. Yasmine sits down a few feet from the tent and listens. That song she recognizes. It's reborn again inside her head, intoxicating her flesh. It floods her with nostalgia. Her mother used to sing it often. Since then, she hasn't heard it. With half-closed eyes, a smiling heart, Yasmine abandons herself to its sweetness.

The woman has seen this girl approaching with furtive steps. Now, sitting near the entrance, Yasmine looks at her with avid eyes. The woman interrupts neither her gestures nor her song, but smiles at her amid her movements and her melody. Without being old, the woman is of a certain age, as evidenced by a few wrinkles, like crow's-feet, crinkling merrily at the corners of her eyes. The dark green, finely inscribed tattoos adorning her cheeks and wrists are the stamp of her origins, the sign of the plateau tribes. From her ears, beneath her large white turban, dance enormous silver earrings. Yasmine doesn't move, even when the woman stops singing. Then the woman smiles at Yasmine.

"Come, come in, my daughter. Don't stay out in the sun. It's treacherous at this time of year. You like the song from what I can see."

Breaking with her normal patterns, Yasmine approaches and enters the tent.

"What's your name, gazelle?"

With her forefinger making cursive loops, the young girl

writes her name on the ground. The woman stops grinding and looks at her, dumbfounded. Then, full of doubt, she asks her: "You don't answer. Don't you talk?"

Yasmine shakes her head no.

"Ya Allah! You don't talk . . . you write!"

Yasmine nods yes.

Hands resting on her millstone, the woman observes this singular girl. Her eyes reflect her train of thought. A sudden shadow darkens them. Then a disconcerted and troubled look, torn between pain and disquiet, steals over them. For a moment the woman stares at the arabesque covering the ground.

"It must be writing. What do you expect me to do with such a thing? And why, at your age, do they still let you run around the palm grove?" she exclaims, disapproving.

Writing, "a thing"?! Looking at her curiously, the woman perceives her chagrin. Bit by bit the crow's-feet crinkle at her temples. They bring the sparkle back to her eyes, filling them with laughter. A smile of reconciliation spreads across her lips.

"Let me guess . . . aren't you a *houria*? A fairy emerging from the silence of the sands thanks to the incantatory power of my song? Is it because of your presence the sun has swallowed its ill temper and miraculously smiles on us? Is it one of your silent words offered to the earth that has made the date harvest so abundant this year?"

With a quick swipe with the palm of her hand, Yasmine erases her name. Immediately, with her forefinger already out, she prepares to write again. But she suspends this automatic reflex response in midair. A spoken-written dialogue, now habit between herself and her father, is useless here, half-amputated. Not to be able even to express herself in writing! While ordinarily she flees questions, here, for once, the torture resides in her desire to answer and her inability to satisfy that desire. Like her voice, writing too now falls behind the bolt of censorship. In this woman's world, writing is "incomprehensible." For the first time, Yasmine becomes aware of the extent of her and her father's solitude, of the life they lead outside the norm. The woman notices this failed attempt to respond. Then they burst into laughter. Beating a rhythm on her grindstone, the woman improvises words to a well-known tune and sings:

"My friends, my neighbors, all of you people of good will, she appeared before me one morning, this girl of silence born from my refrain. This fairy of the sands visited me while in the shade I was grinding my grain. Learned and grave, she lingered but refrained from speaking of yesterday or tomorrow. She does not share her words with our muted ears, her only confidant is the earth. My friends, my neighbors, all you people of good will, this quiet one will seduce you, I'm sure, just as surely as she pleases me . . ."

While talking with the men, Mahmoud's eyes follow his daughter distractedly as she wanders along the wadi's bank. This is certainly the first time in the presence of such a large group that she is taking the initiative to venture so far without him. A moment's inattention, and she disappears from his field of vision.

"A palm trunk is hiding her from view," he assumes.

But for a long time the adolescent remains invisible. Disturbed, the father quits the conversation and watches for her to reappear. After a moment, impatient, he takes leave of the men and strides off to find her.

In the kheïma, Yasmine and the woman hear his calls. The latter stops her improvisation. Regretfully, Yasmine leaves the kheïma. Just outside, she stands still and waits. Quickly, the woman comes to stand by her side. Surprise stops Mahmoud in his tracks. In any case, good manners forbid him to come too close to the tents lest he surprise the women. Mahmoud looks away and coughs to announce his presence. But soon enough he hears he is being hailed:

"Come on, come on! You can approach, sir. At your first call, my daughters-in-law all went into their tents. Don't be afraid. You have before you just a grandmother worthy of receiving you."

Mahmoud walks toward them.

"Salaam 'aleïki. Peace be on you, honorable sheikha who knew how to tame my little wild one."

"Ou 'aleïkoum es-salaam. Peace be on you, happy father of a splendid daughter who speaks only with the earth. *Ou el-nabi*—by the prophet—you are my guests. I am anxious to meet your daughter's mother."

"Alas, sheikha, she is no longer alive. We are orphans, both of us. I am Mahmoud the poet."

Tactfully passing over Mahmoud's first words, the woman cries:

"The poet! Ya Allah! What a rich promise for the evening. I am Khadija of the Hamani tribe. I am the widow of Khaireddine, called El-A'ouar, the one-eyed, because he had only one eye. May Allah keep him in his mercy, now that he has closed forever the other eye, too. I have five grown sons and am more than a little proud to be a grandmother many times over. Sir, you'll spoil a day so well begun if you take her already . . . Yasmine? Isn't that what you called her?"

Before answering, Mahmoud reflects, "I would lack courtesy if I declined such a kind invitation."

"That is indeed her given name," he says. "She doesn't seem to me to be at all predisposed to leave you at the moment. I have no choice but to accept."

"Don't stay there, let's go into *kheïmet-ed-diaf*," says Khadija, leading them.

Behind the tent where she bustles about there are a dozen other kheïmas with children playing around them. They go into one of them. There is a *hsira* made of esparto grass with sheep-skins arranged here and there on it. Nothing else. A child dressed only in a short shirt, belly button showing, appears briefly in the frame of the tent's entrance. A thick layer of snot covers most of his upper lip where flies circle.

"Go tell your mother to prepare some tea! And, by Allah, wipe your nose if you don't want the flies to eat you up to your eyes, and other kids to call you rightly enough *boukhnouna*, the sniveler!" Khadija scolds him.

The child, thus mockingly scolded, disappears quickly. A bit later, an older boy brings them tea. They sip from their glasses. They chat about one thing and another.

"The date harvest is excellent"

"The season of sandstorms was particularly long and brutal this year."

"For at least three years now there have been no locusts."

Like two old friends at the mercy of the seasons who meet when their wandering paths cross, their conversation runs on easily. They tell each other unstitched scraps of their lives, without chronology, mostly inconsequential bits and pieces. They drink tea again. From the outset, they like each other. Mahmoud likes her eyes sparkling with generosity. In her pleasant face, he divines a strength of character. As for her, she is taken by this father like no other she has seen. A man who, instead of taking another wife, has dedicated his life to his daughter. A girl of mixed blood to boot who certainly ought to have been already married off. This strange father was a mystery, a living myth even. The meeting brings a sweetness into Khadija's harsh life. His attitude plays a part in this deed, at once heroic and dangerous. While he believes that thanks to writing he has saved his daughter from solitude, he has condemned her to it, maybe forever. How much Khadija would like to help him.

As the afternoon draws to an end, Khadija's children return one after the other from the palm grove. They are among the workers who climb to the top of the palm trees. Each of them carries three *'arjouns* as their daily salary.

"Salaam 'aleïkoum," they say.

Khadija introduces her guest to them. Sitting down, they talk about their day. The harvest is not finished. Tomorrow will be another pleasant working day carried out amid the general gaiety. More than just another fruit, the date is a staple food in their diet. Thus it is imperative to participate in the harvest and to bag the dates. The women bring them clotted cream. Passing the carafe around, they drink and eat a few dates.

Mahmoud gets up to leave as evening falls. Khadija and her children protest and insist on their staying for dinner. Yasmine, seated by the woman, throws him an imploring look. Mahmoud gives in with good grace. Reassured, Yasmine continues tracing designs on the ground.

Little by little the palm grove empties out. The men who live in the ksar return to their *dechras*. Only the guardians who live in a mechta in the heart of the grove itself remain. Slowly, night falls. Little by little the blue mists of the evening obscure the long, straight trunks of the palm trees while their crowns are still lined with rose from the last rays of the setting sun. The voice of the *muezzin*, half drowned by the noisy confusion of the douar, reaches them. Khadija and her sons soon go to answer the call to prayer. Mahmoud takes advantage of the moment to leave the kheïma. Followed by Yasmine, he takes several steps outside and breathes in the smells. Then he goes to sit down a bit farther away, turning his back to the camp so that his wandering gaze does not bother the women who are preparing dinner in front of the tents. The camels, kneeling nearby, front legs hobbled, complain from time to time as if distressed by the waning of the day.

The evening is mild. Everyone is eating outside by the feeble glow of oil lamps. Several groups are seated on the ground itself around the guessa'as. First there are the men whom Khadija and Yasmine join. A little farther on, and at the moment the only ones making noise, are the young boys and girls. The boys argue over the food that they are scooping with their hands from a common platter. From time to time they interrupt their meal suddenly and move away from the guessa'a to engage in some rough tussling for a moment or two. At that time, a household dog with a sly step and a stealthy eye on the evolving chaos cautiously approaches the platter. Suddenly the melee dissolves. Everyone rushes back suddenly reconciled by the same objective: to grab their dinner and give the dog a thrashing. The dog whines and slinks away before going back to wandering from group to group in the hope of scavenging a little food. In front of one of the kheïmas, the women, hidden by the night shadows, are eating. They have no oil lamp, so the only light comes from the glow of the kanoun. Straining his ears, Mahmoud can hear their low whispers beneath the cries of the children. From time to time, the clear, musical laughter of a girl ripples through the night.

It is evening. Sipping his tea, Mahmoud again takes up his role as storyteller. Behind the men, the children sitting in a row are quiet, enthralled by the adventures of Joha. Only their excited eyes shine in the dark, reflecting the small but steady flame of the oil lamp as they move. But Yasmine, for once, does not listen to her father. She waits for the bells of that cherubic laughter to ring in her ear, amazed by its clarity. She is on the lookout for it even in the limbo of her sleep.

This strange, beautiful, mute girl the color of ripe dates, who is sleeping with her head resting on her father's knees, troubles Khadija. Mahmoud charms her. An idea that has been germinating in her head since the afternoon continues to haunt her thoughts. By the end of the evening, it is burning her tongue.

"Why don't you stay with us, poet and storyteller, with that daughter of yours who writes on the ground? You'll be very useful to us. You could teach some writing to a few little boys. In return, they could take care of your animals. You wouldn't have to bother yourself with women's work. I myself would be happy to help Yasmine. That girl is already a woman! A woman who doesn't know the first thing, however, about women's ways because of your education. She needs to live among women and children. I bet she doesn't know how to work with wool either. I'll teach her those everyday things that fill our time from dawn to dusk and soon make a girl like a mother to her brothers. These useful activities safeguard our sex from the dangers of idleness. Her solitude is not healthy. How do you expect her to adapt to family life, to be a good wife and a good mother? Listen to me, you are on your way to creating a woman who will suit no one, not even herself! If only it isn't already too late. And besides, we need a storyteller among us. My children lack the gift of gab, and I've run out of stories many times over."

"*Ya sheikha*, the first thing I have to do is finish a task outside Aïn Sefra. Tomorrow morning Yasmine and I will leave again. But I promise to take advantage of this short trip to think seriously about what you suggest. Walking is conducive to thought. Living in society, especially with a tribe as welcoming and kind as your own, would be good for my daughter, I have no doubt. But until now, even the sight of others has filled her with fear. She takes refuge in my lap and stays there, reclusive. Her muteness justifies in part her fear of others. However, I have to admit that even when her mother was alive, when Yasmine still had the ability to speak, we did little to prepare her for life in society. We have always wandered alone. Her only access to life outside is through writing. That's why I was so astounded to see her at ease in your company, as if tamed. Teaching children to write would delight me. It is a worthy task for which I am well suited. But I have to say in all honesty that if I take this responsibility, I will not teach them the Qur'an."

"We noticed that you did not respond to the prayer call either at *maghreb* or at *'acha*. Sole judge whose law is inalienable, Allah knows his subjects. It is a matter between you and him. As for the rest, if the children know how to read and write, they will discover the sacred texts by themselves if they wish, *inch'Allah*."

"We'll be gone for two days, three days at the most. If you are still here when we return, we'll give you our answer."

"We'll wait for you. Today is Sunday. We won't leave until Thursday after the market when we'll head toward Moghrar until the end of winter. I hope you'll be part of our group."

Up early the next morning, father and daughter collect their empty goatskins and their camels. When they take leave of Khadija, a quickly repressed expression of pain fills Yasmine's eyes, betraying her sorrow. Moodily, she hurries to follow Mahmoud, pounding across the ground with her bare feet as if to escape the hold of this feeling so new and gently overwhelming.

Before leaving town, she pulls her father toward the Arab cemetery. Each time they pass through Aïn Sefra, the tomb of the roumia Isabelle is an obligatory pilgrimage for Yasmine. Even with her eyes closed she'd be able to find it. She kneels down near the white stone and reads: "El-Sayyed Mahmoud . . ." That Isabelle Eberhardt had chosen the name Mahmoud when she disguised herself as a man and converted to Islam always comforts Yasmine. She sees in it another tie between them, a sort of common destiny. Once again in good spirits, Yasmine follows her father with a firm step. Having filled up with water and loaded palm branches and trunks on the backs of the animals, they set off again following the path of their solitude.

From afar, the sight of the construction of modest proportions but magnificently crenelated makes them drunk with pride. They hurry their mounts to reach it more quickly. As soon as they get there, a fever of activity absorbs them. That very afternoon they put a roof over the tiny room where the graves lie. The tree is now contained in the small courtyard, leaning against the room. Only its hairy fleece of grayish thorns reaches over the wall. They spend the next two days rough casting. What fun rough casting is. With the water hauled on this last trip, Mahmoud dampens and mixes a huge mound of red earth in a solid, compact mortar. He fills two buckets, which he places at the bottom of the wall. For a scaffold, he uses some leftover bricks to climb on. Using both hands, Yasmine grabs huge handfuls of earth from the buckets that she skillfully shapes into balls. Then with a vigorous sweep of her body, she throws them to her father. He catches them in midflight and, with a quick gesture, applies them to the wetted-down wall. The balls line up one against the next, forming a varied, somewhat unequal geometric pattern. From time to time Mahmoud climbs down from his perch and, followed by Yasmine, walks a short distance away to admire the work. With a lively eye and his headdress awry, Mahmoud rubs his hands together contentedly. Yasmine dances with pleasure. The father again fills the buckets with mortar. The daughter, arms covered with earth, joyfully kneads the balls of mud. She throws them to him and, carried away by energy, leaps around, laughing.

Wednesday morning their work is finished. They arrange the remaining bricks to form a small bench. Using a bunch of esparto grass, they sweep the interior of the building and scrape the traces of mortar off the tree. Hoisted up by her father's arms, Yasmine writes on the wall above the door: "Lalla Nejma el-kahla." Then they look around to see what else remains to be done. Suddenly they are at loose ends.

"It is finished. Only pilgrims are missing with their airy *youyous* soaring and circling in the sky and their fantasias on fiery horses whose hooves hammer the plain. One day, either in spring or next autumn, midseason when the sun is less intense, we'll come back to dig a well. Nejma will like that," Mahmoud concludes.

Yasmine agrees and writes on the ground:

"Where do we go now?"

"Wherever you wish, my sylph."

"To see Khadija?" she suggests with her forefinger, confused, continuing to scribble in the sand with her gaze fixed in anxious expectation.

"Why not? We have nothing better to do, right? You know, the other night, while you were sleeping, Khadija suggested that we stay among them. Would that please you?"

Laughter brightens Yasmine's eyes and in response she leaps up happily. They take down their kheïma and fold it. After a last tender look at their construction, they slowly take their leave without regret, memory having been purified. This place that they love for its extreme desolation has become once more a place to return to.

That evening they arrive at the camp of the Hamani. The palm trees have lost their ripe yellow summer jewels. The date harvest is finished. The children swarming around the kheïmas see them coming from a distance and come to meet them. Among them runs a golden, carefree nymph of a girl whose silvery laughter fills the air. Yasmine recognizes this laugh. The other evening, she had tried in vain to see the girl in the darkness. This laughter being linked to this will-o'-the-wisp girl gladdens Yasmine's heart. With a leery eye and a blighted step, the famished camp dog follows them at a distance. Alerted by the joyful shouts of the children, the women take refuge in their tents. Only Khadija remains standing outside to await them.

"Salaam 'aleïki, sheikha. Here we are back, ready to follow you if you still wish to include these two orphans among your family."

"*Marhaba*, I'm very happy to see you again."

The next morning father and daughter go to the market with Khadija's son. Mahmoud must return the tools and the rented camels, and get back his own herd of sheep and his donkey. The

Hamani want to sell some woolen crafts that the women hurried to finish before leaving the oasis.

A confused din pierced by strident nasal tones wells up from the ksar and overflows into the palm grove. It swells the closer you get to the souk. And when you penetrate the atmosphere thick with odors, it spreads out across a spectrum of individual sounds. A few more steps and the overpowering odors, too, open out into a fan of differentiated whiffs: acrid and fetid miasmas of animal waste, the rancid smell of human bodies, the aroma of the spices, merchants' displays that attract the eye, bloom in the nose, and flood the palate. All this overflow, exacerbated by the heat, swirls in the still air. The dust raised by moving feet seems to weave a solid backdrop that captures the dense odors and cacophonous sound.

The Hamani choose a corner for their wares. Squatting, they unroll a small esparto grass mat at their feet on which they spread out some items for sale. Then, joining the noisy atmosphere, they too begin to call out to the mixed crowd of Bedouins and townsfolk. Aside from Yasmine and a stooped grandmother being led by two little boys, there is no female presence. Amid the drab uniformity of somber masculine clothes and the dusty hides of animals, only the luxuriance of the displays of cotton cloth can rival that of the spices, delighting the eye. But it is not so much the riot of colors as the vying of merchants both Jewish and Arab, that captivates Mahmoud for the time being. He watches them with pleasure. Their way of measuring lengths of cloth, with elbows and arm lengths, has always amused him. Oh, yes! It is best to pick a tall one! Watch out for the arm lengths above all! They are likely to get shorter depending on the client or the spirit of the moment. Above all, keep your eyes on the nose of the merchant, which ought to be pointed in the opposite direction from the horizontal axis of hand-wrist-arm. Because, here, the arm length is the distance between the pinch of the thumb and forefinger, arm extended, and the tip of the nose, which in principle should be turned in the opposite direction. So if the buyer isn't wary, a finger, hand, or arm fraudulently bent or a miserly turn of the nose will quickly rob him.

Tugging her father by the hand, Yasmine heads resolutely toward one of these merchants. Reigning over the bolts of cloth, three or four dresses of various sizes light their fires in Yasmine's eyes, which flame with desire. Smiling, she examines them longingly. The merchant, lying in wait with ready words and gestures, unhooks one and brings it down. Soon the dress begins to dance in his hands. He turns it, turns it again, spreads it out, holds it up, flings it out, then brings it to a standstill in front of Yasmine.

"A pretty dress is always sewn with magic. It metamorphoses a homely girl into a woman but . . . on a pretty girl like you, it is only the final touch to her appearance," clamors the man cheekily.

Tactical error. It is not this one at all that attracts Yasmine's gaze. The merchant quickly sees this and takes down a dress and hands it to her without further ado. This dress is a bit short. It scarcely covers her knees. But it is a brilliant red with large white flowers blossoming out into fleshy corollas. Yellow, green, and violet ribbons edge its flounces and flutter on its bodice. Mahmoud tries to persuade his daughter to choose another one that is a little longer. With her eyes obstinately fixed on the one she has chosen and her lower lip pushed out disdainfully, Yasmine shrugs her shoulders and taps her foot in exasperation. Both amused and touched, Mahmoud gives in, laughing at his daughter's caprice. Without waiting any longer and with a baleful air, Yasmine grabs the dress. She can scarcely repress a small triumphant smile. As he is paying, Mahmoud spots a handsome *mendil*.

"We'll buy this mendil to give to Khadija, eh? What do you think?"

So the shawl joins the dress that Yasmine is already clutching to her chest. With the money for the two purchases pocketed, the merchant ventures to say, darting a look at the adolescent:

"Pretty you are, but I pity the man that will be your husband, because . . ."

Yasmine's ferocious look instantly freezes his budding smile. Mahmoud bursts out laughing, turns his back on the man, and leads Yasmine through the crowd.

"You've dressed in girl's clothes again, with the city folk!"

Yasmine replies with a coquettish pout.

"It's true that it would've been difficult for you to buy a girl's dress while wearing boy's clothes! Now go sit with the Hamani and wait for me. I'm going to find Meftah, the man who has our herd. I won't be long. He must be around here. If I don't find him, I'll come back to get you, and we'll go to his house.

Two of the Hamani are fully engaged in the customary rites of buying and selling. They are sitting on the edge of the mat facing their clients. The elfish Bachir, their youngest boy, stays back behind them. He agrees vociferously with them and from time to time exclaims in support of the assertions of his elders. The negotiations are tough. In cahoots, the two sides perform as if in a play, engaging in repartees that they enjoy with the same parsimony, the same delectation, as they do sips of tea. Sometimes, interested passers-by stop and become temporary allies with one side or the other, entering the discussion unexpectedly. Yasmine is entertained by this playful dialectic and follows its evolution closely. Suddenly, a silhouette catches her eye. That man there, the big one, lanky . . . With an ungainly gait, he walks with great strides into her memory. His eyes! There is in his eyes something of the hunted beast. An insanity seen before. His hands! His enormous hands! Suddenly, a dense silence unfurls in Yasmine's head. A curtain falls on the scene of the marketplace. Yasmine is behind a pile of stones. Something hallucinatory, something menacing, vibrates inside her. Then suddenly, her entrails, her chest, her throat explode, erupting into a terrible cry. Before her eyes, the knotty hands of this man are squeezing her mother's black neck.

171

"Ya Allah! Ya Allah! What's gotten into you?" ask the Hamani impatiently.

Yasmine doesn't even look at them. The dress and the mendil, thrown down at her feet, her body frozen, she cries out. Taken aback like the rest by this strident cry that drowns out the noise of the marketplace, the man too is immobilized. Apparently he doesn't realize that this cry implicates him. He doesn't recall ever having seen this girl who cries out like one possessed. But he has committed so many crimes that this look, fixated on him, quickly becomes an accusation. Besides, Yasmine stretches out an arm and points directly at him. The man begins carefully retreating. Astonished eyes are already searching the throng of faces for signs of guilt. The man snakes his way through the crowd and quickly disappears.

Mahmoud is not far away. He hears the cry. He turns around, sees the throng around the area of the Hamani, and hurries over. Pushing aside the men in his path, he hurls himself toward his daughter and kneels by her:

"Kebdi, don't be afraid, I am here!"

"It's him! Him! Him!" screams Yasmine.

"Yasmine, you're talking! You're talking!"

"It's him, it's him!"

A lightning flash of insight supplanting this extraordinary miracle, Mahmoud understands with brute force the meaning of the accusation. He turns to look in the direction indicated. After several seconds, his eyes meet a shifty gaze that he recognizes on the spot: "Hassan!" Elbowing through the crowd, El-Majnoun's servant, who has also recognized Mahmoud, flees. Leaving Yasmine, Mahmoud takes off in pursuit. But with an astonishing swiftness, the other has already disappeared from the souk. Mahmoud searches for him all over the marketplace and the back streets of the ksar. The villain has vanished as does a nightmare before the first glimmers of wakefulness.

"*Oummi, oummi.* Mother, Mother," Yasmine moans now.

Her voice is rough and hoarse. She is overcome by a strange feeling, a bittersweet sensation she is unable to analyze. It is a grief-stricken explosion at the exquisite moment of newfound speech, a shooting pain until then submerged in the unsoundable depths of her being. As if caught in the throes of an immense distress unrelieved for so long by the healing of tears, a liberating sob at last bursts out.

"Oummi, oummi!"

Suddenly she is aware of this mangled, rusty voice—her voice. She is so frightened she goes mute. A furtive thought flashes in her soul: her voice has died with her mother, has been interred with her. It cannot return to her. This voice is only a ghost. It wells up from the land of the dead. It passes through her just for the brief moment of denunciation. Yasmine trembles at the thought. Her eyes search the crowd for the man. Will her father return? She wants to be able to be silent in order to concentrate, to think more clearly. But she is not in control of that voice. It is unruly. She can barely even modulate it.

"Oummi, oummi," she begins again with a whisper at once drunken and lost.

The gathering around the Hamani has dispersed. However, a few curious folks still are waiting. Khadija's sons are unable to give them an explanation, so they await the return of Mahmoud. The Hamani, putting this windfall event to good use, are vaunting their wares emphatically. Bachir, the youngest son, approaches Yasmine, who is still crying and calling for her mother. The young boy, who excels at making faces, does a few of his best grimaces in the hope of getting her attention. Usually these simian pantomimes draw laughter from even the most sullen of children and cause the most preoccupied of women to burst into laughter. But this clowning is unsuccessful with Yasmine. Disconcerted, the boy stretches out a hand to her, the hint of a caress. But Yasmine rears back and turns on him. Bachir's gesture stops in midair.

"Oummi, oummi," Yasmine moans dully.

His inability to distract her from her pain leaves Bachir staring and defeated. Then, struck by a new idea, he gets up and leaves for the far end of the market. A few moments later, he returns with a cheerful step and sits down next to her. His eyes sparkling once more, he offers her some candy.

"Oummi, oummi," she mumbles, her face distorted, indifferent to the boy's efforts.

Vexed by the obstinate girl, his eyes lose for a moment their sweet mischief, and Bachir turns away from her sinking into a gloomy meditation at odds with his mischievous face. Then, to console himself for the vexations he has suffered, he plunges his hand into the depths of his pants pocket and pulls out a flute. It is a small reed flute, simply made. But at its touch, his brooding face breaks into a smile. His fingers flutter over it, caressing the instrument. He tosses it into the air, catches it again, and turns it like a spindle in his hand. Then he brings it to his mouth and drinks its music like an elixir. Its melody streams out like a prolonged sob. It winds its soft meandering about the noise in the marketplace. It flows out and lingers, going from laughter to tears. A magic fluid that mollifies grief. Bachir is a storyteller of the wind. His air flows over Yasmine, calms her lamentations, dries her tears. Yasmine listens to it, silence regained.

After a long and fruitless search through the back streets of the ksar, Mahmoud returns to the market. Diverse ideas jostle one another, occupying his thoughts one after the other:

"Did someone assassinate Nejma because of me? Instead of me, perhaps? Was El-Majnoun the second man?"

All the ghosts of the past he thought he'd banished from his life are there again, befouling the joy of the present. Their menace burdens an already compromised future.

"Filthy assassins! Now that I know who you are, I'll track you to the end of my days."

Mahmoud's return causes a hubbub among the men. They

mill around, gesture, try to approach him, asking each other the questions that are tormenting their curiosity. With unusual calm, given the circumstances, Mahmoud walks toward his daughter. Seated, her large eyes for the moment calm, she stares at the boy with the magical flute.

"I am going to see Khadija. I have several requests to make and some revelations to share with her," Mahmoud says to the Hamani in a low voice, taking his daughter by the hand.

Forcing their way through the unhappy crowd robbed of their moment of anticipated pleasure, the father and daughter leave the market. The sound of the flute winds through the noise and accompanies them for a long while.

The curious scatter. In small groups they return to their lazy sauntering about. The haggling over suppositions and commentaries rises above the crescendo of the noises of the souk. It's about who can invent the most gripping version, the most incredible scenario describing this brief scene without words—a cry, a flight, a pursuit—that they just witnessed.

"Can you still speak, my sylph?" the father anxiously asks, once they are out of range.

The child nods, a wince creasing her face. This sudden hatching of speech now presents a new danger for her. An imminent danger.

"Say one word, just one, any word," her father implores her.

A word. She opens the flask of perfume and breathes it in to drown the words beneath her mother's death. Spoken words? Could these words once again sink into more years of silence? Could they again die and abandon her to written words, the only expression she mastered? But they are there. She feels them in her fear. They whirl around inside her, birds of every kind of anguish, ready to surge up again. Inside her they are bitter, scorching, and rough-edged. They are lugubrious and violent. Blown along by winds other than her own, whether they are fine and light or heavy and crook-beaked; whether their songs are soothing or jarring, they all have sumptuous wings edged with light. The words of others are virtuosos of the first class. Nesting in hidden soft crags of her throat, they play on the rich scales of sounds. Her throat is a gorge that is merely an arid and inhospitable rock. Her words are dross, they only sound the death knell. Like birds of prey clinging to her entrails, they make the cavernous sounds of a ventriloquist. They brood in the depths of her grief that will never die out. Now she knows their treachery. She will no longer expose herself to the work of their claws. She only wants to hear strangers' words, words that nourished her silence and whose resonances feed her writings. As for the words of others, even when anger sounds in them, even when fear is unfurled there, or bitterness stirs them up into a dirty foam, she wants her body to receive them, to feel them vibrate, to let her spirit drink them in and become intoxicated just as she gets drunk on the madness of the wind.

"Say one word, just one," her father repeats.

Yasmine vigorously shakes her head no.

Earlier, in spite of the intense emotion, the rough timbre of several stammered words in her surging cry did not escape Mahmoud's ear. He stops and crouches down, putting his hands on his daughter's shoulders. He looks into the dilated pupils of her eyes. She looks at him, and again there is that mute cry.

"Words aren't guilty. It's that cry earlier. It injured your throat, scratched your voice. Don't be afraid, Kebdi. Don't be afraid of yourself."

She tries to convince herself:

"It is the cry. Father said so."

"The man must be somewhere in the ksar. I know him. He is dangerous. So I must first take you to Khadija before going to look for him."

She bends down and writes: "He must be found now."

Mahmoud shudders. He isn't mistaken, this writing in the

sand is a command. They begin walking again without talking any more.

Khadija, astonished to see them return so quickly, comes to meet them. Yasmine runs to throw herself in her arms.

"Sheikha Khadija, today is a special day: my daughter found her speech again! A wounded speech, but it will heal now, I'm sure."

"*El-hamdoulillah, el-hamdoulillah*! What wonderful news. What a blessed day!"

"It is also a great day because I have finally identified and located one of the two men who assassinated by wife."

"Ya Allah, assassinated?"

"*Ya krima*, that is how Yasmine's mother died, killed in front of her eyes."

"Ya Allah, *ya rabbi*, may curses fall on the criminals."

"I am confiding my daughter to you, ya krima. I am leaving to search for that vile man. I will find him if I have to wander day and night till the last moon of my life."

"But why did someone kill the poor woman?"

"It is an unbelievable story, ya krima. A long ride through the dreams of the dead. An epic of dreams crushed by fortune's inconstancy. A journey plagued by all manner of locusts. Should my life escape their voracious jaws once again, I'll tell you how in the midst of one of their devastating invasions, on a day when the skies were angry, I met the most luminous of women. I am confiding my daughter to you, ya krima. Kindest of women, see that my absence doesn't grieve her too much. I know that in your big heart, there is already a place for her."

"By Allah, do not leave yet—wait. My sons will return soon. When they learn the truth, they'll want to go with you."

"Certainly not! I don't want to mix other people up in my affair."

"But what will you do exactly? Listen, wait a bit. Take the time to think things over."

"Sheikha, for more than six years now one question has plagued my life. Like a rusted pulley that fills the empty throat of a well with its incessant groaning without ever bringing up a mouthful of water."

"We have all known in our lives the cursed invasions of locusts. We all have, buried within us, something that aches. I'm not asking you to stay here for hours. Sit down just long enough to drink a glass of tea. It is ready and fragrant with mint leaves. One doesn't leave a kheïma where tea is being served without tasting it. And even if it doesn't quiet the grating in your heart, at least take the time to put your mind in order."

Mahmoud doesn't answer. Khadija goes to him. One hand on his shoulder, the other holding always to Yasmine's hand, she leads them gently to her kheïma. Mahmoud swallows a gulp of tea and gets up. Outside, he puts a saddle on one of the camels. On the packsaddle of the second, he loads a guerba, what is needed to make tea, and his handsome *hadoun*.

"But why all this gear?" questions Khadija.

"With the men I am pursuing, I have to be ready to travel across great distances."

"Do you want your kheïma?" she asks then.

"A kheïma? When I am alone the dome of heaven is good enough. Sheikha, just now in the marketplace I gave back the camels and the guerbas I had rented. But I didn't have the time to collect the herd I left. They are with Meftah of the Ouled Boutkhile. I have fifty-two sheep. I made him a gift of two of them. As for the others, take them with you. They are not yet sheared. I'll give you the sheared wool, the milk, and half of the herd's increase until I come back. Choose the best of the animals and make a *mechoui* for the children. I'll go by to alert Meftah. How much longer can you wait for me here?

"Eight days, even ten days."

"After ten days, if I'm not here, leave. I'll figure out how to find you."

"As for the *mechoui*, we'll await your return. *Ma'a salaama*."

Her eyelashes pearled with tears and her breathing constricted in grief, Yasmine looks at him. He crouches by her and murmurs:

"Kebdi, all words, all forms of speech, have one side that cuts, another that foams, one face that is bitter, the other sweet. Open them up, open the words. Hoard them as one hoards time. Don't let them control you, these words of time. Turn the silky side of words toward your throat. Into the venom of sorrow, they drip honey. Refuse the plowshare of cries, be they sonorous or silent. Change your fears into plaints. And, in awaiting my return, write down the stories and poems that I have taught you. Explore your imagination freely, inventing others. Write down others that you will hear. Kebdi, in my absence, I also prescribe for you a large dose of dreaming. Dream to escape when what others say to you seems harsh. Dream with spoken words so they will cease to be cursed and become edged with hope. Refuse to submit to reality so you can conquer all the *regs* of life. Learn to taste and savor laughter, too, even in the midst of cares. Whether its bell rings out or clangs, it is always the Milky Way of thoughts. I am assigning you this important task. Upon my return we will go to the Orient, and we will write a collection of poems and stories. We'll entitle it *A Harvest of Elegies at the Gate of Orality*.

They look at each other for a moment in silence. Mahmoud becomes aware of other children around them.

"These lyrical effusions shared between father and daughter must seem at the least ridiculous and extravagant to them," Mahmoud says to himself.

Then, hastily, he hugs his daughter, rises, and leaves.

Mahmoud returns to the souk. It is the end of the market day. The place is empty, its clamor muted. Most of the displays have disappeared. The sellers who have stayed late fold their goods and put them in order. Speedily, they load the packsaddles of a legion of small gray donkeys. In the section reserved for animals, there are only two or three camels left and a few odd sheep. The latter mill around, rummaging with their muzzles through the trash littering the ground. The camels, nostrils flared, breathe in the sky. One could say they were inhaling the irresistible call of wide-open spaces before leaving, at a nonchalant amble, the sedentary world with its hobbled gait. Or is it out of disdain for the meager herd who, muzzles to the ground, breathe in all sorts of offal and excrement, that the camels put on airs and breathe in the horizons?

At this feverish time, one must be tactful if one is going to interrupt the activities of the sellers without buying anything, however, and beware of snubs and sarcasm! Mahmoud helps one of them fold a large rug before asking about his man. But his description means nothing to the merchant, who calls his neighbors. No one seems to remember the guy. Mahmoud is becoming discouraged when Meftah appears:

"I waited for you. Did you get your man?" Meftah asks innocently, repeatedly stroking his moustache.

"Do you know him? Did you see him?"

"I only saw a fleeing silhouette. But after you left for the palm grove with your daughter, he came back to the souk. I never saw him before. He's not a nomad from this region. A man with such a gait, I would have remembered. How can I explain it? . . . He is so supple, so quick, and his face and gestures are so tormented. He seems to float like a dust devil, several spans above the ground."

"That's him!" Mahmoud cries out.

"And then he has eyes that glow like coals."

"That's him, there's no doubt about it."

"I saw him heading toward Khatab, the merchant who sells hides. He spread a large *mezoued* out in front of him. The guy mumbled a few words. Then he left as furtively as he came. I talked for a moment with Khatab. He knows nothing about the man. The previous evening, he'd come into the shop and asked him if he could buy some *ma'akra*. "My wife can make some for you," Khatab told him. "Can it be ready for tomorrow?" "Yes, it can." The man handed him an empty mezoued. He paid and left without giving even his name. The next day when he picked up the full mezoued, he only said: "Thanks, I'm in a hurry. I have to go back north immediately."

"I gave a description at the caravanserai. He had been there for three days, someone told me. He picked up his mount and seems certainly to have left Aïn Sefra. I thought I'd help you by collecting a few clues."

"A thousand thanks, Meftah, for this important information. Do you know if he had a companion?"

"Apparently not. However, I can't say for certain," Meftah comments.

"No, it's unlikely. Believe me, if his crony had been here, he would have stirred up the entire souk. I, too, am in a hurry, Meftah. If I don't return to collect my flock in the next eight days, it's because I have left for an indeterminate time. The nomads, the Hamani, will come to take them off your hands.

9

Mahmoud left the camp at morning's end. Yasmine seems distant and glum. She hasn't even wanted to eat. In the afternoon, Khadija manages to take her along with her toward the wadi. There, Yasmine sits at the foot of a palm tree while the older woman washes wool. But her heavy-heartedness blots out the charm of both the countryside and the newness of her situation. Her eyes wander without fixing on anything, as if the wadi and the palm trees were suddenly transparent. Time stands still, seeming to delight in a thoroughly morbid immobility. The sky mirrors it. A glassy blue eternity. And Khadija's plaintive songs conjure up only endless weariness. Suddenly a voice, still far off and indistinct, disturbs her lethargy. At first she and Khadija can only distinguish terrified intonations.

"It's Bachir, my sprite of a son," says Khadija.

She leaves her chore and stands up, worried. The boy appears at a run around the far end of the palm grove.

"*Jadarmi! Jadarmi!*" he cries out in warning as soon as he sees his mother.

The woman and the girl stiffen and wait.

"Jadarmi! Jadarmi!" Bachir cries out again.

He reaches them. Terrified, he throws himself into his mother's skirts and hides behind her. There are three men dressed in khaki coming toward them walking their bicycles, useless for crossing the palm grove. Rigid in their leggings, like centurions encrusted in their tight jackets and severe faces, they approach full of a sense of power. They stop several steps from Khadija and Yasmine.

"Where is Mahmoud Tijani?" thunders one of them.

"We don't know any Tijani," shoots back Khadija, convinced that it is merely a mistake.

"I think they call him the poet in these parts."

"We don't have among us any poet or any Tijani," the woman counters without losing any of her assurance.

"Someone claimed, however, that we would find him here. He'd have a girl with him."

"Someone is mistaken or is making fun of you," Khadija replies with equanimity.

Disconcerted by her certainty, the man in uniform is silent. Khadija quickly adds:

"Here, there are only Hamani."

"We'll have to do an identity check," decides one of the policemen, speaking to his colleagues in French.

He is the one carrying on the conversation. The others, it appears, do not speak Arabic. He sticks out his chest and announces:

"We're going to check everyone's papers."

"Our papers? What papers? The sons of the great kheïmas don't need any papers to know who they are. Should one of them fancy he has forgotten, one of his elders will be happy to remind him with a few licks of a stick. Paper? I can't even find a scrap when I want to send a handful of tea or black pepper to a neighboring tent. The only paper that crosses the entrance of my kheïma is the one wrapped around the sugar cubes. But . . . that paper I save carefully for the taleb. Because without paper, there can be no talismans!

"I've always maintained that we needed to force them to register, all of them! All we get from these wandering herds is trouble!" the man sputters. "You, what's your name?" he thunders at Yasmine.

"Her name is Yasmine Hamani," Khadija says.

"I want to hear it from her!" the man replies, visibly agitated.

"She's mute. Do you have the gift of making the mute speak? The great *marabouts* to whom we have prayed for so long haven't granted it. If you succeed in giving her speech, we'll raise a qobba dedicated to you. But she knows how to write."

"Then write your name!"

After a moment's hesitation, Yasmine bends down and writes her first name in the sand. The man shrugs his shoulders in annoyance. Anger has clouded his thought. Why expect a nomad girl to write her name in French? It's already a miracle that she knows how to write in her own language. Khadija laughs insolently, repressing with difficulty a mocking ululation. Disconcerted, the man in uniform turns angrily on his heel and walks toward the camp. His two associates, worn down by impotence, trail along in his wake.

"What is your name? What is your name?" he repeats angrily, collaring a group of children.

They all reply:

"Hamani. Hamani. Hamani."

"And her? He asks pointing to Yasmine.

"Yasmine Hamani! shouts out Bachir with a radiant smile, having picked up the lesson from his mother.

"Yasmine Hamani! Yasmine Hamani!" the chorus of children insists.

These assertions are punctuated by the crystalline laughter of the nymphet, 'Aicha.

"But she doesn't look in the least like you! She is much darker," the man in uniform argues with distrust.

"Her mother is black. Do you want to see her maybe?" challenges Khadija.

"This man Tijani, the poet, or whatever, is dangerous. He set a farm on fire, killed a man. He's been tracked for a long time. Someone saw him prowling around here."

The Hamani don't budge.

"What an awful world! His 'logic' is nothing but a fiendish, cynical farce. My father tracked by these men who accuse him of the worst crimes? While he . . . What kind of grotesque charade are these men lending themselves to? What a sacrilege!" thunders Yasmine in her silence.

Khadija has read the anger in her eyes. She goes to her and puts an affectionate arm around her shoulders.

"We'll find him, you can be sure!" barks the man in charge, threatening dire consequences.

Then, turning to his colleagues, he gives the signal to leave. They leave, girded in their leggings and jackets, but with their pride wounded.

"In this climate how can they stand such tight clothes? You'd say that all their pride was lodged there, covered in sweat, squeezed into that khaki cloth and . . . onto that paper, of course. Roumis remain a complete mystery to me," Khadija murmurs.

Yasmine never imagined her father gone. From the time of her mother's death over seven years ago, they haven't been parted for one day, one moment. This first separation makes her heart heavy, robbing her of all volition.

"But why doesn't she speak? Her supposed muteness is only a sham, we know that very well now," the Hamani say, bewildered.

Yasmine doesn't answer. She wishes her voice never returned. Its return is a burden for her today, bringing sorrow and anguish as deeply felt as when it disappeared. The last straw would be to see herself accused of having any responsibility whatsoever for the suffering she had once endured. Although her condition was imposed on her in the past, from here on out she'll be careful not to offer herself up as a martyr. She no longer wants to endure the ferocious caprices of this voice. It flees when she is in desperate need of it. It comes back when she no longer asks anything of it, when she has learned so well to cope with its absence. On words polished by the silence of writing, her voice imposes its harsh sounds, broken on the wheel of suffering, grown hoarse from old traumas. Now this voice is simply an instrument of torture. It is the pendulum of a terror that swings between the extremes of grief. Yasmine will never gain control over it. So, she encloses herself more firmly in her muteness. It is her refuge. She nests there. It seals in her melancholy.

Yasmine feels distant from all these people. Before, when she and her father crossed paths briefly with other nomads or villagers, she realized how different they were. The daily contact with the Hamani gives her the real measure of the gap separating her and her father from the nomads' social systems. To escape from the implacable sense of vengeance dogging their thoughts, and given their perpetual quest for peace and forgetfulness, the father and daughter have thrown themselves into a losing hand-to-hand combat with dreams. They've thrown themselves so far into the fray that they've ended up being overwhelmed completely by dreams. Perfect harmony. They've walked through an unreal limbo, encircled by the nimbus of poetry. Cradled in the hoop of time, stealing small, unspoken, fugitive moments of happiness. Working and reworking the material, the chisel of poetry sculpted for them at last a lively sensibility, an uncommonly pronounced receptivity: an extraordinary wealth, but also a fearsome vulnerability.

So, when the early charm of her affection for Khadija has passed, life with the others becomes a violent shock for Yasmine. It proves to her how unfit she is for life in society. She is too mature to lose herself in the carefree universe of children, too detached to join in the trivial realities and daily concerns of the adults, too educated to invoke without irony their *mektoub*, too rebellious to submit her freedom to their rules. Raised by a man, a poet, she has escaped from the traditional female mold. She is unaware of the taboos that everywhere constrain her sex. She does not speak, she writes in the midst of an oral world. Neither male nor female, she disguises herself. Neither white nor black, she wears the hue of difference and of solitude. Neither black nor white, she wears the hue of condemnation, of damnation. Now she is completely aware of it. So, more than ever, she withdraws and barricades herself behind acts of refusal. The refusal to speak, the refusal to eat, often the refusal to make herself a victim of those whose eyes and words are for her a sort of flagellation. As the days pass, other refusals come to reinforce this isolation, to consolidate the singular character of her personality. As the tribe is not on the move, the need to walk is so great that she goes off by herself. Walking involves a different type of close combat. The physical need to feel the sand and the weariness of the desert, to bump up against stone, against the punishment of the regs, to feel the burning of the light like a fixed gaze, a call to divine liberty.

As time goes by, the continuous efforts of three people, Khadija, Bachir, and 'Aicha, manage to draw her eyes away from the void, to capture her attention once more. Even if she doesn't say a word to them, all three nonetheless have the privilege of attracting her interest for the time being. From Khadija, she hears the voluptuous plaints, saturated with sensuality, that were the breath accompanying even her least gesture. Bachir's flute comes to her, pearls of fresh sound with an intoxicating languor at its depths, like a lamentation, like a sweet sob of love. 'Aicha doesn't come near Yasmine. But from a distance Yasmine watches her with envy. Because 'Aicha thrills, dazzles her. 'Aicha is a gift to the flat life of the plateau. Mischievous and coquettish, her eyes full of gay impudence and shining with pleasure, 'Aicha hums. 'Aicha buzzes around and whirls about. Golden and fragile as a honeybee, she sips the light, and the honey of her laughter sweetens the bitterness of the days.

Drawn by Khadija's songs, Yasmine watches her at her daily tasks, weaving and basket making especially. She admires her dexterity in weaving esparto grass and palm fronds to make dishes, baskets, and couscous holders. The ballet of these hands over the tight woof of the weaving loom fascinates her to the point that she forgets her nausea for a moment. Sometimes, almost as if linked to him by the spell of his flute's sounds, Yasmine follows Bachir as he herds the flock in the quiet of the plateau. The sheep graze, muzzles searching close to the ground, eyes empty. The boy, sometimes a will-o'-the-wisp, sometimes serious, with his large eyes velvety as the wings of night butterflies, intoxicates the day with his music, which he sips insatiably at the mouthpiece of his flute. From time to time he stops and smiles at her. Yasmine doesn't smile. He jumps and capers. The legs of his saroual sketch a clear bubble in the air. They balloon out like wings before falling back. So light and supple are Bachir's leaps you'd think him able to fly. With agility, he lands on his feet again. Yasmine's sad eyes grow frightened. Bachir mimes a comic scene, plays the clown. Yasmine doesn't smile. So, he returns to his music. She resumes walking behind the sheep while the rippling of his flute runs through her mind. But this music awakens in Yasmine a delight that is incomplete. It opens within her an expectation without a clear object: an interrupted deliverance, a roll of thunder whose distant drum promises rain. It passes on, and the sky closes over in immense frustration. The quest for music carries her along. She walks behind something she will never catch or even name.

Mahmoud left twenty days ago. For twenty nights, darkness has spread itself out at both ends and shortened the days. From the depths of an oppressive forgetfulness, it has hauled up winter that settles in bit by bit. The Hamani have no news of Mahmoud. They are growing impatient. The perpetual search for sustenance for their animals doesn't mix well with immobility. It forces nomads to cover large areas. And Mahmoud's livestock, which the men had gotten back from Meftah, have been added to their own. Meftah had told them that Mahmoud had headed north.

"How far north?" they asked themselves. North to Aïn Sefra, to the high plateaus, to the green tell stretching to the sea? His animals will waste away!‘

But the police intervention makes them nervous. Khadija urges them to be patient. Yasmine's gaze so full of apprehension both annoys and paralyzes them.

"We must reassure her that her father hasn't been captured by the authorities before we take to the road again," they decide.

"Meftah has gone to visit his family near Tlemcen," the neighbors say.

No one else knows Mahmoud. Not a single other soul to turn to. On two occasions, Khadija and Yasmine have gone to the village.

"We have to listen to the village gossip in hope of hearing news of Mahmoud," the woman says stoically.

Confronted by the labyrinths of village streets, Khadija, who is never afraid when facing horizontal planes devoid of landmarks on the plateau or in the desert, is completely terrified of getting lost in the city. Her gaze, accustomed to roaming without obstacles across vast spaces, collides with the walls, wounding itself repeatedly. Her thoughts, trapped, go crazy, swirling around in the buzzing of the swarming narrow streets.

Accompanied by Yasmine, Khadija gets lost between one question and the next because of the twisted language of the sedentary people and the hermetic one of the roumis. She ruminates over the same questions to the point of losing her courage and becoming completely disoriented. They have walked from place to place following diverse and contradictory directions, all of them wrong. Crossing the village is a trial as difficult as crossing a flooded wadi.

On the third try, they discover with dismay that the prison is not just a sinister legend intended to make children tremble.

It is a horrible reality. They find the building at the edge of the town. It is an enormous tomb where they bury men, alive. The thought that her father could be in there makes Yasmine shake with sorrow and anger.

The man on guard duty before the heavy, closed door understands nothing of Khadija's words. He tells her she can't stay there.

"Go on, go on, get out of here, Fatma!"

In response to his commanding gestures, Khadija shrugs her shoulders and squats down across from him. The man, surrounded by a wall of indifference, doesn't deign to give her a second glance.

"Why does he call me Fatma? We'll stay here. Someone will have to listen to us," Khadija decides.

They wait. Little by little, overwhelmed by the torpor of midday, the narrow streets empty out. Like a monster satiated with cacophony, the ksar sinks into a digestive lethargy. As if its own progression were linked to the circulation of men, time comes to a standstill when their feet do. It is an abdication in which the sun glories. Hailed by the shrilling of the cicadas, it triumphs and rules alone, a despot. They wait. After a long time, a man covered with hair goes by. A great beard blackens his face. One of his thick, rebellious fleeces spreads out into a large fan. His mouth is scarcely visible beneath the luxuriant tuft of his moustache that blends in with his beard. Dominating this exuberant bushiness are sparkling, elongated eyes gleaming like two black crescents. Jet-black eyebrows outline them, tracing perfect arcs. On his bare torso, beneath his *'abaya*, on his arms, another abundance of hair. A minuscule white cap jauntily crowns the top of his head. He is surely a Jew.

"Salaam 'aleïkoum," he says as he walks by them.

"Salaam 'aleïk," they reply.

He walks on by nonchalantly. They wait. The guttural voice of a muezzin chants the call to prayer: *el-dohr*.

"I will pray tonight. Allah, help us!" thinks Khadija.

In front of the prison, the man in khaki takes refuge beneath the porch. The shadow has shrunk, retreated to the foot of the wall. Yasmine's eyes don't leave the tops of the walls. A grief-stricken gaze. They wait. Khadija covers Yasmine's head with her mendil.

"It too is disdainful and pitiless, even in autumn," she comments, finger pointed at the sky.

They wait. Finally, a man approaches from the distance. He has a great beard. It is doubtless the Jew returning to his business. Soon he is in front of them.

"What are you doing in the sun, poor things? There is no use waiting before closed doors. It's been three hours since I passed by in the other direction. You haven't budged."

"We'd like to have some answers. But no one even listens to our questions."

The stranger fumbles around in the depths of his beard with one hand. These pathetic faces paralyze him. He stands there, embarrassed, his indecisive fingers both caressing and pulling on his beard.

"Where are you from," he inquires.

"Far from walls and prisons, far from the confusing, cold ways of settled peoples," Khadija says with a sigh of resignation.

"Come into the shade, in my *hanout*, for a moment. It's nearby. There you'll find at least some cool water in the *qolla*.

They are very thirsty. So, without even glancing at each other, they rise to follow the man. He has a shop just outside the souk. There is a little of everything in this *hanout*: first, a line of burlap sacks. Some contain grain, flour, semolina; in others a bit smaller, spices, henna, *ghassoul*, benzoin . . . Hanging from the ceiling are several *'arjouns* of dates, several goatskin bags. In a corner, there is even an *'oud*, a superb lute with a high sheen. Yasmine looks at it, a lute so noble and silent, so fragile in the midst of everyday supplies. They drink. Happy to have found a friendly ear at last in this town, Khadija talks about their worries concerning their friend, Yasmine's father.

"From time to time I've done small services for the soldiers. I'll see what I can find out. Come back to see me in three or four days. My name is Benichou."

Two days later they are sitting in front of one of the kheïmas. Khadija has brought out all the washed fleeces, signaling that it is time to work the wool. There is a huge pile, a great wealth to be sure. One of her daughters-in-law stays behind to make the bread and prepare lunch. All the other women—mothers, aunts, and cousins, as well as the little girls—come to help. Yasmine is spellbound as much by the organization as by the virtuosity of the work. The little girls do the first step. Already expert and agile, their fingers separate, untangle, and air the tufts compressed by washing and long periods of storage in tightly packed piles of bundles. In the process, they pick out the many twigs and wadded hair, separating out the rare tufts of brown, red, or black in the white fleeces. These naturally darker colors are precious. They will be used for the making of *jellabas*, *hadouns*, and *kheïdous*. Men will wear these both to show off and for protection against the cold. Three women work with large combs whose handles they've weighted with heavy stones. Many strokes of the long teeth will be needed. Two other women lay hold of large carding combs with multitudes of closely set short teeth, brushing and refining the work begun by the combs. Then, in large layers, the carefully carded wool is pulled from between the teeth and rolled up in bundles, ready to be spun. Two more women apply their bare legs and the happy, moving arcs of their arms to the fascinating spinning of the distaff. Crazily, they twirl around, making a line through the brown legs. They make the *kholkhals* on their ankles ring, and their silvery trills twist in harmony with their hands winding the thread on high. In the tent with flaps raised, Khadija's fingers are intoxicated by the threads of her loom, an enormous harp, harmonizing the dance of the women to the rhythm of her song. Wild little 'Aicha is lazy. Drunk on the violet light, she's only concerned with finding the most radiant and joyous notes.

"Yasmine, my gazelle, do as the other girls are doing," Khadija suggests with an engaging smile.

Yasmine turns away from the women, and with her index finger to the ground, finds the thread of her own craft, writing in the sand.

A man mounted on a donkey suddenly emerges from the palm grove and rides in their direction. The women abandon their tasks and disappear into the kheïma. Khadija leaves her thread for a moment and goes out. When he gets nearer, she sees a black beard beneath a white chéchia.

The Jew?

Yasmine gets up. He approaches, his small donkey trotting, his body dangling, as if asleep, hidden in the shadow of his beard.

"Mahmoud is not in prison. I can promise you that!" he announces before stopping his donkey.

Yasmine almost throws her arms around his neck. Khadija welcomes him with a radiant smile.

A detour by the caravanserai. Not that Mahmoud doubts Meftah's revelations, but he wants to reassure himself that Hassan hasn't pulled one of his diabolical feints. There, he gets confirmation that Hassan left the premises early in the morning and hasn't reappeared. So Mahmoud heads up north, too.

"I'll find both Majnoun and him! I'll force them by whatever means to admit their crime before roumi law. I'll never have any peace otherwise. I'll try to find the address of the teacher Meunier in Constantine. Otherwise, I can write to him at the school! I'll tell him the whole truth. He will help me. He'll find me a lawyer who isn't shady. And now that Yasmine has her voice again, she must study French, too, with Meunier or someone else. I'll work it out with her," he swears to himself.

These resolutions made, a curious sense of comfort relaxes Mahmoud. Does it come from having finally destroyed personal vengeance as the end of this project? He sinks into a somber calm and walks, humming a traditional lament.

The journey back north takes him across a chaos of rocks chiseled by the frost, blown to fragments by enormous thermal extremes. Then, the pulverizing regs. Finally, the steppes of esparto grass, the short but dense green grass turned rusty by the long summers but regenerated with the first rain. With the smallest puff of air, the esparto grass rustles and trembles, skimmed by long phosphorescent ripples whose spreading waves move out to caress the infinite ether filled with powdery light. Two days' camel ride farther to the north, the maquis begins. But that is already the tell. Another world.

Softly rocked by the gait of his mount, Mahmoud thinks of Yasmine. The evocation of this girl, fleeting as it is, troubles his peace and reawakens a dull anxiety. But now that he knows the identities of the assassins, he can no longer take her with him without endangering her. Luckily, they met Khadija at a crucial moment.

"Khadija is a woman who will know how to look out for her," Mahmoud tries to console himself.

This thought, though it does nothing to soothe the wound of their separation, still reassures him about his child's future in his absence. Already he misses Yasmine. Until this moment, Nejma's child has been the concern and delight of every moment. Her absence makes him feel completely empty. Those beautiful eyes, sometimes dreamy, sometimes terrifying, always consumed by thought, always eloquent. Seeing in his mind her small forefinger poking at the ground with the feverishness and grace of a bird in search of a beakful fills him with tenderness. Her words written in the sand, which she always looks at with a sort of joyful and eager surprise, with the solemnity required by exceptional gifts, make Mahmoud proud. Yasmine in her entirety, with her enigmas and questions, Yasmine fragile and introverted, Yasmine formidable in her silence, Yasmine and that newfound voice, a voice of sand and crevices. Yasmine is part of him, like a shooting pulsation. His throat grows tight:

"I will return, Kebdi."

He raises his head, looks into the distance. Like the camels, he breathes in the sky. In his case the indomitable need for solitude and limitlessness living within him actually is a kind of survival instinct, a mysterious dynamic that binds him to nomadism simply to protect him from others and to save him from himself. With the rhythm of his steps or the cadence of camels, he sounds the infinite depths, stripping himself of pretentious cares, cutting down to size the itch of pride. From walking he draws a saving exhaustion, a sort of drunkenness imbibed from the vast spaces, that completely consumes him. The barrenness of the regs and *hamadas* purifies his thoughts, lends them a true asceticism.

His food, already frugal when he is with Yasmine, is reduced to a minimum without her. No preparation is needed beyond the making of mint tea. In a mezoued, he keeps some ma'akra that the good Meftah offered to him before he left. In a small bag he carries tea, dried mint, a block of sugar, and a lot of peanuts. Hanging on one of his packsaddles is a guerba full of water.

Each evening, when the sky turns purple and the shadows of the camels and his own stretch out to immense lengths, he stops, puts his packsaddles on the ground, and hobbles the camels. Then he starts looking for dried twigs for a fire, the longest part of preparing tea. Squatting by the fire, he eats three or four balls of ma'akra and a fistful of peanuts while drinking tea. He loves this curious mixture of ma'akra and peanuts in his mouth. At one and the same time salty, sugary, and peppery, combined in the softness of the dates, full of butter and washed down by tea, it is incomparably delicious. It provides energy that reinvigorates his body instantly. Then, leaning on one elbow on the ground, Mahmoud opens his tobacco pouch, rolls a cigarette made of tobacco and kif, and smokes while sipping several more glasses of tea. When his legs stop moving, he always has the strange sensation that something continues walking inside him at the same pace, with the same peace, as his own steps. Is it the simple setting in motion of his spirit at last freed from the iron rule of mechanical motion? Is it the fantastic trot of his dreams always headed off on the craziest epic journeys? Is it the resolute stride of death approaching?

Night falls, sudden and opaque, like a deep sleep. The yelping of jackals, no doubt drawn by the fire and the smell of the animals, rends the silence. Mahmoud lies down on his back, reassured by these familiar signs that soothe away the worries brought on earlier by the dark shadows. His body molds into his bed on the ground, pressing down with all its weariness. He admires the sky, a field of stars crossed by ripples as if beneath gusts of wind. Their twinkling engenders poems in Mahmoud, sparkling above his nostalgia. Tonight for him the stars are a harvest of the distant laughter of women. His fatigue is swallowed up by the darkness. His body grows light, floats under the dome of constellations. He is inside a cozy womb. He is a child of the plateau:

"One day, I will meet another women I will love." A shooting star carries him into the land of sleep.

Four days later he arrives at Mecheria. The round of several stalls informs him that no merchant has seen Hassan.

"Could this man have gone toward the South? Or was he in such a hurry to get back to the tell that he didn't stop along the way? Maybe he has a reason for always avoiding this town?"

Mahmoud can make all the conjectures he pleases. He is left, nonetheless, with one sure thing: Hassan hasn't passed through here. Because here, as in the other *ksour* of the plateaus and the desert, while the women in the mechtas are engaged in multiple tasks, men have no other occupation than to "hold up the walls."

As soon as they've drunk their morning tea, they go out, slowly arriving one by one. After a brief "salaam," they squat down or stretch out, leaning on one elbow in the shade of the north wall in summer, in the sun of the south wall in winter. And, sunk in a sort of plaintive hebetude, they scrutinize the void. They are so motionless you'd think they were asleep. But from time to time, one of them makes a comment that, as if by a sort of contagion, draws from the line of hoods a buzz like clouds of flies. All bits of news, all miscellaneous facts, fall like beads come unstrung in this way, anonymous complaints trapped at the foot of the walls. Beware the foolhardy who expose themselves to their surveillance! Nothing escapes them, ever, in their feigned somnolence. The only way to escape the *mounchars* of their tongues capable of decapitating even the hardest heads is to join them, to "hold up the wall." In fact, to be there among the very first! Because this tribunal of the ksour, sitting against the wall, is pitiless, and its only impartiality is that it spares no one. That is how the men of the plateaus are. There are those who walk for a lifetime, and those who sit with their backs glued to the wall.

"Whether we squat against walls that dissolve into mud at the first rain, or we abandon them to go on quests, upright in the midst of the impossible, life touches us all equally with her dagger of hunger," advocates the antiquated philosophy of the *jema'a* of the *hittistes*. "And like a bad hostess, she delivers us thus, dried out skin and bones, all wrinkled, to her eldest son, death. So, although we escape neither hunger nor death, and although we live with empty stomachs, the least we can do is save ourselves from futile weariness by sitting and nourishing ourselves with stories about others. And above all, make sure you keep your viper-women locked up at all times and their hands always busy with wool, lest they weave a web of treachery against you, making of you, without your knowledge, a cuckold, the butt of laughter rippling along the foot of the walls."

"Yet another wild goose chase!" rages Mahmoud.

Despite the absolute solitude he had just been through, he feels in no mood to chat any longer. He uses his extreme fatigue as an excuse to decline all invitations. He leaves his animals at the caravanserai. The *maghreb* call for prayer has scarcely finished anchoring its call in the red anguish of the evening before Mahmoud is in the hammam.

"You are the first customer. Say 'bismi Allah' and enter at your leisure," the proprietor tells him.

Mahmoud takes off his clothes in the dressing room. He helps himself to one of the foutas provided for clients, wraps it around his waist, and enters the hot room. It has been almost two weeks since he really bathed, other than the furtive "washing" in the morning with water from a small calabash. Certainly, economy in water, more than any other resource, is a vital necessity for nomads. Even so, he would have had many chances to bathe during his brief stays in Aïn Sefra had he wished. But building the qobba absorbed his spirit too fully.

The *tayyab* is busy in the hot room. Mahmoud can barely distinguish his familiar brown silhouette in the dense, cottony fog. The only spot that emerges clearly is his red fouta. The rest of his body, blurred as if erased by the thick vapor, seems to float, almost unreal. The man is throwing great pitchers of water on the floor to clean it after the women's visit. Cold water on overheated stone. Then, with a great whoosh, a cloud bursts from the stone, enveloping the frail body with its fouta before absorbing it completely. After a few seconds, when the thickness of the vapor diminishes and spreads out, the fouta reappears, followed by the man blurred and gesticulating like a spectral apparition in a whirlwind of fog.

Fascinated, Mahmoud stands there watching the scene. But surreptitiously, this mist, that immerses him as well, tells him stories with its odors to the point of distraction. His nostrils quivering, he breathes in the moist nakedness of woman. The perfumes of the various parts of her body are there, captured, in the droplets of mist that envelop him. He recognizes them and breathes them in one by one: the smell at once acrid and musky of her armpits, those of ghassoul and henna in her hair, the aroma of hot sand and gorse from her belly, the aroma of waterfowl, moist and peppery, from her sex. Mahmoud's senses, for so long limited to a meager regime of furtive embraces in a few scattered villages of blacks, cry out their need and rebel suddenly against this inhuman treatment, treatment they refuse to submit to any longer. Beneath his fouta his sex is swelling and rising. Troubled, Mahmoud sits down by a column. To hide his state, he takes cold water and dowses himself. But the tentacles of these essences are there, holding him from all sides like a woman maddened with passion. His imagination plunges him precipitously into the vertigo of his fantasies.

"The hammam is home to all my deliriums," Mahmoud thinks with a smile.

The tayyab brings him a bucket of steaming hot water.

"Do you want me to give you a short massage, rub your back?" he asks.

Mahmoud certainly would have liked that. He knows the tayyab's dexterity when it comes to soothing knotted muscles and relaxing the body. But with his heart thumping, his sex persisting on brandishing its rebellious erection through the fouta, his mouth so dry despite the great dampness of the place, the man would be able to sense his arousal. He might mistake his motives. Mahmoud responds with a shake of his head. Luckily, other clients are arriving. The tayyab goes over to them, leaving him in peace.

"After the bath, I'll go eat a big couscous with meat. Then, I'll go to the 'big house,'" Mahmoud murmurs to himself, hoping to liberate his body from the grasp of his senses.

"And then tomorrow I'll continue north, I'll look for El-Majnoun," he adds after a moment's thought.

With the promise of satisfying both the needs of the body and the spirit, the rushing of blood eases in his head. His breathing becomes calmer bit by bit. A sort of communion between all his parts, in the expectation of being satiated, leaves him at peace. At last he begins to wash himself.

Living in a kheïma is like inhabiting the bed of the wind. At the least breath, it comes inside, importuning. Its odysseys raise and fill the sails of dreams. Its songs intoxicate you with the longing to move on. The kheïma tosses, pulls at its ropes. The camels complain, the whites of their eyes showing, their nostrils quivering. Even the sheep raise their heads at the wind's passage, and their bleating vibrates suddenly with an unsuspected tremolo. The nomads recall the wind's follies. It blows across their wake and erases their footsteps. Like the wind, they are here, they are there, they are beyond all frontiers. And, just when you think you've got them, they are already far away. Their kheïma does not even protect them from cold. It is only a chimera where the winds sing, a pretext for sleep, a quilt made of dreams, folded up upon waking when it is time to follow the wind along paths leading nowhere.

Mahmoud says to himself as he walks, "El-Majnoun even has this wind in his head. How am I going to find this madman again? In spite of the scant resemblance of his life to the usual life of nomads, he is an authentic nomad nonetheless. A nomad who is *bezef* eccentric, *chouïa* thieving, *chouïa* too rich. A wanderer tacking between folly and extravagance, always outside the paths of reason. He lives in the tell, far from the nomads. His kheïmas stick up insolently in the midst of the settlers' large buildings. He stimulates his deliriums by disturbing the daily lives of sedentary people, whether bourgeois or poor. He avoids the nomadic migration, which he thinks too boring and fruitless. He follows his hallucinations to the point of trespassing into areas where there have been no nomads for a number of years because the settlers, working all the land, have pushed back the maquis day by day. After the expropriations, they'd also cut away at the spaces where the herds grazed. So the pastoral nomads were left with only one set of alternatives: either become sedentary and work for the roumis or go elsewhere, to uncultivated lands, to the high plateaus, or the desert, or scatter to the four winds."

Luckily Mahmoud remembers the location of the small Arab farm where El-Majnoun thought he'd find a horse after his escape from prison. He hopes to get some information there and to pick up his trail, and even that of Hassan.

Two days later, at Aïn el-Hajar, he leaves his camels with a peasant farmer. From that point on it is horse and mule country. The ambling of the camels would draw attention now. No point in arousing curiosity by taking them farther into the tell. The farmer, hesitant at first, ends up giving in to his entreaties and agrees to rent him two horses. In his stable there are three donkeys, two mules, and three horses: two black and one bay. The past suddenly overwhelms the present. Discharged from his memory, other scenes erupt inside his head: his meeting with Nejma, the night of the mad squalls spent on a carpet of dung. It is all there before his eyes and in his nostrils, while in his ear Nejma's voice whispers to him the legend of "the man on the bay horse."

"Magnificent, aren't they?" the farmer brags, thinking him struck by the splendor of his animals.

"Oh, yes," Mahmoud agrees obligingly. "The bay has a superb coat, my favorite color."

The deal concluded satisfactorily, Mahmoud takes to the road again. Once again he is on a journey through the past, on a red horse but without locusts. The fertile fields are there once more. The tell is there once more.

"One's gaze can settle here. Anxious eyes finally find rest here. All these fragile tints, like flowers, bloom. Burning eyelids are soothed. They feel like the velvet of rose petals all of a sudden. On burning skin, stamped by the imprint of incandescent days, the cool air feels like dew. Ears, enclosed for so long by silence, shed their oakum and fill with gentle rustling. Nostrils, beneath the usual veil of sullen dust, quiver, flair, and breathe in the perfume of autumn, a harvest filled with the sap of an entire summer. Thought escapes at last from the pitiless sword of derision, from the stranglehold of eternal landscapes. Teasingly, it dallies between hill and forest. The rushing of water in the streams, the awakening of shivers, heighten their prose. Nature unfurls her excesses, veils her desires for the infinite. She caresses herself, calm and serene. And in her gentle lap, she rocks men with soothing dreams," Mahmoud sings.

He admires the eucalyptus trees. How he loves these disheveled giants, their oblong leaves spreading out with fragrant murmurs. And the olive trees with their incessant shimmering and constellations of fruit. The autumn light, with its violent contrasts, sets ablaze the leaves of the forest that whirr when the wind soughs, and packs black shadows tightly around their trunks.

Mahmoud easily finds the little farm once more. It belongs to three brothers. In reality, the occasional aid they give to El-Majnoun is born neither of cowardice nor of any kind of complicity. The eldest was married to a relative of El-Majnoun. So, their contact with him was limited to the propriety required by this affiliation. But the woman died some five years ago. Little by little, they'd lost sight of the man. However, they'd heard that he'd left the region. Perhaps he'd be able to get more information from Zeyneb bent Lahmar, a woman whose liaison with El-Majnoun had lasted a long time.

Now she lives in the village of Tolga, between Sebdou and Tlemcen.

The men offer tea to Mahmoud but maintain their reserve, not saying anything one way or the other about El-Majnoun.

What an astonishing woman that Zeyneb is. She lives in a modest but attractive and well-maintained house. A pair of elderly servants see to the upkeep of the house. She has no children. No one in town knows where she came from. "Surely from some bordello," they say. "Where else could a woman alone and with money have come from? She bought the house three years ago. After renovating it, she moved in." While they don't know about her past life, they do know that for the past two years, rich and powerful lovers have been protecting her. It is even rumored that one of them is a roumi.

The servant lets Mahmoud in. He then climbs a narrow stairway leading to a terrace, onto which the room for *diffa* opens. It is a salon without any furniture, with walls hung with velvet and a floor covered with a thick carpet. Cushions of all sizes and shapes offer themselves to your body. Mahmoud sits down comfortably. As soon as the servant disappears, a woman's silhouette fills the doorway. She stops on the sill and looks him over. Mahmoud can only see her shadow. Then the woman comes forward. She is no longer youthful, but what he sees above all, and especially what is suggested by her body, which seems to undulate rather than walk, is a sensuality that almost suffocates him. She smiles. Her smile shows she is used to this reaction, to this gleam in men's eyes, which she receives like a flower. Then, in a soothing voice, she says:

"Salaam 'aleïk."

"Ou 'aleïki salaam," replies Mahmoud, regaining control of himself. "I am Mahmoud Tijani, from the days of . . ."

"The man on the bay horse!" she exclaims with surprise. So here you are then? But where have you been all this time? El-Majnoun looked for you everywhere! Do you know that in these parts you're a hero of epic proportion? Women sing of you."

"If only they knew what a sad and piteous man their hero is. If they only knew!" Mahmoud thought with irony, before saying:

"Yes, yes, I know the legend, although I didn't know it was

so important. However, the only thing I have in common with the myth is the color of my horse."

"And the same name and the same itinerary beginning with a certain ride when red was not only the color of your horse. Friend, I find it very foolish of you to have come back here. Especially mounted on a bay horse! It's a provocation that could cost you your life! The people from the Sirvant estate, exasperated by the inability of their policemen to find you, have been offering for years now a large sum of money for whoever finds you. Since then, I myself know of at least one who . . ."

"El-Majnoun?"

"No, that's not his style. But it is exactly like Hassan. El-Majnoun would have liked to find you, too, certainly, for other projects. I don't know what they were, but from his impatience I gathered they were important. To tell you the truth, I don't know which of the two was more dangerous in your case."

"Where can I find them? Where is El-Majnoun?"

"El-Majnoun? It will soon be five years since he left."

"Where did he go then?"

"Oh, long before he left in body, he was already in that land from which there is no return . . ."

"You know that red, that conflagration—I had no part in it. It was the work of El-Majnoun. Did you know that?"

"Back then I didn't wear myself out anymore by trying to distinguish what was true in what El-Majnoun said. He had already been, for a very long time, in that country where the borders are closed, where I could no longer follow him: madness. Did he tell you that his grandfather was a pirate?"

"Yes, he took great pride in it, it seemed to me."

"This grandfather was his pride and joy, his role model. One day the idea occurred to him to become a pirate himself, but better, a king of the desert! He maintained that the women of the desert were more liberated and more rebellious than those of the tell. His idea was to convince them to break away from their men and to form an army around him that would capture desert caravans and hold them for ransom. In spite of all my affection for him, I couldn't follow him. No woman has lived around him for very long. They all end up fleeing in complete terror. All except for me. I was always there. I'll tell you why. Maybe it is my own kind of madness. I stayed despite my fear of him, despite my fear for him. I was a woman who lived in fear. However, back then he would have brief moments of lucidity from time to time. A sort of calm amid the fury of satanic desires that pierced him. Then he was truly marvelous. But it didn't last. As years went by, the moments got rarer and rarer and finally disappeared altogether. At the beginning of our liaison, I followed him everywhere. Then I forgot about that, preferring not to know about his activities. He'd disappear for months on end. One evening he'd reappear, unshaven, thinner, and often even wounded, but always with all sorts of booty. And much more abundant even were his clouds of words. Words that were jeering, arrogant, cruel. Words suggesting all the vices . . .

"Did he leave with Hassan?"

"Yes. I never understood their strange relationship. Everything was a pretext for El-Majnoun to heap scorn on Hassan. At the same time, he acted as if he couldn't get by without him. Such that if Hassan was the valet of all his whims, the outlet for all his bitterness, he was equally indispensable for any long trip. Hassan, you know, no longer has all his wits. But his insanity is more unpredictable. In other words, more dangerous, in my opinion. The mere sight of him gave me the shivers. He seemed to have an implacable hate for El-Majnoun, mixed at moments with an undeniable veneration. Impossible to fathom! Some saw in it a case of extreme jealousy and suggested they had homosexual relations, saying El-Majnoun took his valet when he didn't have any women. And often he didn't have any. But you, why are you looking for them?"

"I have an old debt to settle."

"Oh, I guess I'd rather not know."

"You haven't seen them since?"

"No. Every once in a long while, I hear news from travelers returning from the south, especially from a certain Behi."

"It seems to me I saw Hassan a little more than seven years ago around Mecheria, and three weeks ago in Aïn Sefra."

"Are you sure?"

Her astonishment seems sincere.

"It's been five years, probably. That would match with their journey to the south. But . . ."

"I will find them again."

"Friend. Why chase the tempest when it has spared you? Go back where you came from. There you are safe from the law of the roumis, the Sirvants, El-Majnoun, and Hassan, because none of them has managed to find you."

Mahmoud is careful not to reveal his motives. He looks at this disconcerting woman. Questions about her crowd his thoughts. He silences them. Her skin is amber and there are sparks of gold in her eyes. She has the smile of a woman certain she is being looked at. They drink tea in silence.

"Friend, would you like to be my guest tonight?" she asks after a moment.

"Nothing would please me more," he quickly replies in a voice that reveals his excitement.

She gets up and leaves the room. Mahmoud continues to sip his tea. A great peace reigns in the douar. The door is opened onto the sky. A violet blue sky so intense, so profound, that it seems to be hung like linen over the white terrace. Without the white splotches of sun, without the coating of dust from a hard day, the blue dusk smelling like warm honey has the color of purity. The muezzin's guttural voice rends the silence, turns back on itself, fills with anguish and spirals up through the dying day. The sky remains calm, spreading before the door the arrogant splendor of its steel blue.

After a time, the woman returns with a *meïda*. The servant brings dishes: an aromatic *h'rira*, a tajine of olives smelling of coriander, caraway, and cinnamon. A small pitcher of cool wine is there. Zeyneb serves him. While he drinks, words that were written the first evening he experienced intoxication flood into his mind, and he recites them for his hostess:

"Grapes? Dry—from this time forward, my friends, I do not want them that way ever again, even to sugar my couscous. I do not want them green, firm, and fleshy like the nipples of nursing women filling with milk. I want it only as the blood of that final fermentation. I want it as the red sun of my thoughts. I want the world order to be overturned by it . . ."

He drank more and more. It was a smooth wine that left an aftertaste of bitter tannin on his tongue. Cool on the palate, it heats up as it descends, pouring its warm breath over his relaxing body. From mouthful to mouthful to the bottom of the pitcher, it is an enchanted voyage through a strange country. Night comes and wraps the terrace in its black folds. The house is a ship that pitches on the obscure swells of the evening.

Mahmoud, drunk, loses all track of time. . . . It is not without pain that a week later, he manages to tear himself from the arms of the beautiful Zeyneb to return to his long journey to the south. But he swears, promises, to come back to lose himself there again and again.

10

Mahmoud is not in prison. This knowledge frees the Hamani. Thus, the decision to leave for the winter pastures is made quickly. The Jew Benichou, who has come to bring the good news, is about to leave when Yasmine gets his attention. Noting her feverishness, he looks at her. She bends down then and writes on the sand:

"I would like some paper."

Benichou comes closer and reads her sentence out loud. Then he looks around at those gathered to find an explanation for this request, which is curious to say the least.

"She has now found her voice, if it was ever lost! We've heard it. So, what is the meaning of these affectations? Who else around here besides her father can understand her? Why does she refuse to speak to others?" one Hamani asks indignantly.

"Her voice is still injured. She has to nurse it," Khadija explains. Then turning to Benichou:

"Before leaving, her father charged her with writing the tormented history of her family.

"Write the history? And . . . by a girl!"

This was the first time they'd heard of such nonsense. What need is there of writing, a paper shroud for transmitting facts? In the realm of orality and of nomadism, the only human vestiges are tombs, and even they do not last for long. The sands retain only the tracings of the wind. The sands are the writings of eternity. Speech itself is living memory. It weaves the burning links of gazes along the thread of generations.

Given their consternation, Khadija realizes how inspired she has been to invent this white lie. If she had told them that the father had asked his daughter to write down poems and stories, they'd have been even more dumbfounded. His fingers fumbling in his beard, Benichou smiles. He is the only one smiling. After a moment, he breaks the silence:

"I'll give her some paper. Do you want a lot?"

Yasmine nods her head.

"Bachir, take the donkey Kherbiche and accompany *Si* Benichou," Khadija adds quickly, cutting short all discussion.

Bachir, happy to render some service to Yasmine, rushes toward his small donkey.

Now the days are short and the long nights glacial. In the early morning, athwart the frosty stubbornness of the sky, the sun seems pale. You can see it, but you can't feel it. Cold sticks to your skin, runs down the rusty spine of your back for a long time. With its fictive presence, it deceives you at the break of day by the false light the color of lunar tin. It freezes the landscape, sketching its flat spaces with a line so cold it takes on a ghostly aspect. Children don't budge. They are in a sort of stupor between sleep and numb awakening. You have to wait. When the warmth finally beams down and chases the last shivers of cold from your body, life returns gently. Your limbs unknot. Your spirit comes to life. Women light the kanouns, preparing tea. This hot liquid pours other splashes of sunlight down your throat. Only then do the day's activities begin.

They've left Aïn Sefra and crossed the magnificent gorges of Moghrar, a land of blasted black rocks forever caught in a moment of petrified anger. As the day progresses, the sun orchestrates a dazzling score of metallic tints. Coiled amid the chaos of rock is an oasis that lends this harsh, magnificent setting a note of coolness. The violence and contrasting colors of the desert. Then Hajerath M'guil and its wadi full of esparto grass, pink acacias, turpentine trees, and lentisks. Higher up on the plateau, the grass is more plentiful, certainly, but winter is more unforgiving there and the daily extremes of temperature murderous. They will await summer to go back to the esparto grass of the steppes. Their survival is thus a continual struggle against the ferocity of desert summers and the murderous winters on the high plateaus, an eternal compromise between entrancing aridity and excessive temperatures.

Yasmine uses up paper. Holding it, caressing it, feeling it, crumpling it, and hearing its whisper were delightful. The children watch her with half-intrigued, half-anxious faces. The men spy on her with suspicion and disapproval. The women, for want of having been able to reshape her and fashion her in the mold of their traditions, watch her closely and criticize her.

"Won't she bring trouble upon us?" asks one of the wool carders with honest anxiety.

"You know how her mother died! Allah protect us!" respond the spinners in a chorus, distaffs bobbing.

"Let's hope her father comes back soon to take her off our hands," the littlest of the wool workers chimed in all together.

Behind the screen of her loom, that absolute emblem of the companionship of wool working, Khadija refuses to participate in the condemnation, extending her protection to Yasmine. Yasmine's other ally is the young shepherd Bachir, who vows his unlimited admiration for her and cheers her with his wild flute. Sometimes 'Aicha whirls about her at a careful distance. She throws her mischievous looks, teases her silence with ricochets of laughter. She minces toward Yasmine, risking now and then brief interludes of provocation or seduction. Her naïveté always comes up against Yasmine's gravity. Then 'Aicha shakes it off. She rears back, spins about, and with a lively step, goes to spread her joyfulness far from this mystery.

When the warm breath of the sun unknots her limbs, Yasmine leaves the kheïma. Carrying the small satchel that Khadija has woven for her under her arm, she sits at a distance. The bag contains her precious flask of perfume and her writing desk: her pen, object of her most jealous attentions, some *midad*, two notebooks, one for poems, the other for stories, and finally her *louha*, the wooden slate used by students at Qur'anic schools although she has always preferred the convenience of sand. Sitting crosslegged, the *louha* propped on her knees to serve as a support for the notebooks, she writes. She writes in a small, tight hand to economize on paper use. She concentrates hard, sticking out her tongue. Sometimes she stops, raises her head, and smiles. In her ear her father is whispering the plot of her story. She lowers her head and continues. She is completely happy in these moments. Moments that she prolongs at leisure, as long as the biting of the cold does not drive her back to the camp.

She swings with the beat of her heart from poem to song, swings with the arc of her dreams from story to legend, transforming solitude into conquest. She writes down her father's stories. Her favorite is the story of the "daughter of the dog," which she narrates in her own fashion. In it her mother becomes the daughter of her own imagination, her own myth. She imagines her . . . She imagines her as the illegitimate daughter of the chief of a white tribe. She imagines this fellow would probably have killed her because he had many daughters and no son. Four women repudiated, and seven others living in his kheïmas, have definitively destroyed in him all hope of having a son one day.

"It's a fiendish plot of women who wish me ill!" he had the habit of thundering.

Neither scholars nor magicians had been able to cure him of this terrible curse. So he became embittered and ferocious toward all those linked to him by allegiance. She describes his tyranny and his misogyny. She imagines that the black mother abandoned her child in the hope of preserving the child's life in the face of her husband's murderous fury. The child, saved by the milk of a dog who stayed by her after the departure of the tribe, will be rescued by other nomads and will become a storyteller of great renown. She will be a woman who walks in the desert and in songs, followed by her dog in search of her father's tribe. She finds this "father" whose dignity has been crushed by an avalanche of daughters. He likes her songs and invites her to come entertain him amid his tribe. Entertain? Why, yes! She came just for that! Then, after a few pure Andalusian songs, she sings him one of her own creation:

"Son of a she-dog, son of a man so overwhelmed by having only daughters that he becomes completely disinterested in the pregnancies of his wives. So they avenge themselves by leaving the only son he ever had by a spring . . . Nursed by a dog, the boy survived. He was already barking when a tribe found him. They say on nights when the moon is full, he still howls out his hatred, cursing his unknown father."

A seed of doubt is planted. The singer of the story disappears. In vain the man rushes off to find her. He chases after the legend of this son for a long time and dies in despair. The storyteller, avenged, tastes her joy from afar.

Yasmine's thoughts dally, intoxicated by words. The words flare up and clothe the nakedness of straight lines with the relief of dreams. Then Yasmine also tells herself the story of Isabelle Eberhardt. A belle called Isa, whose fair skin is bronzed, haloed by intelligence. Dressed as a Bedouin for freedom of movement, she walks outside the beaten path. And on nights when the moon is opalescent, Isabelle has the ebony tint of her mother and her father's brio to tell her life story. When that happens, all the dead of the desert, both man and beast, rise up, throwing off their coverings of earth and, dressed in light, come on foot to the dune of Aïn Sefra to hear her.

From afar the others watch her:

"The way that girl behaves is a sacrilege!" pontificate the combers of wool.

"Who knows what she is writing?" say the carders, the vengeful teeth of their combs biting into the wool.

"Won't she cast a spell over us? Won't she dabble, like all women whom misfortune has cast outside the circle of daily life, in the occult?" grumbles one of the spinners, suddenly yanking her spindle in a fit of imagination.

"She needs a man, one with some *lahia*!" decide Khadija's sons, beside themselves.

Only Khadija, Bachir, and Merbouh, the old dog, go now and then to join her, for they always see her with their hearts and admire her.

The Hamani cross paths with the Ouled Khallil one day. The two tribes have known each other for a long time. These meetings, which set the rhythm for their respective wanderings, do not happen just by chance. They are part of a ritual long awaited and celebrated. But these reunions are so dependent upon the exigencies of the grazing of their herds that sometimes they are reduced to the sharing of tea to mark friendship or to a brief exchange of goods and news. At other times, when grazing permits it, the two tribes spend several days together. That allows them to carry out diverse projects: circumcisions, marriages . . .

This reunion intimidates Yasmine. By the extent of their herds, the number of their camels, and the imposing size of their kheïmas, she imagines that these are well-off folks, and from that she draws a second dose of anxiety. She watches them unloading the packsaddles. Then she gathers up her little satchel, and with the old dog Merbouth at her heels, she distances herself from the agitation of the camp that is being set up. Forgotten by the others, she writes, forgetting herself. The sun is a hot kiss on her body, which offers itself to it. And the sky is a tender eye. The dog, sitting down on the ground, looks at her. From time to time she caresses it with a distracted hand. Used to being the target of small boys' aggression, the animal rubs against this friendly hand and wags its tail to show its gratitude.

"The two useless ones have found each other: the hartania who writes and the mangy old dog that doesn't guard anything anymore," say the mocking children from a distance.

How long is she absorbed in writing before a faint sound right next to her makes her jump? A man from the Ouled Khallil is there, just a few steps away. Standing with hands behind his back, he is watching her.

"You are writing?" he asks stupidly.

He is about the age and size of her father. But his body is heavier. His fleshy face lends him a certain smoothness. As she does not answer, the man adds:

"What are you writing?"

He pauses.

"Do you know you are very pretty?"

Yasmine looks fearfully at him. His stiff gentility, his drawling, guttural voice augur nothing good. Almost upon arriving the Ouled Khallil heard about the girl who writes . . . the hartania.

"For some obscure reason she walls herself up in an impenetrable silence. So be it. At least her muteness protects her from the nonsense women love to feed on," the man thinks. "But writing? And that gaze at once candid and shameless, that doesn't lower itself before mine. At her age, any other girl would have bent her head, lowered her eyes, and blushed from confusion. What does a girl without obedience and modesty to honor her tribe amount to?"

A gentleness quite alien to his intransigent personality reins in the man's sermons and muzzles him. Fascinated and deeply troubled, he stands there paralyzed, his eyes riveted on her. And instead of righteous anger, a different flame rises dumbly within him. Vexation at feeling himself suddenly so vulnerable in front of this strange girl, and propriety toward his hosts, oblige him to turn away from her and go back, with slow steps, toward the camp.

As soon as the sun is at an oblique angle, its embers glow red but no longer give off heat. Coming out of nowhere, a perfidious cold lodges harshly in the soft flesh of a body left imprudently uncovered. And the fires of the sunset are still consuming the skies when the first shivers begin piercing through to exposed flesh. Yasmine puts her paraphernalia in her satchel. She takes out the small flask of perfume, opens it, and inhales until it burns the depths of her nostrils. Eyes closed, she breathes in again until her memory thrills and her heart warms. Then she closes it, hides it in her satchel, and goes toward the kheïma.

She hangs the satchel on the beam of the tent and pulls on her jellaba. It is the only piece of men's clothing that she has managed to preserve from Khadija's confiscations. Thus clad, she strolls among the tents. The arrival of the cold has driven the others into the kheïmas. In the largest of the Ouled Khallil tents, the men are sitting around kanouns. The women in small groups are preparing dinner. Some are rolling couscous, others are cooking bread on tajines. As she passes by, the conversation stops. This unusual silence stops Yasmine in her tracks in front of the tents. Through the raised flaps, eyes made feverish by the glow of the embers pierce the violet shadow of the interior, rest on her, and cling to her robe.

"A girl in a jellaba? Why doesn't she put on a fouta or a mendil appropriate for girls? To be sure, this one has accumulated all sorts of eccentricities!" scold these eyes.

But one gaze stands out from this silent and dark fury—that of the stroller who, a bit earlier, had come to watch her. That man devours her so voraciously it makes her shiver and go away to escape him. The murmuring starts again around the braziers like drones buzzing round candle stubs.

Yasmine goes back to the kheïma she shares with Khadija and

Bachir. From a small wooden chest she takes out her favorite books, the *Roba'yat* of Omar Khayyam and *A Thousand and One Nights*. She smoothes the paper, straightens the curled edges, smiles at them. Then, with greedy eyes shining, she begins reading. After a moment, Bachir, bursting with overexcitement, joins her:

"Ahmed Khallil wants to marry you. He says that he'll give sheep, camels, and carpets. My brothers are pleased. But Khadija is not in favor!"

This last phrase is beaded with joyous laughter. He does a somersault, rolls across the ground, and crouches down in front of her. Yasmine shares neither his exuberance nor his high spirits. She is suddenly tense with worry.

"Mama said no!" the boy repeats trying to persuade her.

And to give weight to his assertions, he energetically shakes his head no. But a glimmer of suspicion remains in Yasmine's eyes.

"If she had said yes, I would have come to get you, here where you are. I would have taken you on Kherbiche, my small donkey. Just you with your writing and your perfume. We would have gone to the Jew Benichou or farther, as far as the place where the locusts come from. They would not have found you. But Mama said no! She said, 'If you wish, I'll give you 'Aicha, but not Yasmine.' He said, 'It is the hartania I want!' She said, 'You'll take 'Aicha!' All the others are afraid of Mama. Mama is a real man!"

Yasmine smiles. He is so unaccustomed to this smile that he retreats, intimidated. With the suppleness of a cat, he sits down in the opening of the tent and taking his flute from the pocket of his jellaba, offers its joy to the silence of the night. At the first notes, 'Aicha appears wavering and ruddy in the glow of the oil lamp. She gathers her dress up around her tapered legs, taps her feet, clinks her *kholkhals*, and bobs her head. The sight of

216

her invigorates Bachir's flute. Her eyes sparkling with laughter, her movement drunk with pleasure, 'Aicha dances. Soon her radiant nymph's body and the music seem to merge. Fascinated, Yasmine forgets about reading. Suddenly, a fouta covering her head, 'Aicha's mother, one of the shrewish spinners, comes running. She slaps her daughter violently and pushes her inside the kheïma. There she joins her and pinches her with a twist of the hand:

"Have you no shame! Do you want to ruin my reputation? Viper! I could wring your neck! I'm going to marry you off right away—that'll fix you."

'Aicha is crying. Her mother goes out muttering all sorts of threats. 'Aicha isn't a rebel. Rebellion isn't the reason 'Aicha hasn't internalized the taboos. She's just heedless. But if slaps and scolding sometimes bring large tears to her eyes, they seem only to make her laughter more iridescent, laughter that flashes out, mowing down censure. 'Aicha is frivolous. 'Aicha is a firefly flitting above these small dramas.

"Why don't you take the roumis' *el-machina* to go to the south? You'll get there quickly with less fatigue!" Zeyneb had said to Mahmoud when he was leaving her.

El-machina is what people from the region call the small train that stops down there, bumping against the black dunes of the mines of Kenadsa in the desert. In the late 1930s the nomads still looked at it apprehensively as it crossed the high plateaus. Every day, that devilish wood and iron reptile violates the regs and the hamadas crucified under the sun. It runs on, following the blinding obstinacy of its rails, bringing the armed roumis into the heart of this silent land. At each station, it spits, farts, burps, and from all its orifices, defecates the men in yellow who infest the place like locusts. Not only are they the color of locusts, they are also as voracious and have a propensity to move about in clouds that devastate the very dignity of the 'arbi. They have peppered the rail line with forts. And starting at Kheïder, the lone stations disguise themselves as small forts.

"El-machina moves almost as fast as the wind," said the nomads.

At first sight, it had terrified the nomads' children. With passing years, they've become used to its panting whistle, to its distant crawl as it slithers along the horizons. And while the nomads, who fiercely reject all inventions of sedentary folks and all intrusions into the country of baroud, refuse to use it still, its use is nonetheless widespread among the people from the towns and ksour.

"With el-machina, one morning you're listening to the song of the sea, and the next your ears are filled with the oakum of the desert," they say.

Crossings that take even the best caravans at least several weeks can be done in just a day and a night. And if some travelers complain about headaches they get from the fracas that goes with it, all admit that the body is less shaken than by the lurching of camel caravans.

"But these are the opinions of people who know little of travel by camel," thinks Mahmoud. "As for speed and saving time! Time has always tied the tightest of the knots around the dreams of sedentary people. Their whole lives long, those uptight citizens of towns think that only speed can master the flight of time." Then, furious at himself, Mahmoud realizes, "Wait, maybe it's because of that cursed train that I've always lost Hassan's trail! What an idiot I am that that idea never even occurred to me."

To find Hassan he'll have to find El-Majnoun again in any case. His meeting with the beautiful Zeyneb, in addition to its other advantages, has assured him of one thing about his risky pursuit: he has to go to Adrar to find someone named Behi in order to know how to find El-Majnoun. As for Hassan, Zeyneb knows of no family, no attachment anywhere other than to El-

Majnoun. Another of Zeyneb's revelations encourages him to go toward the desert:

"Both of them follow the prudent principle of always announcing that they are heading off one direction, and then systematically they go the other."

And Hassan had insisted to one of the merchants at the ksar in Aïn Sefra that he was heading north.

The Hamani are no longer at Aïn Sefra. A harsh wind convulses, rages, and flays the dune into long strips of sand. Under the whip of its frenzy, the leafless and spectral silhouettes of the poplars creak as if they were metal. Stripped of the yellow adornments of summer, the palm trees look naked before Mahmoud's sorrowful gaze. And without the bluish, phosphorescent blur of the orchard leaves to bolster their great height, the palm trunks look fragile, in danger of breaking. They pull themselves upright, stretch themselves, and dip their crests into the bowl of the sky, stirring up the blue with a crackling like sparks. The ksar is paralyzed, huddled behind its sordid walls. Cold and the absence of Yasmine put a chill on Mahmoud's solitude, and he feels suddenly prostrated and dispossessed.

"It's already been two months since I left," he realizes.

During his return to Aïn Sefra, the desire to see his daughter is so strong it hides the onslaught of doubts. Absence and distress burn courage to cinder. For a moment, Mahmoud dreams of going to find her before taking the road south. It was as if, by some compelling power in the magic of her silence, this girl could, despite the distances, enter into the most secret of Mahmoud's thoughts, detect his smallest failings, her gaze rising out of the sands to home in on him. What does that look say? How will she react to the return of a father who is once again empty-handed?

"With a glum muteness more expressive than a thousand condemnations . . . surely," Mahmoud says to himself.

Already those eloquent eyes disturb him with their reproaches.

Already they are looking down, lids heavy with weariness and disappointment. Already, they begin to torture him.

"No, better the most boring of solitudes than their disaffection. Yasmine, my nymph, are you talking? Are you writing?"

He gets up. Walking behind the camels with resolute strides, he enters the ksar.

"I'll put the animals in Meftah's care. Tomorrow, I'll take el-machina to Bechar. And from there, I'll find a caravan going to Adrar," he decides.

The sight of him moves the placid Meftah. Scarcely is the door open when he grabs him by the burnous and hauls him inside the courtyard. Then, without a word, he sticks his head out cautiously to inspect the street. Luckily, the call to prayer has emptied it out. Meftah quickly bolts the door and, still rolling his eyes fearfully, lets out a noisy sigh of relief.

"Brother, you mustn't show yourself in this town! Men in uniform are looking for you. They have your exact description."

"Hassan, that rat!" Mahmoud hisses between his teeth.

Meftah tells him how the Hamani woman and Yasmine came to know the Jewish merchant Benichou during his absence.

"I've got to go see the man, if only to pay him for the paper and to thank him."

"So be it," says Meftah. "But you'll see him here. It's useless to run the risk of getting yourself caught. Benichou is a good and wise man. He'll come."

Invited to Meftah's home, Benichou meets Mahmoud that evening. He tells Mahmoud of his two meetings with his daughter, the anguish she felt in front of the prison, her strange request, and the explanations given by Khadija.

"In addition to paper, I also gave her some old books I had. I will try to get some more for her next trip here.

"A thousand thanks, kind man. But why such devotion to a stranger?"

"I asked myself the same question and was at a loss to order and understand my own motives. How can I explain it to you? One thing is sure . . . she exerts a compelling force, a sort of violence that waylays your gaze in a moment, that stops you in your tracks. At least it was that way in my case. And once I discovered the extraordinary language of her eyes, I was captive to their fire. A gaze a million miles from childhood, tradition, obedience. Writing is only one of the ways she keeps her distance from others. She incarnates otherness, and even the color of her skin bears the mark of difference. Look at how I'm talking to her father, I've forgotten my usual caution about being circumspect."

Mahmoud's unspoken distress doesn't escape Benichou, who hastens to add:

"Man of culture and poetry, please don't take my remarks as a sign of disrespect."

"Did she speak to you?" asks Mahmoud.

"No, to the great displeasure of the Hamani."

Mahmoud winces, giving his smile a sad and enigmatic air that increases Benichou's embarrassment. But Mahmoud encourages him to continue with his story.

"And then there was that woman, Khadija, with her eyes full of laughter, with her charmed speech so unctuous and fragrant.

"You poor victim of women," Mahmoud jokes, now completely at ease.

Relieved to see him find his bantering tone again, Benichou laughs heartily before continuing:

"Finally, your story as a hunted man, tracked both by settlers and by men in uniform, intrigued me. Any rebellion awakes in me an ancient echo of jubilation. As far back as I have been able to trace it, my family history is a series of flights. Fleeing Spain and the Inquisition, they settled on the Moroccan coast. Their descendants barely escaped the massacre at Tétouan in the sixteenth century. They took refuge in Tlemcen. And there, in 1897, my father, pursued by vicious settlers, only saved his skin thanks to a caravan of nomads who had come to buy supplies from him. He spent a number of months living among them on the high plateaus. Behind my mother's back, the whole family whispered that he had fallen madly in love with a nomad woman and had, wittingly, prolonged his visit.

"After having vented all their wrath against the wealthy Jews, the settlers' rage finally abated. By then not only did my father run scant risk of returning to a sedentary life, but he had in addition become himself a danger for the clan. One day they indicated to him that he had to leave. Three men were delegated to take him to Aïn Sefra and leave him there. In the face of the brazen laws of religions, affections disintegrate, alas, into dust. You know very well that our two races have lived in harmony for centuries, but they have hardly mixed with one another. They say that my father was on the verge of madness, that he gave himself over to all sorts of debauchery for a long time."

He is quiet for a moment. His eyes are a dark dream in which softness and flame move. His nervous fingers fumble around in the fleece of his beard. Mahmoud respects his silence. Soon, flicking his *chechia* back on his head, Benichou continues:

"To tell you the truth, I have always felt myself in the debt of nomads. Whether it is a true debt of honor or just frustration, I really have no idea."

The pitcher and the meïda arrive just in time to break the heavy silence that suddenly weighs on the two men. During the meal they carry on a banal and easy conversation.

Their complicity is woven on the loom of their affinities. Late into the night they are still there, sitting on the sheepskins, talking, baring their hearts. One after the other, the sounds of the house die out. In the only other room Meftah's wife and five children are stretched out against one another under one cover. Meftah, muffled in his jellaba, sleeps with his head resting on one arm. It is a sleep burgeoning with snores, broken by brief abrupt awakenings caused by the laughter of the two men. The late January wind grips the night. It hurls itself against the walls of the dechra. Its freezing venom seeps in under the door. The glowing of the kanoun has disappeared beneath a bed of cinder. From time to time a pernicious gust of wind disturbs it and illuminates an ember that bursts into flame suddenly, like an eye brutally aroused from a gentle somnolence beneath the soft cover of cinder, one which opens wide, half dazed, half infuriated. An ephemeral gleam gapes at the room, soon to be covered again by a crumbling eyelid. At the bottom of the large teapot, there is probably still a bit of tea, barely warm.

"Listen, I think I've just come up with an excellent idea. Are you registered with the state?" Benichou asks suddenly.

"Of course, my family couldn't avoid that. And also, I needed papers to travel outside the country. It would seem I am all too clearly registered in the accursed paperwork of the settlers."

Benichou seems confused. After a moment of reflection, his face lights up again:

"It's all the same after all! You need only to hide those pieces of identity and to file for a false identity. Necessity brings poor wretches everyday to ask for identity papers. By changing your appearance a bit, you could travel freely through towns without fear of being stopped. Believe me, this is wise council."

Elated by the birth of his ingenious idea, Benichou, deaf to the protestations of Mahmoud, puts the finishing touches on his idea:

"Wait! Wait! You must replace your turban with a chechia. You can keep your saroual, if you wish, but no more 'abaya. You will wear a shirt and coat."

For several moments the flow of his words suspends itself. Afire with intrigue, his eyes scan his listener anxiously, without shame.

"Fixed up in that way and letting your beard and hair grow, you'll be unrecognizable!"

As if struck dumb, Mahmoud doesn't say a word.

"Stay here a couple of days with Meftah or with me, as you

wish. As soon as a beard darkens your face, you'll change clothes and we'll go together to the mayor's office. I have several acquaintances there. That will protect us from any snags. I'll say that you have been my employee for a short time, that you've recently become sedentary, and that you are going to travel with me for commercial reasons. You'll play dumb. Choose names for yourself, your father, and your grandfather. Family name? Say you forgot it. You'll invent the name of a tribe, and then, after a moment's hesitation, another. You'll see a mocking disdain blossom on their faces. Then, without any more hesitation, they will name you, just like all of your brothers who know nothing of their jargon: Senpé!

"Senpé? Why Senpé? I never heard of such a name!" Mahmoud protested.

"Yes, yes, Senpé! From now on, you'll hear it a lot. That's the name given to many nomads forced to become sedentary. The roumis stick them with this name. And they accept it, thinking it is all part of the rules concerning sedentary life. My friend, Senpé pronounced in Arabic is in reality S.N.P., the abbreviation for "sans nom patronymique"—no family name! Contempt of this enormity touches on absurdity."

"And you want me to name myself that! No way!"

"You're really one of your race. What pride! When it comes to freedom, pride is an extremely poisonous luxury. You know who you are. What does Senpé matter if it helps you avoid prison?"

In the face of Mahmoud's stunned look, Benichou bursts into sonorous peals of laughter, rudely awakening Meftah.

"Look," he continued. "Mahmoud is a rare first name, quite Eastern. How's this: Senpé Mohamed ben Ahmed, for example. Thus, you no longer stand out from the run-of-the-mill Arab."

The laughter escaping bit by bit from Mahmoud's stiff lips ignites suddenly as he joins in the hilarity of his companion.

"It's not such a bad idea," he finally admits.

With false solemnity, the framework of his plot now hatched,

Benichou picks up the teapot. He raises it on high and pours. A thin golden thread cascades into the glass, its pearly froth hissing. Benichou's eyes shine with pleasure. He sips the tea noisily in small gulps, clacking his tongue. He yawns, his spirit satiated by this original idea.

"Before leaving, I will give you a letter for my daughter. Could you give it to her when the Hamani pass through here next?"

"You trust a Jew?" Benichou says with irony.

Then seeing Mahmoud's suddenly weary face, he adds:

"You can count on me."

Mahmoud is now called Senpé Mohamed ben Ahmed. To prove it, he possesses a new card in roumi writing, penned by a stranger's hand. Stapled to it is a photograph taken that week, of a different Mahmoud. A Mahmoud all bearded and hairy in his prison of paper. But a Mahmoud with the same eyes. Eyes that recognize him and stare at him with an air of complicity and amusement. In defiance of the power of the strange writing, ignoring the jacket that seems to envelop him, their gaze succeeds in sharing their secret. It proves gently that his true identity is in no way sold out by the simple fact of his being disguised. This lettering does not signify any obedience. It is, on the contrary, a delicious prank against the established order, reducing the authorities to the role of forgers. His truth is contained in the depths of those eyes that remain true to themselves at the center of a face in disguise.

He takes el-machina to reach the desert. If he must live like a city dweller and suffer his constraints, why not take advantage of his resources as well? The train moves off with a clatter of a metal. Accustomed to the silent motion of traveling by camel, Mahmoud is first impressed by the composite, rhythmic noise. The roaring, the panting, the squeaking of wood and metal pounded by pistons. To the accompaniment of this strange concert, the countryside unrolls before the empty gaze of travelers whose shapeless chèches sway. His body brutalized by the rudimentary wooden bench, Mahmoud already misses the familiar comfort of the saddle. But most of all what he misses in front of his gaze is the camel's head with its disdainful and roguish muzzle that, atop the long curve of its neck, concentrates on ignoring, with all the philosophy of a recalcitrant traveler, the ground that tortures it. It is very strange to submit to the paralysis of sedentary folk, who stay frozen in a somber daze as the land unrolls beyond the windows of this monster of wood and iron.

Jagged rocks, phantom redoubts hazardously perched on lonely *bordjs*, open their empty sockets upon cosmic necropolises, crimson hamadas, and cheerless and poignant regs, magnificent in their desolation. The dry hills are colored an unreal sea green, and the sky of metal has an undertow of pitiless light, sometimes a white hot, sometimes an infernal blue, sometimes the color of blood. This rapid uncoiling of empty landscapes blasted by sandstorms, quartered by demonic horizons, scorched to the point of nothingness, clears the head of the last particles of thought and leads painlessly to disincarnation.

At Béchar, the train stops. Movement on the platform. A motley crowd. Béchar, a garrison town with streets laid out in a grid, would be a bastard place without attraction were it not for its wadi, its palm grove, its dune, or its small ksar with twisting, narrow streets and walls of reddish-brown *toub*.

Mahmoud walks slowly toward the wadi. The image of Yasmine immediately flows into his head. He remembers her half fearful fascination with the wadis, which, like magnets, attracted their feet. Here as elsewhere the wadi gives rise to a prodigious flow of stories where a delicious fear throbs, where tumultuous waters roar only in moments of terror or in nightmares. Stories of ravaging flash floods that leave in their wake only tears and misfortune. So, as long as their muddy blots remain in memory, no one will venture into the riverbed even if the only thing filling it is the continuous croaking of frogs. No one, until the days of oblivion, until once more men and beasts are dying from the dream of water that haunts them.

His spirit reinvigorated by a few steps, Mahmoud suddenly becomes aware of the hunger dully kneading his stomach. He hurries toward the shops on the periphery of the ksar, buys some bread and dates, and finishes his long journey at a *qahouaji*'s, under the arcades that encircle the great square of beaten earth. It is there that the biweekly camel market, for which it is named, takes place. It is there that the nomads of the region come to sell off the increase of their herds and to get provisions. It is there, that very week, that Mahmoud finds a caravan leaving for Adrar.

February finishes off the agony of winter with a succession of sandstorms. Suffocating death rattles that, with a few ventings, wipe out all illusion of spring and hurry March directly into the full fire of summer. His footsteps following those of the long silhouettes whose blue 'abayas pitch in the trembling air, Mahmoud walks on in silence. He thinks of nothing other than how to not let himself be left behind by these devils who unwind skeins of dust over nonexistent roads with the ease of merchants unrolling bolts of cloth on a counter. A dozen men alone. Their families have stayed in Adrar in order not to slow their speed. On these burning regs, the rhythm of these commercial caravans is far more rapid than that of pastoralists on the high plateaus. Still, nearly two weeks will be needed to cover the six hundred kilometers that separate Béchar from Adrar.

The frantic rhythm of the pace of the Regueibat wears Mahmoud out. In their wake, he doesn't even have the leisure to think about their evening stop when he'll finally be able to drink tea and relax. He walks. In the effort of the moment, he forgets all else. A merciful weariness that, while wearing out his body, imposes its blinders on him and fills his head with one hypertrophied goal: walking. If the glimmer of a thought manages at times to pierce the blankness of his mind, it is quickly submerged by the amnesiac drift that sweeps his entire being along. And if Yasmine's face emerges here and there along the way, it causes him no pain. Quiet and evanescent, it flits across his fatigue with the lightness and grace of a butterfly, according to its fancy.

It's not so much the men's exhaustion as it is the discovery of a rare bit of grass that, like a sort of tropism, halts the caravan at the end of the day. Sometimes, before the hint of a shadow covers the burning day with its cinder, it happens that the packs are already unloaded. Other times, evening only hurries their long strides. And if they find no grazing, they stop only when they bump up against the night. Mahmoud likes it when aridity pushes and harasses their footsteps into the depths of the shadows. Between the engagement of the mind in the blankness of the hours gone by, and the collapse upon halting into sleep, there is hardly any time for the influx of thought.

Reaching Adrar and finding Behi at last, Mahmoud learns to his consternation that he could have avoided this long and quite purposeless journey across these burned-out flat spaces. El-Majnoun is at Kenadsa, right next to Béchar. If he had taken the time to ask questions at Béchar. If he had . . . Because who in the entire Saoura doesn't know El-Majnoun? From Béchar to Tindouf as far as the Moroccan Touat, his intemperance, his madness, are a windfall for storytellers. Knowing El-Majnoun to be capable of the most grotesque escapades and the cruelest of machinations, of every excess and in every fight, you can easily imagine the fertile repertory of legends that swarm and buzz around his name. Trumpeted thus, the diverse allegories of his epic all have the same ending: although the different myths of El-Majnoun sweep furiously along the paths of the desert, the final phase of his dementia has limited his days to a grotto on the rocky crest that crowns La Barga, the strange dune of Kenadsa where he lives as a hermit.

Some, the most credulous or puritan, no doubt think him a sheikh or great vagabond. A *majnoun Allah*, in short, who wanders the desert, the Maghreb, and black Africa, along the paths of renunciation, *fi sabil Allah*. These same want to see in his present condition only the wisdom of a successful quest, the expression of an asceticism that has finally attained the absolute.

The dreamers and romantics create for him a life adorned with poetry, the pounding of galloping hooves and above all the mark of a passion as grand as that of the famous Majnoun Leïla. With all the lyricism found in anthems, they cast him out upon arduous roads in pursuit of an inaccessible ladylove.

Among all these myths, there is one that Mahmoud finds at least anchored in reality, if indeed reality had a sense for El-Majnoun. In any case, its theme connects not only with the words of the beautiful Zeyneb but even more with the remarks of El-Majnoun himself one day.

This story claims he'd gone off armed with several guns to kidnap the nomadic desert women from their husbands. And although his entire army was reduced to his ghostly but nevertheless demonic valet, Hassan, numerous camels trailed behind him, transporting among other riches guerbas filled with wine. He took up his position at a place where the paths of nomads cross, and waited. The first tribe that came by was so flabbergasted by his baroud that the males quickly raised their hands in surrender. Disappointed by their docility that deprived him of the hope of resounding exploits, El-Majnoun took revenge on them with much disdainful laughter. Immediately he proclaimed himself their king and began to harangue the women. When evening came, he was served couscous. He ate and drank a great deal of his wine. It was a torrid night. In spite of Hassan's repeated attention to the guerbas, continuously cooling them with water, the wine was hot and vinegary. It was the knockout blow, putting an end to El-Majnoun's chatter by plunging him into a most profound sleep. In the morning when he woke up, he, who had gone to sleep a monarch, was so astonished he could not master his confusion: the tribe had vanished, taking with it all his supplies, his water, and Hassan. It left him only a mangy camel and a guerba full of sour wine. Hassan, liberated three days later at Beni Abbès, retraced his path and came to his rescue with water and food. When he found El-Majnoun not far from the place where he'd had to abandon him, the last shreds of his mind were done for and his body was shattered. As soon as El-Majnoun had emerged from his alcoholic stupor, he'd had such a great thirst that he drank more of his wine and passed out again. The sun, sovereign despot in these countries, gave him the coup de grâce. This legend holds that while El-Majnoun eventually regained his strength, the sour wine had forever gotten the better of his shaky lucidity at the bitter end. Hassan brought El-Majnoun to Kenadsa where Hassan had some acquaintances who could, in his absence, watch over El-Majnoun. Fleeing the ksar and the mere sight of any guerba, El-Majnoun took refuge on the dune. Now from the heights of his throne of sand, he fixes his empty eyes on the barren, rough, incandescent regs upon which no mortal human will ever reign.

Waiting for a return caravan, Mahmoud takes the opportunity to rest and consoles himself by collecting and writing down the stories of El-Majnoun.

"Kenadsa? It's the train's terminus. You need only to get back on it, and it will go huffing and puffing until it bumps against black dunes heaped up from the bowels of the earth. But if one day's travel doesn't make you balk, take the pilgrim's path following the famous dune, La Barga. It will take you to the ksar while avoiding both the coal mines and the roumi quarter," the proprietor at the baths in Béchar tells Mahmoud, who'd stopped there again two days before.

Up early in the morning, Mahmoud asks the man at the hammam to mail two letters addressed to the Jew Benichou. The night before a youth had written the addresses in French for him. After saying "salaam" and "thank you," he leaves the still-sleeping ksar. The sun is just rising over Jebel Béchar. Encircled by a blood-red corolla, it showers down powdery gold rays beneath which the blue of the *jebel* takes on a sulfurous phosphorescence. Mahmoud turns his back to it. The west is clear. Pushing his elongated shadow along in front of him, Mahmoud walks in that direction. On his right, perpendicular to the crest of the Jebel Béchar, La Barga rises up. Mahmoud has never before seen such a dune, inlaid with ocher and white rocks, between which gigantic breasts of sand swell up. A rocky table, hollowed out into caverns here and there, overhangs it all. To Mahmoud's left is the dismal reg.

Yesterday at the end of the afternoon, some locusts had speckled the sky over Béchar.

"They are at the forefront of a great wave that won't arrive until tomorrow or the next day," the wise old people predict.

This morning they form masses that blister the earth here and there. Cold-blooded beasts, frozen in their copulation, they await the warmth of the sun to unsolder their bodies at last so they can fly away.

"There are always locusts in the vicinity of El-Majnoun!" Mahmoud thinks.

The sun has been blazing down for quite a while and the rubbing of the wing sheaths of the locusts is tearing the silence unceasingly when Mahmoud reaches Aïn-Sid-Sheikh. The small bouquet of palm trees surrounding the spring offers only a narrow shadow riddled with fire and bursting with cursed insects. It is nonetheless a sanctuary for Mahmoud. His strength drained, Mahmoud decides to wait here until the more merciful hour of dusk. Kenadsa is nearby. He can see the minaret of the mosque of Sidi M'hammed ben Bouziane, the somber ksar, and to the left, the traces of the gardens, black against the whiteness of the light.

At dusk, the minaret pierces the crowded skies with its red coral dart. The dune lets its curves of bloodstone flow around the dark purple of the rocks. The crests of the palm trees turn red amid a vapor of blue smoke. While walking, Mahmoud continues to scrutinize La Barga in the hope of seeing the silhouette of El-Majnoun. Only the angular flight of some sparrow hawks, profiting from the windfall of the locusts that they swallow in midair, stands out as they glide over the rocky table. Kenadsa emerges ocher in the soft mauve light. In approaching thus from the east, along the dune, Mahmoud passes behind the Jewish quarter and crosses the cemetery peaceful in its barrenness. The sweep of the tombs marked out by stones is concentrated around the qobba of Lalla 'Aicha. Mahmoud at last reaches the ksar of narrow streets, a labyrinth of shadow invaded by fine sand. Across from the Jewish quarter is the roumi quarter into which Mahmoud will avoid venturing. As usual Mahmoud prefers staying at a hammam over the other possibilities. Here, as the sensitivity of the *chorfa* requires, the *zaouia* is the inevitable refuge for pilgrims and travelers. Mahmoud pays it no heed.

The next day, following a bath, as Mahmoud prepares to leave the hammam, a fellow named Tahar with whom he strikes up a conversation invites him to have tea at his nearby house. Their first exchanges are about the massive invasion of locusts, which, as predicted, has arrived. The drinking of a glass of tea seems to Mahmoud an opportune time to gather information about El-Majnoun and Hassan. Besides, the air already torrid and buzzing with insects hardly encourages a walk to the ksar, which would have allowed him to glean some information.

In the streets, will-o'-the-wisp swarms of children armed with pots swirl around with joyful chaos, regrouping and then dispersing, trapping bunches of insects in their pots by victoriously clapping down the lids. The locust hunt has begun. Tahar's wife is in the courtyard before the entryway where a great cauldron is steaming. She is a tall, tanned woman wearing a *melehfa*. Given her dress and especially given her natural ease in front of a man, even a stranger, Mahmoud guesses that the family is from the

Doui Minaï, one of the desert tribes whose customs still bear strong traces of black Africa. The children push open the door and come in. With much pushing and shouting, they offer the woman their flittering harvest. She laughs and dumps the locusts into the boiling cauldron. She adds a great handful of salt. Soon a greenish-yellow foam rises and threatens to overflow. A putrid odor fills the air. Farther away, exposed to the sun on a cloth ringed with all sorts of dubious stains, the locusts already cooked are a deep maroon color, scrawny and gleaming. Tahar takes a fistful, swallows a few and offers some to his guest. Mahmoud clenches his teeth. Like the foam in the pot, his nausea is mounting. Thus, at the risk of offending his host, he runs to a room whose door is open. The thick shadow welcomes him and calms him. After a moment his host joins him with some tea.

"They're good and crispy, dried locusts! You people of the tell, you eat snails, ugh! One could call it snot!" he comments, laughing.

He gives him some tea. At Adrar, Mahmoud resigned himself to this strong tea without mint, a sort of tannin for the gut. He drinks it, and although his nostrils are still assailed by the fetid odors, swallow by swallow his nausea recedes slowly. Now Mahmoud knows where to find El-Majnoun.

Outside the air is aflame, sputtering with insects. It licks Mahmoud's face. The legs of the locusts remain stuck to his clothes. Mahmoud's nausea rises again when inadvertently he touches the underside of their wormlike abdomens. A plague of insects. Even the virgin sands are infested with them. They clump together and form, here and there, long flows like brown lava along the curves of the dune.

Mahmoud climbs. The burning sand and the multitude of locusts oblige him to keep his sandals on. The friction of the sand makes abrasions on his skin, sets his teeth on edge. But this is no time for sensitive teeth, nor for the sensuality of feet and their nuptials with the texture of the sands. Mahmoud concentrates on putting one foot in front of the other. His mouth opens all by itself, desperate, and inhaling only fire, suffocates. His body staggers and is wrung dry at each of his pores. Henceforth, Mahmoud will know that one doesn't walk on this dune at any old time with impunity. Right now it is simply a volcano in eruption covered by a cloud of locusts.

The bottom of the dune is imprisoned in a network of rocks, some of which bear the imprint of shells, an immemorial Eden. Mahmoud hoists himself up to the line of ocher rocks that form a belt midway up the dune. Beyond that, the sand wins out over the rock, pushes it back, and throws itself forward, spreads itself out, swells, and piles its mounds against the rocky table at the summit. Dazed, Mahmoud lowers his head and becomes engrossed for a moment in contemplating the laborious progression of a line of ants who are hauling a dead locust. Certainly nature is prey to all sorts of excesses.

He returns to his climb. His clothes, though loose, run with sweat and stick to his body. A sensation of vertigo glazes his eyes with a phosphorescent coating and fills his ears with whistling. Reaching the summit, he lets himself collapse in the stingy shadow of a rock and allows himself, at last, a sip of water from his gourd. The tepid, slightly brackish water is a disappointment for his thirst.

The flight of the locusts, so different from the rustling sound they make in the tell, draws his attention. Here, the myriad of flashing wings seems to burn longer in the sky like fiery, flying ashes. A large lizard tinted a gleaming reddish color emerges from a crag and imprints itself on a rock. The play of insects excites and maddens it. It opens its wide triangular mouth, breathes, inflates its neck and belly. Its rough skin dancing with tints spreads out like a tuberose. Mahmoud gets up. Frightened, the lizard disappears.

El-Majnoun must be just a hundred feet from here in a cavern that opens to the north. Mahmoud follows the line of the crest.

Suddenly the echo of laughter rings out and ricochets from rock to rock. El-Majnoun is very near, rising up like a monolith in front of a grotto. A hairy beard covers his neck with a dirty frill in which insects nest. A fleece like oily sheep's wool covers his bare head, reaching his shoulders. His skin is now too big. It hangs in long flaccid folds from the protuberances of his bones. With a haggard eye and anemic mouth, indifferent to the plague of the locusts, he's absorbed in a hermetic monologue.

II

Ahmed Khallil wanted Yasmine. They give him 'Aicha. Yasmine is from another kheïma and her father is away. Yasmine is not only unusual but rebellious. Yasmine is older. The flightiness of 'Aicha's personality is a sign of youth. She will be more malleable, adopting the habits her future family gives her.

A quintal of wheat, another of barley. A sheep and the whole fleece of twenty others. A *zarbia*. A *farrachia*. Five large handfuls of tea. Ten loaves of sugar. A damask embroidered by a renowned Jew from Tlemcen. A piece of velvet, violent purple crimsoned with fire. A length of cotton cloth for dresses for all the women of the tribe. *Kholkhals*, silver earrings and anklets bleeding with inlaid coral . . .

"Ahmed Khallil is a generous man. 'Aicha is a *merbouha*."

Grimaces of compassion triumph over the requisite expressions of complicity as the women of the tribe hand the girl over to the care of Ahmed Khallil's senior wife.

"My new *darra* will be like my daughter. Every daughter is a cause of pain. Pain when she is born, pain when she is given away, pain when she is received," the woman avers with the acid philosophy of those beaten down.

'Aicha's husband is older than her father. Like him, he already rules over a harem squealing with children. But chagrin has yet to touch the honeyed bubble of 'Aicha's adolescence. Does she even understand what it means? She is so flighty that all she sees in it is a celebration where she'll be queen. She's happy about it.

One morning, the women take charge of her still prepubescent body. *Messouak*, kohl, and henna. A purple dress, twice-dyed, brings out the luster of her amber skin. Heavy jewelry of coral and silver add the finishing touches to this dressed-up doll. Their pitiless pinches and repeated threats succeed that day in muzzling her laughter. Brutally, they lower her eyelids even more over her delighted eyes. They are the first to blind her shameless joy. A little nymph perched on a departing palanquin, they veil her face a bit more to hide her irrepressible smile. The slow and languid steps of a camel carried 'Aicha away. Ululations on wings wet with sorrow accompanied the procession for a long time.

Yasmine will never see 'Aicha again. 'Aicha snuffed herself out to escape the tragedy of a hopeless future full of violence and taboos. Death like a final burst of laughter freed her from the snare of tradition. An escape by death from the spider web of years that traps women. To take on the abnegations of a wife and the responsibilities of a mother? To drink, day after day, from their cup of resignation? How could she? It was much too heavy for her fleeting, fragile wings. Torpid fever. Rapid flight. At the end of two months, 'Aicha passed on, a child riding with her natural, happy laughter along the road of final refusal, toward other skies more merciful and more hopeful. They say that in the final moments of her feverish delirium, her breath stopped in the middle of a dream upon which her smiling face and heavenly gaze are forever fixed.

Forty days later the two tribes meet to conclude the funeral in accordance with the *char'ia*. While preparing the *'acha*, the women shed tears. Tears bitter as wormwood because of so many other sorrows. Tears to disarm suffering and undo its perversions through communion. Tears caused by what fate has in store for them. After the customary couscous, the talebs, with their hypocritical airs of devotion and phony litanies, intoned verses of the Qur'an for a long time. Then, Ahmed Khallil with his dapper moustache and guttural speech asked for Yasmine again.

"Maybe . . . It has been a number of months since her father left . . . Wait a bit," the Hamani reply.

The heat returns, but it does not bring back her father who'd left with it. To find him again, to while away the period of waiting, Yasmine writes poems and stories. In order to talk to him, she invents them . . . She tells him about 'Aicha, of the flying fragments of her laughter stung by her silence, of days wounded by the broken crystal of 'Aicha's joy. 'Aicha banished from existence because of her inappropriate joy. 'Aicha suffers, she believes, the same misfortune as the "little princess of salt." Where did her father find the story of the "girl of salt," expelled from her tribe, from her country, because she dared say to her father, a powerful and revered king, that she loved him as much as salt? From *A Thousand and One Nights*? Yasmine doesn't know anymore. All the salt in the world vanished into thin air in the wake of the girl who was exiled from the kingdom. All desire was burned off like stubble in a field. Life lost its flavor, the country became a desert, because men and beasts lost their desire to eat or drink, seeing themselves dying for lack salt. And so the childhood of the Hamani tribe was snuffed out along with 'Aicha's laughter.

Yasmine also writes about her mother, magnifies her accursed color:

"She was the ebony of flawless nights without stain. To better display its texture, she illuminated the sweet voluptuousness of darkness with the daylight crescent of her smile. She was named Nejma, star! A black star that shone by day. She was herself both day and night, finally reunited by the grace of love."

The discovery of tribal life is for her an inexhaustible source of stories and revolts. Yasmine's mind, innocent of the damage wrought by tradition, sharpened by the skill of observation that sustained her in her muteness, accustomed to debates by the crucible of her writing, recorded with bewilderment the weight of all the castrations that, from their earliest years, mutilate the days of women, that they themselves perpetuate with a resolution that Yasmine finds masochistic.

Frequent meetings with the Ouled Khallil foster a feeling of menace in her. A multitude of questions stirs up her fear.

"*Baba*, why do they stifle laughter, forbidding girls from singing and dancing? Why do they applaud all the caprices, all the cruelty of little boys, especially when they are carried out against their little sisters? Baba, is that why you always clothed me in a jellaba rather than a fouta? I thought it was to better protect me from the cold. What were you trying to protect me from in advising me to dress always like a boy? Baba, would Oummi still be alive if she had, like the roumia Isabelle, disguised herself as a man? Baba, sometimes a terrible desire for violence cries out in my silence. Strident, it burns my guts and slashes my thoughts. It turns my writing into diatribes, into pamphlets that become soliloquies. Baba, my words fight one another. The words in my belly are in shreds. I fear that their anger may one day transform me into a ventriloquist. Baba, my words quarrel with me, they devour me. I thought they were sealed within me forever. But they prove invincible and take me for their target. They wear my gestures and speak in my place. Right now I am the one who is trapped in their fury. The others, even when their mouths shut on their wounding words, scold me with their eyes, disapproving of me. They have taught me I am different. And even my silence no longer works for me. So I write, I write to spit out the nauseating pain that swells and rises up within me. I write to resist. But I keep in my guts something that torpedoes me.

Baba, men, whether they are skinny or big and fat, highwaymen on the great roads or among the pious mumbling their rosaries, clumsy or agile, mischievous or moronic—men are in agreement indeed about bullying women. They don't even wait for some indiscretion before accusing women of being whores. Baba, when they get up in the morning, the first breath women draw is about needs: fires, tea, the crowding around of children who need a mouthful. The growl of the grindstone beneath the effort of an arm that won't take no for an answer. More tea, always tea for the man who sits at a distance in order to hold forth in peace. They make him tea in an effort to protect themselves from his mischief, to keep his anger at bay. Ferment the whey, leaven the dough for bread, turn it while it cooks and the couscous pot steams. They carry out their daily plots, these fantastic utensils, in league against the housewife. Baba, if women had five pairs of hands, they would all be busy. And when the hearth finally grows cold, wool working begins in a fury of spritelike fingers. Wool to wash, clean, comb, card, spin, dye, and weave. Wool masterfully shaped into rugs, and clothing for men. While women wear themselves out, the men fight, parade, or dilly-dally, and then go sell the woolen goods in the souks, never giving the women a cent. Baba, what about the heavy loads of wood and water they bring back, bit in their teeth, bent double beneath the burden? Baba, when it is time to move on again, they are the ones who carry the smallest children. The days fade away beneath the whip of labor, break the body on the wheel of years, tarnish the light with sobs of grief. And on top of all that, Allah doesn't even exempt them from prayer! Baba, why this evil fate? I've come to the conclusion that Allah is just an idea brandished to legitimate secular injustice.

Baba, they confront and confound grief dry-eyed, teeth clenched against warlike challenges, but they cry at a trifle, so full are they of suppressed suffering. They cry even when they should laugh and then immediately laugh at their tears. Baba, in the land of sand, rocks, and dust, the women are full of dew. Like the oleanders that dot the wadis, they are full of bitter milk, broken and uprooted by floods, bent by the winds, harried by all weathers. You'd think them burnt to a cinder, dead! But watch out! At the least smile, the least heartfelt look, how they rise up, how they give generously. Baba, they are so tragic they become magical. And when I would like to strike ferociously at their abnegation, when I would like to hate them because of their excessive passivity, I surprise myself by loving them. And when I want to be different from them, a thousand leagues away from the whirlwind of their days that engulf them without pity, they are inside me, serene or flayed, threaded into my sensibility. Are they my destiny? I know already that escaping with my feet will serve no purpose. Already, without my knowledge, they monopolize my words. They will always haunt my dreams and torment my writing.

Baba, my fingers will never touch raw wool. A vampire is hidden inside there in its suffocating heat, in its animal oils. A vampire that sucks the energy of women to the last gasp. In the craft of unbearable silence, on the dense loom of my sensations, I want only to weave words. Never will my days be harassed by running from kanoun to guerba, tajine to guessa'a. Never will my life be sacrificed to those insatiable ogres, bellies! Never will my belly carry a child! With their angelic looks, children chain women down, participating in their immolation. The succession of births and deaths, the laughter that stifles suffering, carve deep lines in the resigned souls of these women. Baba, I am the daughter of a slave suckled by a dog and of a solitary poet. A rebellious slave, a hunted poet. A mother assassinated. Our life wouldn't fit into any normal pattern. It is only a succession of small moments of happiness and great tragedies, only good for opening up spaces for flamboyant imaginings. I want to gallop through the most impossible of dreams; must I tear myself apart there? They will not kill me, Baba, neither the wool, nor the children, nor the men, nor all those leechlike objects stuck to women's fingers, nor even the fatalism of women. Thanks to you, I escaped the education of girls and women. And just like you, I am as clumsy at submission as I am at recognizing reality. You've got to come back. We have to flee the trap of vengeance in which, without calling it that, we have been wandering for so long. We will go to a foreign country where I'll be able to wander and write like the roumia Isabelle, where you can tell wonderful stories in full freedom."

Yasmine no longer follows Bachir now except during migrations. Every morning when he leaves camp to follow his sheep, she stays to write. Before leaving, Bachir, ever aware of her evasions, comes to dedicate a dawn serenade to her on his reed flute. His music pours into her, opening the earth and the sky to a sweet wandering of the spirit and sketching on her lips the flower of a smile. Satisfied and happy, Bachir leaps up to leave, dancing along in the stream of his melodies like a sylph of light. Upon his return in the evening, he sees her from afar, a small dark smudge at a remove from the others. He runs toward her and from the pockets of his saroual and the sacks of esparto grass that the small donkey Kherbiche is carrying, Bachir brings out all sorts of offerings as if all day he wandered with only that goal in mind. A branch of violet euphorbia or amaranthus. A bitter apple that spreads, clinging to the nudity of the reg, and offers to the resigned gaze, as aridity's final prank, its pretty little melons, bitter because in their pulp of a juicy soft green is concentrated all the gall of the earth. A white lily of the desert so ephemeral it astonishes your gaze like a spark flying up from earth set afire. Or . . . a sand rose, the concretion of time in petals of gypsum, the only flower whose slow blooming reveals a corolla immune to fading. An eternal rose. Sometimes Bachir brings back a large lizard with a back of vivid yellow or red, the rest of its body black and pot-bellied. Or maybe it is the lamb of the day, with hesitant steps on legs still shaky and stiff, with fuzzy wool still warm from its mother's womb, with a bleat like the cries of a newborn, that Bachir, jumping with joy puts down in front of Yasmine. Yasmine's eyes light up and the flash of her teeth adorns her smile. Bachir's eyes sparkle with tears of joy.

After supper the exhausted children fall asleep pell-mell, often outside, sometimes even where they were playing. Freed from the network of their buzzing, the evening wraps itself in a silence suddenly deepened. The feeblest of sounds then become audible as if the dark has transformed itself into an echo chamber in which the least of sounds is revealed by an amplified echo. Such that whispers, typically masked by the noise of day, treacherously penetrate the screen of night to spread out, sometimes even without the knowledge of those saying them, even unto the hearing of those whom they hope to avoid. Thus it is that one night heavy with silence, Yasmine's sleepy ear is unexpectedly assailed by a proposition involving her.

"Ahmed Khallil wants her. We must give her to him. Her father will only thank us if he returns. Given her conduct, odd to say the least, this is perhaps the only time in her life that a man will be foolish enough to want her in an honorable way. Who is going to marry a woman just to look at her? Those whom her beauty arouses will only sleep with her in beds of sin," decrees a spinner.

"As for me, I tell you, her father wanted to get rid of her. He's never coming back," pontificated a carder.

"Her masculine dress hides her curves. But in a dress . . . In keeping her, we are flirting with danger," another carder warns.

"Her gaze is perverse. The eye of the wisest male gets engulfed there," says the distant voice of one of the combers.

"Even Bachir, the will-o'-the-wisp who's barely lost the last of his milk teeth, brandishes his flute like a penis," the second spinner adds.

"Have you seen how she becomes languid as if she gloried in lasciviousness beneath the sound of his flute? Khadija, I warn you, your son is already bewitched," cautions the keeper of the kanoun.

"My sprite likes her a lot, as do I. But he will marry obedient and hardworking Fatma of the Ouled Khallil. That is a promise made long ago. My sons are in agreement with the rest of you. In a few days we will meet the Ouled Khallil at Aïn Sefra for Mouloud. At that time, I will put everything in the hands of Allah by agreeing to Ahmed's request," Khadija's voice finishes weakly, convinced by the arguments of the chorus of wool workers.

This sentence puts an end to the treacherous whisperings. The only sound is the scratching of the carding combs tearing apart the clumps of wool. Yasmine remains still, oddly calm. Their words don't affect her, they don't concern her. She herself is only a spectator who refuses to descend into the women's arena because this *mektoub* they accept without balking, she rejects. She wants to flee these lands and these tragic lives. She wants something else. What? What? If she only knew! But she knows that the decision she made long ago remains firm. She thinks again of 'Aicha.

"Since it will not be me, what other girl will they sacrifice to that ogre Khallil? Zahia, the little housewife already somber and accomplished at eight years old? Probably!" she thinks with indifference.

She gets up and walks toward Khadija's kheïma. She lights the oil lamp and sits on her bedding. She gets out her flask of perfume and puts it next to her. Then her hands slip once more into the opening of her dress to cup her breasts. Just a few months ago, they had suddenly pushed out their two aureoles, scarcely larger than a couple of date pits. Now they fill her palms with their perfect roundness. At the touch of her fingers, her breasts harden. Her caresses move next to her armpits, fingers brushing their down. The first stirrings of desire fill Yasmine with a disquieting languor. She pulls out her hands and grabs a book, taking refuge in the *Roba'yat* of Omar Khayyam.

As usual, Bachir comes to sit at the opening of the tent. In the wavering light, his red chechia stands out against the coal black of his hair. His eyes are oblong, darkly moving. Lips pursed with a melancholy joy, he brings out his flute and serenades Yasmine. At the first notes, Yasmine stops reading and listens.

A quick, silent step stirs in the night, approaching. Khadija's silhouette materializes behind Bachir. With a brutal gesture, the mother tears the flute from her son's mouth and, with a rage so alien to her usual manner, breaks it in two.

"You, get out of here! Here, take this! From now on you'll sleep with the boys!" she fumes, throwing a mattress and a pillow outside the kheïma.

Both frightened and stupefied, Bachir backs away, collects his bedding and disappears into the darkness.

When Yasmine had left it, Aïn Sefra was chilly, filled with the clapping of sharp winds. Today, she barely grants even a distracted look at the landscape. Nonetheless, the gold of the dunes is warmer, more voluptuous. Their masses satiated by the heat, all drowse in the abandon, in the plenitude of their majestic curves. The trunks of the palm trees rise up and stretch out aimlessly, twirling their fronds beaded with young fruit beneath nostalgic skies. The leaves of the orchards are a froth of blue shadow on the red bosom of the sand. Those of the fig trees look like large hands downed with silver in the light reaching out as if to caress the dunes, accompanied by the rustling of the poplars shot through with sunlight. Even the most slender of branches of the oleanders are snow white with an abundance of flowers enclosed in a net of golden bees.

All the Hamani are busy unloading the packs, putting up the kheïmas. In the excitement of arrival, no one pays attention to Yasmine, who turns her back to them and goes off immediately toward the ksar.

Sitting relaxing on a small bench in front of his shop, Benichou chats with a neighbor. An unusual shadow appearing around the corner of the street draws their gaze. It is a young girl, dark-skinned and bare-headed. Something standoffish gives her gait an allure that is lofty and disillusioned, despite her haste. A few seconds more and there can be no doubt—it's her! He gets up and waits at the door to his shop:

"Salaam 'aleïki! I have a letter from your father for you!" he tells her right off.

She follows him inside. Benichou gets out two sheets of paper, simply folded, from beneath his counter. He blows on them to get rid of their dust and hands them to her. While she is quickly skimming the missive, Benichou can't help watching her secretly.

"A belle, a belle, with the salt of rebellion as well," he thinks.

She's finished reading. Her contented fingers caress the paper while her eyes return to the beginning of the text.

"Hey! Here is another one, hot off the press."

He holds out a clean envelope that he has hidden behind his back until now.

"The first one was left with me by your father. This second one arrived the day before yesterday from Béchar.

The indecipherable roumi writing on the envelope brings distrust to Yasmine's face. She takes it, examines it circumspectly, turns it over and over.

"Wait, wait, it's inside!"

The man takes the envelope in his hands, tears it open, and pulls out a sheet that she pounces on as soon as she recognizes her father's writing. Then she raises her radiant eyes to the Jew and rewards him with a smile. Suddenly in a hurry, she stuffs the letters inside her bodice and gets ready to leave when she sees some *gasbas* hanging from the ceiling. She goes over to admire them. Suddenly, by means of association, she remembers the lute. She turns around. *El-'oud* is still there, round-bellied and hidden, surely gestating with some intoxicating melody. She smiles.

"Benichou plays the lute," she says to herself. Then she turns her eyes to the flutes.

"Do you want one?" asks Benichou.

She nods yes. The man brings down one of them and offers it to her.

"Do you play?" he asks her.

With a shake of the head, she leaves the shop without further ado.

"Will you come back soon?"

She is already gone, her eyes on a distant dream.

"I will be at Kenadsa, there where the train tracks stop." Her father's words beat, throb in Yasmine's head like a pulse. She forces herself to cross the French quarter of town as far as the railway. Lingering, she stares at the gleaming track with an enigmatic air. Then she turns, and with a hesitant step, leaves slowly. In the streets, men's eyes, intrigued, fix on her. Whistles, hot looks, praise, and obscenities burst out in her wake. She doesn't notice them. What is happening to her? Has making this decision plunged her into a state of lethargy? Is it magic, the touch of the flute between her mute fingers, that penetrates her and bleeds inside her? Is it the antique gold of the light that her body is drinking in through all its pores inundating her suddenly with a new sensation? An indefinable torment, at once sweet and heart-rending, invades her whole being. Anxious waiting grips her heart, cinches in her breath. Is it hope? For the first time, Yasmine feels a desire to experience the vertigo of dance, the folly of trance, part joy, part suffering. A desire to tear open the straitjacket of silence, to hear this body resonate with the clamor of words resuscitated after a long demise, just like dead leaves rustling in the wind. A desire to risk damnation on the rupturing of reefs, on the shivering of danger, in the burning of stings. A desire to laugh, too. What does it matter if her laughter does not have the tinkling sound of a cherub, the right tone.

What does it matter if it sounds like a sob compared to that of 'Aïcha! So long as it emerges, melting with pleasure, splitting open the pain cowering in her depths. What does the sneering of the oh-so-austere, oh-so-stay-at-home Dame Solitude matter either. She will overwhelm her with lampoons, the wench. She will save herself by kicking over the traces, moving toward the most impossible of beauties only to return in haste to her chapel like a sinner whose faith has been purified in the flames of sin. And from treason to devotion, in a mocking tour de force, she will drag the wench along to share her own bitter brew, the price of absolute liberty. Then, no matter how false the joy of their reunions, their shared libations of poison nectar will surely have a heady savor.

The Hamani have looked for her on the dunes and in the orchards without any luck. They will not inflict upon themselves the humiliation of going to poke around in the ksar to find a young girl! Full of threats, they waited for her at the camp. All afternoon Khadija has mulled over her grievances, planning to abandon Yasmine to them as just punishment. But seeing Yasmine's unsteady step, her disdainful mouth, the weary fever that burns in her eyes, Khadija, in spite of herself, is compelled by affection to protect her.

"I am saving you once again, one last time," she grumbles, exasperated by her own weakness, while putting herself between Yasmine and the anger of the men.

She pushes her inside the tent to protect her from blows:

"Stay there! Above all, don't budge, don't leave this kheïma. Showing yourself will only set off their indignation. Your father really made you into a boy! A girl, a woman, never leaves her people except in marriage or in death! See how those older than you and those younger than you behave. This cannot go on! It causes too much worry for me in my old age. We will marry you off. Ahmed Khallil will arrive tonight or tomorrow. Let him do what he wants with you!"

With a scowling face, hidden in the shadows of the kheïma, Yasmine does not write, she does not read. She listens to the noises outside. She listens, inside herself, to the progress of her resolutions. Bachir stops in front of the tent and takes a furtive look inside. Yasmine makes a sign for him to come in. Her power over him is such that repeated threats do not curb the ineffable delight he feels in answering her summons. He goes over to her. She gives him the flute and, without giving him the time to savor his pleasure, gets up and starts a strange pantomime. He watches her with anxious eyes. He thinks he has understood what she is asking. He thinks he has even guessed what her project is. A last resort! A cloak of sadness covers him and mists his eyes. The rumors circulating within the tribe the last few days have not escaped him. They've made him lose appetite, sleep, and his smile. So if indeed he must resign himself to a life without Yasmine, better to become her accomplice in this project, better to gather from her lips a last smile. Had it been anyone other than her, this possibility wouldn't have even touched him. But how can she be compared to the others? She is not and will never be a woman. She is his muse, a muse enamored of poetry. Perched in her silence, pedestal of the gods, the sole purpose of her presence in the tribe was to inspire his flute, to call upon his prowess. Now that thanks to her he excels, she wants to move on to other destinies, leaving in her wake an inconsolable loyalty sublimated in music.

With a flick, Yasmine signals him to leave, putting an end to his meditation. He gets up and submissively leaves the premises. But he is not long in coming back to give her the things she has asked for, which he has carefully hidden beneath his 'abaya. Yasmine hides them beneath her pillow and then checks the contents of her satchel. Her writing board is there with her father's books and those given her by Benichou. Only the *Roba'yat* of Omar Khayyam is missing. It is there on the small chest. She packs it. The letters from her father and the flask of perfume also.

Everything is now ready. With a sign of her hand, she dismisses Bachir. He backs out, his large eyes speaking to her of the torture of saying goodbye.

At suppertime Khadija comes into the tent and puts a plate in front of Yasmine.

"Even Merbouh the dog is more careful than you are about the ways of the tribe. It wouldn't occur to you to feed yourself if I didn't bring you your bowl, apart from the others, like a quarantine animal," she grieves. "How are you going to manage later on?"

⁂

Trapped in his madness, El-Majnoun is at this point unreachable. Mahmoud penetrates into the grotto and decides to wait hidden there for the arrival of Hassan. Hassan is in Kenadsa. Mahmoud has gotten confirmation of this from Tahar, the man with whom he had tea. The shadow and the relative coolness of the grotto are a benediction to his body and burning eyes. The water in the pitcher set against the wall is cool. Farther off, a dirty plate covered with the remains of a meal is on a rock: stale bread, dried dates. El-Majnoun seems to get regular provisions. Mahmoud chooses a carpet of sand on the bed of rock as a place to stretch out. Soon all the weariness of his continuous traveling weighs down upon him. He falls into a deep sleep.

The cavern rings with the satanic laughter of El-Majnoun. Then a long, long sigh is emitted upon which a rosary of uninterrupted snores is strung. Suddenly the grotto is nothing more than a den, a belly that gurgles, prey to frightening growlings. Everything about El-Majnoun that Mahmoud had fled from is there in those beastly and invasive exhalations. In comparison, his own breathing seems to him so feeble. Trumpeted off of the dome, the void fills up and suffocates him little by little. Mahmoud's body is sweaty, weak, tossed down like a rag on the sand. His head is boiling. Suddenly a face is there looming over

250

him, its eyes cruelly hilarious, its features contorted by a sort of massive rale. Unbearable torture. A flash of lightning and loud crack. The taste of blood in his mouth. Then nothing, everything goes black. Jerking awake, Mahmoud has slept until deep into the night and hasn't even registered the furtive visit of Hassan.

His thoughts flow smoothly: "Am I dead? Death by insignificance! Dead for not having even known how to defend myself against the madness of El-Majnoun," he thinks with irony.

Now he is nothing but a feather, an amputated locust's wing that drifts towards Nejma.

He tries to move his limbs. Miraculously obeyed, he sits up. With the cautiousness of an invalid who doubts his strength, Mahmoud gets up and goes out of the grotto before his fears return.

Once outside, he walks away in order to avoid hearing the snores of El-Majnoun. But other faint sounds come to disturb the silence: the vibrations of the wing sheaths of the locusts frozen in their nocturnal hypnosis, the furtive steps of some small animal, a stone split from a rock that falls with a dull sound on the sand. Then a noise that he cannot identify.

The moon surprises him. It is globular like a glassy eye in the corpse of the sky that drops down onto the earth long brown tatters like some mammoth octopus. The stars are yellowed, drowned in the moon's pallor. The dune is blistered with ghastly rocks. To the south a slag heap displays its sturdy silhouette, its somber note settling in as if brooding upon the darkness from which true nights would hatch, alive with shadows.

Another succession of small, strange noises. Mahmoud turns around and scrutinizes the contours of the dunes. Is it a hallucination? It seems to him that something moved over there. Beneath the milky moonlight, the stone fixed and unmoving in the dune attracts his eye. Hallucination? Now another noise behind him. Mahmoud pivots. Still the same immobility, and it is always behind him that the noise occurs.

"Who's there?" Mahmoud asks weakly.

A number of shadows emerge from the rocks.

"Police! Turn yourself in!"

Mahmoud takes off across La Barga. Quick, quick, the shelter of the rocks. A first burst of gunfire drowns itself in the clamor of El-Majnoun's shouts and laughter. A second burst. Mahmoud drops down. The taste of blood in his mouth. Then very quickly, everything disappears into a white fog. Relief. The sweet sensation of leaving, drifting away on the shroud of the moon.

"Stupid bastard, I told you to aim at his legs!" thunders a uniform.

"I aimed low."

"You aimed low? Did you think he was walking on his head maybe!"

A third turns over the inert body.

"This way, at least, the Sirvant affair is finally settled," he concludes against the backdrop of El-Majnoun's demonic laughter.

❧ ❧ ❧

The last sounds of the sipping of tea from glasses, the claws of the carding combs, and the dull shock of the weaving fork die out. Khadija, yawning, wishes them all:

"Tassabhou 'ala kheïr."

There is the indistinct murmur of other women as they spread out toward their kheïmas. Khadija enters her own. Yasmine pretends to be asleep. The woman goes over to her and covers her with a *haïk*. Then she fixes her own mattress, plumps her pillow, stretches out, and falls asleep almost instantaneously. Yasmine waits a while longer. The light of the moon outlines the opening of the tent with ivory. In the camp the silence is profound. Yasmine sits up. She grabs Bachir's 'abaya and saroual, hidden inside her satchel. She takes off her dress, stuffs it inside the sack, and slips on the boy's clothes. She knots her hair and hides it beneath a light *haouak*. Khadija's breathing is completely calm. Her satchel strapped across her chest and her jellaba over her shoulder, Yasmine glides furtively outside the tent. She waits for a while at the doorway, her ears pricked up, her eyes alert. An unmoving state of well-being filled with snores. The kheïmas look like large tortoises dozing beneath the shadows of their carapaces. Taking a long breath, Yasmine speeds off across the palm grove. Immediately there is a light footstep behind her that doesn't go away. She turns, her heart beating wildly. Oh, it is only the dog Merbouh.

"Merbouh, Merbouh, you want to go with me? Okay, I'll certainly need your company, you whose name means 'lucky,'" Yasmine's eyes say in the dark.

With Merbouh at her heels, she goes on. One step, two steps, light strides, the caress of the sands of freedom on her feet. At her passing, the palm trees stretch their trunks, shake out their ethereal hair, and accompany her with a celestial murmuring. In the gardens, night has heaped up their dark flakes and sucked in their essences only to breath them out in small gusts: mint, basil, and jasmine line the path of the runaway.

No obstacles while crossing the ksar and the roumi quarter. Only a few dog barks flare up every now and then. As if he had an intuition about the importance of the moment, Merbouh concentrates on ignoring them. Soon the railway cuts into the gray monochrome of the night with its two metal tracks. Yasmine casts her flight along this iron guide and smiles at last at her accomplice, the night. At the end of these tracks, she will find her father.

She walks on. As she goes along, the vertigo of this stolen, nocturnal liberty stirs with renewed strength in her all the sketchy sensations that plague her. She walks, fatefully attracted by a distant trill that draws her steps irresistibly toward it.

Suddenly there is a noise. Yasmine stops, listens attentively. The wind! The sirocco! She recognizes its groans swelled with churlishness, bursting with the grapeshot of sands. In squalls, it thunders in the distance, scrapes the regs and the hamadas, claws at the sky, crams space with its fury. Soon the dune will rise up in seething ground swells, a hurricane. Yasmine loves and fears this wind. It fascinates her. She hasn't gone three steps when its tidal wave breaks upon her, opaque, bitter, and shrewish. It erases the tracks. It buries the stars. It snuffs out the moon. It blinds Yasmine. The night grows denser, growling and erupting. A trance of shadows. Monstrous orgasm. Yasmine moves on, bent double. She goes where the wind blows her. The wind slaps her around. It claws her and snaps its whip in her ears. Her skin heats up, burning from the carding of the sand. Her throat is raspy, scratched by dust that sticks to her palate, grates on her teeth. Yasmine is so thirsty. She didn't even think to supply herself with a bit of water for her trip. She only thought about leaving. Leaving, that was all. Now she has nothing to drink but the hot breath of the wind. Her satchel is weighed down by books and notebooks. The raging of the gusts adds to its ballast. The violence of their bucking pushes Yasmine backward, off balance. The bandolier is cutting into her shoulder. Yasmine grabs the satchel in her two hands, holds it against her chest, and wraps her arms around it. Bent in two, she walks into the wind, sustained by the knowledge that at the end of the tracks, at the end of the wind, Mahmoud awaits her. But she can't open her eyes anymore. She grabs onto her haouak and tries to cover her face. It is impossible to go on like this. She doesn't want to lose the tracks and get lost in the angry wind. She stops, feels around with her foot, finds it, steps over it, and descends the embankment of the railroad bed. She sits with her back to the wind, its angry darts going straight to her heart, its harsh gusts on her neck, its plaintive whirling giving her vertigo.

The satchel imprints the hard shape of the bottle of perfume on her chest. Soon Yasmine reaches her hand in to look for it. Her fingers seize the flask. The smoothness of the polished glass comforts her. She knows its contents are the amber color of tea. She brings it out, pulls out the cork, throws back her shoulders, and inhales. The strong fragrance clears her nostrils. Yasmine brings the bottle to her lips and drinks a mouthful. She shivers. It's like a flow of lava in her blood, the echo of the sirocco, the torrid blood of the roaring sands. Another gulp, and again, and again. A tempest of flames is inside her body as if she had imbibed all the violence of the outside. Yasmine reels and capsizes at the mercy of Aeolus, a sweet sensation. She is nothing more than an incandescence carried by waves of wind into the strident night. Yasmine sings a lament. Words, exhumed, ignited. Birds of purple, jade, turquoise, birds of golden and silver light, owls of the shadows, messengers of dreams, all the words spoken cease to be cursed and take flight, liberated by the lover of the dunes, the wind. A jubilant song of deliverance. A song of rebirth.

"Yasmine! Yasmine!"

Yasmine falls silent, hunkers down in her terror amid the black fury of the wind. Hallucination? Drunk with singing?

"Yasmine! Yasmine!"

It's a man's voice wavering and haunting the gusts. Yasmine is still as a stone.

"Yasmine, don't be afraid. It's me, Benichou, I only want to help you! I heard your song. I know that you are there—answer me!"

Yasmine's fears dissolve. Soon she perceives close by the voice of Benichou who is prodding his donkey:

"Errr! Errr!"

Yasmine turns around, taking a great breath.

"I am here," she says.

"Blessed be this sirocco that carried your voice!"

Benichou stops turning his back to the wind. "You must return to Aïn Sefra to wait for el-machina. But as soon as dawn pierces through this tumult, we'll be on the road to Kenadsa. I promise you."

Yasmine comes up and touches the donkey.

"The boy Bachir alerted me. He suspected your plan and watched for you in the night. His sobs choked him, drenching his words. His grief was so strong, as strong as the sobbing of the wind. A remarkable boy, he will say nothing to the others. His secret is a treasure for his suffering. Get on the donkey. I will walk alongside pushed by the wind. We still have time."

Benichou helps Yasmine climb up on the donkey. Then he continues on, yelling so she can hear:

"We have to talk, to talk. But what I have to say is so difficult. . . . I was going to come see you tomorrow morning. Yesterday, after you came by the hanout . . . Several pieces of bad news . . . But maybe all that can wait for a while . . . Yes, yes, wait until daytime when the sirocco's died down, when the words will be less bitter . . . You have a wonderful voice, Yasmine. Your song was so beautiful even in the midst of the harshness of the tempest. . . . I don't want to spoil your happiness tonight . . ."

"What does he have to say that is so terrible?" Yasmine asks herself. Anxiety is rising again within her, filling the silence.

"Me, too, I must leave here. You know, over there, on the other side of the sea, it is war. The Germans have invaded France. They want Europe, all Europe, but without Jews. So they are killing the Jews. One of my friends from Aïn Sefra went to France for a short stay. He didn't come back. Now his family has been without news for a number of months. Today the police came sniffing about my hanout when I was out. A French friend warned me. I didn't go back. They asked my neighbors all sorts of questions. They said they'd come back. They won't find me. My ideas and my activities are suspect. They say that the methods of the Germans are terrible, terrible."

"Ejjrad?" asks Yasmine.

"Yes, it's the same, ejjrad! You are right, my gazelle, they plague the Jews like locusts."

"Mahmoud says that they devastate even dignity."

"Yes, even dignity. And they think those who are different from them deserve only death."

They reach Aïn Sefra. The railway station is deserted. The window is closed, but two men are sleeping in the small room. One of them jumps up when he sees them.

"My brother," Benichou announces.

The other is a roumi.

"Ferrand, the doctor," says Benichou giving him a friendly tap on the shoulder.

"So you write poems and stories in Arabic?" asks the roumi. Yasmine doesn't answer. She stares at him intensely.

"When you come back to Sefra, would you teach me to write in Arabic? In exchange, I could teach you French."

"She finds him handsome and smiles at him. He interprets the smile as consent. Against one wall of the room, a bundle and the lute from the hanout are leaning. The men spend a long time greeting each other. A few murmured words, muffled by the wind, and they separate.

"I hope that we'll see you! Don't forget my suggestion!" says the doctor, bending down in front of Yasmine.

Benichou's brother unties the donkey waiting outside. The roumi has a bicycle. The two leave on foot because the two-wheeler is useless in this weather.

Yasmine and Benichou sit down with their backs to the wall. Benichou starts to talk again. He tells her about his meeting with her father and about their ruse for getting Mahmoud another name.

"The uniforms will be very happy to find a solid indictable count against me: aiding and abetting a murdering Arab. As if Mahmoud were capable of that."

The dawn dirties the beautiful black stridency of the night with its murky glow. Benichou can see the features of the young girl. They are contracted with anxious waiting.

"Yasmine, Yasmine, they've killed Mahmoud!" he resigns himself to whispering finally.

Yasmine jumps up, runs, leaving the room howling.

"Baba! Baba! *Baba habibi!*

The wind sobs. Her inconsolable heartache stirs the soul of the sands, the wind.

"Baba, Baba, I want to see you, Baba!"

Hoarse is the wind, and Yasmine's despair sifts into the glaucous light of the dawning day. She whimpers and suffocates. Moaning, the wind rears up, knocks about, and leaves noisily. Yasmine's sobs are absorbed like dust in its monstrous whorls. It dries her tears on the threshold of her eyelids. It sculpts them into rings of sand. Suffering would never see her pupils wet. The wind watches over her, the wind blows on her, exerting itself to keep her eyes shut to an impossible reality. Yasmine stands stock still, suddenly attentive to this body to body, grief to grief contact with the sirocco. The wind cries for her, rages for her, lays blame in her stead. Interpreter of her interior tempest. Expressed by it, her suffering acquires a strength, a timeless and cosmic dimension that tames her and goes beyond her. The wind is a virtuoso appropriating her sorrow and transforming it into tragedy. Yasmine faces the wind, rears back, and sings:

"Baba, Baba! Baba is not dead! He lives in me, vibrates in my broken voice!

Baba! Baba is not dead . . . i'

Always the same phrase. Just that phrase hammered out tirelessly as if in a duet with the wind. A strange contest of despair. Yasmine's voice is rocky like the regs. There is in it the roughness of grasses dried out from birth and dead before they have matured. The wind exhausts her sorrow, weighs upon her words with all its snarling, dusts her incantations with weariness, sharpens the tension. Yasmine collapses onto the ground. Benichou runs to her. Carefully he raises her head and puts her satchel beneath it as a pillow, and then with the tenderness of a mother, keeps watch over her in her prostration.

Little by little the railway station emerges from the fog of dust, lonely, spectral, and empty. After a few moments some soldiers and townspeople show up, hasty blurs amid the gusts of sand. With a whistle milled by the fitful wind, the train erupts into the red clamor of the breaking day. Benichou wakes Yasmine and helps her to climb into the train car. The travelers give way in the face of this pretty girl dressed as a boy, her head bare, holding her haouak in her hand. She stops at the first bench, lies down on it, and immediately falls into a deep sleep. Around her the men maintain silence, glancing at her now and then with admiration and disquiet. El-machina groans and drags itself into the endless tunnel of the sandstorm.

They say that the train stops when it collides with the austerity of the desert. At the gateway to this realm of silence, from which its metallic fracas is banned, it drops them off. They say that in the land of all trances and all bewitchments, a mysterious story awaits them.

They say that the policemen who had fired on Mahmoud at the summit of the dune committed the indiscretion of coming down, all three together, leaving the body where it lay, but that they only rushed down La Barga quickly with the idea of sending stretcher bearers right back up immediately to get him. They maintain that they were no sooner at the bottom than a sandstorm unleashed itself. It would have been pure folly, as everyone there knows, to climb back up to the top of this dune higher than a hill when the sirocco was raging!

"Let's wait until dawn at least, which is in less than an hour," the ones chosen for this tedious task would have protested.

They say that in this way it happened that misfortune overtook them. When they climbed back up, the body was no more.

"It was the wind! It was the wind! Up there, the tornadoes are surely capable of burying even a live and active person so much do they accelerate around the rocks and suck up the sand," the uniforms guilty of the indiscretion claimed.

With reinforcements armed with batons, they sounded the dune at the spot where Mahmoud had fallen and then all around, right up to the entry to the grotto of El-Majnoun. Nothing. The camel corps, dispatched to search the environs, came back as well, sputtering and shaken.

They say that suspicion next shifted to El-Majnoun.

"That devil must have buried the body somewhere on the rock-studded crest," some suggested.

But how was one to get any information, any clue out of a man enclosed in a hermetic soliloquy, punctuated only by de-monic laughter? So who's to blame? El-Majnoun's madness or the wind, the dementia of silence? The good weather brought no key to unlock this enigma, which remained complete. And now some are guessing, to the great fury of the police, that maybe Mahmoud wasn't dead, that after their departure, he had simply recovered his strength, dealt with the pain of his wound, gotten up, and gone off into nearby Morocco.

Whatever the case, the perfidious sandstorm had once again erased all traces. What proof do the police have of their work? An identity card in the name of S.N.P. Mohamed ben Ahmed while the name of the guy they were looking for is Mahmoud Tijani!

They say that for once the warring Doui Minaï and their fierce enemies the Ouled Gerrir put aside their secular hatred and united against the misdeeds of Hassan. They whisper that, aware of their plan, Yasmine took part. The story goes that she lined her large eyes with kohl and, adorned in the most beautiful finery, she awaited the evildoer in ambush to trap him. They say that she abandoned him to these men who, turning their noses up at the idea of obedience to roumi law, swearing against both *caïd* and *cadi*, hanged him from a fig branch in the labyrinthine heart of the ksar.

His cries ringing in her ears, she walked toward the dune of La Barga with a dispirited step. They say that at the summit, her gaze drunk with the unearthly light and staring into the blinding sleep of infinity, she sang the songs of Mahmoud. They say her voice made the great dune sacred, a steppingstone for the sidereal quests of dreams, a royal tomb for Mahmoud, the poet of time and of dreams. They say that from the funeral procession trilling with angelic ululations, to the diadem of pearly rocks that crown La Barga, a sparkling anthology of echoes shattered the indigo of the skies.

They say that then her eyes wandered toward the hills of Morocco and that she smiled as if she had seen Mahmoud. Some claim that it is in that direction her wanderings took her, followed by the Jew Benichou. They say that he filled her bottle of perfume with absinthe and that she always drank it to be able to sing. They say she was nicknamed *Riha*, perfume, and that she intoxicated the lute of Benichou who always accompanied her laments, just as the loyal footsteps of his friendship never failed to follow her. Some claim that from caravan to caravan she crosses the desert toward the black native source of her mother. They say that there in ancient Africa, she nourished her songs on black rhythms. They say that she goes from lover to lover because no love can hold her or satisfy her. How could they do so when even writing, for her, is just a wandering toward the far corners of her losses? And if as she gets older, words reach deeper and deeper within her to express her joys and suffering, they will never reach the unspeakable hurt that gives rise to them. They say that she consoles herself for that by arguing that she lives as a free woman as did her role model, the roumia Isabelle. They say that all her happiness is knit together with pain, but could it be otherwise for those who want always to keep their hearts and minds as open as the wide spaces they travel through?

They whisper even that she would have found her father in that neighboring maghreb . . . But . . . But should one believe the discourses, whether whispered or spoken aloud, that run along the foot of the walls of these magical ksour? Words are nothing more here than elegiac complaints, derisive odes to conjure the magic of silence and the orisons of the wind. And the odysseys of the imagination that, like all illuminated myths, ride the light and traverse the desert furiously are but false migrations when the body is trapped by its greatest terror, immobility. Should we believe the stories told by those in the ksour, when they themselves are nothing more than the stories and mirages of the burning regs?

GLOSSARY

'abaya: *gandoura*; a summer dress made of light material, no sleeves.

'abd(a) / *'abid* (pl.): slave; also worshipper, when used in names.

'acha: dinner; evening prayer; funeral wake.

Allah ijib: May God grant it!

'arbi: Arab.

'arjoun: bunch, stalk (of dates).

'atouch: palanquin.

'aziza: darling; dear.

baba: father.

baluchon (Fr.): a mat used as a satchel.

baroud: literally, powder; by extension, arms, combat.

bendir: traditional tambourine.

bezef: a lot.

bismi Allah: in the name of God.

bordj: fort; citadel; bastion; tower.

boukhmouna: snotty.

cadi: judge, at the town or village level.

caïd: tribal leader.

calame: reed pen.

caravanserai: an inn with a large courtyard and stables for animals.

chakoua: lambskin in which to churn and preserve milk.

chari'a: law, understood to be Qur'anic.

chberr: span.

chèche: headdress worn by a man.

chechia: felt hat worn by men, especially in Tunisia.

chorfa: plural of *cherif*, a descendant of the prophet.

chouïa: a little.

couscous: staple food of North Africa. Also rolled semolina and flour mix; pasta for the dish.

darra: pain, used by women to indicate the other wives of their husband.

dechra: simple house, usually made of mud brick with a roof of palm or reeds covered with dried mud.

diffa: invitation; festivity.

douar: village.

Doui Minaï: tribe from the region of Abadla south of Béchar.

ejjrad: locusts (singular: jarada).

El-Azhar: Islamic university in Cairo.

el-dohr: midday prayer.

el-hamdoulillah: blessings to God; praise to God.

el-machina: the train.

el-maghreb: west; sunset.

el-mashreq: east.

el-'oud: Arabic string instrument (definite case with prefix *el-* or *al-*, indefinite without prefix).

el-rih: wind.

El-Sayyed: mister, expression preceding man's name.

erg: area covered with dunes in the desert.

fajr: literally, daybreak; also dawn prayer.

farrachia: rug.

Fatma: generic woman's name used by colonial settlers to refer to a Musim woman (derogatory).

fi sabil Allah: on God's path.

fouta: rectangle of multicolored cloth that Berber women wrap around their skirts and attach to their belts; napkin.

gandoura: see *'abaya*.

gasba: literally, reed; a flute carved from a reed.

ghaïta: a sort of clarinet or thin wind instrument with a high nasal sound.

ghassoul: clay for washing hair and wool.

guelta: pool.

guerba: goatskin bag.

guessa'a: the large dish, usually made of wood, used for mixing and serving couscous.

habibi: beloved; dear.

hadoun: cape of pure black wool (natural color).

haik: white veil worn by women in North Africa as a full body cover.

hamada: rocky desert plain (as opposed to *reg*).

hammam: Turkish bath.

hanout: shop, store.

haouak: turban of light cloth.

hartani(a): person of mixed race.

henna: orange natural dye made from henna leaves used to decorate hands and feet, especially during celebrations, and to color hair.

hijab: veil, protection.

hittiste: ironic Algerian name for "those who hold up the walls"; the unemployed who gather at the foot of walls.

houria: angel, but also liberty.

h'rira: soup.

hsira: mat, traditionally made of esparto grass.

Ihoudi: Jew.

inch'Allah: God willing.

jadarmi: policeman ("gendarme").

jebel: hill.

jeich: literally, army, but often used to designate all groups of armed men defending a region; a tribe or group out to pillage.

jellaba: Moroccan overall robe.

jema'a: literally, Friday; by extension, Friday assembly, a saint's day, or any meeting or reunion.

jinn, *jnoun* (pl.): genie, genies

Joha: legendary person known for being mischievous.

kanoun: brazier; barbecue.

kebdi: my liver, an expression of filial affection different from *qalbi*, my heart.

kelb(a): dog

khayi: my brother.

kheïdous: cape of pure brown wool (natural color).

kheïma: nomad's tent, usually made of wool and camel's hair.

kheïmet-ed-diaf: guest tent.

khlii: mutton seasoned with herbs and dried.

kholkhal: silver ankle bracelets.

khourda: waste; manure; rubbish.

kif: marijuana.

kohl: black cosmetic used to highlight the eyes.

ksar, *ksour* (pl.): village; old part of town.

lahia: beard.

lalla: lady; mistress.

Lalla 'Aicha: female saint named 'Aicha.

Lalla Nejma el-kahla: Lady Nejma the Black.

ma'akra: mixture of peppered grilled semolina, dates, and ewe's butter.

ma'a salaama: peace be/stay with you.

maghreb: time of prayer, at sunset.

majnoun(a): insane person.

Majnoun Allah: a Sufi, spiritual lover of God.

Majnou(n) Leïla: "Leila's smitten lover," a name given to Qays ibn al-Mulawwah, who with his ladylove are among the legendary couples in Arabic literature (Islamic period).

maquis: a type of thick scrub brush.

marabout: saint. Also saint's tomb.

marhaba: welcome.

M'cha: He's gone.

mechouis / *mechoui*: barbecued meat.

mechta: hamlet.

medersa: school.

meïda: low table.

mektoub: it is written, destiny.

melehfa: a rectangle of cloth used by women in the South to wrap themselves, as Indian women use their saris.

mendil: large shawl, traditionally of woven wool.

merbouh(a): he, or she, who brings good fortune or who is lucky; a thing that is won.

messouak: bark of a nut tree that can be rubbed on the lips and gums to color them orange.

mezoued: a bag, made from an entire goat, to carry flour or semolina.

midad: ink, in this context, hand-
made.

Mohamed: Generic man's name
used by colonial settlers to refer to
a Muslim man.

Mouloud: Name of a month in
the Muslim year. Also, birth. Used
alone, it designates the birthday of
the Prophet.

mouna: food staples, mainly grain.

mounchar: saw.

muezzin: the person who calls be-
lievers to prayer.

Nahdha: literally, reawakening; Arab
renaissance under the influence of
Djamel ed-din al-Afghani and the
Egyptian Mohamed 'Abdou.

narghila: water pipe.

nasrani: Christian.

nejma: star.

ou'ada: a saint's feast celebration
that requires offerings be made to
the poor.

Ou 'aleikoum es-salaam: greeting answering *salaam 'aleik(oum)*.

Ou el-nabi: by the Prophet.

Ouled Gerrir: tribe from the southern Oranais region near Béchar.

Ouled Sidi Sheikh: tribe from
the southern Oranais region near
Labiod-Sid-Sheikh.

oummi: mother.

qahouaji: coffeehouse owner.

qahwa: coffeehouse

qobba: cupola or dome.

qolla: water jug.

raï: popular music from the Oranais
region.

Ramadan: Muslim holy month.

reg: rocky desert.

Regueibat: inhabitants of region of
Tindouf and the Western Sahara.

rob: cream made of a puree of dates
cooked in ewe's butter.

Roba'yat: the quatrains of eleventh-
century Persian poet and mathe-
matician Omar Khayyam, celebrat-
ing the delights of the senses as a
way to conquer anguish.

ronda: card game loved by Algeri-
ans, inherited from the Spanish.

roumi(a): Roman, and, by extension, Christian.

salaam: peace.

salaam 'aleik: may peace be with
you, in dialect.

salaam 'aleiki: may peace be with
you, addressing a woman.

salaam 'aleikoum: may peace be with
you, addressing a group.

salamalecs (slang): greetings.

Saoura: river valley south of Kenadsa.

saroual: pants.

sebkha: salt marsh sometimes completely dry.

seguia: trench; irrigation canal.

sfifa: sugared couscous.

shahada: one of the five pillars of Islam, the recognition of the oneness of God.

sheikh: notable man, one who has memorized the Qur'an.

sheikha: feminine of *sheikh*, head of a tribe; a wise and respected leader in the group.

si: dialect diminutive for Sayyed, that is, mister.

sloughi: North African greyhound.

smalah: Abd al-Qadir's nomadic capital.

soubressade (Fr.): pork spread eaten by French colonial settlers, who are referred to as *pieds-noirs*.

souk: market.

tabib: doctor.

tajine: earthenware pot.

taleb: master; professor.

tapenade (Fr.): spread made from olives.

tassabhou 'ala kheïr: literally, may tomorrow find you in peace, good night.

tayyab: man working inside a *hammam*.

tell: the humid regions near the coast.

Touareg: Saharan tribe (Blue Men).

toub: mud bricks.

touisa: collective work; mutual support.

wadi: riverbed; dry riverbed.

ya Allah: Oh, my God.

ya krima: Oh, generous woman.

ya rabbi: Oh, my God.

ya sidi: Oh, mister.

youyou: cry of women to indicate joy.

zaouia: religious complex (chapel, school) with lodgings for pilgrims, constructed around the tomb of a saint.

zarbia: large rug of thick wool.

zriba: round enclosure, usually covered with reeds or palm fronds and dried mud.

IN THE EUROPEAN WOMEN WRITERS SERIES

The Human Family
By Lou Andreas-Salomé
Translated and with an introduction
by Raleigh Whitinger

Artemisia
By Anna Banti
Translated by Shirley D'Ardia
Caracciolo

Bitter Healing
German Women Writers, 1700–1830
An Anthology
Edited by Jeannine Blackwell and
Susanne Zantop

The Edge of Europe
By Angela Bianchini
Translated by Angela M. Jeannet and
David Castronuovo

The Maravillas District
By Rosa Chacel
Translated by d. a. démers

Memoirs of Leticia Valle
By Rosa Chacel
Translated by Carol Maier

There Are No Letters Like Yours: The
Correspondence of Isabelle de Charrière
and Constant d'Hermenches
By Isabelle de Charrière
Translated and with an introduction
and annotations by Janet Whatley
and Malcolm Whatley

The Book of Promethea
By Hélène Cixous
Translated by Betsy Wing

The Terrible but Unfinished Story of
Norodom Sihanouk, King of Cambodia
By Hélène Cixous
Translated by Juliet Flower
MacCannell, Judith Pike,
and Lollie Groth

The Governor's Daughter
By Paule Constant
Translated by Betsy Wing

Trading Secrets
By Paule Constant
Translated by Betsy Wing
With an introduction by
Margot Miller

White Spirit
By Paule Constant
Translated by Betsy Wing

Maria Zef
By Paola Drigo
Translated by Blossom Steinberg
Kirschenbaum

Woman to Woman
By Marguerite Duras and
Xavière Gauthier
Translated by Katharine A. Jensen

Hitchhiking
Twelve German Tales
By Gabriele Eckart
Translated by Wayne Kvam

The South and Bene
By Adelaida García Morales
Translated and with a preface
by Thomas G. Deveny